NOWHERE TO HIDE

Sunshine glittered on the lake, and the morning looked crisp and clear, so Guy decided to walk the few blocks to the Gare. From the lakeside he took the angled street to the Rue des Alpes and began treading its rise to the almost visible station.

Behind him a car slowed, and Guy glanced around to see a taxi pulling toward the curb. For a few moments it stayed even with him, then drew ahead and stopped parallel to the curb, engine running.

Doors opened and three men stepped out, facing him.

Sensing danger, Guy thought of the gun in his attache case, but the nearest man pulled a machine pistol from his overcoat and pointed it at him. "Get in," the man snapped, and as Guy hesitated he heard the action cock, a shell snap into the firing chamber.

Guy dropped his luggage and moved toward the open door . . .

D1059207

PINNACLE'S FINEST IN SUSPENSE AND ESPIONAGE

THE DUBLIN AFFAIR

P. S. DONOGHUE

PINNACLE BOOKS
WINDSOR PUBLISHING CORP.

PINNACLE BOOKS

are published by

Windsor Publishing Corp.
475 Park Avenue South
New York, NY 10016

First Pinnacle Books printing: December, 1989

Printed in the United States of America

This book is for
Odette Artime de Worrell
With a father's love

In my Father's house are many rooms;

S. John 14:2

BOOK ONE

BOOK ONE

One

In a darkened ninth floor suite of New York's Harkness Pavilion an elderly man lay motionless beneath an oxygen tent.

His shallow breathing grew labored, he stirred, and the nurse watched the heart monitor apprehensively. As the spikes and valleys began leveling she pressed a button and presently the cardiologist hurried in. With a glance at the monitor he picked up a prepared syringe, the nurse lifted the transparent enclosure while the physician injected adrenalin into the patient's heart. Presently heart action steadied, the nurse lowered the tent and the patient's gasping eased until he was breathing regularly again.

The cardiologist shook his head. ''There's a limit to how often I can bring him back, nurse. Please send for Mrs. Ryan.''

''Yes, Doctor.'' She picked up a nearby phone and began dialing.

The cardiologist studied his patient's sallow face. Old Sean Ryan's eyes were closed, lips bloodless. Nearly gone, the cardiologist thought—and wondered which way the market would head when Ryan's death was known.

He looked at his watch—well after midnight. Eerie how man's life forces dwindled during darkness.

11

The nurse said, "She's coming in, Doctor."

"From Southampton, isn't it? By car that's a couple of hours."

"Mrs. Ryan's had a helicopter standing by. She expects to be here shortly."

"Did she say anything about calling a priest?"

"They brought a priest from Ireland for the last rites. A Father Fallon."

"Then I'll wait in the other room, get a few minutes' rest. I should talk to her about a heart-lung hookup."

"They can afford it if anyone can," the nurse said with a trace of envy.

"And she'll probably want their children here." He began walking toward the other room. "How many are there?"

"Three, I think—one in New York."

As he passed windows he could see part of Riverside Drive, the chains of moving lights on the George Washington Bridge. Glancing south he made out the diffused halo of Grant's tomb. Familiar sights all.

When he was young the area had been quiet, affluent, attractive. Now, the great hospital thrust upward from decayed surroundings that had become a wasteland of bums, gangs and violent criminals. Only infrequently did he come back at night, he reflected as he stretched out on the comfortable sofa, and then to attend persons of prominence such as Sean Ryan, isolated in his plastic enclosure.

Remarkable, he thought, how the old man had survived. Emphysema had overburdened an aging heart, and he could sense death hovering in the shadows. Had Sean Ryan made prudent disposition of his conglomerate or would heirs and survivors commence a bloodletting struggle for control? What should he do with his own RyTech shares? Sell? Buy to the hilt on margin? Would his insider's knowledge of Ryan's impending death be valuable? Couldn't reach a broker for eight more hours. Damn!

He remembered, as he occasionally did, how he had taken up medicine impelled by a compulsion to serve mankind. That had been his motivating force until his last year as cardiovascular resident at this same hospital. As though it was yesterday, he recalled the middle-aged bypass patient from Texas on whom he'd operated. The man had become wealthy from oil and real estate, had been flown to New York in his private plane. His suite was always filled with relatives and expensive gifts, and on the Texan's last day, during the pre-release exam he said, "Doc, I really appreciate what you done for me. I guess you don't get much salary, so here's something you can enjoy." He then handed over a crumpled bag that contained—a dozen colored gumdrops.

Flushed, humiliated, he'd taken the bag, left the suite and tossed the gumdrops in the trash. After that he rethought his motivation, and decided to go for the gold—and had, ever since.

The nurse was so right—the Ryans could afford him if anyone could. Twenty grand would cover his daughter's last law school year, and if Mrs. Ryan would make out the check to Columbia Law he'd avoid tax liability. Wouldn't hurt to ask her for the accommodation, say after the funeral.

With those agreeable thoughts he dozed off, woke to the sound of an opening door and got up to greet the dying man's wife.

Long before meeting her professionally the doctor was familiar with her face from society pages and magazines that covered the very rich. She was, he thought, a native American aristocrat, and the fine molding of her features would have suggested generations of selective breeding had she been dressed in rags. Hair almost white, mouth a little taut from stress, she bore her slim body erect, almost defiantly.

"I'm sorry," he said, "but I thought it best to alert you."

"Thank you, Doctor. What happened?"

"It was another—spasm," he told her gently. "Unless I

13

put him on life-sustaining equipment the end could come at any time."

She closed her eyes and seemed to sway. The physician steadied her arm until with a faint, apologetic smile she said, "How curious that we accept the concept, the inevitability of death, though never the timing." She looked away. "Is he conscious? May I see him?"

"Of course, Mrs. Ryan—he may respond to your voice."

"I—I understand. Thank you, Doctor—at this hour you must be very tired."

He shrugged, saw her move through the doorway to the bedside, heard her call, "Sean, Sean, it's Marguerite—your wife."

The doctor went back to the sofa.

After a while she came out and said, "He knew me—I'm very grateful."

"He spoke, then?" The doctor was surprised.

"Yes—asked for his son, Guy."

"Is Guy in New York?"

"No, somewhere off Haiti."

"Then—forgive me, Mrs. Ryan—we should consider life-prolonging measures."

"My husband is in your hands, Doctor. Anything you recommend."

Forty feet beneath the Caribbean, Guy Patrick Ryan braced his feet on the sandy bottom and wrestled the bucking impeller tube. Eight inches in diameter, the jointed metal pipe jetted a high-pressure stream at a tape-marked area, blasting sand and coral fragments into the distance.

Sometimes current lifted his black-finned feet from the bottom but he continued gripping the iron hand-holds and regained footing, always peering down for traces of the long-lost treasure ship he had spent six months trying to find.

And during long hours of bottom time Guy Ryan had

wondered whether others had come before him, a century or more ago, and plundered the bones of *Nuestra Señora de Compostela*. Or if wet-suit divers like himself had found the ancient vessel, looting the gold, silver and precious stones his Seville researches told him the King's brigantine had loaded at Cartagena.

So far he had raised only a small coral-crusted brass cannon that *could* have been mounted on the vessel's poop rail. By now his salvage crew was disgruntled, the other two divers worked perfunctorily, and the feeling of expectancy all shared when he first dropped hook off Hispaniola was gone with the winter storms, the treacherous bottom currents and the unpredictable tropic winds.

Less than a hundred yards distant stretched a great rift in the ocean floor, and Ryan's recurrent fear was the *Nuestra Señora* lay broken on its unreachable bottom. Were that so, future salvors would have to mount an immense deepwater expedition whose cost neither he nor his in-laws could meet.

By his calculation they had clean-scoured half a square mile of bottom, finding old storm debris and rusted relics from the Second World War, reef-shattered boats and broken cases of Prohibition rum. But of Spanish treasure—*nada*.

Back, shoulders and arms ached. Hold on, he thought doggedly, another twelve minutes to go.

The current raised and dropped him, swirled sand toward the chasm, and when he settled again he noticed two chunks of coral the pipe-stream hadn't moved. He poked one with the tip of a fin, and as it turned over he saw the underside was oddly blackened—and his heart seemed to choke his throat.

Holding the jet-pipe under his left arm, he knelt to grip the object in his gloved hand, bring it nearer his face mask.

The first clue had been the discolored underside of the coral chunk; the second was its weight.

He jerked hard on the signal lanyard that ran along the

pipe, and in moments the jet stream ceased. Leaving the pipe Guy picked up the second chunk and found its bottom-side, too, dark gray.

On his knees, he dug both hands into the sand, feeling hard objects below, clawed out several and found them smooth and free of coral. He lifted one toward the filtering sunlight. A stubby bar of blackened metal.

Silver.

He clenched it hard, unbelievingly. Then he dropped it in a mesh waist bag and grubbed in the sand for more, uncovering a jumbled mound that reminded him of turtle eggs. Sitting back, he felt like shouting through his mouth-piece. *Silver.* Yes, the mint-markings would determine where it was cast, and when.

Would there be royal seals stamped on the bullion? Had he finally found the wealth of the king's own treasure ship?

The silver ingots were fine—but what about the gold bis-cuits and *escudos?* There should be pieces of eight, as well—cobs, the coinage was called.

Remembering the pressure stream he yanked twice on the lanyard and almost before he could grip the hand-holds the water jet resumed.

He aimed it at the nested silver, clearing away sand, scat-tering pieces of wood that had been the carry-chest, then scoured the radius, noting more clusters of shell and coral that looked promising. Another hail of rotten wood, and Ryan was gazing at a scatter of glinting coins.

Gold. No sea growth marred their pristine perfection.

With a sense of awe he scooped up a handful and placed the *escudos* in his mesh bag. Automatically he checked tank air pressure and found the gauge at 700 psi. Time to as-cend.

He jerked the lanyard three times and lowered the blower end beside his latest find. Then, bleeding air into his buoy-ancy pack, he began ascending to his trawler, rising even with the smallest exhaled bubbles.

Sunlight was piercingly bright as Ryan hauled himself onto the weathered dive platform. He peeled off his face mask and stared around blinking at Roy Shammas, who was lifting off his heavy tank.

Fins in hand, Ryan stood up, swaying with the rolling swell. "I found it," he said hoarsely, and lifted his mesh bag.

With a whoop, Shammas grabbed him in a bear hug, and they danced around the tilting platform. By then Simón Bernal, the third diver, two crewmen and the cook had gathered at the stern railing. "What is it? What's wrong?" one of them shouted.

"Nothing's wrong," Ryan called back, pausing to unfasten his waist bag and heave it at Bernal. The Mexican lunged and caught it, nearly toppling backward from the unexpected weight, saw the gleaming gold and burst into a series of Sonoran yips and yells.

Then they were all together, crowding close to the precious metals on the wooden deck, picking up the coins, rubbing them even brighter, hefting ingots in their hands, murmuring at the unexpected climax of their long search.

Ryan looked at his dive watch—not quite nine o'clock. Good weather, and a full day's diving ahead.

In a choked voice Shammas said, "How much is down there, Guy?"

"God knows—a lot. Take down a buoy line and mark the site."

"Sure." He swallowed. "By the ship?"

"There isn't any ship. It must be down in that deep crevass. The treasure, being heavier, dropped through when the wooden hull was pushed along by the current." He shook his head. "That's a guess—unless we find cabin artifacts."

"No jewels, huh?"

Ryan smiled. "Don't expect me to do *all* the finding."

17

He filled his lungs with clean salt air, stared at the Haitian coastline. "Just when I was beginning to give up hope."

"Me, too," said Shammas grittily. "*And* the others."

"Then let's get organized. Take down balloon cages and start sending up the stuff. Nobody takes souvenirs until everything's been inventoried by the Haitians, right?"

"If you say so."

"That's my agreement with their Treasury."

Shammas grinned. "Just my luck to work for an honest salvor."

Ryan peeled off his wet suit, feeling the breeze cool his wet body. Just then he was aware of a stranger among the others. A woman in blue-jeans and khaki work shirt, staring down at the treasure. She lifted a camera to focus on it when Ryan shouted, "*You*—what the hell are you doing here?"

Unperturbed, she clicked a picture, clicked another and faced him with a smile. White teeth, freckled face, wind-blown chestnut hair. "Have you forgotten, Mr. Ryan? This is interview day. I'm Jenny Knox from *Scuba Magazine* in New York, and it seems I picked just the right time."

He *had* forgotten. *Damn.* He'd wanted to savor this moment with his crew—*just* his crew. "All right," he said slowly, "you're here, and I'll honor my commitment."

Gazing at him she laughed abruptly. "You look the way Tarzan must have looked—*sans* loincloth."

"You don't have to look," he snapped, and made his way to the wheelhouse cabin. Damn girl, he thought, as he got into his khakis and deck shoes, toweled water from his hair's dark ringlets. He'd give her the interview—but it would be a short one.

Automatically, he peeled black tape from his West Point ring, whose glinting gold could bring a 'cuda's slashing jaws. And while he was combing his thick hair the engineer came in with a radio message form. "Bad news, Guy," he said, "so brace yourself."

He snatched it from the offering hand and read the un-

18

even printing: FATHER DYING, ASKS YOU COME AT ONCE. URGE YOU GRANT HIS LAST REQUEST. RYTECH JET AT PORT-AU-PRINCE AIRPORT. MEET YOU NEW YORK COLUMBIA PRESBYTERIAN HOSPITAL. PLEASE COME, GUY. FOR ME. LOVE, MARGUERITE.

He stood alone in the shadowed cabin, clenching the message. Years since he'd even seen his father, never expected to see him again. But for Marguerite, he wouldn't.

Memories, most of them cruel, flooded his mind. He'd go, not to see Sean Foley Ryan on his deathbed, but because Marguerite, his stepmother, would need him there. Her own children, his two half-siblings, would be little enough support, but to him she had always been unfailingly kind. For his remembered life she had replaced the mother who bore him, whose death his birth had caused. Marguerite was the only mother he had known.

Rapidly he packed a small bag, grabbed his pea jacket and went down on deck where the journalist waited. "Plan's changed," he told her and handed her the radio message as he went aft to find his captain.

To the captain, Bernal and Shammas, Ryan gave detailed instructions. A strict log was to be kept of everything recovered. For the balance of the day they were to bring up as much treasure as possible. Tomorrow, the bottom area was to be photographed and grids installed. "You know the drill, skipper, you've done it before."

The captain nodded. "When will you be back?"

"Don't know—soon I hope."

"There'll be—the funeral. You'll stay for that?"

"Yes, though I doubt he'd have come for mine."

Returning to the visitor, Ryan said, "I'm flying the chopper to the airport. You can come with me—or stay."

"Wouldn't miss the chance, Major."

He glanced at her. "At sea we don't use army rank."

"It's yours—why not use it?"

He shrugged, walked amidships to where the two-seater Hughes 269 was toggled to the deck.

After tossing bag and pea jacket beside his seat he freed the skids and said, "Get in and belt down."

With a glance at the flag for wind direction, Ryan buckled into the pilot's seat and started the four-cylinder Lycoming. As the main and tail rotors began to turn, she said, "Where'd you learn to fly choppers?"

"Fort Rucker."

Pad in hand she began making notes. Ryan checked the instrument console, took the control stick lightly and applied power. Like a dragonfly the chopper lifted from the deck, and he saw his crew waving goodbye, the divers signalling with upturned thumbs.

The route was one Ryan had flown often before—for supplies, conferences with government officials, for a rare night on the town. He looked at the compass bearing and put on headphones, handed her the companion set. He switched to intercom so they could talk free of engine and rotor noise.

As they crossed the coast he said, "The village down there is Grand Goisier. that mountain peak ahead is Mont La Selle."

"I see it—how high?"

"Nearly nine thousand—so we'll fly carefully past—leave climbing for another day."

She looked down. "Just jungle, isn't it? Not much else. Remind you of Vietnam?"

"Some."

"Care to talk about some of your experiences there?"

"No."

"*What* can I get you to talk about?"

"You were to do a photo-story on our search for *Nuestra Señora.*"

"You've found it—I can always go back for pictures—but with your father dying, I really want to talk about him. He must have been a fabulous man."

20

"So they say." La Selle was coming up on the right. He banked and steered safely left. Altitude three thousand two.

"You and your father weren't close?"

"From childhood I hardly ever saw him." Ryan turned to face her. "Look, I don't want to talk about it. You're here on false pretenses, anyway. I thought J. Knox was a man."

"Chauvinist, eh? You can't think too badly of all women—you married one."

Ryan said nothing as he guided the Hughes over the central Massif. That high, he could make out the island's northern coast.

"Will your wife meet you in New York?"

"Unlikely. She's in Paris."

"With your daughter, Gloria, right?"

"You know a good deal about me."

"I started with *Who's Who.*"

"Sounds like a good place to end."

"You don't like me, do you, Major Ryan?"

"Nothing personal, Miss—I've a lot on my mind. Getting us to the airport is numbah one."

"Look—I have to get back to New York, anyway. Can I go with you?"

He considered. As a West Point athlete and Heisman candidate he'd had experience of the press, learned to be wary of reporters looking for an offbeat story. But—maybe they could compromise. "Come along," he said, "with the understanding you'll write only about the expedition. I don't want anything to embarrass my family."

She thought it over. "Your finding the *Compostela* is an exclusive for me. That's luck enough for one day."

At the airport he arranged for hangar space for the Hughes and guided the girl toward the flight line where a sleek Lear 35 with the RyTech logo was waiting.

21

As they neared the plane Ryan noticed a man getting out of a parked black sedan. The man waved and began walking toward them.

"Reporter?" Ryan asked Jenny.

"Could be—don't know every ink-stained wretch in Gotham—but I'd guess not. Clean shaven, wears a hat, too well dressed. Executive type. Maybe from RyTech?"

"The pilot will know." He eased Jenny into the plane and indicated seats. "More likely, the word's out on Sean Ryan, and that vulture wants an interview."

"Little knowing I have an exclusive," she said prod-dingly.

The co-pilot stowed his bag and raised the stairway sealing the narrow cabin. Outside, the man was waving wildly and shouting. Ryan couldn't hear his voice and ignored him.

"Let's go," he said, and looked around.

Carpeted and tastefully decorated in shades of green, the cabin had four single seats, a double, and a wood-grained table.

The co-pilot said, "We'll be flying nearly four hours at an altitude of forty-thousand feet, four-forty knots. There are hot meals aboard, and assorted liquor."

Jenny said, "After takeoff I'd like a Bloody Mary."

"Black Label on the rocks," Ryan told him.

"Certainly, sir. Seatbelts, please." He ducked forward and took his place beside the pilot. Cool air rushed from vents as the turbofans whined. Outside, Ryan knew, the screech would be earsplitting, but in the soundproofed cabin it was only noticeable as vibration.

Airborne, Ryan looked back at Port-Au-Prince, and then the Lear shot skyward, shoving him back against the soft, upholstered seat.

When the plane reached cruising altitude the co-pilot brought back their drinks and said, "How soon would you like to eat?"

"I'm hungry now," Ryan told him, "been diving all morning."

Jenny nodded. "Famished."

As they were eating shrimp cocktails, she said, "What inspired the treasure expedition?"

"Well, you probably know I was an Assistant Military Attaché in Madrid."

"After Vietnam."

"Yes. A soft post for a wounded grunt. I learned Spanish, did the diplomatic circuit—and met my wife."

"From her pictures she's very beautiful. But what's she really like? Do you want to tell me about Consuela?"

He dipped another shrimp in cocktail sauce. "No, she's not relevant to your story."

She said, "After marriage you left the army. Why?"

"Let's say the thrill was gone."

"The thrill of combat?"

"Well, I was given to understand I'd been designated for the fast track—Army War College, then Leavenworth Command and General Staff School. After that, probably Harvard. But I didn't want to be an armchair soldier—that's what my future held."

"Because of your Rhodes Scholarship?"

"The Point doesn't get a lot of Rhodes men, so there's prestige attached to it."

"But you studied only two years at Oxford, not three."

"There was a war in Southeast Asia, and my classmates were there." He finished the last of his shrimp, set the cup aside. "Let's get back to the expedition. After resignation I had time to kill while Consuela was pregnant. One day in Seville I wandered into the General Archives of the Indies and found myself looking at old charts and ships' logs. They were a challenge to my Spanish, so I decided to improve it by reading about the treasure fleets from New Spain. I con-

23

sidered doing a monograph on the fleet of 1593, read up on it, and found that most of it had reached Seville—minus the vessel carrying the king's portion—*Nuestra Señora de Compostela*—which was older and heavier than the other ships, and had become detached from the main convoy due to a storm off Windward Passage. According to three survivors, the ship was gutted on a reef off Hispaniola. Its log was lost, but the treasure manifest reached Spain—and eventually the Archives.''

The co-pilot served rare filets mignon with Lyonnaise potatoes and endive salads.

''So,'' she said, ''the treasure list fired your imagination.''

''To put it mildly. I began looking for other accounts of the voyage, read admiralty statements by the survivors and studied old charts of Hispaniola. I compared their coastlines with current hydrographic studies and located the most likely reefs.''

''While doing all that you were living in Seville?''

''No. My wife wanted to be with her family, so we were staying at La Rocha—very comfortably, too.''

''La Rocha's near Seville?''

''Northeast—between the Guadalquivir and Genil rivers.''

''A large estate?''

''Thousands of hectares. My father-in-law raises Arabian horses, grapes for the winery, cattle and fighting bulls—*toros bravos*. Actually, my sister-in-law, Cristina, manages the Arabian stud—some of the bloodline goes back to Moorish times, before the *Reconquista.*''

''And your father-in-law's name?''

''Don José, Marqués de Palafox y Urriaga.''

He helped her with the spelling as she wrote it down. Looking up she said, ''So your wife is a marquesa.''

''As elder daughter.'' He cut into another portion of juicy filet, chewed thoughtfully. ''I had the general search area electronically dragged for nonferrous metals, found a promising zone and began organizing the expedition.''

"Financing shouldn't have been hard—with RyTech behind you.''

He shook his head. "Don José and Cristina put up most of the money, my stepmother the rest.''

"Good Lord, you'll share a huge fortune.''

"The Government of Haiti gets the top fifteen percent.''

"*Those* bandits?'' she said. "I'd rather you hadn't made a deal.''

"Better than having my trawler confiscated or sunk.''

For a while she wrote. Ryan said, "Your meal's getting cold.''

"This is more important. Now—before West Point, where did you go to school?''

"Switzerland—Vezelay.''

She whistled. "Very select—*and* expensive. Of course your father paid for that.''

He shook his head. "Sean wanted me at Canterbury or Priory—he's very Irish Catholic. When I declined, he said I could go to hell. Instead, I went to Vezelay, thanks to Marguerite.''

"West Point was her idea?''

"Mine—so no one would have to pay for my education.''

"What was your father's reaction?''

"Negative—he preferred Georgetown or BC.'' He looked aside at the clear, cloudless sky. "There's an old saying—a true Irishman sits on a stool with four legs: pigs, potatoes, priests and poteen.''

"What's—?''

"No more family talk—you're not to use it, anyway.''

"I know—and I won't. Even so, it's a fascinating glimpse inside one of the country's most powerful families. Authentic greenbloods.''

Ryan decided not to react to the condescending term for Irish-American aristocracy. Instead, he finished his steak,

25

drank a glass of milk and stretched out across the double seat. He was dead tired—drained from diving, the exaltation of his treasure find, depressed by his stepmother's message. Not that he felt affection for the dying man who'd cast him off almost at birth, but he respected Sean's accomplishments, the way he'd risen from Irish poverty to titanic stature in America—with the help of Marguerite's money and old family connections. He regretted Sean's passing because Marguerite loved him so deeply, and because her own children were disappointments even to themselves.

But they'd be at their father's deathbed, he was sure— Gant, the wastrel; sister Nicole of the body temperature IQ and compulsive spending. Neither worthy of their parents.

As sleep began to wash over him, Ryan wondered how his father was distributing his wealth and multinational holdings. For the sake of the family name, Ryan hoped Sean had made intelligent decisions.

For himself, he wanted only to return to his trawler and the treasure being recovered from the bottom of the sea.

"We're approaching Kennedy, Major. Seat belt, please."

Ryan rubbed his eyes, sat up and reached for the belt buckle. Ahead, Jenny Knox was sipping a *demi-tasse*. Groggily he wondered if she'd managed a nap.

Through the window he could see the eastern tip of Long Island between gray clouds. Soon they'd be flying above Eastover, Marguerite's family estate where generations of Hillyers had lived in genteel opulence. Her line went back almost to the Pilgrims, and Ryan often wondered how she and his father—polar opposites in almost every way—had joined and found happiness together. Well, no accounting for love.

No more than he could calmly assay what he felt now for his own wife—their wants, their ways had so diverged since

Gloria's birth that he could hardly remember how strong his love had been . . .

He had dealt with alienation the only way he knew—by not acknowledging it, and letting Consuela have her way. Most of his love he reserved for his only child.

On the ground he helped Jenny into the waiting limousine and watched wipers carve arcs in the late afternoon drizzle until she said, "In the unlikely event you need a bed I'm on Bank Street in the Village. Phone's listed."

"As J. Knox?"

"To avoid heavy breathers. My boyfriend won't mind."

"Thanks, but the family has an intown place on Park near the Racquet Club. There may be room for me."

"Of course—well, it's been great, Major—and thanks for everything."

"Glad you were along. Will you be coming back to Haiti?"

For a moment their gaze met. Looking away she said, "The mag will certainly want more pix. I think you can count on it."

When Ryan entered the hospital suite he found Marguerite resting on the sofa, an afghan thrown across her body. Going to her he knelt and kissed her cheek. "I'm here," he said softly. "Is he still alive?"

"Yes—but drifting away. More than anything, Sean wanted you here, Guy. Go to him now—reconcile if that's what he wants and it's within you. Go—" She pressed him away, and as Ryan rose she gazed up with tear-streaked cheeks. "Oh, Guy—I've loved him so."

He went to the doorway and looked in. The room was silent but for the hum of life-support machines.

Inside the transparent enclosure lay his father, a network

27

of wires and tubing extending from his shrunken frame. The once-handsome face, grizzled now with white beard, looked more dead than alive. Twelve years since he had seen the man whose seed had fertilized his mother's womb. Dying now, his many secrets with him.

Moving close to the oxygen tent, Ryan spoke. "You sent for me, father. Well, I've come."

Two

Sean Ryan had lost track of time and hardly cared whether the world beyond the plastic envelope moved by night or day. His sleep lay always on the edge of wakefulness so that he was vaguely aware of motion around him, sounds filtering through the hum of machines that he had come to realize now sustained the fraying fibers of his life.

Whenever sedatives abated, his mind began to clear, and he likened it to surfacing after a voyage submerged. Drugs again, and he sank in a dark gelatinous sea where memories played like warped and twisted ribbons until he was too confused and tired to sieve and grasp reality.

But of the green fields of his youth he was sure. They were a constant—and the gray sea tonguing Cloghy's gray-black cliffs, whirling seabirds and spindrift pelting his face before a gathering storm. Warm hearth and porridge, his mother's careworn face, soft Gaelic syllables, cowbells, the creak of wooden carts at dawn . . . all so long ago, so buried in the lower levels of his mind, that only now while he was drifting, floating without purpose, could the freshening take place.

He remembered sorrow, the women keening by his father's bier. The rough, caring men who brought him to the Brotherhood and taught him how to fight and take his father's place.

Ah, the fighting. Bodies, rivulets of blood washing the cobbles. Hiding in fear . . . night whispers, flight. Another land, a foster family. The secret that was to have been sealed became known outside the Brotherhood.

29

No, he would not think of that again, not now when the hushed voice of his wife had lured him from the past. His son would come, she said, the son he'd cast aside and shunned for thirty years in revenge for his mother's death. Sweet Molly, ah, dear lass, the true love of his heart and irreplaceable. So strong yet yielding lovingly . . . weeping beside her coffin he'd wanted to die . . . join her in that heaven of which even now, as he faced the end of everything, he was not sure. Fergus, his own father, had scant use for priests, arguing that if there were a God He would not permit cruel England to exist. And God— in holy vengeance?—had let a British bullet strike him down. So— what was a lad to think? In what could he believe?

Still he'd been awed by the Church—the solemn priests, the ancient symbols spread across the face of Ireland, and so he'd feared not to believe. Twice he'd married in the Church and tried to give the son of Molly a Catholic education. In that he'd failed—as in all else with Guy, who was his mother's child far more than his.

But now he saw it for the best. He loved his Marguerite, good Catholic that she was, but from her womb had come that girl and boy who'd never measured up despite her loving care, his stern instruction. Was it the money, his wealth that stopped them short? Or something strange beyond his ken?

No sense in ruminating, scarce time to face his son at last, if only he would come. For Guy was the best, and worthy of my murdered father, Fergus. Made his way despite me, become a man, excelled. He's never known the Ireland of my youth. The Trouble that seared my blood, or taken arms against Ireland's ancient enemies.

He'll never forgive the lie I lived . . .

The dying man heard the door's soft opening, sensed the room light growing somewhat brighter. Opening his eyes (were they open all along?) he made out a tall, dark profile at his beside, heard *"You sent for me, father. Well, I've come."*

Sean wet his lips. "And glad I am to see you. Was it a hard journey, son?"

"Son?" Guy laughed thinly. "How long since you called me that? How many years?"

"I know, I know . . . don't make this harder than it must be. At least you came. I'm grateful."

"Marguerite asked me to be here. I am. What have you to say?"

For a time Sean was silent as though gathering the remnants of his energy. Guy pulled over a chair and sat down. His father said, "I loved your mother, lad, you'll never know how much. Her dying made me do things I . . . Well, I was wrong to treat you the way I did."

Guy said nothing.

Voice lower, hoarse, Sean said, "It's useless I know to ask forgiveness for those sad years of neglect . . ." His voice trailed off.

Guy said, "You went your way, I found mine."

"And I'm proud of you for that, have always been. Lad, you'll watch over Marguerite?" A trace of the Irish accent fogged his words.

"Of course."

Again he fell silent. "It's a sad thing I've never seen my granddaughter."

"That it is," Guy agreed.

A sigh filtered through the transparent enclosure. "Too late, too late." The words were wistful.

"Far too late," Guy replied, and stood up. "Is that all?"

"I've confessed to Father Fallon, sought forgiveness for my sins."

"And now you feel better about everything."

"A bit," he acknowledged. "When you're in Ireland, visit the Father, ask about me."

"Why would I be visiting Ireland?"

"Because I have associations there, interests you'll now take over."

Guy shook his head. "Not I," he said. "Business is not my way of life."

31

"But it will be, Guy—and that is why I wanted you to come. It's all arranged: you'll take my place at RyTech."

Again Guy said, "Not I."

As though he had not heard his son's refusal Sean went on, his breathing more labored. "It's in your name, Guy. With Marguerite you'll control it all. A tremendous legacy . . ."

"I don't want your legacy."

"You'd have it go to Gant and Nicole?"

He shrugged. "Let them sell it."

"Ah, lad, so ignorant of the world. Since you care not for the money, you'll find the work of interest and importance. For years I've built things for the Pentagon."

"RyTech and a hundred other corporations."

"But none does the work of mine. Or can."

He was breathing deeply now, Guy noticed, and heard him gasp, "You *must* take over. There are secrets . . ." His voice trailed off as he seemed to be gathering strength to say more. Guy waited quietly, feeling his own throat tighten. For this was his father, all else aside, his father dying, gasping out his life to transfer all his wealth and secrets to his Irishborn son.

Guy saw the near arm lift, fingers beckon. He leaned close to hear his father whisper, "Above all . . . save sceptre. Don't let it—" The arm fell, Sean's eyes bulged and breath rattled in his throat as nurse and doctor hurried in. Rising, Guy stood aside, turned to meet Marguerite at the doorway. He tried to hold her but she brushed past and stood beside the doctor, who shook his head and shrugged.

Guy went to the anteroom and waited, hearing her cries of sorrow and despair. The lump in his throat was choking. He tried to swallow water, spat it out and went to the window, staring blindly at the icy river. When he heard Marguerite's footsteps he took her in his arms and held her close while she sobbed brokenly. Finally she dried her cheeks and said, "Did you—were you reconciled?"

32

"Yes," he lied.

"Then you know you're to head the corporation."

"So he said, but—"

"You must, Guy—there's so much at stake."

This was not the time or place to argue with her, tell Marguerite he had no skills for business, that he'd found a different life, one he preferred to offices and meetings. Instead, he said, "Sean said something—his last words, but I didn't understand."

"What did he say?"

"That I should, above all, save—I think the word was *sceptre*—but his voice was so faint I'm not sure. Does it mean anything to you?"

Slowly she shook her head, tears welling in her gray-blue eyes. "That was all?"

"Perhaps his last thoughts were of Ireland, it would be in keeping with his life. I—" he swallowed—"thought of the sceptre of Brian Boru."

"Ireland's legendary king," she said softly. "Yes, Sean loved the legends, the myths of Ireland. It's so strange he never returned."

Guy stared at her. *"Never* went back?"

She shook her head slowly.

The doctor and nurse came out, closing the door. To the widow, the physician said, "If you'd like I can prescribe something to help you through this bad time."

"Thank you, but I'd rather not." She looked around vacantly. "There's nothing more you can do—why don't you go home, get some rest?"

"Later—but I'll be in the lounge if you need me for anything. I'm very sorry, Mrs. Ryan."

"So am I."

When they were alone she said, "We must go on, mustn't we?" With a final glance at the closed door she drew back her shoulders, took Guy's hand and left the room.

In the lobby her chauffeur was waiting. He stood smartly

33

but she motioned him to wait. Then, drawing Guy aside, she said, "Tonight I want to be alone at Eastover."

"I understand." He pressed her hand.

"Do you mind staying in the apartment?"

"Not at all. But I want to be with you as much as possible these next few days. You're—the only mother I've ever known." He felt his eyes moisten.

"And you're as much my son as if I bore you."

Strange, he thought, that neither had mentioned her own two children, but then with him, she seldom did. As he held her close she said, "Please honor Sean's wishes for you."

"It's—early to make a decision. And you know how different my life has been."

"Yes—always alone, Guy," she murmured with a wistful smile. "Is—Consuela well? And little Gloria?"

"I believe so."

"Then I'll ask no more." She turned to leave, paused. "There's a special reason Sean wanted you to manage RyTech. For a long time he's felt things were going wrong in certain ways."

"How wrong?"

"He—his words were 'rotten to the core.' But the firm is too immense for him to look into everything, as he did at the beginning. Besides, his health was failing. Death concerned him more and more."

Guy decided to plant a thought. "You can find a better corporate head than I, Marguerite. Any headhunter firm could produce one from industry's top levels."

"True—but your father was determined that RyTech remain in the family—under your control." She glanced away. "Perhaps it was his way of trying to make up for past neglect."

"A poor way," he said, regretting the words at once. "I'll come to Eastover tomorrow."

She nodded. "The funeral's two days hence, and then the reading of his will." Taking his arm she strolled with him to the doorway which the chauffeur opened. Outside stood a gunmetal Rolls. Guy walked her to it and opened the rear door. She kissed his cheek and said, "Between us we can do what's right for everyone. But you must be careful from now on."

"Careful? Why?"

"Sean feared—and I agreed—that you would be in danger."

"I don't understand."

"When so many millions are involved the transfer of power gives rise to—risks. I shouldn't want to lose you, Guy." With a nod at the chauffeur she sat back and Guy closed her door.

Almost without sound the Rolls pulled away, and as Guy watched its tail lights vanish he thought of her warning, deciding as he hailed a waiting cab that for him it held no meaning. Old people worry, he told himself, and gave the driver the address on Park, sat back and finished the thought: often needlessly.

Still, he had to respect Sean's judgment, and if his father believed that taking over RyTech placed him in danger, that was additional reason not to become involved.

In 'Nam, with the Long Range Recco Team, he'd had more than his share of danger. He still craved adventure, but as spice for a quiet, rewarding life.

The taxi gained Riverside Drive, sped south through the fading night.

No doorman on duty. A lobby security guard admitted Guy, saying he'd been alerted to receive him. He turned over a door key and walked to the elevator. After punching the call button he scrutinized Guy. "Ain't you that Army footballer?"

Guy smiled tiredly. "I was, but how did you know?"

"I keep a West Point scrapbook. I'm retired army—tech

35

sergeant. And how I loved watching you run with the ball. You shoulda got the Heisman—how come you didn't? Politics?"

"That was a year for quarterbacks," Guy told him, pleased to be remembered.

The guard persisted. "You coulda got a pro contract, why din'cha?"

Guy stepped into the elevator, touched the 10th floor button. "I had one—with the army. Three years, renewal options." As the doors closed he gave the guard a wink.

Fitting his key into the lock, Guy reflected that it had been seven years since he'd used the family *pied-à-terre*. Then, he'd stopped over on his way back to Madrid to marry Consuela, having resigned at the Pentagon.

And so much had happened since—not much of it good. Except for Gloria's birth.

He went inside, turned on the light and immediately recognized the scent of marijuana.

From 'Nam he knew the odor, associating it with surly grunts and misfits who muttered about fragging officers—but seldom did.

The apartment comprised a large living room, sunken dining room and three bedrooms, the master somewhat larger than the others. Bathrooms for each. He carried his bag to the nearest bedroom, glancing into the master as he passed the open door.

The king-size bed was rumpled; someone sleeping there. The marijuana scent was stronger. He turned on a table lamp.

His half-brother's long brown hair fanned across one pillow, and as Guy approached he saw a crest of jet-black hair, face hidden by the coverlet. Gant had company—girl or boy?

He pulled down the cover, exposing the slim, naked body

36

of an Oriental girl—under sixteen, from the meager development of her breasts. Angrily, Guy flung back the coverlet and the girl woke with a cry. She stared at Guy and pounded a small fist on Gant's back until he woke and stared around groggily. "What the—?"

Guy snapped, "Pay her off, get her out of here."

Gant grinned idiotically. "Hey, bro', what's the big problem?"

"Statutory rape's the problem, bro', something the family doesn't need just now."

Gant sat up, peered around as though seeking a roach. "My big, macho army half-brother," he said, sneering. "Where the hell do you get off ordering me around?"

"Because I'm your big, macho army half-brother. Tell Suzy Wong to beat it." The girl-child had retreated under the coverlet.

Gant shrugged, "We've done our thing, anyway." He nudged the girl and glared at Guy. "What ill wind blows you to Gotham?"

"Guess."

Gant's hands spread vacantly.

"Our father's dead."

Paling, Gant struck his forehead with his fist and fell back. "Oh, God," he whimpered, blinked at the ceiling and shoved the girl toward the edge of the bed.

Guy left the room, slamming the door. Splendid reception, he thought, and went to the next bedroom. Too tired to shower he got into bed and was seduced by its soft embrace. Before sleep washed over him he thought of the days ahead, the family gathering for the funeral, the reading of the will.

A lot of people are going to be surprised, he told himself, but they needn't worry. No way I'm going to take over Sean's corporation. No way at all.

Three

The telephone woke him. A man identified himself as chief of RyTech's air operations, and said a helicopter would ferry him to Eastover at his convenience.

"Give me a couple of hours," Guy told him. "PanAm Metroport?"

"Right, sir. Two hours."

Still far from rested, Guy shaved, put on his travel clothes and had breakfast-lunch at a counter eatery around the corner. From there he walked to J. Press and selected clothing from the rack: Chesterfield, dark blue three piece suit, white shirts, black tie, hose and shoes. Also, Cambridge-gray flannels, an Orkney tweed jacket, wool socks, a striped, and dark blue shirt, regimental tie and brown blucher shoes. After he signed for the purchase the clerk checked his file and came back. "It's been a while since you bought here, Major."

"Quite a while."

"I'm sorry about your father's death." He tapped a folded newspaper.

"Yes," Guy said, "a lot of people are."

The clerk handed him two large boxes. "Pleasure to serve you, sir."

Guy glanced around. "Marty Rosen still here?"

"Yes—but today he's home with the flu."

"Tell him I said hello."

"I'll do that. He'll appreciate the message."

From the store Guy taxied over Sixtieth Street to the East River. On the helipad waited a Bell *Long Ranger* with a RyTech logo across the cabin side. He walked through gusty wind to the lee side. After greeting him the pilot said, "It's been a busy morning. I just flew Miss Nicole and her husband from JFK to Eastover."

"Gant?"

"Haven't seen him."

He'd been gone when Guy wakened. Lord knows where, Guy thought, but surely his half-brother had enough innate decency to attend the obsequies. Or maybe not.

He buckled into his seat. At least Nicole had come promptly. And her husband, Thibaud de Neuville, who managed RyTech's interests in France. Thibaud was a slim, rather handsome Polytechnique graduate who was working at the Ministry of Commerce when Nicole married him. Sean didn't tolerate incompetence even in a family member, so Guy supposed Thibaud had delivered adequate performance. Still, Guy had never cared for his brother-in-law's Continental style; he dressed impeccably, and looked as though his wavy hair had never been ruffled. And his French-accented English was delicious. The debonair Thibaud would have plenty of reason to be concerned about the direction RyTech would now take, perhaps nominating himself as Sean's successor.

The prospect displeased him.

The helicopter lifted gently, flew east across the river, gaining altitude above the smokestack factories and sprawl of industrial Long Island. Then residential areas and soon the coastal beaches, abandoned in late winter cold.

Watching the sea reminded him of the work he had left behind, and he wondered how much treasure had been recovered, whether the crew was taking proper inventory, and if any problems had arisen with the Haitian Treasury. Well, he'd soon be back to all that—this time not to search unendingly, but to savor and divide the gold. Then, on to another project—which meant more research in Seville. The next expedition he'd finance alone.

It would be nice, he thought, to have his wife and child along, but Consuela would be repelled by all the sweat and heat, the discomfort of cramped quarters, living communally with the crew, the limited cuisine. Still, it would be an educational experience for the daughter he hardly knew, and he decided at least to extend the invitation.

Below, the forested expanse of eastern Long Island, sectored by roads and highways, the white fences of gracious old estates. Eastover's helipad was in a clearing well away from stables, and hidden from view of the main house. The Hillyer squire who built it had copied it from the English estate he had been forced to flee by Goerge III after his pro-American sentiments became a thorn in the king's side. While at Oxford, Guy had visited the original mansion and found it managed by a Trust that lodged visitors to the countryside.

After landing he thanked the pilot and carried bag and boxes down the wooded path that led to the rear of the manse. The brick was weathered and somewhat faded, but dormers and trim were gleaming white, and Guy wondered how many restorations the place had seen in the past two hundred years.

He went in by the service entrance and was taken in charge by a houseman who showed him to a third-floor room. There he changed quickly into mourning and went down to Marguerite.

She was seated in a side parlor surrounded by family and people from RyTech whom Guy did not know. After embracing his stepmother he kissed Nikky and shook hands with her husband.

"Sad thing," Thibaud intoned. *"Très triste."*

40

Guy nodded, realizing it was going to be difficult not to be a hypocrite. Nikky said, "It's good you were here, Guy. How've you been keeping?"

"Well."

"And the treasure hunt?"

"Successful."

"Really! How marvelous."

"The fruit of long hard labor."

"And—you'll return to it?"

"As soon as possible." He looked around. "Your brother here?"

"Gant you'll find at the bar. Incidentally, RyTech's PR man has taken over one of the front parlors, set up an office for press releases and such. The wire services are here, financial journals, all speculating on what's going to happen to RyTech."

A camera flash blinded him, and when his vision cleared he saw Jenny Knox tucking away her camera. "Dammit," he said, "what are *you* doing here?"

"My job."

"This has nothing to do with the treasure hunt."

"Exactly. Today I'm working for the Brooklyn *Record* syndicate. And I must say you look a good deal more presentable than yesterday."

"Sleep does wonders."

"Will you help me get a photo of Mrs. Ryan?"

"Absolutely *not.*" Taking her elbow he drew her aside. "You're presuming a lot, Jenny. If I had my way the press wouldn't be here."

"RyTech has a life of its own. Barry Gunderson is making us welcome."

"Gunderson?"

"Head of PR for RyTech—my, you *are* out of touch."

"It's how I want to be."

"Then let's have a drink together."

41

"Early in the day for me—but you journalists have hollow legs."

"Now, that's a worn-out cliché—but I'll concede we drink our share. C'mon, escort me to the bar."

He followed her, noticing that she was appropriately dressed in a dark cheviot suit and matching shoes, hair nicely coiffed and a flouncy bow tie over a white blouse.

The bar had been set up in the near end of the solarium, and two bartenders were laboring to meet press demands. Guy noticed Gant at the far end, too-long hair, brown corduroy jacket and string tie holding together the collar of a rumpled Madras shirt. Since early morning he had managed to wash his face, shave, and comb his hair. Quite an accomplishment for Gant, Guy thought unkindly. Their glances met and Gant grinned vacuously.

To the bartender, Jenny was saying, "Champagne cocktail, please."

"Right away, Miss. You, sir?"

"Fruit juice—V-8, anything."

After they were served, Jenny touched her glass to his. "Chin-chin. Like old times, eh?"

"Like yesterday," he said, and smiled. "You *do* get around."

"Have to scratch for a living. Not as if I were some playboy's bauble, y'know." She sipped the bubbling drink and looked around. "Speaking of yesterday, *I* was asking all the questions. You showed no curiosity about me at all."

"I was taught it's impolite to be nosy. Also, if one waits long enough most questions will be answered.

Her laugh was light. "Shrewd observation, Major. But I'd have held it polite if you'd asked even a few."

"Where should I start?"

She sighed. "I'm a sage twenty-eight, divorced three years from a fellow journalist I shouldn't have married . . . let's see—I come from Kansas, graduated from Missouri Journalism, and went to work for Time, Incorporated."

"Which part?"

"*SI—Sports Illustrated.* I learned a lot, but the jock atmosphere became too much for me. So, I decided I'd entrust my talents to the free market."

"Successfully?"

"I pay the rent and eat where I choose, go to the theater when I'm able to splurge. And I share my apartment with a very nice guy who treats me right."

"Satisfied with your life?"

"I guess so, though I have aspirations to be another Margaret Bourke-White."

"Laudable ambition," he said and saw Gant approaching. His half-brother's face was flushed and he said loudly, "Who's the lady, bro'?"

With a glance at Jenny, Guy said, "Name's Knox. Miz Knox to you. Jenny, my half-brother, Gant."

He leered alcoholically. "You a reporter?"

"Sort of." She was reaching for her camera but Guy's hand clamped around her wrist. "Leave that to the *National Enquirer,*" he said in a hard voice, and finished his juice.

Beckoning him aside, Gant said, "No reason to mention our earlier encounter to Mom, is there?"

"Not on a day of mourning."

"Good." He patted Guy's arm fraternally. "I was out of line—but, shit, I don't ask every chick for ID."

"Better start—or you'll spend years staring at a striped moon."

While Gant figured it out, Guy steered Jenny from the bar. She said, "I gather you two don't like each other."

"Whatever makes you think that?" He pointed at his half-sister and said, "Go snap Nikky, she'd love to have her picture in the papers."

"Can I say so?"

"By all means." He moved away and found himself face to face with a solid-looking man whose plump face and curly ringlets gave him a cherubic appearance. The man thrust

43

out a meaty hand and said, "I'm Roy Stoner, RyTech General Counsel. Sorry about Sean's death, we were very close."

Guy nodded and Stoner went on. "Also sorry we've never met, but I suspect we'll be talking a good deal over the next several weeks."

"Have to be by radio," Guy told him, "because I'm going back to my boat."

Stoner looked astonished. "You can't be serious?"

"Absolutely." He saw the attorney beckon to a thin-faced man whose well-trimmed hair was almost snow white. "Major Ryan, I'd like you to meet our executive vice president, Paul Edmonds. Paul, Guy is Sean's son by his first marriage."

"Pleased to meet you, sir," Edmonds said crisply. "Whenever it's convenient for you, I'm at your disposition."

"Thanks—but, for what?"

"Why, to brief you on our far-flung operations, fill you in."

Guy shook his head. "I appreciate the offer but I've never been interested in RyTech and—if you'll forgive me—I'm not now."

"But you *must* be," Edmonds said firmly.

"Why?"

"Because—well, certain things your father—your *late* father said."

Guy shook his head. "Whatever he may have said I'm not responsible for—nor am I bound. I came for the funeral. I'll go back where I came from as soon as Marguerite can spare me."

"I see." Edmonds gazed thoughtfully at Roy Stoner. "Then I can only say we were misinformed."

"So it seems." Guy was about to leave when a short balding man with button eyes confronted him. "*There* you are," he exclaimed jovially. "Been lookin' everywhere for

44

you. Word's out among the press that the mysterious elder son is here, and they're clamoring to meet you.''

"Ah," said Guy, "you'd be Gunderson."

"Right, Barry Gunderson." He seemed pleased by the name recognition. "If you'll just step over here with me—"

"Hold on—why is the press so anxious to see me?"

"Because—well it's obvious you're heir apparent."

"But I'm not," Guy told him with finality, "and if I were I'd put an end to this—this circus. The bar, press releases, hors d'oeuvres—my God, a catered affair. Where's respect for the dead?"

Gunderson swallowed. "You don't understand—the transfer of power commands attention. This is as much for RyTech as for Sean."

"Then you should have held an office party," Guy said brusquely, and made his way back to the parlor where Marguerite sat between Nikky and her son-in-law. His stepmother was wearing a black silk dress, a black lace shawl across her shoulders. Her only ornamentation was a gold wedding band, and Guy inwardly approved her lack of ostentation. Had to be *some* balance in the house. To Thibaud he said, "Mind?" and waited until his brother-in-law rose and ceded the chair.

"Not at all," he said stiffly. "In fact I need a drink."

"There's plenty," Guy told him, and took Marguerite's pale hand. "All the food and drink reminds me of a wake."

"You don't like it? Neither do I."

"Who laid it on, for God's sake?"

"Paul—Paul Edmonds. He persuaded me, said it really had to be done."

"That's his opinion. How are you holding up?"

"Fairly well, though I don't care to stand endlessly. After all, the 'viewing' isn't until later. Are you rested?"

"Pretty well." How characteristic of her to be solicitous of others at a time like this, he thought, and said, "There's

45

widespread expectation I'm to replace my father at Ry-Tech—I assume you didn't start the rumor.''

"Hardly." One hand briefly touched her throat. Then she smiled bravely and greeted someone who bent over to murmur condolences. Others came and went; occasionally Guy was introduced as 'my stepson, Guy,' and after a while Thibaud came back with a drink for Nikky.

After speaking with Marguerite a thin-faced man with a long nose and a ferret look introduced himself to Guy as "Farley Johns, sir, and I have the honor to be comptroller of RyTech."

"Glad you could come," Guy said agreeably.

"Essential—wouldn't have done otherwise—and I'm looking forward to conferring with you in days ahead."

"About RyTech? There's misinformation about. I will not be joining RyTech."

The comptroller looked startled. After pursing his lips he said, "Then who is it to be?"

"Haven't the faintest." Guy felt Marguerite covertly pinch his knee to signal displeasure. As Johns drifted away Guy whispered, "You can't change my mind."

"We'll see." She patted his knee. "Did I hurt?"

"Dreadfully."

Marguerite acknowledged the sympathies of another visitor, and Guy realized that reporters were moving past, staring curiously at him. He ignored their gaze, and after a while Nikky came over and said, "Is Consuela coming?"

"You both live in France, I thought you might know. Did you tell her?"

"I tried, Guy, but she wasn't home so I left a message with the maid." She shrugged. "Perhaps she'll decide to come."

I'd rather she didn't, he thought, but said nothing.

"After all," said Nikky, "this rather changes the equation for her, doesn't it?"

"How so?"

"Well, if you take father's place then she'll have all the things she wanted, a way of life suitable to a marquesa."

"She married me for rich or poor," he said thinly, "and did badly with the poor. I'd rather not see what she might do if she were rich."

"I think she'd do very well. After all, her family aren't exactly field hands tilling barren acres. She was accustomed to a good deal, Guy, you can't overlook that. And she *is* the mother of your child."

"Speaking of which, when are you and Thibaud going to produce?"

Her cheeks colored. "We—haven't decided. Besides, that's very private."

Meaning, Guy thought, that one of them abhors the idea of children. Probably her husband. With a glance at Thibaud he rose. "I return your chair. Need to stretch my legs."

Marguerite said, "I believe we've been here long enough. I'd like to rest before the viewing. Guy, will you see me to my room?"

As they neared the wide staircase he noticed an electric chair running along the railing. "Sean's?" he asked.

"Yes, it was installed nearly a year ago after the first—episode. In time I expect it will also be useful for me."

"You're sound as rock, don't talk that way," he remonstrated and heard her say, "Ah, that's what your father would say. Like it or not, dear, you have much in common with him."

He held her arm gently as they went up the staircase and down the wide, carpeted hall to the master bedroom. At the door she kissed his cheek and said, "Again, thank you for being here. It gives me strength." Then she placed her hand on the doorknob. "I'll continue staying here, so much of my husband is in the room. I want to . . . nourish the memories."

"Of course you do—and will."

He waited until she was inside and then he went up to his own room on the floor above. There he took off coat and vest, loosened his tie and lay back on the bed. He hadn't been prepared for the mass intrusion but Marguerite was handling it well. Probably she'd ask him to stay until the Board selected a new chief operating official, then he'd be free to go back to his boat.

His mind was reviewing what it had been like working on the bottom those hundred of hours when, through the old ventilation register, he heard two men speaking. Their voices were hushed, distant, but he heard one say, ". . . mighty alarmed when I heard he was coming, but that's over with. Turns out he's just another army simpleton, not his father's son at all."

"Thank God," the other voice replied. "So there's no danger for now."

"Not the slightest. We hang tight and make sure an insider gets the job."

A short chuckle, then: "What if the bastard changes his mind?"

"Hell, *you* know the answer. He'll have to disappear."

By then Guy was half off the bed, listening close to the vent. Evidently the men had moved away because he heard nothing more. He didn't recognize the voices, and the conspirators could have been speaking from almost any place in the house.

As he lay back, Guy reflected that chance and proximity to an ancient heating-ventilation system had confirmed his father's insight about one important thing. At RyTech something was very, very wrong.

Four

At the funeral home the family paid their respects before others were permitted in. Guy knelt beside his father's open casket, said a brief prayer for his soul, crossed himself, and joined Marguerite where chairs were arranged at an angle from the flower-decked coffin. More flowers and wreaths arrived, and Guy contrasted the array with the grim body bags he'd seen too often in Vietnam. The flowers were a symbol of life, their presence denying the perpetuity of death. The calculatedly sterile setting created the impression of a smooth, painless transition from life to the grave. Cotton packing in his father's oral cavity restored the shrunken cheeks, and other cosmetic touches shed years from Sean's appearance.

The room was filling now. Attendants maintained an orderly line of viewers, and soft music filtered in. Some Irish song, or hymn, Guy supposed. A prelude to the wake.

A youngish priest was circulating among the mourners, exercising the burdens of office as he greeted some, blessed others, whispered a consoling word to those whose sorrow was obvious. A stooped, elderly man with a strangely curled cowlick over his forehead conferred with the priest, who responded deferentially.

Something about the old man was familiar to Guy, and

49

as he tried to recall the snag-toothed features, he recognized the man as an Irish Republican militant who, a few years ago, had been charged and acquitted in Boston of smuggling arms to the IRA. What was the name? Conor . . . Conor Counihan, that was it. A shrewd, heartless old devil, he mused, who, absent imprisonment, should at least have been deported.

Yet here was old Counihan himself, directing a pair of brawny lads who carried between them a huge wreath mounted on an easel. Fluttering green ribbons were stamped in gold with Gaelic words unknown to Guy—and with the priest's acquiescence the floral tribute was placed behind Sean's bier to dominate the setting.

To Marguerite, Guy whispered, "I don't like Counihan being here. Why is he?"

"Your father knew him, Guy, contributed money to his defense. I suppose this is the old man's way of showing appreciation."

"But he's a murderer," Guy said, "a terrorist".

"Shhhh—your father was romantic about the Old Sod. Giving money to Irish patriots was a safe enough way of indulging nostalgic fantasy." She patted his hand. "Though Sean hated everything English he made an exception for my English blood—probably because I was Catholic."

Guy watched Conor Counihan and his aides withdraw from the bier, move slowly back toward the door, and he wondered how deep had been his father's involvement with Irish revolutionaries. The answer, he decided, was something he would never know—yet the floral tribute represented something vestigial, an occult trace of his father's life just now, in death, breaking surface.

As the evening wore on Guy was introduced to scores of people, many from RyTech, others neighboring landowners come to offer non-commercial sympathies. Roy Stoner was on hand, chatting easily with a RyTech group, while Paul Edmonds stood isolated from the flow. Barry Gunderson, the day's impresario, was probably back at his temporary office, ingratiating himself and RyTech with the press, milking the occasion for every possible advantage.

To Guy it was significant that he sensed no empathy with any of his father's senior associates—for what had he and Sean ever agreed on? Sean must have chosen staff in his own image, yet none seemed to possess his father's inner iron. So he could dominate them, Guy decided; typical of what he had inferred of his father's character.

Back at Eastover, he mused, the kitchen would be busy preparing for the all-night wake. Bartenders restocking to tend the fifty-odd friends invited by Marguerite. To Guy, the whole idea of a wake was barbaric; surrounding the corpse with mortals to fend off evil spirits. To him the custom represented superstition linked with Ireland's ultra-Catholicism. A ritual burdening the living.

His semireverie was broken by a familiar voice. "Guy, I'm so sorry about your loss." A firm handclasp, and Guy looked up at the face of Jake Needham, one of his closest friends at the Point, a tight end on his team. Rising, he said, "Jake—thanks for coming." They hugged impulsively and stood back to survey each other. "You're looking fit," Guy said. "How've you been?"

"Very well. Located in New York, and practicing law."

"Law? I thought—"

"Failed promotion to major—heart murmur—so I settled for bars, not stars, and it's been all to the good. Took my GI Bill to Yale Law, and it's been upward ever since." From his wallet he extracted a card. "If you ever need legal services, please call, no matter how trivial."

Guy saw Jake's engraved name above the name of his Wall Street firm: Hay, Hughes, Wriston and Van Wickle.

"We do mostly corporate work," Jake said, "but occasionally we accommodate a private client—if he or she can afford us."

"Jake, I can't tell you how good it is to see you. Except

51

for family members I'm lost in a multitude of strangers."
He tucked the card into his wallet.

"Then I'm particularly glad I came. FYI, I've got a long-suffering wife and three small children. You?"

"Wife and one."

"She here?" Needham looked around.

"Paris. We—well, we haven't been living together for some time."

"I'm sorry," Needham said gravely.

Guy put his arm around his classmate's shoulders. "I'm glad you've done well, Jake. Before I go back we'll at least have lunch, talk about old times, have a general update."

"Look forward to it."

"Can you stay for the wake?"

"Wish I could, but I'm expected back in Manhattan. Came here from the office, and my wife and children need my reassuring presence. By the way, anything to the rumor you'll be joining RyTech?"

"Like I'll be joining the astronaut team." He shook his head. "Not for me." They shook hands again and the lawyer made his way to the bier.

Marguerite touched Guy's arm. "I'm ready to leave for the house," she said. "I need to repair myself before the casket arrives."

He filed out with the family, as behind them attendants closed the coffin and began removing floral pieces for tomorrow's transfer to the cemetery.

Guy saw Marguerite to her Rolls where she was joined by Gant and the de Neuvilles. He was walking alone toward an estate car when someone approached him in the half-light. "Major Ryan, may I have a word with you?"

Halting, he said, "Not if you're a reporter."

"Far from it." He showed Guy a Pentagon credential: Defense Security Agency. The name was Wilke. Face and photo matched.

Guy said, "What have I done now?"

"Nothing—though you managed to elude our man at Port-Au-Prince airport."

"So that's who he was. I figured he was press."

"Naturally enough. I realize this is a poor time to brace you, but our business can't wait."

"Our business?"

"RyTech. You must know the firm does millions of dollars worth of business with Defense every year."

"Frankly, I know very little about RyTech." He gazed at Wilke. "How did your people know I'd be at the airport?"

"The National Security Agency monitors the airwaves, extracts radio messages from and to prime contractors like RyTech. We felt it was important to get to you before— well, *others* did. Have you had any buy-out offers, Major? Any threats?"

"Buy-out offers? I have no stock in RyTech."

"But you will, won't you? I mean, it's set you'll be taking your father's place."

"I understand that was his wish. It's not mine."

Wilke frowned. "That's unfortunate. With so much at stake we must have someone completely dependable at the helm."

"And my father wasn't?"

Wilke looked away. "Your late father's role was a complicated one. He had many interests, a lot of them abroad. Obviously he couldn't stay on top of everything, so it's not a question of distrusting him. What I'm trying to say, however badly, is that some disturbing things have taken place at RyTech."

"Such as?"

"Technology transfers to the East Bloc."

"My father wasn't a Communist sympathizer."

"He sympathized with, and to some extent supported the IRA, some of whose factions have had Communist connec-

53

tions for many years. More recently there've been PLO involvements.''

''I can't believe my father would condone anything like that.''

''I'm not saying he did. Still, Conor Counihan was here, fact is fact, and RyTech's specialized work is too important to leak to our enemies.''

Guy thought it over. ''How specialized?''

''I'm not a liberty to say more than that a RyTech subsidiary, the Institute for Strategic Research, developed a system or process invaluable to national defense. If it should get away from us, we'd be vulnerable to a lot of unpleasant things.''

''In the nuclear area?''

Wilke shrugged. ''You'll be asked to a briefing in Washington.''

''When?''

''After the reading of your father's will—when it's known where you stand.''

''Well,'' said Guy, ''if you're thinking I'll take over RyTech, I won't be.''

''The briefing may change your mind.''

''No way.''

''You're a patriot, Major, fought for our country. I can't see you turning from something so important. Meanwhile, we ask that you keep an open mind. You'll be pressured by certain interests either to stand aside from RyTech or sell them your stock. In the event you decline, your life may be in jeopardy.''

''Seems all the more reason not to get involved.''

''Except that you're needed there. You've taken risks before. Defense is asking you to take another—perhaps the most serious you've ever faced. But you're a man of proven courage. Combat infantryman, Silver Star, two Bronze Stars, Soldier's Medal, Purple Heart. We need you at RyTech.''

54

Guy smiled despite himself. Was Wilke trying to flatter him into accepting the RyTech position? Well, he'd have to come up with a better strategem than that. "You'll have to find someone else," he said simply and began moving toward the Mercedes roadster he had driven from Eastover.

"Final thought," Wilke called. "Keep an open mind."

As Guy got behind the wheel he remembered the voices overheard through the ventilation flue. Now they seemed to fit in with Wilke's ominous warning. He'd never even heard of the Institute for Strategic Research, had no idea where it was located. And if he had his way, never would. Starting the engine, he let it warm, then steered out of the parking lot and gained the high-crowned rural road to Eastover.

Patches of ice slicked the asphalt. The frozen road snaked through woods and fenced fields, illuminated ahead by the half-moon's gray light. Headlights bounced and Guy realized he was driving too fast for the treacherous surface. Ahead, a sharp turn. Slowing, he stepped on the brake pedal, felt no resistance. Angrily he pumped it, but nothing grabbed. He turned into the curve and felt the rear end slither. The car spun around and as its front wheels cleared the iced shoulder Guy saw black trees ahead. He was going to crash.

As the car turned over Guy switched off the ignition and covered his face. Body-shattering impact. Metal grinding.

Nothing.

Consciousness returned and he smelled gasoline. The car had rolled over and ended up on the driver's side. His ribs ached from the seatbelt. His first thought was to get free.

Grabbing the wheel for leverage he eased strain on the belt and punched it loose. Then he shoved the door upward and crawled out, gasping for air free of fumes. Miracle the car hadn't exploded, he thought—but it could if gas reached the heated engine block. Thank God he'd turned off the juice before impact.

He looked around.

The car roof was lodged against the bole of a tree, roof dented inward as though clasping the immobile wood. Groggily he made his way up the bank, slipping and falling on ice and frozen weeds until he reached the crest. As quickly as he could he walked from the wreckage, half stooping from rib pain that shot hot lances with every movement.

He was trudging toward the village when the roadster's tank let go. A hundred yards from the wreckage he felt the blast concussion, saw flames shooting high, towering above the gaunt and leafless trees. He turned his back and walked on.

Headlights shone behind him, elongating his shadow eerily across the road. Turning sideways he gave the hitchhiker's sign and heard the car begin to slow. As it pulled up beside him a voice called, "Your car? Anyone in it?"

"No." He made out the driver's face: Jenny Knox.

"Well, Major," she said in a show of good humor, "we meet in the oddest places."

"Don't we, though?" He swallowed. Gas fumes still wafted up his nostrils. His throat and mouth were dry. "Coincidence? Or were you expecting—?"

"Don't be funny—get in."

Painfully, he eased his body into the Datsun and the car lurched ahead. "The coincidence," she said stiffly, "derives from my lingering to talk with some of the neighbors about your late father. Then I phoned my apartment but my boyfriend was on the phone. So I had to wait to talk with him." She glanced at Guy. "I know you were heading for the wake. Lucky the son's wasn't added to the father's."

"Apparently I've forgotten how to handle a car on ice. Now if you'll just get me to Eastover I'll be very grateful."

"Gratitude or not, you're for the nearest doctor, after which I have to compose a story on the day's happenings."

Ahead was an illuminated lawn sign: *Dr. Trevor Provost, G.P.* Slowing, she turned into the drive, shut off the engine. Guy said, "I don't need this."

"That's for the doctor to determine." She got out, walked around and opened his door. "This is the second exclusive you've given me."

"My—accident?"

"What else? And let's hope it was just that—an accident."

She helped him up the steps, while on the road a cawing fire engine hurtled by. "Just like Manhattan," she remarked and pressed the bell. A gray-haired woman peered through the door pane, opened up, and said, "I'll get the doctor."

They went into the waiting room. On the lamp table lay an old issue of *Life*, copies of *Popular Mechanics* everywhere. Guy found himself wondering whether some *un*popular mechanic had tinkered with his brakes, his life . . .

"You okay?" Concern tightened her face.

"Sure. Tension, I guess."

"Well, I hate to go, but you're in better hands than mine."

"Thanks for your help. I appreciate it."

"We're even, Major. Read about it tomorrow." She went back through the doorway as a ruddy-faced middle-aged man appeared. "I'm Dr. Provost," he said cheerily. "What seems to be the problem?"

Two hours later, bruised ribcage taped, right wrist in an elastic bandage, facial cuts treated, Guy taxied to Eastover. Taking his Chesterfield, the houseman sniffed. "Gasoline," Guy told him, "so try to air it out."

"Yes, Major."

Inside, the wake was well underway. Skirting the crowd, Guy made his slow way to the bar and was rewarded with a double shot of Black Label. A few moments later old Counihan hobbled up and requested Bushmill's. Guy decided to get away, but as he was leaving, Counihan lurched over and clutched Guy's lapel. "Ye're the *true* Irish son," he intoned. "Descendant of a fine Irish patriot."

"My father was American," Guy retorted, pushing aside the clutching hand.

"Ah, but they's things ye don't know about yer fayther," Counihan persisted.

"And I don't want to know them."

"Ye must fill the gap, lad, we're countin' on ye."

"Who's counting on me?"

"Why, the Brotherhood—who else?"

Guy stared at the worn, drawn face that looked dead but for sharp, malicious eyes. "Fuck the Brotherhood," Guy snapped. "You're a gang of murdering terrorists who ought to be lined up and shot."

"That's yer English eddication," said Counihan, his shrill voice rising. "But peel away the English muck an' yer an Irish lad. Take up the struggle, say we."

"Old man," said Guy in a clear voice, "You're talking rubbish. I want nothing to do with you or what you represent."

Eyes blazing, Counihan stepped back.

Their voices had caused the room to quiet. From nowhere came the easel-bearers, who steadied their chief and drew him from the bar. Guy strode past them and found Marguerite sitting in the parlor. She glimpsed his bandaged wrist, his treated face, but before she could speak Guy said furiously, "Counihan's here, babbling about his glorious cause, desecrating my father's name. Who let him come?"

"Ah, Guy, it was your father's wish."

"I can't believe it."

"Oh, it's true enough. Conor was never convicted of those gun-running charges."

"Ever hear of an Irish conviction in Boston?"

She smiled tolerantly. "Calm yourself and tell me what happened to you. I've been worried for hours."

Swallowing, Guy sat down and blamed the accident on ice and too much speed. Tenderly she kissed his forehead, squeezed his hand. "Thank God you're safe. I couldn't bear to lose you."

"The car's a total loss—I'll pay for it."

"No, no, I'm sure insurance will cover. Besides, I won't believe it was your fault. Don't think of such a thing." She patted his hand comfortingly. "I know you feel alien to this wake, but you've made an appearance, and now I want you to go to bed and get some rest. Tomorrow will be worst of all."

"If—" he said hesitantly—"you can spare me."

"Of course I can—with so many loyal friends here—"

He kissed her cheek and went up to his room. Undressing was painful, but the Scotch was beginning to work. When he was finally in bed, staring up at the dark ceiling, he wondered if the explosion had left enough of the car to tell whether the brake line had been sabotaged. He thought of Wilke's words and tried to put them in focus. The DSA man had been specific about some things, silent on others. But how much did he care to know? As his eyes closed and pain began to fade he saw himself being sucked into a whirling maelstrom from which he could never struggle free.

Five

Guy rose early, had a light breakfast in the kitchen and took an estate wagon into town. The police station turned out to be two rooms of the town hall, and Chief Weston was drinking coffee from a foam cup. Guy introduced himself and said he'd been the driver of the burned Mercedes.

"From the tag we connected the car to Eastover, but I wasn't goin' to bother anybody for a day or so." He was a young, intelligent-looking fellow who might be taking a correspondence course in law.

"Appreciate the courtesy," Guy said, declining an offer of coffee. "Wreck still there?"

"Yeah, I'll have it hauled in later."

"Is there a good mechanic around—one you can trust?"

"Might be. What's on your mind?"

Guy described the brake failure and said, "So I'd like the brake lines checked—if the explosion left enough to check."

Chief Weston leaned forward interestedly. "Suspect sabotage?"

"The way things happened it seems possible." On the wall behind the Chief's head hung a framed parchment decorated with the 101st Airborne insigne. Guy felt he could trust Chief Weston. "I'll pay for the expertise."

"Might not have to. If foul play's suspected it's police business."

"I don't want to upset my stepmother, so if anything's done I want it kept quiet—among the three of us."

Weston nodded. "You're staying at Eastover?"

"For a day or so."

"Shouldn't take long to get an answer from Charley Ferris. I'll let you know." As Guy rose the chief pushed back his chair. "What if there was wrongdoing?"

"Mainly, I want to know."

"Any enemies? Suspects?"

Guy shook his head.

"When I heard the fire truck last night I went out there myself. Helluva blaze. Either way, you were mighty lucky to come out so light."

Guy turned away, paused and said, "Ever get to Hue?"

"Sure—after the slaughter. Poor bastards. I see your Pointer ring, so I guess you was around."

"Later—I was working up north at the time."

Weston whistled. "Yeah, you look like you got the guts for that. Pleasure to meet you, Mr. Ryan. We'll do what we can." He levered himself from the chair and came jerkily around the desk to shake hands. "Left part of me in that fuckin' jungle," he explained and went with Guy as far as the door.

At a newsstand Ryan bought the Brooklyn *Record* and read Jenny Knox's story as he walked back to the Cherokee wagon. Tastefully done, he thought, and noticed that his accident was mentioned without innuendo and almost as after thought. She was a talented reporter who honored facts—which gave her, he thought, not much of a future in the reporting trade. He started the engine, backed around and drove back to Eastover. Slowly.

Green tarpaulins concealed earth from the freshly dug grave. Priest and mourners assembled beneath a canopy, for

61

the sky was gray and threatening. Cold wind fluttered the canopy, lifted tarpaulin corners. Guy stared at his father's casket, hardly hearing the priest's eulogy. To Guy's irritation Conor Counihan and his two bhoyos stood at the fringe of the crowd. All the RyTech executives he'd met were on hand—including Gunderson, who had a handful of press in tow. No Jenny Knox.

Through the black veil he could see Marguerite's reddened eyes. Occasionally she dabbed her cheeks with a black-edged handkerchief.

Nikky wore a chic costume and Thibaud appeared staunch in Homburg and Oxford gray. As usual Gant looked disreputable in a stained trenchcoat and knitted ski cap. God gives us our relatives, Guy mused, but allows us our own friends. A heavenly dispensation.

Through the cold air floated the priest's nasal words, eulogizing Sean's rise from humble birth to envied success in America, praising his concern for family and friends, his benefactions to Church and charity. A man to be emulated by all who prized the loving, caring spirit of Christ.

Typical of Sean Ryan's humility, the priest continued, was his wish to forego formal mass in church. So, with a sprinkling of holy water, the priest consigned the coffin to the earth, Sean's soul to his Creator.

As the coffin silently lowered, Guy took the widow's arm and led her back to the waiting limousine, first in a long, gleaming procession. He rode with her and her two children back to Eastover, through the dark deer park, past stark statuary and frozen fountains, into the manse where a roaring fire, a buffet table, and lawyers waited.

When family and servants were assembled in the drawing room Roy Stoner made a prefatory statement and began reading the will of Sean Foley Ryan. Bequests to Eastover's fourteen retainers were generous, and Guy saw pleased expressions on their faces as each name and sum were read. Good for Ol' Dad, he thought.

After pausing for a sip of water, Stoner said, "As for the deceased's real property it is left in its entirety 'to my beloved wife, Marguerite Hillyer Ryan, in whose prudence I have full confidence.' " He paused again. "Paragraph Eight 'I distribute my sixty percent of RyTech's voting stock as follows: ten percent to Marguerite Hillyer Ryan, unconditionally. Fifty percent to my elder son, Guy Patrick Ryan, on condition—' " Gasps interrupted the lawyer, who waited for Nikky and Gant to compose themselves. Guy felt eyes upon him and stared straight ahead. Stoner said, "To repeat—'fifty percent of the voting stock to my elder son, Guy Patrick Ryan, *on condition* that he assume the presidency and direction of RyTech. In the event that he does not choose to follow my wishes his portion will revert to my wife, Marguerite Hillyer Ryan. My son, Guy, is to make his decision known within fifteen days of this reading, after which it becomes irrevocable.' "

Gant muttered as Stoner began reading the final paragraph. " 'My daughter Nicole and my son Gant already possess ten percent each of RyTech's voting stock, neither having done anything to deserve it. My wish is that their shares not be sold, hypothecated or transferred to persons outside my immediate family, and that their shares be always voted in accordance with the wishes of their mother and half-brother."

Rising, Gant blurted, "The old shit!" and left the room, knocking over an empty chair. Marguerite shook her head sadly. Nikky drew her fur collar around her pale face and stared rigidly ahead. Thibaud shrugged expressively.

Stoner said, "That completes formal reading of the will and much of the speculation concerning RyTech's future." Rising he strode to Guy and extended his hand, pretending his conversation with Guy the day before had not taken place. "Welcome to RyTech. You'll find all operating officials eager to cooperate with you."

Uncertainly, Guy clasped his hand. Marguerite whispered, "Together we control eighty percent, dear, so you've got clear sailing."

"I've also got fifteen days."

The servants were leaving. Nikky came over and kissed Guy tentatively, "I suppose I should congratulate you—at least I wish you well."

"Thanks."

Thibaud shook his hand vigorously. "Good *show*, Guy. Look forward to showing you my operation as soon as you'd like."

Guy nodded, feeling the world had suddenly dropped on his shoulders. At his side Roy Stoner said, "Should I tell Paul you'll be in charge?"

"I've fifteen days, so hold off."

"But we really should—"

"I have other responsibilities, a life that's far removed from corporate management. I guess Gunderson has press releases prepared? Have him hold off, too."

Stoner frowned. "This uncertainty will have a negative effect on Wall Street, you know."

"I don't exist for the Street," Guy said. "I'll do things at my own tempo."

"Of course—your privilege." He stepped back as Marguerite took Guy's arm. "Let's have a cup of tea—chat a bit."

Nodding, Guy let his stepmother lead him toward the sun room where a houseman interrupted him. "Sir, there's a telephone call for you."

"Press?"

"No—a man who said he was at Hue." He gestured at an extension. Guy excused himself and picked up the phone. "Ryan here."

"Guess you know who's talking?"

"I do."

"Okay. I took the mech to the spot and had him go over things. Unfortunately, heat and blast destroyed the brake lines."

"I was afraid of that."

"How*ever,*" he drawled, "the master cylinder survived. Charley showed me a nice puncture that let the brake fluid drain out. Hole the size and shape of a cold chisel."

"Enterprising," Guy remarked.

"Yeah. So, what do you want to do about it?"

"Pay Charley and forget it."

"Twenty will cover."

"I'll stop by—and many thanks."

"Always glad to help another vet."

Marguerite said, "Nothing alarming, I trust?"

"Garage calling about the car wreckage."

They seated themselves in the parlor where Marguerite poured tea and offered him small butter cookies. After sipping she said, "There must be a good deal on your mind."

"There is. My first obligation is to my salvage crew."

"I'll have Roy put the jet on standby."

"Thanks, but I probably ought to fly commercial. From Haiti I need to go to Paris and Seville."

"It's your plane, after all, take it where you will."

He smiled. "Seducing me with luxurious corporate perks?"

"It will accelerate things for you—no waiting around airports for delayed flights."

"There's that. Well—if you don't need the Lear for a while?"

"When I flew it was always with your father. So—" She left the thought unspoken.

Stoner came in. "Forgive the interruption, but I've been talking with Paul and we agree Guy should have protection—at least for the present."

"Protection?" Guy asked.

"Security guards. These days it's fairly customary for corporate heads."

"I survived 'Nam," Guy said. "I wouldn't know what to do with civilian guards—they'd be in my way."

"Also it affects our kidnapping insurance. Unless you're guarded it could be canceled."

"If I take the job I'll consider it."

Stoner left the parlor and Guy said, "Roy drew up Sean's will?"

"Yes—but the provisions were your father's, not his."

"Point is, Roy talked about the contents—otherwise there'd have been no rumors of my taking over."

"Or perhaps the typist gossiped."

"Result's the same. I'm of the school that holds classified info should stay classified."

"Well, it's in the open now—and Roy certainly seems eager to serve you."

Guy stirred his tea reflectively. "If you can spare me I'll leave for Haiti tomorrow."

"With my blessing and thanks." She sipped from her cup. "Gant behaved badly, wouldn't you say?"

"I'd prefer saying nothing."

"That's charitable of you, but I can understand his disappointment. He wants funds to produce a music video of some group he's invested in. I've declined to oblige so he resents me more than usual. Should he approach you, Guy, don't feel under any obligation on my account."

"I won't. He knows where we stand."

"If only he'd been more like you," she sighed.

"And if I'd been more like Sean . . . ?"

She smiled. "Point made. Nikky—*there* you are. Tea, dear?"

"Thanks, Mother, but if we leave now we can just catch our flight to Paris." Bending, she kissed Marguerite. "Thibaud's doing last-minute packing, so I'm including his goodbyes." She stepped back. "Will you be all right?"

"I'll be quite fine, don't worry about me."

"Guy, we hope you'll come soon. Lyon's an agreeable place, really." She kissed his forehead. "If you like I can phone Connie from Paris."

"That would be nice."

"Goodbye, then." She waved a gloved hand and swirled away as the houseman entered. "Call for you, sir. Not the press—someone in Washington."

When he hesitated Marguerite said, "Come, it could be the President."

Guy picked up the phone. "Guy Ryan."

"My name is Hoskins," the man said, "and you were seen by a representative from DSA."

"Right."

"He mentioned a forthcoming invitation?"

"He did."

"How soon could you come to Washington, Major?"

"I'm leaving for Haiti tomorrow, then Europe, so it could be quite a while. Anyway, it's far from established that I'll succeed my father, so—"

"Haven't agreed, eh? Well, what you'll learn here could be decisive. Trouble is it can't wait, so let me urge you to stop here for a few hours en route to Haiti."

Guy considered. "All right," he said reluctantly. "Where's the meeting?"

"Over the phone I'd rather not say. You'll be coming in at General Aviation, I assume, so I'll have transportation waiting."

"Lear 35, RyTech logo."

"Good, Major, I look forward to meeting you."

The line went dead, and Guy finished the rest of his tea.

"Pentagon?" Marguerite inquired. "Sean was forever attending those meetings. Now you. Part of your new responsibilities."

"It's on the way south," he said, and got up. "I've some things to take care of, but we'll dine together."

"Of course—do what you must."

Under the staircase stood a built-in telephone booth. Guy closed the door and fished Jake Needham's card from his wallet. He called the law firm office and after piercing two secretarial barriers finally heard Jake's voice. "Guy! Glad you got back to me. Lunch tomorrow? Calendar's clear."

"Good. I need you for the day. Can you manage it?"

"Sure, but—what's up?"

"A meeting in Washington—you should be back home for dinner."

"No problem. Metroliner?"

"RyTech jet."

"Sounds good. What time?"

"Ten o'clock, Kennedy General Aviation."

"I'll be there."

Guy hung up. He was getting boxed in and he needed advice from someone he trusted completely. Jake Needham filled the bill. Besides, there wasn't anybody else he could talk to. Last night's sabotage persuaded him he could no longer ignore warnings. Someone wanted him dead, and he was resolved to stay alive.

In his bathroom Guy soaked his sprained wrist and grimaced at the mirror. The butterfly clips on cheek and forehead looked bizarre, he thought, as though he were a bionic man. The tape around his torso was beginning to itch. He drew a hot tub and soaked for half an hour, feeling the rib pain diminish.

While he was dressing his extension rang, and it was Jenny Knox. "Feeling better today?"

"Considerable."

"Then you haven't heard the news?"

"Guess not—what news?"

"I was right to call you—and please don't kill the messenger. I just read an AFP cable from Port-Au-Prince. Your boat's been seized, treasure confiscated."

"Damn! Why? What reason did they give?"

"Fiscal irregularities. Guy, I'm *so* sorry."

The news crushed him—all that time, money and effort wasted. He couldn't believe it. Either the government of Haiti had taken up open piracy or his crew had tried to short-change the Haitians. After a deep breath he said, "I'm flying there tomorrow—want to come?"

"Don't think I'd be much help—besides, I'm tied up here, so I wish you luck. And be careful down there—those Ton-Tons can get pretty nasty."

"I can get pretty nasty myself," he said without conviction, for short of an armed raid how could he free the boat? Sue—and watch the World Court dawdle for years. While Haiti spent his hard-won gold. Negotiations? What leverage did he have? *They* had possession. Jesus!

Finally he said, "I appreciate your letting me know. I had a legal arrangement with the Haitian Treasury. If they've abrogated it I'm not sure what I can do."

"Let me start the ball rolling."

"How?"

"I'll call the Haitian Embassy, demand details, put the blast on them. Let the bastards know they're screwing with American public opinion. Couldn't hurt."

"Guess not, and thanks."

Slowly he continued dressing. No need to distress his stepmother with the news. She had enough on her mind already.

What a rotten development. How in hell could he set things right?

He rewound the Ace bandage around his wrist, got into his tweed jacket and went down to dinner.

Six

Beyond Philadelphia the co-pilot served coffee in Wedgewood china, a midmorning snack of pecan waffles, maple syrup and mild sausage. Jake Needham said, "Man, this is *living*. Sally won't believe it." He smacked his lips. "Not like the Point, eh?"

"Or 'Nam."

"Okay, we're airborne—why am I here? Is this a junket or is business involved?"

Guy drank from his cup and set it down. The Lear flew so smoothly the china didn't rattle. "To begin with I have the problem of RyTech—taking over or walking away. Yesterday morning I planned to do the latter. By nightfall I was wavering—and this is why." He told Jake of his boat's confiscation. "That wipes me out—not to mention my in-laws' investment. I planned the expedition, put more of myself into it than I'm willing to admit, and for the present at least, everything's taken from me. Under the circumstances what would you advise?"

Jake scratched his cleft chin. "Well, I'm no expert in International or Admiralty law, but I always like to begin with the facts. So far we don't know them. If your people were pilfering, that's one thing. If the seizure was unwarranted, that's another. Only find out when you get there."

Guy nodded. "Can you come with me?"

"I'd like to—let me phone the office from Washington, check with my seniors."

"I don't want a substitute, Jake—has to be you. Tell them that."

"I will. Now tell me about RyTech."

He told his friend everything that had occurred since his arrival at Eastover: the overheard conversation; the Mercedes sabotage; his encounter with Counihan; the talk with Wilke of DSA; the provisions of Sean's will. When he finished, Needham whistled. "If your father thought RyTech was rotten to the core, why didn't he do something about it?"

"Perhaps he was too old, too sick, too far removed from what was going on."

"Or—threatened?"

Guy shook his head. "I don't see my father taking kindly to threats. He didn't reach the top by being intimidated."

"By *rotten,* we might infer he was thinking of technology transfer to the wrong users. That's an ongoing industrial problem, you know. What was your father's request—'save sceptre'? There could be an association." He looked at Guy. "Who's seeing you in Washington?"

"Don't really know. No address, no phone number."

"Well that's how delicate things are done. I suspect you're to be briefed on some critical aspect DSA is concerned about—which your father didn't live to resolve." He took a coffee refill from the co-pilot. "How much do you know about RyTech's activities?"

"Next to nothing."

"That's what I figured. So, I checked with my brokerage house and a couple of sources that contract regularly with the Government." Opening his briefcase he took out a sheet covered with handwriting. "Total worth of RyTech isn't known—but the estimate is three to four billion."

"Billion?" The sum staggered Guy.

"Repeat: billions. RyTech's organized as a sort of holding company for foreign ventures—that's why a true worth figure's not available. Let's see—in South Korea there's an outfit developing alternate high-protein foods: krill, kelp, that sort of thing. Started as lab research and a production plant is now building. In France—near Lyons—your brother-in-law manages a plant that produces high-grade industrial computers—hardware, computerized navigational systems. It's also developing robotics which, I guess you know, is the harbinger of automated production."

"If you say so."

"Near Geneva there's a RyTech subsidiary turning out lasers, and if rumor's correct, laser weaponry. The Sovs would be interested."

"Too interested."

"Yeah, the Swiss sell to anyone who can pay. Okay—in England and Ireland RyTech labs are conducting medical research for eventual new products."

"Like what?"

"Biogenetics. The rules there are less restrictive."

"My father never visited Ireland—I wonder why?"

"On the U.S. side a corporate subsidiary deals with Government contracts: army, navy, air force and NASA. In Houston you have oil exploration, marine salvage operations and a training program for executive protection."

"Salvage," Guy muttered. "I could have used some help. That's all in the U.S.?"

"Well, there's also this think-tank called the Institute for Strategic Research—ISR. Probably one of those places where a bunch of non-tenured eggheads sit around and try to come up with answers to problems that don't yet exist. Lot of speculation about ISR, but in the time I had I couldn't track anything solid. Still, it sounds harmless." He replaced his notes in the briefcase. "Bottom line—quite a legacy, pal."

The co-pilot cleared their table and said Washington National was in sight. Banking, the Lear began to slow and Guy felt brief shudders as wheels and flaps went down. Presently he glimpsed the Capitol, the gleaming Potomac, the Mall and the riverside runways.

The Lear skimmed down like a swallow, alighting with hardly a jar, and when Guy stepped onto the tarmac a long black limousine drew up beside the plane. The door opened and a well-dressed man stepped out. He looked in his late forties, with graying sideburns and penetrating eyes. Approaching Guy he said, "Rob Hoskins. Thanks for coming."

They shook hands and Guy said, "This is my attorney, Jake Needham. He'll be accompanying me."

"Afraid that's not possible, Major—no offense, Mr. Needham, but it's a question of clearances."

Guy pointed at radio antenna atop the car. "While we're going wherever we're going you can call for an index check. Computers should clear him in about two minutes."

"I—" Hoskins began, but Guy said, "It's both or none."

"Very well—but it's irregular." The three men got into spacious seats, and Hoskins wrote down Jake's DPOB and West Point class, and while he was calling in the limousine headed not toward the Pentagon, as Guy anticipated, but toward Washington.

Hoskins replaced the radio phone. "Pleasant flight, gentlemen? That's a fast aircraft—I'm used to meeting your late father, Major."

"I understand he did considerable business with Defense."

"Yes—and I trust you'll be taking his place. Last night Wilke said you were undecided."

"Still the case," Guy told him. "What I know about industry, computers and robotics you could stick in the bowl of a pipe."

Hoskins chuckled and Needham said, "If I might, I'd like to call my New York office."

"By all means. Know the system?"

"I've got one in my car."

While Jake was getting through, Guy scanned the winter landscape. He liked Washington, but hadn't returned since the day of his army resignation. New construction everywhere. Some day he wanted to tour the new Smithsonian. As Needham talked, Guy said to Hoskins, "How long is this going to take?"

"The briefing? It's eleven now—we'll get started, take a luncheon break and continue. I'd say you could be wheels-up for Haiti by three o'clock. What takes you there, if I may ask?"

Guy told him about the expedition, the treasure find and confiscation. Hoskins listened, then shook his head. "Bad people. What are you going to do?"

"Whatever my lawyer recommends." He glanced at Needham, who was replacing the phone. Jake said, "The partners agree, but this is going to be hellishly expensive for you."

Guy smiled. "We'll bill RyTech."

Hoskins said, "Do you have a card, Mr. Needham?"

"Ever met a lawyer who doesn't?" Jake handed him one, and as the limousine turned onto Constitution the radiophone buzzed. Hoskins answered, and after a few moments replaced it. "Mr. Needham has a provisional clearance—when we get to the building he can sign a secrecy agreement."

"Glad to," Needham said.

Hoskins' expression was thoughtful. After a while he said, "Without being presumptuous, I feel I should explain and clarify a particular area of DSA responsibility as it impacts on RyTech and certain other specialized defense contractors."

"Go ahead," Guy said, "I've been wondering about it ever since Wilke spoke to me. Why should Defense care

74

who heads my father's firm? My late father," he added in afterthought.

"Because of the highly sensitive and secret nature of RyTech's specialized work for the Department of Defense. In addition to the usual intelligence collection you're familiar with, DSA has a special responsibility for overseeing the physical security of private installations that perform classified work. Also, DSA is required to make sure that industrial secrets are secure, that they don't travel East. Of course, RyTech and similar contractors supply their own plant guards and maintain classified material in secure areas—at least they're supposed to. But DSA has the overall responsibility of making sure that defense contractors fully comply. To that end we make spot checks at plants, and of course all personnel clearances are processed through DSA."

Needham said, "Meaning your people can come and go as they choose, check files and overall security wherever there's a classified contract?"

Hoskins nodded. "It's an essential bond between Defense and private industry. Without it there would be few secrets remaining." His face turned away as he looked out of the window. "I wanted you to understand the relationship, gentlemen. There are no exceptions."

Guy looked at Needham and said, "If that's the way it is, that's how it is. I never realized how closely Big Brother is watching."

The trip ended at the west side of the Ellipse in front of one of the restored Georgian Colonial buildings. From the steps Guy could view the south face of the White House, and as he walked to the entrance he saw a polished brass plaque engraved with the legend: *Joint Study Committee*.

Nice noncommittal name, Guy thought, and waited for Hoskins to open the door. Inside were two uniformed guards. The three men signed the register and Hoskins gave Needham a printed security agreement to read while they hung their coats in the cloakroom. To one side a large Ori-

75

ental urn held two umbrellas. Guy liked the British touch. Needham signed his name and said, "God knows how this will affect my future." Hoskins witnessed and handed the form to a guard. "If you continue as Mr. Ryan's attorney, very beneficially, I'd say. Gentlemen, shall we go in?"

At the end of a passageway doors opened into a sort of airlock, and Guy found himself in an elevator that began to descend. Doors opened on an airspace with a heavy metal door. Hoskins punched an electronic sequential lock and the door slid aside.

Guy was now facing a dimly lighted room with a long boat-shaped table at which several men were drinking coffee. The room was sound-proofed and the far end was almost covered by a glass projection screen.

"We'll dispense with introductions," Hoskins announced. "Our visitors have further travel today, so I suggest the briefing begin." He indicated table seats for Guy and Jake, brought over a coffee carafe and cups.

In a low voice Jake said, "Why the anonymity, Guy?"

"Because," Guy said, "I haven't agreed to take over RyTech, so at this point I don't need to know their names."

At military intelligence school before his Madrid attaché assignment he had learned many things. Among them the practice of limiting classified information to those who could demonstrate a need to know.

After they were seated the screen brightened into blue sky across which sped a missile trailing smoke. It soared higher, altered course and the camera cut to a striped missile heading in the opposite direction. From the table a voice said, "The striped missile is the interceptor. The aggressor missile was launched from Saipan, the interceptor from White Sands."

The camera view cut to high space, looking down at earth. Guy saw the interceptor veer to correct course and close

76

with the aggressor. They impacted in a ball of orange-white smoke. The screen went blank. The voice said, "What you've seen is state-of-the-art interception of one land-based missile by another land-based missile. We've had the capability for some time, so has the Soviet Union."

There was now enough light that Guy could identify the speaker as an air force major general whose voice continued: "Both powers have recently come to the realization that earth-launched missile capability has been neutralized by earth-launched interceptors. Thus, the long reach into space.

"Perhaps our most valuable and closely guarded secret is our ongoing development of High Side—an integrated defensive system forming MDS, our country's Missile Defense Shield. The shield is intended to neutralize missiles launched from space."

The screen displayed simulated satellites positioned in space. From a distant space platform a missile shot forth, erupting into a cluster of warheads that broke away and sped toward targets. Ruby beams flashed from the interceptor platform and three warheads dissolved. Another interceptor platform picked off the other three warheads. To Guy it looked almost like a video game.

The major general said, "That represented optimum scenario, resolution of an uncomplicated problem. Suppose a swarm of decoys confronted the interceptor? At present, a percentage of decoys *and* warheads would reach targets in the US. So, with a limited number of interceptor platforms in space, how do we solve the problem? In theory we solve it by enabling the interceptor to discriminate among potential space targets: between decoys and mirved nuclear warheads, between their satellites and ours, their missiles and ours—and do it in fractions of a second before taking out the warheads, destroying them in outer space." He glanced back at Guy. "Only by upgrading High Side can we attain a fully invulnerable Missile Defense Shield. And that's

77

where Sceptre comes in." The screen cleared. Guy blinked and looked at the speaker.

"Sceptre is a product of RyTech's Institute for Strategic Research," he continued, "whose brain is a unique microchip, capable of processing data thousands of times faster than the human brain. To produce it, lasers etch the aluminum oxide surface in lab conditions of near zero Centigrade. On it, vapor-deposited tungsten 'wiring' creates the microprocessor named Sceptre. It can be programmed as the manufacturer desires. At present, Sceptre forms the core of an integrated space defense that in time will see laser beams replaced by neutral-particle beams that travel sixty thousand miles a *second*. The system will be independent of earth commands, for our assumption is that prior to hostile launchings our conventional communications systems will be disabled by EMPs."

Guy said, "What's that, General?"

"Electromagnetic pulses generated by nuclear explosions."

"How would they be delivered?"

"By Soviet missile-firing submarines. Hence the need for an independent MDS."

"You can't defend against the subs' ballistic missiles?"

"At present, no absolute defense. We'd try to eliminate them by conventional means."

The vice admiral said, "Plans to enhance that capability are on hold, thanks to budget constraints." His voice was bitter. "However, RyTech's Swiss subsidiary is developing a means whereby we can communicate with our own submerged submarines despite EMPs. That will give us the capability of ordering our submarines to fire retaliatory missiles."

"What means are those, Admiral?"

"Laser, sir. Laser Deep Communications, LDC. Transmitted from distant aircraft. Aircraft that survive the initial missile assault." He cleared his throat. "Of course, all

RyTech work is sensitive, but developing reliable LDC is classified in the highest degree."

"So, despite Sceptre and the MDS we're still vulnerable to nuclear attack from the sea."

"Unfortunately," the major general replied, "but no one ever said war is bloodless."

"Cold comfort," Guy remarked.

Hoskins said, "Even less comfort in this, Mr. Ryan. Although a reasonable cover story was formulated to explain the detonation of our space shuttle, there is technical evidence that strongly suggests that a Soviet submarine off Cape Canaveral zapped the shuttle with a laser weapon."

"My God," Guy said. "If that's so, why not tell the public?"

Hoskins shook his head. "Can't, without revealing the satellite data that provided the information. Now, before you ask why the US hasn't retaliated, it was the President's decision to suppress the truth."

"In the interest of detente?" Guy said, his disgust obvious.

A man in civilian clothing got up and looked at Hoskins. "This might be a good time to break."

Hoskins glanced at his watch. "I agree."

Lunch arrived on a room-service-type hot wagon: tomato juice, filet mignon, salad and mint sherbet. There was hardly any conversation during the meal, and Guy found it a relief from the concentrated input. To Hoskins he said, "Could you give me an idea of what this group represents? What does it report to? How authoritative are its decisions?"

Hoskins smiled. "You won't find Joint Study Committee in the Federal Register. I can tell you that it's part of the executive branch, reporting to the Joint Chiefs of Staff and the President through his science adviser." He nodded at the man in civilian clothes who'd spoken before. "Also, the Joint Chiefs liaison informs SecDef on major matters, so we're pretty well plugged in." He looked around. "Everyone finished? Let's get coffee and resume."

Hoskins went to the far end of the table and began to speak. "Gentlemen, you've heard the basics of High Side, MDS and the critical significance of Sceptre. When deployed in space and integrated into the planned missile shield, Sceptre can be the great peacekeeper, eliminating the threat of nuclear war in our time."

Until, Guy thought, the Sovs develop a countering system.

Hoskins said, "For some time the Defense Security Agency has been deeply concerned over the transfer of our advanced technology to the East Bloc. Some of what's leaked has been classified, but not all by any means. In recent years the Soviets have gotten more than forty thousand samples of Western production equipment, weapons and military components; and half a million technical documents, classified and not. Through espionage arrests we know that Silicon Valley is the KGB's prime target in the US. Why? Because by stealing our research products and equipment the Soviet Union saves billions of research dollars each year and an estimated five years in their research cycle. They gain hard information on our manufacturing processes and the technical advances we've made. Having one of our desirable items, all they need to do is copy it.

"Our export laws were designed to prevent illegal shipments, but Customs is undermanned, and with profit still a capitalist motive, evasion takes place. It's hard enough to police US-based manufacturers, but to control the export to Russia of what's manufactured abroad is a near impossibility. Europe and Japan take a more relaxed view of the USSR than we do—they sell what they make to the high bidders." He gazed at Guy and Jake. "RyTech's French subsidiary, Systèmes Aeronautiques, is a case in point. To be blunt, SA has been extraordinarily helpful to the Russians; it's not just a leak, it's a rupture, considering the flood of gear that's gone East: computers, Loran, robotic devices. In fact, there's hardly any product of SA that hasn't reached the USSR."

Guy sat forward. "What did you do about it?"

"We informed Sean Ryan, provided documentation and proof of thirty-two violations. We requested he clean house at the Lyons plant, which son-in-law de Neuville manages. *Still* manages, as you know."

"Has SA violated French export controls?"

"Not that we know of. Considering the depressed state of the French economy, the Socialist leadership is eager to export to anyone with hard currency."

"You're suggesting my father did nothing to cut off the flow."

"He gave lip service—but in Lyons nothing changed."

"How do you account for it?" Guy asked.

Hoskins cleared his throat. "Because I know your relationship with your late father was less than cordial I feel I can speak frankly. As men age, they change, become forgetful. Perhaps he thought he'd told Thibaud de Neuville to tighten up, but failed to. Or, he may have been reluctant to fire the son-in-law responsible for that appalling situation."

"My father was a hard-nosed industrialist. If he blamed Thibaud for screwing up he'd have fired him without a second thought."

"So we assumed—only it never happened."

Guy considered. "If I were to take over RyTech you'd want me to replace de Neuville?"

"We'd want you to shut off the flow of SA products to Russia by whatever means you chose. In our country's interests."

"All right, I understand that. But you didn't get me down here just to talk about the plant in Lyons."

"Hardly. What all this has led to is our ultimate objective—that nothing concerning Sceptre ever reach the East—no plans, no technical data, much less the microchip itself.''

"How do you estimate the danger of that happening?"

"Very real, if not immediate. Suppose someone other than yourself replaces Sean, he-or she—might for a variety of reasons allow that to happen. Or ISR could be physically penetrated and critical material stolen. Already three such attempts have surfaced—how many others, we don't know. Or, in the event you become RyTech's chief executive officer, you might be given a financial offer for your stock you couldn't refuse. If you sold, it wouldn't be illegal, but it would be disloyal.''

"Of course. But I'm not part of RyTech."

"In addition to the Lyons situation we've an ongoing problem with the Swiss subsidiary. Overtly it manufactures lasers for commercial application; it also produces beam lasers for military use. An unspecified number of those have slipped away from us although we've managed to recover a few before they reached the end user. Of more importance, though, is the firm's R&D on the neutral-particle beam which will complete the MDS space array."

"Why not relocate the firm to the US?"

"Because Switzerland possesses unique conditions for experimentation: unlimited amounts of hydroelectric power and deep, mountain-shielded tunnels. It's not feasible to conduct the work here. Still, we can't have particle-beam data going to the Sovs."

"My father knew of the Swiss problem?"

"He was informed; again, he took no corrective steps. Charitably, one might assume his mind deteriorated beyond decision taking."

The room was silent. A coffee cup grated its saucer. The air force general spoke. "You've heard of Stealth aircraft?"

Guy nodded. "Planes designed to make radar detection more difficult."

"Not only the design, but the construction material—a

82

carbon and epoxy composite that absorbs radar beams. Where RyTech comes in is the special coating for our planes, satellites and missiles.''

"Some sort of invisible paint?"

"You could say that. The forerunner was devised for German U-boats. Their snorkels were coated with a radar-absorbing substance that made them difficult to detect by the radar we used in those days. Your father got hold of the German formula and gave it to your Swiss subsidiary to perfect against modern radar capability. As you can imagine, the new formula has inestimable value. If our planes, missiles, tanks and satellites can't be spotted by enemy radar they can't be attacked by his tech weapons systems, and we gain a terrific advantage in battle.''

"Do the Soviets have anything like it?"

"They have the old German formula, but as far as we know they haven't developed it as RyTech has. So, as is their custom, they would very much like to steal G-371. The *G* stands for German, and the number represents the number of formulae tried before settling on the present one. We call it 'Ghost.' Applying the substance is called Ghosting.

"We Ghosted a B-51 and sent it over the Swiss Alps, where mountain peaks reflect sharp radar outlines. The B-51 reflected a signal no larger than a child's kite—hardly enough to alert enemy radar observers. So, we're very pleased with the development. Among other things Ghost enables us to make our aging bombers nearly radar-proof, while waiting for the coming generation of Stealth aircraft to replace them.''

Guy said, "You've given me a good deal to consider. How can I get back to you?"

"There'll be no need to—until we know you've taken charge of RyTech. Until such time, we request that you not discuss these matters with anyone, including relatives.''

Guy rose stiffly, feeling his injured ribs. "For argument's

83

sake, suppose I don't take RyTech—how would you handle the Swiss operation?"

"We'd eliminate it."

"And Sceptre—the same?"

"If necessary."

"I appreciate your candor." Guy glanced at his watch. "One way or another I have to decide in fourteen days. If that's all, we'll head for Haiti."

Hoskins walked to him, shook hands with Guy and Jake. "Thanks for listening," he said. "You had car trouble the other night. Take the warning and be careful. Good luck in Haiti—you'll need it."

He escorted the visitors to the elevator and through the passageway where they paused to collect their coats. Hoskins opened the limousine door, said goodbye again and the big car drew away from the curb.

As they neared the Lincoln Memorial, Jake said, "Quite a session—wasn't prepared for anything so heavy."

There were youthful skaters on the Reflecting Pool. At the far end thrust the Washington Monument, pure and white in the afternoon sun. A symbol of the nation he had served and which deserved his loyalty. No easy decisions, he mused, just hard choices.

After a while they pulled up at Butler Aviation and walked through the ready room where pilot and co-pilot were waiting.

Cabin heaters warmed the air, and while the Lear taxied for takeoff Guy scanned what he could see of the city, and wondered when he would come back again.

Turbojets screamed and the Lear shot down the runway like an arrowhead. As the plane gained altitude Guy looked down on the silver reaches of Chesapeake Bay. The pilot turned east to round the tip of Cuba.

Relaxing over drinks they played blackjack until Jake said, "I think something other than a frontal approach to the Haitians might produce better results."

"Such as?"

"Divide and conquer. You stay in the hotel and I'll hit the streets—you could be subject to arrest, you know."

"And while I cower under the bed what will you be up to?"

"Start with the AFP guy who originated the seizure story, find out what else he knows." He waved a fifty-dollar bill between his fingers. "Then a call on my firm's Haiti correspondent, Avocat Henri LeSeur, to determine how the land lays, solicit his advice. You tend to impatience, friend, and down where the banyan grows that ain't the way to play."

"What would I do without you?" He added Scotch to his glass. "Suppose I go with RyTech—would you come along?"

"As what?"

"General Counsel."

Jake whistled. "I'd have to give it some heavy thought, Guy. I've been building seniority at my firm, competing for partnership."

"When?"

"Two years."

"And if you didn't make it, where would you go?"

"Where failed lawyers go—Street and Walker. But I've a good shot at partnership, I've worked hard, kept my nose clean. I'm not a drunk and neither is my wife. But it's not easy to maintain a family in Manhattan on an associate's salary."

"Well, think about it."

"Hell, you haven't made the basic decision yourself." He cut the cards. "Your deal."

Guy played, mind only partly on the game, reviewing the secret information he'd been given. He understood now why Sean had called the company "rotten to the core." But why hadn't his father purged it? Especially when Sean's last thoughts were of saving Sceptre. Well, if the time ever came

85

he'd deal with the dilemma. Meanwhile, he faced the problem of boat and crew. For himself the treasure meant little beyond achievement of a dream that had consumed him over the years. But for Cristina and Don José it was different. Their two hundred thousand dollars was serious money that had to be returned—with interest. So he couldn't walk away.

With or without Jake's help he was going to liberate his men and what belonged to him. He'd dealt with guerrillas before. He wasn't accustomed to defeat.

Seven

The long-vacant room stank of mildew. The air conditioner rattled loudly but produced no air. A ceiling fan turned slowly and impotently. Sheets were damp to Guy's touch. This was the Mansion Royale, painted with peeling pastels and facing the Port-au-Prince waterfront.

Tub water was slightly above body temperature. Guy relaxed in it, hoping the aircrew's airport accommodations were more confortable than his. But compared to his boat crew's cell this had to resemble paradise.

After a while he left the tub, toweled and lay naked on the bed near the open window. The thin curtains were motionless and perspiration formed on his body. Distantly came the sounds and rhythm of a steel-drum band. Playing for whom? he wondered, for he'd seen no tourists on the streets, just the usual ragged beggar boys. It was a country whose principal product was misery, whose deposed ruler had lived in isolated luxury befitting an Arab oil sheik. Ironic that in front of the National Palace stood a bronze statue of a slave sounding the conch shell call to revolt against French rule. Further work to be done here, he thought. If you're seeking a social conscience outlet this is one place to come.

Better hotels were set in the residential hills behind the port, cool and remote from the dust and wretchedness of the city, but he'd selected this one to be near government offices, the waterfront where, he assumed, the trawler had been moored.

Nearby were stores where he'd bought provisions and supplies; one could be a refuge should sudden need arise. He'd pointed them out to Jake as the *publique* drove them in.

Now, he must turn his mind to sleep. He needed rest, and depending on what Jake learned the night could be a lively one.

Outside the window it was dark when Needham woke him. Guy turned on a bed lamp and sat up slowly, unrested by the nap, body slick with moisture. Sitting on the other bed the lawyer pulled off his tie. "Good news and bad," he said. "The good news is your boat's over there, tied up at the far end of the pier. The bad news is it's guarded and your crew is in jail." He pulled off coat and shoes and lay back. Staring at the idling fan he said, "I found the AFP stringer in a bar down the street—name of Mercier, Jules Mercier. He wasn't aboard the Government gunboat so he can't say what took place. Maybe your folks were dipping into the treasure pot, maybe not—but he says it made no difference. Whoever wanted your boat and treasure simply took it."

"Who's responsible?"

"He says the Treasury subsecretary for Maritime Affairs, gent by the name of Coulou, Auguste. Reputation for avarice and violence. Lavish lifestyle—needs moolah to support it. Keeps a *petite amie* back in the Petionville hills."

"How's the crew doing?"

"Jules hasn't been allowed to visit them, but he says general conditions are pretty bad. It's a jail-jail, no a/c, no color TV; eat what you catch on the wall or scrape from the floor. Do your business in a bucket that's seldom changed.''

Guy grunted. "All six in the same cell?"

"He assumed so—they're charged with the same crimes, so for convenience sake they're kept together. Says that's the usual practice."

"LeSeur should be able to find out. Did you see him?"

"When Henri heard why I'd come he got scared as hell, said he'd talk to me later—at his home. He asked me to leave his office on the double. He'll send a car for me."

"For *us*. We may have to play Good Guy-Bad Guy."

"Car's due at eight. Let's try room service, eh? *Pommes frites* and *biftec* suit you?"

"If room service is as bad as the room, forget it. Still, I ought to share the suffering."

"I bought a flask of Barbancourt and bottled water. Should I ring for ice?"

"Not if you value your gut." Guy found two glasses in the dresser drawer along with candle stubs for power failures. He opened the rum and water, poured two drinks. *"A la votre."*

"Beat Navy." Needham swung his legs over the bed edge and grinned broadly. "When I left home this morning I couldn't have believed I'd end up in this lousy hole by nightfall."

"You needed a break from dull routine."

"Did I?" He chuckled. "Whatever—it's reality now."

Guy sipped the tepid drink and peered through the glass at the light. "Getting back to subsecretary Coulou—did your informant mention his lady's name?"

"Yes, he did as a matter of fact. Her name is Manette and I'll bet she wears pink garters with a whiff of Fleurs du Mal."

"Easy, please order before that rum hits harder."

Needham picked up the phone.

While Jake was talking with the waiter in a mix of French

89

and English, Guy stayed in the bathroom. After the waiter left, Guy got into trousers and shirt and saw the lawyer shaking his head. Jake said, "Know what that boy thought? He figured we were a pair of predatory queers looking for subteen kids. He was disappointed when I declined his offer to produce as many as we wanted. Jesus, what a place."

"I should have warned you about the juvenile brothels. They've lost some popularity because of AIDS." He took money from his wallet, handed the wallet to Jake. "Back shortly," he said and left the room. He went down by the back stairs and followed a side street two blocks until he reached a store where he had purchased marine supplies. The owner was closing up, but he recognized Guy and shook his hand. "They take your boat," Jacques said softly. *"Je regret.* You one good customer. No more boat, *hein?"*

Guy motioned him toward the back of the store. "I need a gun. Handgun." He flashed green bills. "With shells."

Jacques' eyes widened. "Very risky. If Ton-Ton Macoutes find out—they separate my head."

"Not to worry. Show me."

Jacques turned off store lights, locked the street door, and set the protective grill. Then motioned Guy to follow.

Inside a cluttered office he closed the door, toed aside a worn rug and removed a square of wood floor. He reached into a metal box and drew up something wrapped in oily rags. "Good quality," he said, handing it to Guy. "See for yourself."

Guy undid the wrappings and found a cheap Star 9mm pistol. Bluing was worn from the barrel and the grip was chipped. Guy extracted the magazine and found it loaded. He slid the receiver back and forth, satisfied with the action. How much?"

"For you, four hundred."

"For this? They stamp these out in Spain for ten bucks apiece." He twirled the pistol before handing it back.

Slyly, Jacques said, "We not in Spain."

"Three hundred, tops."

"Trois-cinquante."

"With an extra magazine."

"No got, only shells."

"Bon. Also your shirt."

Jacques spread his arms, looked down at his worn, dirty shirt. His head moved wonderingly, but he began to take it off. Guy counted out three hundred and fifty dollars and said, "Wrap it," handed over the money, and tucked the pistol under his belt, next to his spine. Jacques wrapped the shirt in brown paper, tied it with twine, and gave the parcel to Guy with some cartridges. They shook hands. Jacques said, *"Bonne chance,"* and let him into the alley. Guy went back to the hotel.

Needham was eating at the movable table. "Thought I'd lost you."

"Not likely. I know this town." He dropped his package, washed rag-oil from his hands and joined Jake at the table. After a while he said, "This was an old cow and I'm glad they put her out of her misery."

"Yeah, don't chew too hard—suck the juice."

The french fries were limp and cold. The coffee was air temperature, but coal black and syrupy. Well packed with caffeine, Guy thought. He added sugar and stirred. It was also yesterday's brew, his taste buds told him, but he swallowed it down thinking it could be a while before he had a better cup.

The pistol prodded his spine uncomfortably. There were guns aboard the trawler, but by now they would have been found and removed by the pirates—thus his overt purchase.

Jake said, "It's close to eight. Time to see LeSeur."

Guy nodded, picked up his parcel.

As they went down to the lobby the hotel lights flickered out. "Helpful," Guy remarked, and as they stepped outside he saw the streetlights were out, too. While they waited, the hotel's generator cut in and dim light penetrated the lobby.

Fifteen minutes later an old Peugeot pulled up and the driver motioned at Jake. They got into the rear seat and the car chugged away. "Could do with a ring job," Jake suggested.

"A whole new engine."

They were silent as the Peugeot climbed up into the cooler air of the hills. Twenty minutes of lurching ride and the Peugeot pulled into a slanting drive where it gave up. The driver pointed at a two-story house surmounting a gentle rise. They got out of the car and followed steps that wound through flower bushes, well-trimmed shrubs and lush lawn. Jake rang the bell and in a few moments the door was answered by a large white-shirted Haitian who wore a white beard and goatee. "Welcome," he said in perfect English. "It's too seldom that I see a colleague from the mainland. This is the boat's owner, Mr. Ryan?" They shook hands, and Henri LeSeur led them into a book-lined study decorated with primitive wooden sculptures. Framed by two of them hung a law degree from St. John's. LeSeur closed the study door and sat heavily behind his desk. "A complicated affair," he said. "Mr. Ryan, you have a signed agreement with our Treasury?"

"It's on the boat."

He shook his head. "Perhaps a certified copy?"

"In Spain, I'm afraid."

"Where it will be of no benefit, alas. You see, you and your men are charged with theft of public treasure; accordingly, that treasure has been confiscated, your boat as well, and the guilty persons jailed for trail. With the exception of yourself."

Jake said, "They follow the Napoleonic Code here. It's a little different from our law—you have to prove yourself innocent."

"And that could take considerable time," LeSeur said.

"Is the treasure still aboard the boat?"

"It was left in place as evidence—under guard." His

fleshy fingers resembled Vera Cruz cigars. A gourmand who indulged the finer things of life.

Guy said, "I sense that confiscating my treasure may not have been an entirely official undertaking."

LeSeur said, "What do you mean?"

"I mean it has the earmarks of a personal initiative. Who is the responsible official?"

"Subsecretary Coulou."

"Who could have been acting on his own, for his personal benefit."

LeSeur shrugged. "Given the confused political situation here that is at least a possibility."

Guy said, "Seems to me the treasure should have been off-loaded and stored in some government vault. That it wasn't suggests Coulou wanted it handy, where he could plunder it piece by piece or sail it away intact." He glanced at Needham. "Who placed the charges?"

"Subsecretary Coulou," the *avocat* said.

"And he can dismiss them?"

"Naturally."

"How much?"

LeSeur's eyes rose delicately. "Pardon?"

"How much?" Guy repeated.

LeSeur's eyes became calculating. "Fines could exceed the value of boat and treasure combined."

"I don't mean fines—*fines* are legal. This confiscation was illegal. What, I mean, is Coulou's *price?*"

"*Sub rosa?*"

"Exactly."

Jake laid a restraining hand on his arm.

"Perhaps you might care to discuss that with Coulou," LeSeur said.

"I might," Guy replied, "but you can earn a fee for representing my interests."

LeSeur looked at Jake, who nodded. The Haitian rose, said, "Pardon me a few moments," and left the study.

Jake whispered, "Jesus, what the hell are you up to? This guy represents my firm in Haiti—you can't involve him in bribery of a public official."

"He's involving himself," Guy told him. "He can't wait. Relax, and agree with everything I say."

"For *this* you brought me along?"

"For this—and more." He helped himself to a shot of dark rum, poured one for Needham. "Good stuff," he said, smacking his lips. "I feel better already."

"Please take it easy—you could get us both in jail."

"Admit it—this is better than torts and writs."

"Maybe for you—but I've got three Class A dependents." Shuddering, he downed the liqueur rum.

LeSeur returned. "The subsecretary will see you presently—and guarantees immunity from arrest."

"Was a price mentioned?"

LeSeur shrugged, licked his lips. "He thought two hundred thousand would balance things out."

"Bucks?"

"Yes, dollars."

Guy said, "Sounds exaggerated but negotiation is customary. Would Coulou take your bank draft backed by Needham's word and law firm?"

"You mean—I would advance the money against repayment by Hay Hughes Wriston and VanWickle?" His thick lips pursed. "I believe so—plus my fee, of course."

Guy said, "Assuming we reach agreement on the sum involved, Mr. Needham will write you an IOU. Please inform Coulou."

LeSeur nodded. *"D'accord.* Mr. Coulou is spending the evening nearby—at the home of, shall we say, a close friend? I'll have my driver take you."

"Appreciate it." Guy strode over and firmly shook the *avocat*'s out-sized hand. "We'll get back to you."

"I trust things will go well."

"No more than I." Taking his parcel, Guy followed

Needham down to the car. Before they reached it, Needham said, "Holy God, are you *serious?*"

"I'm serious about reclaiming what is mine." Guy told him. "If you want out, now's the time."

"Hell, I'm no quitter. Well, here goes nothin'—or everything." They got into the car and the driver returned with LeSeur's instructions.

Guy looked at his watch: nearly nine. The drive to Coulou's home-away-from-home took seven minutes. The house was a one-story cottage set back on a grassy ledge. Before getting out Guy peered around for roving guards. None he could see. Passing a ten-dollar bill to the driver he said, *"Pourboire."*

"Ah, *m'sieu, merci, merci."* He clutched the bill delightedly.

In French Guy said, "Take your time—we'll be at least three hours."

"Merci," the driver repeated and drove off as soon as they left the car.

Needham said wonderingly, "You're some operator. You weren't like this at the Point, Guy."

"Sure—but we learn as we grow." Together they went up the rock staircase to the front door. A generator humming behind the cottage explained the lights within.

The man who greeted them was short and thin, with scimitar sideburns and a pencil mustache. He wore a white linen suit, no shirt. Guy felt he had interrupted something. "I am Auguste Coulou," the host proclaimed. "Mr. Ryan, I remember you from when you were at Treasury some time ago—negotiating, I believe."

Guy followed the subsecretary into the living room. In a large wicker chair sat a voluptuous light-skinned woman, twenty-five or so, Guy thought. Manette, the *petite-amie.*

Without making introductions Coulou spoke to her in Creole. Lazily she rose, ground out her cigarette, and flounced out of the room. A distant door closed. Auguste Coulou spread his hands and said, "Please be seated."

Needham said, "Your English is excellent, sir. Did you study in Britain?"

"Actually, I shined shoes in Miami. There I learned many things—some of which have come in very useful."

"I can imagine." Guy leaned forward so he could reach the pistol if need arose. "You mentioned my visits to your Treasury."

"So I did. A shame you were unable to conclude an agreement with the *proper* authorities. Then"—he shrugged—"none of this need have happened."

Needham opened his mouth to speak, but Guy shook his head and Needham shut his eyes, Guy said, "Lamentable, but I'm now prepared to pay for that oversight. For crew, boat and contents."

"Bon."

"Did Avocat LeSeur explain the process?"

Coulou nodded. "He called me back. Your friend's firm will replace his funds."

"My problem is this—the price is too high. I'm not a wealthy man, though I aspire to be. Let's agree on a hundred thousand."

Coulou shook his head. "The treasure itself is worth millions—and there is more in the sea."

"You can get that on your own," Guy told him. "We won't be back to claim it."

"Two hundred thousand."

"Half that. Now. Tonight."

In the dark eyes avarice gleamed. The subsecretary moistened his lips. "Hundred fifty."

"Done. I'll want the crew out of jail at once, guards removed from my boat so we can sail away. Leaving you to enjoy a large fortune in dollars."

"First, LeSeur's draft."

Guy shook his head. "Issue the orders and I'll go down

96

to verify they're carried out. Meanwhile, you'll have Mr. Needham here to guarantee payment.''

Coulou thought it over. "I prefer this wait until tomorrow."

"Things agreed by night don't always endure by day. We'll do it now or never." He stood up. "If you're afraid I'll cheat you of your due, you'll have Needham. His firm will pay for his freedom. How can you lose?"

For a moment Coulou stared at Guy's guileless face. Abruptly he got up, went to a telephone, and phoned the jailer. He made a second call, this to an army outpost. Then he came back to the seated men. "It's done," he said. "Your men will be escorted to the trawler and put aboard."

"You didn't say that. Get it right this time."

"Ah, you understand Creole, Mr. Ryan?" His face grew thoughtful as he went back to the telephone. Guy listened to the conversation, and when it ended he rose, nodding.

Coulou rubbed his hands together. "Now to call Le-Seur?"

"Not yet," Guy pulled out his gun and pressed the muzzle under Coulou's chin. The man's eyes rolled whitely and Guy thought he was going to faint. A shiver coursed his body and his lips babbled a prayer.

Shocked, Needham stared at the scene. "God, you've done it now."

"One of us has to tie and gag the girl. You're elected, Jake. And make damn sure she'll stay put and silent."

Like a sleepwalker the lawyer moved toward the rear of the cottage. Guy heard a drawer open, the sound of metal. Jake would show her a knife.

With his free hand he dragged Coulou to the sofa, slammed him face down. "Killing you would be a pleasure, Coulou, but if you follow orders you'll survive the night, see dawn and live to bang Manette forever."

Kneeling on Coulou's legs he dug the pistol into his spine. "Here's what you're going to do. You'll drive us to the waterfront. If my men aren't on the trawler you're in bad trouble. If there are guards around, you're dead. *Compris?*"

"Yes, yes, I drive you to your boat, see you safely off."

"Exactly." He's caught the loophole, Guy thought with satisfaction. Thinks this is just a short delay. Having hope, he'll be easier to handle.

He got off the sofa and sat down. From the rear of the house, surprised shrieks, a scream, muffled moaning. Silence.

Coulou's face was pained.

They gazed at each other until Needham returned, butcher knife in hand. "She's tied and gagged," he reported. "And I can't believe what you've got me into."

"So far you've done fine." To Coulou he snapped, "Get up, we're going. Jake, turn off lights and cut the generator." He pushed Coulou ahead of him and around the side of the house to a black diesel Mercedes. "Behind the wheel," he ordered, "start the engine."

Without protest Coulou did as ordered. Guy took the seat behind the driver and pressed the pistol to his head. "If there's trouble I'll shoot you through the seat. There better not be trouble."

Hoarsely, Coulou said, "You heard me give the orders."

The house generator cut off. Guy glanced at the dark cottage and saw Needham jogging toward the car. When the lawyer was seated beside him, he laid the barrel against Coulou's cheek and snapped, "Let's go." The car backed down the sloping drive.

"No mistakes," Guy warned. "Take a chance, and it's your life, not mine."

"Sir, I'm cooperating fully," Coulou said.

Guy sat back and spoke to Needham. "Too bad about your Haitian correspondent. He's minus a good fat finder's fee."

Needham sighed. "Everything was on the up and up until you mentioned bribes."

"I read him," Guy said. "Read him as greedy enough to go along. Flexible as a Kowloon solicitor."

"Well, you read him ten by ten. How do we get out of here?"

"Trust me," Guy told him. "Keep a tight grommet as the night unfolds."

﹡

As they neared the port Guy transferred the pistol to Jake and changed into the old work shirt. Needham watched him and said, "You're full of surprises. I wonder what it would be like to work for you? Full time, I mean?"

"Well," Guy said, "I can't promise this much fun every day, but we'll have our moments."

Needham chuckled softly. "Sundays off?"

"Unless I need you."

Resignedly, Jake returned the pistol. "Hell, why did I hesitate?"

Coulou steered the car along the wharf to where the trawler was tied up. "All the way," Guy told him. "If I see one guard you're dead."

"They stopped alongside the trawler. "Out," Guy ordered, and guided Coulou to the gunwale, called. "Who's aboard?"

Suddenly an unshaven face appeared in the companionway. Shammas. "It's okay," Guy called. "All hands aboard? Bernal? Captain? Cookie? Chief?"

Hoarsely, Shammas called, "Present and accounted for."

"Start engines, prepare to cast off. I'm coming aboard." Dim light in the pilot house. He shoved Coulou over the gunwale, walked him to the companionway where Shammas stood unbelievingly. *"This* is the bastard who took us."

"Right. Where's the treasure?"

"Below. Jesus, Guy, what you been up to?"

Needham groaned, "You wouldn't believe."

"All right," Guy said, "Mr. Coulou will be your passenger, treat him as he deserves."

The captain appeared, shook Guy's hand fervently. "Thank God you came. They treated us pretty bad."

"How's fuel—enough for Kingston?"

"Easy. But what about gunboats?"

"If any Haitian boat tries to stop you, display Coulou. I'm confident he'll cooperate. Right, Auguste?"

"Yes, yes." He turned to Guy. "You didn't say anything about this . . . voyage."

"You didn't ask."

"You said you'd free me."

"You expected I'd turn you loose and try to leave. You figured to bring us back. Well, fuck you, Auguste. Have a swell trip." Still covering the Haitian he drew the captain aside. "Refuel at Kingston, enjoy some R&R and head for Grand Cayman—George Town harbor."

"Right—why Cayman?"

"Bank our loot. Radio okay?"

"Haven't checked."

"Report from Kingston and George Town."

"Aye, aye."

Under deck planking the engines were throbbing nicely. Tide nudged the hull against the pier. "Did they take the guns?"

"And scuba gear. Listen, how'd you manage it?"

"With this." Guy passed him the pistol. "Better keep him tied up until you land him. Where is up to you. Meanwhile, for what it's worth, I'm damn sorry all this happened. I'll try to make up for it."

Shammas grunted, "You have."

"Better get moving." With Needham he climbed back to the pier. Freed, the trawler headed for open water. Shammas shoved the Haitian out of sight.

Guy got behind the wheel, started the Mercedes. Beside him, Needham said, "Where to now?"

"Airport."

"Yeah, before things get unstuck."

The trip was three fast miles over the best road in Haiti. They found the crew shooting pool in the transient lounge. To the pilot, Guy said, "Let's move—I'm in a hurry."

He put down the cue. "Have to file a flight plan, sir, get a weather brief." He looked at the wall clock. "Could be too late. Airport's about to close for the night. Immigration, too."

"You flew Air Force?"

"Navy."

"Ever land on a darkened carrier. Take off?"

"Of course." He pulled on his jacket. "You're the boss."

Pilot and co-pilot carried their gear bags outside. Guy and Needham followed at a distance. The runway lights were off, control tower dark. "See," Guy said, "no permission needed."

When they were buckling into their seats Jake asked, "That lousy looking shirt—what for?"

"If things soured and I had to run I didn't want to be conspicuous."

"Ahhh," said Jake and lapsed into thoughtful silence.

The jets warmed, screamed, and the Lear trundled to the flight line. Wing lights whitened the runway. From the base of the control tower a truck was coming toward them. The Lear vibrated until, brakes released, it shot forward as though catapulted. While they gained altitude a searchlight fanned up from the truck.

"You *did* it," said Jake. "By God, you brought it off."

So I did, Guy thought, with luck, help and ingenuity. RyTech, however, would be something else. A quite different challenge.

Somewhere, at some point since leaving Washington, he had come to a decision. Despite threats and dangers, his unfamiliarity with industrial management, Guy had decided to do what his father wanted—take his place at the helm of RyTech. He knew that he was influenced as much by Marguerite's wishes as by the unique nature of the challenge implicit in Sean's legacy.

Throughout all of Guy's adult life he had received and issued orders; he was accustomed to discipline, to a precise and organized existence. Those factors, he thought, might compensate for what he lacked in managerial know-how. And he could learn.

Besides, he reflected, he wasn't going to stay with RyTech forever; just long enough to get RyTech back on track again.

The Lear shot into cloud cover, sped through the black of night.

BOOK TWO

BOOK TWO

Eight

Haynes, the young office manager, was visibly nervous as he stood in front of Guy's desk. "Have a seat," Guy told him. "How long have you been with RyTech?"

"Nearly three years, sir."

"Family?"

"Yes, sir. Child due in May—our first."

"Good, wish you well. Does your wife work?"

"No sir—I'm studying for CPA. At night."

"Makes a long day," Guy remarked. "After certification, please consider remaining with RyTech."

"I—I will, thank you, sir. If there's a place for me I'd want to stay."

Guy scanned the office. Paneled walls were hung with scrolls and civic tributes to Sean, a number from Irish and Irish-American societies. "I have some changes in mind. This is a dark office, I prefer a well-lighted place. My father's memorabilia should be removed—carefully—and taken to Eastover. This desk, too. I want ample working surface but no drawers. Things get lost and forgotten in drawers. Bring in an office designer or decorator, or whatever they're called. I'll want some sketches to choose from when I get back from Europe."

"Yes, sir." Haynes was making notes on his pad. Guy

liked notetakers, and said, "From my military background I'm accustomed to giving orders—once. If there's a problem I expect to be advised, otherwise I'll assume things are happening. Okay?"

"Yes, sir—and I'll pass the word along."

"These heavy window drapes look like Renaissance tapestries; sell or discard them. The chairs and carpets are Victorian. Out. I don't want a space-age setting, just modern, clean, uncluttered."

"I understand."

"Bring in a desk and a chair, telephone for Mr. Needham, whatever else he needs. He'll be working out of here for the present. Both of us are fond of brewed coffee; have it available plus attractive china."

Haynes made another note. "Yes, sir."

"For now, that's it. On your way out, ask Mr. Needham to come in."

Presently Jake opened the heavy door and took a seat near the desk. "Here's some reading material for you—stories about your takeover in *Forbes, Business Week,* the *Journal.*" He laid them on the desk.

"What's the general tone?"

"Skeptical of your ability to run RyTech. But you expected that. Next item—apparently Gant's retained a shyster to contest Sean's will."

"Not unexpected. Do whatever's necessary to sustain it."

Needham nodded. "How long will be you gone?"

"Ten days—two weeks. Depends. While you're still functioning as my executive assistant, before I give Stoner notice, I want you to survey the Houston operations and prepare an evaluation. Same with ISR."

"Sure."

"I'll be replacing Edmonds, too, so very quietly start an executive search outfit looking around. Keep our name concealed."

"Good thinking. I'll check Paul's contract to see what it'll cost RyTech to fire him."

"Run a cost-effectiveness study on our transportation fleet; see how many cars and planes we really need, whether we should own or lease."

"I know the right man for that."

"After you're general counsel I'll want you to have *all* RyTech operations scrutinized in the same way. Anything unprofitable or unnecessary, we unload."

"Right. Guy, a young lady's waiting to see you."

"I know. Now, as soon as you can, and before anything else, I want you to get down to Grand Cayman and take care of the crew and trawler. Give the crewmen substantial advances on their treasure shares, sell the trawler and hire someone to appraise the treasure."

"How do you plan to dispose of it?"

"I want some coins as souvenirs, the rest goes at auction."

"I suggest Sotheby's. They could send down an appraiser."

"I'll leave it in your hands. I'll be with my in-laws in Spain, then Lyons and Paris."

"Switzerland?"

"If there's time to look over the laser plant."

Needham looked uncomfortable. Slowly he said, "Probably I shouldn't ask, Guy, but why are you visiting Seville before—"

"My wife? Easy. Don José and Cristina backed the treasure hunt—Consuela opposed it. My backers deserve an account of what went on, and an assurance that their faith is about to be rewarded. They took a big gamble on me and my dream." He looked away. "Anything else?"

"Have a good trip."

"Ask Ms. Knox to come in."

When she entered Guy rose, noticing that she carried camera bag and tape recorder. "You won't need those,

Jenny, no interview." He came from behind the desk and pulled up a chair opposite her. "What do you earn at the *Record?* Guild scale?"

The question caught her off balance. "Uh . . . a little better—plus extras for feature pieces. Such as the one I expected to do on you." Her lips tightened in disappointment. "Updating the treasure story. Apparently, what went on in Port-au-Prince needs some explaining. Better not go back for a while."

"Don't intend to. Now, what I've seen of you suggests you could be useful to RyTech."

"Doing what?"

"Chief of Public Relations."

Her eyes widened. After a moment she said, "That's a big job."

"I'm confident you can handle it. I believe in corporate public relations—emphasis on product, not individuals, which is what Gunderson's been doing. He's making seventy thousand plus perks. You'd start at the same."

Sitting back, she stared openmouthed.

"And choose your own staff."

"I—I can't believe this. If you're not serious I'll have a heart attack."

"I'm serious. If you're willing when could you start?"

Drawing a deep breath, she exhaled slowly. "Two weeks?"

"How about one?"

"I—I suppose I could work it out with my employers."

"I'll depend on it. You live in the Village, so moving's no problem. Shake on it?"

They did and Jenny rose. "I've got to be the most astonished person in New York."

"And I'm one of the most pleased."

"Why—how on earth did you pick me?"

"Instinct. The peaks and valleys of our lives occur because we happen to be in a particular place at a particular time.''

"Another way of describing coincidence, isn't it?''

"I suppose so. In any case you'll have direct access to me. When you join us Gunderson will be gone, his office ready for you.''

"I'm—overwhelmed. How can I thank you?''

"By doing the job.''

She pinched her wrist. "I'm awake—it's *true.*''

"Promote our accomplishments, keep our executives out of the media.''

"Including you.''

"Especially me. I'll be in Europe for a while, we'll talk when I return.'' He walked her to the door. "I'd prefer you not mention the change until you report in.''

"Of course not. And thank you again. I'm going to treat myself to a gourmet lunch at Twenty-One.''

"*Bon appetit.*''

From LaGuardia he telephoned Marguerite to say goodbye. Tremulously, she said, "Did you know Gant is trying to break your father's will?''

"I know—we're countering it, so don't be concerned.''

"It's—despicable of him, Guy. To even *think* of such a thing.''

"Nikky may do the same—I expect to get rid of Thibaud.''

"Guy—is that necessary?''

"Would I consider it if it weren't? While I'm gone, please take care of yourself.''

"I shall. Love you.''

Attaché case in hand he left the General Aviation terminal and got into the waiting Lear. During the flight he studied RyTech's organization and corporate reports, leaving the plane to stretch during refueling at Gander and Reykjavik.

Watching the sleek Lear suck up jet fuel, Guy reflected that much had happened to him in a very short space of time. From vagabond treasure hunter he had become ruler of a huge industrial empire whose employees numbered in the thousands, and whose skills and technological discoveries could protect and benefit millions.

For the first time in his life money had ceased to be a problem. At his disposal were jets and helicopters, boats, limousines, apartments, the best restaurants. He had set himself the task of defending Sean's legacy, extending RyTech's reach and profits, and if he compensated himself accordingly he made no apology. Critics would find their answer in his achievements.

He had lived the spartan life at the Point and in 'Nam, long years of it; now, all that was changing. He watched the co-pilot engineer complete preflight checks, and then he got back into the plane.

It was close to midnight, London time, when they landed at Gatwick. To compensate for jet lag they slept overnight in an airport hotel, and took off for Seville in the morning.

Toward noon he looked down on the broad, high Sierra Morena range, and a few minutes later made out the Guadalquivir winding through the stately old city. Then they were on the ground.

From Seville, he told the crew, the Lear was to go to Madrid for routine maintenance. While there he urged them to enjoy themselves.

A rental Audi had been reserved, and Guy took the wheel to drive over familiar roads to La Rocha, an hour away.

Passing through the ancient stone entrance posterns he saw Arab horses grazing in the warm sunlight, drove past a section of the vineyards, adjacent servant quarters and stopped in front of the Palafox hereditary manor. Its foundations were huge stones on which Moors had raised a for-

110

tress. Half destroyed in the *Reconquista,* the edifice had been rebuilt and added to over the centuries. If architecturally eclectic, the Palafox family seat was impressively solid, durable as the blood line of their noble strain. Winter and summer the massive stone walls maintained an even temperature within.

Beyond the *barranca* he saw a bareback rider coursing a white Arab. She wore jodphurs, high-necked blouse and traditional Sevillian black hat—round top on flat brim. Below it flowed dark tresses, and as he watched his sister-in-law he thought he had never seen a young spirit so bright and free. Cristina reined her mount until it reared. The vise of her thighs kept her body from slipping down as she forced the horse to pivot on rear hooves. However slight her body, he reflected, Cristina was physical like himself.

Down the broad steps came a jacketed houseman who opened the car door and took Guy's bag. *"Bienvenido a su casa, señor* Guy,*"* he said with a sweeping bow. *"Para servirle como siempre."*

"Gracias, agradecido," he said, getting out as his father-in-law descended the steps to greet him.

"Mi hijo," he said emotionally, and clasped Guy in his arms.

"Don José," said Guy, "I've missed you, missed La Rocha."

"As you should—is this not your home?" He put his arm on Guy's shoulder as he led him into the mansion.

"Don José, you're handsome as ever," Guy told him, admiring the patriarch's thick gray hair, the full white mustache, his unseamed olive skin.

In the anteroom they found a carafe of cool house wine. The *marqués* filled two glasses. "My condolences on the death of your father."

"Thank you."

"I've always regretted never knowing him, but he was surely a giant, a titan of industry. Guy, your inheritance is

111

a proud one. I drink to it, to your departed father's eternal rest, to you and your future." He touched his glass to Guy's. "In your honor we've prepared *paella*—Cristina will join us shortly." They moved to a window overlooking broad pastures.

"So young to be widowed," Guy said. "How is she?"

"Well enough—keeps active to avoid grieving. Though—" he added in a lower voice—"it was a match that never should have been made. An indolent Monégasque whose passion was car racing—a fatal passion, it proved."

"Still, to marry René Puig, Cristina must have loved him."

He shrugged. "With Consuela married she may have felt it was required of her to follow lest she be scorned as *soltera.*"

"No one could possibly consider her a spinster—with her beauty."

The *marqués* nodded. "In her I've long discerned an inner beauty, an echo of her mother's." He crossed himself in respectful memory. "May God console her spirit."

Dutifully, Guy crossed himself. He seldom observed the outward tokens of his faith, though he had absorbed many of its teachings. And he was in a Catholic land, perhaps the most Catholic of all. One had only to see the awesome grandeur of the Valle de los Caidos, the Escorial, to comprehend the soul-consuming faith of Spain.

The *marqués* said, "How is my daughter, Consuela? Did she attend your father's rites?"

Guy shook his head. "I'll see her soon in Paris. With our daughter."

Don José's face lightened. "A lovely child, Gloria, as bright as she is beautiful. Perhaps now in your new situation you'll reconcile, the three of you again become a family."

"That's my hope," Guy told him as Cristina hurried in. Hat hanging behind her head, she peeled off dusty gloves and went to his arms. On tiptoe she kissed his cheek, hugged his shoulders. *"Cuñado,"* she said, "you've been too long away. I've missed you."

"And I've missed you. I would have come for René's services but I wasn't told until too late."

"I know, I know." She spun aside to survey him. "No one in Spain," she proclaimed, "has a brother-in-law as handsome as this *caballero.*"

"Or as wealthy," said Don José with satisfaction. "Guy, you'll not forget us *campesinos?*"

"How could I? I married one."

They laughed and the *marqués* turned to his daughter. "Cristina, make yourself presentable. *Corre,* and hurry back. So distinguished and infrequent a visitor must not be kept waiting for his lunch."

She wrinkled her nose, blew Guy a kiss and ran off.

As the men finished their wine, Guy shook his head admiringly. "She's something—always has been."

"Algo, indeed," the *marqués* agreed. "Not quite as insubordinate as her mother—may God give her eternal rest—but the strain is there for all to see. Without her companionship I'd be a lonely old man, so for me—and I shouldn't say it—her widowhood is a blessing."

The Palafox sisters, Guy mused. Consuela, beautiful and haughty; Cristina, perhaps even more beautiful, and coltishly unaffected.

When he and Connie were married, Cris was seventeen, face high-cheeked, bony like Audrey Hepburn's; just freed of her English convent school, shy, unaccustomed to the outside world. Now she was a stunning young woman who needed no cosmetic aids to accent her natural allure.

Next time, she needed a *real* husband, not a fop like René; a man to climb mountains with or journey on safari, share scuba diving or sail around the world. A man, whose blood when joined with hers, would bring handsome children worthy of her heritage.

113

Don José's voice interrupted his thoughts. "My son, we'll be seeing you more often?"

"I hope to come more frequently—but until I know what I've got into I'll have to spend most of my time in New York."

"You must convey my condolences and respect to your stepmother. Her visit here last year was all too brief. Tell her to consider La Rocha her home in Spain."

"She'll be immensely pleased, and I'm sure she'll want to come. In fact," he said, "I proposed she travel for a while. Take a world cruise, see new places and people. Just now she's devastated by my father's death."

"I understand—as I was when my Mercedes died."

Oval face glowing healthily, hands scrubbed, wearing a fresh starched blouse, Cristina appeared at the dining room door and beckoned them in.

The table was set in the same crisp elegance as when he lived at La Rocha with its elder daughter. Swedish crystal, Rosenthal china and burnished sterling that had survived fire and revolution. He noticed that Cristina—*dama* now— seated herself at the head of the table, father on her left across from Guy. They bowed their heads while Cristina said grace. After she nodded servants silently began serving the midday meal.

Don José said, "Guy, you must tell us of the treasure adventure."

"Yes, please," Cristina chimed. "Suspense has been destroying us. You found it, lost it, recovered it—full details or there'll be no sherbet for you."

He described the thrill of his find, how he'd been abruptly summoned back to New York, learned of the boat's capture. He credited its recovery, treasure intact, to fast work by a Haitian lawyer. "So it's in a vault at George Town waiting appraisal." He sipped wine. "A *large* vault."

114

"Marvelous!" Cristina clapped her hands. "And I thought I'd never see the money again."

Don José shook his head. "Not so, Guy—*I* was the doubter. Cristina maintained you'd find *Nuestra Señora*—and you did. My apologies." He lifted his glass to his son-in-law. *"Saludos."*

"Escudos," said his daughter, happily.

Guy smiled. "Clear case of casting your bread upon the waters and having it returned tenfold."

"Guy," Cristina said, "with that expectation of large profits I'm going to Dublin and bid on Al-Emir for syndication."

"How high will the bidding go?"

"Oh, three million—perhaps three and a half million dollars."

Don José cleared his throat. "For a single Arab horse frenzy—a quarter of a million registered. Overall, a five billion dollar business. You see, it has to do with American tax shelters and investment credits. An Arab is fully depreciated in five years, but a good stud can keep producing for years and years. Let's say I buy Al-Emir for three million. In a year he can easily cover a hundred mares at a breeding fee of thirty thousand dollars each." She spread her hands expressively. "That recoups the original investment. From there it's pure profit."

Don José said, "I know what I'm putting *my* treasure share into—agricultural equipment, new wine-making machinery."

"To do what we've always done? How dull. Come, Father, join my syndicate."

"Well—maybe a small investment—to show my faith in you."

"Guy?"

"Of course," he said. "Glad to return your favor."

"In Dublin there are syndicators to advise me, do the legal work. I don't want a lot of small participants," she said, eyeing her father. "I'd prefer four or five substantial partners."

"Count me in," Guy told her. "I'll take whatever isn't snapped up."

"Espléndido." She gave him her small, strong hand. "After *siesta* I'll tell you about Al-Emir."

He lay on the bed he'd shared with Connie early in their marriage. The room was light and cheerful, breezes from the river tossing the curtains. After a bath his body was cool, refreshed. The treasure expedition was behind him now; dividing the spoils would be routine. He was satisfied with his decision to hire Jake. A loyal friend all these years, he would remain loyal now.

Jenny Knox was more of an acquaintance, a casual professional contact; she'd impressed him with her alert mind, her background credentials, her honoring agreements, her tact. He expected her to do well, soften RyTech's overly imposing image. Gunderson he sized up as an expense account cheater, a coarse intimidator of secretaries. No loss to RyTech.

As for Stoner and Edmonds they were mainstays of the *ancien régime;* he wanted men whose loyalty was to him, who would act without hesitation. Needham was one; replacing Edmonds would not be difficult.

He thought: I suppose the truth is I want to delegate responsibility, select the right men and let them do their jobs—always with accountability. I want to eliminate whatever structural weakness there is, then build something of enduring worth for Connie, Gloria and me. Starting on Sean's foundation—his legacy to me.

Turning, he gazed beyond the window at the distant Sierra against the pale blue sky. As much as any place he'd ever lived he loved La Rocha. It was real, it was solid, it was home. And he admired no man more than the genteel

116

Don who'd fought against the Anarchists, suffered for his faith—yet never mentioned those cruel, barbaric times when Spain was torn apart.

Connie was of his blood, and Gloria. Cristina, too, he mused, now her father's acting son and first lieutenant. She *was* something else, so unlike her elder sister and most Spanish females he'd known around Madrid.

Only once had he met her husband, René, disliking him at once for his femininely handsome face, his pale skin, his unstable temperament. What the boy lacked, he told himself, was character. But a convent-bred girl wouldn't have known that.

Hell, he thought, we're all entitled to one major mistake in life.

His was—what? Marrying Consuela? No, he couldn't concede that yet, he loved the Palafoxes too much, felt absorbed in their lives, their land. La Rocha was his home, Don José the father he had always hoped his own would be . . .

When he first saw her at the Argentine Embassy Ball, Consuela had come up to Madrid for the opening of the diplomatic season. At his request, the Naval Attaché had introduced them and he remembered how stunning she looked, the contrast of her dark hair and the white lace evening gown. Like a princess, regal and diffident at first, warming slightly as they discovered similar likes and interests while they danced and shared champagne.

And he had been drawn to her, he remembered—impelled, really—because in Consuela he sensed a tantalizing blend of contrasting strains: Old World coquetry and the unspoken but implied sensuality of the Mediterannean race.

For that season Connie was staying with the Condesa de Villamor, the opulence of the hereditary mansion quite naturally complementing her beauty. He remembered taking her to the *tapa* places off the Gran Via, sharing wine and snacks; strolling through Retiro Park afterward, finally holding hands. His embassy work was undemanding and largely social, so he became her constant escort as the season wore on. They began to share an unspoken intimacy that was consummated one afternoon in his apartment by the Prado. That he found her virginal only increased his love for the young woman he wanted as his wife.

The next weekend they drove down to La Rocha where he met her father and asked for Consuela's hand. Initially, Don José later confessed, the idea had not appealed to him, but he gave them his blessing and welcomed Guy into the family. With restraint.

Engaged, they visited the Costa Brava, Valencia, the Costa Azul. And as Guy lay there, he remembered orange-scented evenings at Alginet, the fragrance breeze-blown across the patio where they held hands and kissed when no one was watching. His love had overflowed, and in that lover's stupor he neither sought nor would admit her faults. So it was not until after Gloria was born that Consuela's love of possessions and position, her impatience and petty criticism seemed to manifest itself.

Lying there, he vowed to put the past aside, go to Paris and do what was necessary to bring Connie back into his life. To keep on living apart was a rude denial of love.

He tried to analyze his feelings for Consuela . . .

The attraction derived not from her beauty alone, for he had made love with other beautiful women long before that first glimpse of her.

Was it that she sensed his lifelong inner loneliness? He remembered how even in those first tentative weeks he had felt whole while in her company, complete while she was at his side. And how desolate he had felt in the hours without her presence. Consuela had filled a need that before her he had not even recognized. Her light, easy laughter lingered in his mind long after their partings, and he remembered how the touch of her hand and lips thrilled even in memory.

But it was more than that . . .

Without prying she had understood the workings of his mind. At first he had been startled by her sensing what he was going to say, by the occult way Consuela could anticipate his needs and his desires. And he remembered how subtly their relationship had changed, she taking the lead in many things, he following contentedly, glad to minimize the role of warrior-male that he had lived so long.

She had been different from all other women he had known in her rejection of cloying dependence. As Guy reviewed Consuela's traits he acknowledged that her independent spirit had been a powerful and enduring attraction.

And it was that very independence of hers that drew her away from him—to Paris. With the child born of their love.

Until now he had not permitted his mind to dwell on Consuela and their marriage. For a long time he had thought their problems insoluble, then RyTech and his treasure boat demanded all his powers of concentration. But by inquiring of his daughter, Don José had opened the barrier to a flood of thoughts that Guy had long suppressed.

Silently he acknowledged that he still loved his wife, that the obstacles between them were as much his fault as hers. They were two different people, individuals, and he should never have expected Consuela to become his twin.

Their common bond was love. And Gloria, their child.

For months he had kept them from his mind, but now as Nikky said, things could be different. He missed his wife and felt a lover's eagerness to be with her. And Gloria had been too long without a father. The time had come, he told himself, for all of that to change.

As he himself was changing.

On the breeze came the strains of a distant guitar; an Andalusian melody, gypsy-inspired in antiquity. It soothed his burdened mind, lulled it into sleep.

* * *

When Cristina pounded on his door he woke, finding it late afternoon. "Up and out, *lagarto*," she called. "We have business to discuss."

"Give me ten," he called, sitting up.

"Are you decent?"

"No."

"Then I'll leave your riding apparel at the door." She went off humming *"Cuando Te Veo En Tu Blusa Azul."*

He splashed cool water on his face, pulled on doeskin jodhpurs he'd forgotten, and found them comfortable. His jodhpur boots were shined and supple. He strapped them on, got into an Andalusian shirt with embroidered cuffs and collar.

Cristina, with two dappled Arab mares, was waiting by the carriage door. As of old he laced his fingers for her boot and helped her mount, then swung into his well-remembered russet saddle.

Crossed over Cristina's shoulders were two leather wine *botas*, refreshment for the ride. "I'm thinking of taking up polo," she told him as they started off.

"Don't—it's not for girls."

"Girls play in Madrid—at Puerto de Hierro."

"Let them," he said, and drew his mount beside hers. "It's dangerous."

"For a Palafox," she chided, "nothing's too dangerous."

"Courage isn't involved, prudence is. Without you what would your father do?"

She said nothing.

They followed the worn trail past the corrals, around the base of a low hill and through an ancient olive grove. Watching Cristina he recalled what a superb horsewoman she was; her body flowed into her steed as though of common flesh. Her hips moved easily in the saddle, but her torso remained erect, shoulders level. Connie was a competent equestrienne, but far below her sister's mastery.

Now they neared the broad fields and pastures of the fighting bulls. Coming over a crest he saw a group of five;

120

black, red, buff, *pintado,* with their uniformly heavy bodies, wide horns and bulging muscle humps. Not beef cattle, but fierce descendants of Aurochs, Stone Age monsters whose outlines had been scratched into the walls of Altamira's caves. One seed bull to every fifty cows, was the ratio he remembered, prolonging the old Miura strain. Beyond, roamed other *toros bravos,* grazing. With sufficient rainfall pasturage would support four hundred, though at any time no more than sixty were heavy enough for the ring. In any *plaza de toros* Palafox fighting bulls were prized by spectators—though feared by *toreros* for their viciousness and indominability. Living in Madrid, Guy had educated himself to appreciate the spectacle with its old rituals and traditions, the *rejón,* the flashing *trajes de luces* of posturing stiff-legged swordsmen, the blood-red *muleta* . . .

Cristina called, "We'll stop at the river where we used to swim."

Beyond the tumbled ruins of a Moorish watchtower there was grass and a shady grove beside the river bank; coarse sand and crystal water swirling. He thought of Haiti's clear offshore depths as he dismounted.

They let the horses drink and graze, then Cristina handed him a *bota.* Guy tilted it and squeezed. The first spurt splashed his chin, but the rest of the thin stream hit the roof of his open mouth, his throat, and he swallowed thirstily.

She sat on a flat rock and drew papers from her blouse, handed Guy a color photograph of a nearly white stallion. "My stud-to-be," she said. "Isn't he magnificent? Seventeen hands, built like the prince he is. Just two years old."

"You don't have to convince me, Cris, I'm in for the trip."

"But I want you to see what you're investing in so you'd understand there's absolutely no risk. Before we take possession he'll be fully insured. I can't tell you how excited I am."

"Looks magnificent," Guy agreed. "When's the auction?"

"No date yet—that's up to the Saudi owner—but probably in the spring."

"Let me know—I'll attend if I can."

"That would be marvelous." A gloved finger traced idly in the sand. "I'll enjoy having an escort." Her gaze met his. "Will my sister come?"

"I'd like that," he said, "but with Connie one never knows."

"True, she's always been so—unpredictable. Still, I hope the two of you work things out—if that's what you really want."

Guy lifted the *bota* and drank more dry, tingling wine.

Reflectively Cristina said, "When I first saw you I wasn't quite seventeen. You were my sister's *novio,* handsome in your uniform, the first real *man* I'd ever seen."

Guy said, "Even as a child you were lovely, Cris."

"Was I? I'm not so sure, but thank you." She smiled and he saw her forthright mouth, her uncompromising chin.

"I shouldn't have married René," she said softly. "Can you forgive me?"

"It's not something for me to forgive—or anyone. You shouldn't think about it that way."

Under long curling lashes her dark eyes regarded him. "If you'd said not to marry him I wouldn't have."

"Wasn't my place—that was up to your father—or you. Besides, Consuela didn't seem to object."

"She was always indifferent to me, her sole concern was that I marry a suitable aristocrat. She never even talked with me about René, asked if I loved him."

"But you did."

Slowly she shook her head. "In retrospect I realize I made myself think so. René seemed the best choice at the time—since you were gone."

"You mean, I wasn't around to offer advice?"

"I mean that you were unavailable, married to my sister." Her voice lifted.

"I'm not reading you," he said. "What is it that—?"

"Oh, Guy, you're such a fine man and such an *idiot!* I'm saying I was in love with you and shouldn't have married at all."

He patted her hand. "Puppy love."

Patches of color appeared on her cheeks. "Don't patronize me. If it was puppy love at the beginning it matured, Guy, don't you understand? I'm *still* in love with you. I hate Connie for taking you, for what she's done to you, your life. And I feel guilty about René—I never loved him, he knew it, and he's dead." She brushed a tear from her cheek. "So many nights I prayed you wouldn't marry Con, that you'd turn from her to me. God, I was inwardly begging you to smile in my direction, even glance—" She swallowed. "Your few words were . . . a treasure. But you saw me only as a child, not the woman I could be."

Between them fell a heavy silence. At length he broke it, saying, "How could it be otherwise? You were the kid sister, Cris—be realistic."

His sharpness seemed to break her reverie. "I know, I know," she said apologetically. "You were older, a man who'd been to war. I was gawky, all hands and uncoordinated feet. And you were—honorable."

He took her hand. "I still am," he said gently. "And so are you."

"Am I? When Consuela treats you so coldly—don't you understand that affects me, makes me fantasize what might have been? Guy, some day you'll know how different I am from my sister. I'm stronger, more sensitive, yes, more capable."

"I understand now," he said. "And there'll be a man deserving of you. In all this world you're unique, Cristina, and—"

"—if there were no Consuela?"

"Don't," he said, "this isn't doing either of us any good."

Turning back she took his hand and kissed it. "Don't worry, Guy, I'll never speak so frankly again. This was the only chance I ever had."

"I'll always value you, care for you, be concerned with everything you do."

"I know," she said, sighing, "only please don't go on treating me as the unformed child of yore. It's been a long time since I was that."

He managed a smile though her declaration of love had given him an uneasy feeling—unsettled him in a way he hadn't expected.

Rising, she brushed sand from her jodhpurs. "Since it's your wish we'll pretend I never spoke; this—episode never occurred."

"That might be best," he said in seeming agreement, but realized with the truth spoken it would always remain between them. There was no going back.

He helped her into the saddle, mounted up, and as their horses followed winding trails she pointed out improvements to the land; new fencing here, power irrigation there, a modern method of fertilizing the endless Palafox vineyards. Guy responded interestedly, impersonally, until as a distant peak impaled the setting sun they turned back for cocktails with her father.

Nine

The main dinner course was *corderito asado,* lamb fragrant with wild herbs and as delicious as any Guy had ever enjoyed at Botin's in Madrid. Asparagus with mayonnaise, pan-roasted potatoes, lettuce-tomato salad, red and rosé wine decanted from bottles that bore the Palafox y Urriaga label.

As démi-tasses were served Don José said, "Your return adds years to my life, Guy, depth to my enjoyment. Try to spend part of every year at La Rocha. The *perdiz* hatch was good, we destroyed nine foxes, and the shooting should be exceptional." He glanced at his daughter. "Cristina's grown accustomed to your matched Sarasquetas, cleans and oils them as though they were her own. And she shoots like a man."

"With you as teacher, Don José, I'm not the least surprised."

She said, "Last year I took second place at the *tiro de pichón* club at Seville. This year I'm determined to win first."

"I'm pleased you did so well with my guns," he said, "and I look forward to shooting with both of you."

"Then I'll count on you in October," the *marqués* said. "I don't easily accept disappointment, Guy."

"I'll come in October," he promised, and saw Cristina's

lips form a small, contained smile. "And bring Consuela."
Her smile disappeared.

The *marqués* said, "If you don't mind an arthritic companion we'll ride together in the morning."

"Gladly," he said. "My thighs are stiff, need loosening." *Her* supple body, he thought, wasn't suffering like his.

"I'll join you," Cristina said, "make it a family outing; early ride, breakfast back here."

Don José said, "I thought Agregado was coming to select bulls for Ronda."

"He never arrives before noon—in time for lunch. Don't worry, I'll attend him as I always do. I'll sell him a dozen, even if some are underweight."

"That's not right, daughter."

"Let him fatten them himself," she said with a wave of her hand. "Agregado's a scoundrel who always complains of underweight—I know how to handle him."

"Well—if you say so." The *marqués* turned to Guy. "Your *cuñada* is less scrupulous than I who strive to maintain La Rocha's unstained reputation."

Cristina placed her elbows on the table, set her chin on joined hands. "Father, what would you say if I took a place in New York, spent a season there?"

"Why would you want to do that?"

"Because I've only lived here and in London—and the convent was hardly living. I think I should learn the ways of American society."

"My reply is that it would be highly improper for a young Spanish widow to do so."

"Guy would be there as chaperon—wouldn't you, Guy?"
Reluctantly he nodded.

"Guy will have no time to accommodate your whims. He's faced with managing an industrial empire, something he's never done."

Guy said, "If you come, Cris, Consuela and I will be delighted to have you."

126

"Still," Don José said, "the truth is I can't spare Cristina. She's needed here. Without her everything would come apart."

"Not so," she said. "That's an excuse to keep me penned here like a damsel in a tower."

In severe tones her father said, "I allowed you one mistake; I'll not be responsible for another."

"Meaning," she said, bristling, "you can't trust me in New York?"

"Trust is not the question. It's what is proper and what is not. Appearances are still important."

"Ticiticitici," she countered. "Not in this day and age."

"Enough," said the *marqués* irritably, "we'll not discuss it now."

"But discuss it we will," she declared. "Guy, more coffee?"

"No, thanks, I need my sleep."

"Father?"

He shook his head. "Guy, we'll take liqueurs in my study."

Servants drew back their chairs and Guy followed the *marqués* from the dining room. As they reached the study door Cristina called, "I enjoy cognac, too."

"Another time," her father said and watched her walk away. Shaking his head, he entered with Guy and closed the door behind them. "As you may have realized, Cristina displays a certain persistence." He picked up a silver-clad carafe. "Orange liqueur?"

Guy nodded and they took seats.

After tasting the liqueur, Don José said, "I feel I must apologize for Cristina's conduct."

"In what way?"

"Can it have escaped you—the way she's forcing herself on you?"

"I hadn't noticed," he lied. "Surely you're mistaken."

"Well, it's uncomfortably obvious to me. It's not as

127

though you were an eligible suitor. You're married and your wife is my daughter as well as Cristina's sister."

"I'm well aware of that."

"Even though you and Consuela have been living apart, you remain married in the eyes of the Church—and mine." His fingertips drummed the chair arm. *"Mi hijo,* this is difficult to say—I begin by acknowledging that Cristina is a daughter any father would be thankful to have—she's become almost a son to me. But, like a boy, she's not easy to guide, much less control. She married against my will. Now, as a widow she seems determined to act out her juvenile fantasy."

"What—fantasy?"

"That she has always been in love with you. That your marriage to Consuela was a mistake. That somehow—illogical as it may be—she and you are destined to be together."

Guy swallowed. "I think you may be inferring far more than may possibly exist."

"Perhaps—but what may seem nonsense to you and me may exist in her mind with perfect clarity. Guy, you know I love and admire you. Man to man, I ask that you not encourage her obsession, much less violate your marriage vows."

"I never have," he said, "and I have no intention of it—certainly not with my wife's sister."

"Your assurance eases my mind." He breathed deeply. "With regard to Consuela, you and she have had your disagreements—but situations change, and it is my prayer the three of you will form a family again."

"That is my hope as well. I'm going to make every effort to persuade her to leave Paris and join me in New York."

The *marqués* nodded.

Through the window came the clatter of hooves, a rider cantering away. Don José shrugged. "Cristina," he said without further explanation.

* * *

In his room Guy lay sleepless. He tried to blame it on strong coffee but realized his thoughts were tormented by Cristina's riverside confessions, her allure, her resolve.

Avoiding temptation was better than subsequent regret. As he reviewed the thought he decided he would leave for Paris and Consuela sooner than he'd planned. That would solve his problem, ease Don José's concerns as well. Healthier all around.

Because he slept lightly, restlessly, he heard the pebble strike his windowpane. Curious, he went to it and looked down. In the soft moonlight stood Cristina in a long fur robe. She waved and beckoned. Silently her mouth formed the words *Come down.*

His impulse was to return to bed. Then he reasoned that by talking with her he could dissuade her from her—obsession as her father termed it.

He pulled on shoes and clothing, went quietly down the stairs, passed through the dark and silent house and met her in the shadows. Drawing him further from the house she said, "I couldn't sleep. I had to know—was Father discussing me?"

"Your name was mentioned." The night air was chilly, he couldn't stay long without shivering. "We discussed several things—including my marriage to your sister."

She shook her head. "Don't you realize that's over?"

"I don't believe that."

"Oh, she may rejoin you because you're wealthy now, but she'll never be the wife you ought to have. Never love you as much as I."

He looked at her upturned face, her moist eyes. "I understand what you're going through, Cristina. Your world crashed with René, you turned to the trusted, the familiar. Nostalgia's a refuge for us all—if it's not neverending."

Petulantly she said, "You're questioning my mental stability, absolutely refusing to acknowledge the simplicity of the situation: I love you—seven years I've loved you, and nothing can alter it.''

"This is a dead end.''

Resolutely she shook her head. "Can't, or won't you admit you want me?'' Parting her robe she pressed against him and he realized she wore nothing more. "Whatever else I may be, I'm honest, Guy, no hypocrite.''

Desire rose. Before it overwhelmed him he forced their bodies apart, glimpsed the white perfection of hers, the pink-tipped breasts, the slightly mounded belly . . . "No,'' he made himself say, trying hard to do the right thing. "Please don't ask me to betray your family.'' He swallowed down the lump in his throat, stepped dizzily away.

Abruptly he turned and strode back to the house. Undressing in his room, he looked down and saw that she was gone. He got back into bed, angry he'd gone down, trying to erase the memory of her body. Next time they were alone together—if ever—he couldn't predict how he'd react. The truth was there. Submerging, forgetting what he could have without asking, was up to him. Cristina would never help.

In the morning he saw his mirrored face haggard from shallow, fitful sleep. He dressed for riding and went down to the study telephone. There he phoned Barajas Airport and left a message for the pilot: come at once to Seville.

Then he went out to join his in-laws, already mounted and waiting for him to ride.

As he got into the saddle he noticed a small white handkerchief crumpled in the grass where they had embraced. Cristina saw it, too, wheeled her horse and cantered away. Wordlessly, the *marqués* glanced at Guy.

When they returned there was a message from the pilot, giving Guy the aircraft's ETA at Seville. Over breakfast

Guy mentioned it and his father-in-law said, "Some unexpected emergency? I'm sorry, but I must remember you're a man of world affairs."

Guy avoided Cristina's questioning gaze, but after breakfast she came to him and said in a low voice, "You're running away from me."

"I'm inexperienced at affairs of the heart," he said. "If I stay, things could only get worse."

"At least let me drive you to the airport."

"No."

"I'll come anyway."

And she did, following him in her yellow Ferrari as his hands gripped the Audi's wheel until his knuckles were white.

He walked briskly through the airport lounge but she caught up with him at the departure gate, kissed his cheek and quietly began to cry.

After the Lear was airborne Guy looked down and saw her yellow car on the road to La Rocha, trailing a plume of dust. When he could no longer see it he sipped coffee and tried to think how best to reestablish relations with his wife and child.

First, though, he had to deal with his brother-in-law.

And Nicole.

Ten

Thibaud de Neuville said, "Guy, if you'd only let us know you were coming, Nikky and I could have prepared a proper reception." His tone was a mix of obsequiousness and irritation.

"It's not a social visit." Guy sipped the aperitif his brother-in-law had forced on him.

"Still, you'll be staying with us? Let me call our sister and let her know."

"I appreciate the courtesy but it's not necessary." He looked at his watch.

"Of course—you're familiarizing yourself with your holdings. I insist on showing you the assembly lines and production." He got up from behind his desk.

"I walked through coming up here. Everything spotless and functioning properly."

"No strikes in two years—our relations with labor equal those of any comparable industry in France—considering government resolve to give unions all they demand."

Guy nodded.

"Output continues at a nearly twenty percent annual increase. Our profits have been exceptional."

"I'll take your word," Guy told him. "Sean wouldn't have kept you as manager if you hadn't produced."

Stretching, he sat back. Through the large window came the suppressed sound of machine tools, the assembly lines. "You're manufacturing high-technology products, right?"

"Of course—and doing extremely well."

"Granted. The technology was created in the United States. The plant was established here to simplify problems in meeting European demand. To serve European customers. Not the East Bloc." He put down his small glass.

Thibaud's face stiffened. "I don't believe I understand the point, Guy."

"The problem lies with some of your customers."

"I don't sell to proscribed countries."

"Some of your customers do—they're mere intermediaries with no more substance than a Dutch or Belgian mail drop. You ship computers to Rotterdam; in the free port they're relabeled and trans-shipped to Stettin, Gdansk, Libya. Computers, digital navigational equipment, inertial guidance systems—hardware that can be used against the United States . . . and Europe."

"Sean never objected—and it's not illegal," he said defensively.

"Not by French law—but you've had compliance inspectors here from Washington. Not once but four times. On every occasion they expressed dissatisfaction over your indiscriminate sales and shipments. Each time they issued guidance lists covering what should not be transferred East. What was your response? Business as usual."

"That's not so, Guy," Thibaud said. "I consulted Sean—your father."

Guy grunted. "And he said, carry on?"

"He told me to follow French practice."

Guy's impulse was to call him a liar. Instead, after a few moments he said, "Can you document that?"

"Nothing was written or sent. Transatlantic calls."

"How convenient," Guy remarked. "Happen to have a witness?"

133

"My wife, Nicole." De Neuville picked up his desk telephone. "Call her now—question her. Guy, Nikky was as baffled as I was, I swear it."

Thibaud *could* be bluffing—or Nikky would respond supportively, by pre-arrangement. Guy said, "I can't believe my father would condone what you've been doing. Why would he—if he did?"

Thibaud gave a Gallic shrug. "Perhaps he was less concerned about America's defense and more interested in profits."

"That's all you can offer?"

"It wasn't my place to question Sean's motives. If you learn them I'd be obliged to know." Again he offered the telephone to Guy, who shook his head. "We'll leave that pending. Thibaud, I came here prepared to fire you, but if what you've told me is true your job is safe."

"But how can I prove it if you won't even question your sister?"

"I'll accept results beginning today. You'll stop all shipments, recall what you can and cancel all contracts with shadow firms—the trans-shippers. You'll observe compliance guidance as though it was holy writ, and I'll expect detailed reports on your actions. There'll be inspectors here to monitor the turnaround, and unless they're satisfied, you're gone." He got up. "You're on probation. It's up to you whether you remain with RyTech—are we clear on that?"

Thibaud swallowed, cheekbones unusually pale. "I—I understand."

"And I expect you to improve plant security so there is no chance of theft. Where are robotics designs kept?"

"In the engineering design section."

"If there's no secure vault, install one, and I mean now. Institute random searches of personnel when they leave the plant. As far as I'm concerned this is a Defense installation. Unless it's totally secure I'll eliminate it as a menace."

134

De Neuville nodded, then nervously cleared his throat. "I should telephone Nicole, say we'll be four for dinner."

"Four?"

"Gant arrived yesterday—didn't you know."

"We don't communicate, and I like it that way. What's his problem?"

"Money, of course."

"Well, I won't take advantage of your hospitality. But if Nikky joins Gant in trying to break Sean's will, it could have serious consequences for your future."

"Shall I tell her so?"

"It's your future, Thibaud, you know what's expected of you."

"You're leaving?"

"I have similar problems in Switzerland."

"I see—I thought there might be. I'll drive you to the airport."

"You haven't time to spare. Your driver will do." He pulled on coat and gloves, followed his brother-in-law down to the exit where a salon Citroën waited. From low gray clouds came a light, chill drizzle. An unappetizing day. Thibaud shook hands stiffly and stepped back. Guy got into the rear seat, said, "Airport," and the big car splashed away.

He found the aircrew in weather control, glumly watching the postings. The pilot said, "We're socked in and Paris is even worse, including Le Bourget. Runways iced, zero visibility."

Guy glanced at the wall clock; a few minutes after four. "What's the prospect?"

"Poor. A front's moving east from the Atlantic—this is going to be an all-Europe winter storm. I'm sorry."

"Hell, it's not your fault. I'll travel by surface. As soon as flying's safe, go back to New York. I'll return commercial. Radio working?"

"Yes, sir," the co-pilot said. "Satellite link okay?"

In the cabin Guy drank a warming cognac while the co-pilot patched him through to the Washington terminal. "I'll need my bag," Guy told him as he took the radiophone, and when he was alone he asked for a number provided by Hoskins.

The answering voice said, "Duty officer. How can I help you?"

"Hoskins there?"

"No, sir. Who are you?"

"Wilke?"

"Afraid not."

"I'm Guy Ryan, I'm in Lyons and I want you to tape the following for Hoskins."

"Yes, sir. One moment." A slight click, then, "Tape's running."

Guy summarized his findings at Systèmes Aéronautiques and itemized the orders he'd given. "Meanwhile," he went on, I recommend close watch on the plant—in case my brother-in-law tries to make last-minute shipments. If he does, your people are authorized to stop them—and lock him out of the plant."

He taxied to the central railway station and paid for a compartment on the high-speed TGV express. Half an hour's wait and he was relaxing in the compartment with hot *hors d'oeuvres* and a split of chilled white wine. Outside, the gray winter scenery rocketed past. After a while Guy pulled down the curtain, stretched out and went to sleep.

The two-hour trip ended at the Gare de Lyons. He took a taxi through dwindling traffic along the West Bank, crossing the Seine by the Pont d'Alma. Around the Etoile traffic was badly snarled by sleet-fall and fender-bender disputes, so it was close to eight when he reached Consuela's apartment building on the Avenue Foch.

The doorman took his bag into the entrance and rang for the concierge. The burly, middle-aged woman recognized him. *"Tiens, tiens, m'sieu,"* so long absent. Is madame *la marquise* expecting you?"

"No, but you might call ahead."

"With great pleasure. That child of yours—what a great beauty she will be." Guy smiled, and tipped her for the compliment.

He went through tall oak doors to the open-grill lift, set his bag inside and punched the top-floor button.

A maid was waiting in the corridor. Taking his bag she said, "I'm afraid madame is not here, sir."

"When is she expected?"

She shrugged.

"My daughter?"

"Yes. Gloria has just had dinner. Will you dine, *m'sieu?*"

"I'll wait for my wife," he said and entered the apartment. At the far end the skylighted *atelier* was dark, but on the walls he noticed four of Consuela's paintings that had not been there on his last visit. At least, he thought, she's doing her thing, and moved to the kitchen.

There at the table sat his daughter in nightgown and Pooh-Bear robe. Pausing, he studied her childish beauty, her perfectly combed dark hair, the arching Spanish eyebrows, and felt his throat thicken. On the verge of tears he went toward her. His unexpected appearance startled her, but in a moment she smiled and cried, *"Papa,* oh, *Papa,* I've missed you so," in perfect French.

Taking her in his arms he hugged her, held her out, then drew her back to kiss her face and forehead. His daughter, his only child. They'd never be apart again. Her arms wound tightly around his neck as she sobbed with joy.

Then a flood of questions: where had he been? what had he been doing? would he stay with them now, forever?

He carried her to the living room, set her on a sofa and sat down beside her. Holding her hand, he said, "Yes, we'll always be together, but not in Paris. We'll be moving to New York where we'll have a beautiful place to live. You'll have your own pony and we'll ride together."

"Does *Maman* know you've come?"

"No—but I hope she'll be glad to see me." He told her about the treasure search then, explaining it as the cause of his absence.

"And may I have some of the treasure, *Papa?* For my very own?"

"Of course. Old Spanish gold coins, perhaps a jewel or two if you do well at your *école des jeunes filles.* In this family we earn our rewards."

"Then I'll work very hard."

"I'm sure you will. Do you have homework to do?"

"It's done—but you can read me a story. Nurse does if she feels like it, then puts me to bed."

"I'll do the honors," he told her. "Bring me your book."

Capote Rouge was her favorite tale, so Guy read the story with dramatic vocal effects while Gloria mimicked Red Riding Hood's fright at discovering the wolf in *grandmère*'s bed.

When the story ended Guy asked if she liked her school. Gloria nodded but her lips set firmly before she said, "Some of the girls don't like me and I don't like them. Mariette and Esmé twist my arm when *madame* is not looking. The pain makes me cry out and *madame* blames me."

"Does Mother know?"

She nodded. *"Maman* says I must not fight back because I have noble blood and fighting is un-unbecoming."

Guy kissed her forehead. "Forget the noble blood. Punch 'em in the jaw, that'll stop them." When Gloria looked up in surprise Guy said, "Anyway, your blood is only half noble. Mine is—well, Irish and that's all there is to say."

"But *Maman* told me you come from Irish kings."

Guy couldn't resist laughing. Then, seeing his daughter's distress, he said, "I suppose it's true. Anyway, it's what Irishmen like to think and say. But since we're talking about nobility let me remind you that your mother, not you, is the *marquise*. *You* are Gloria Ryan, and never forget it."

"I promise. But *tante* Cristine—is she a *marquise*, too?"

"No, and may never be. Now, further to this noble subject you should understand that a great deal is expected of you. You must be kind to those less fortunate, and always help the weak. It is an obligation."

Her forehead furrowed. "As when Mariette pokes Geneviève who is much smaller?"

"Exactly. Pull Mariette away and poke her if necessary." He kissed the back of her hand. "Always have courage, never be afraid. If you always do right you need fear nothing."

For a few moments Gloria considered his words. Then she said, *"Papa,* don't ever go away. I want you with me, always."

"We'll be together," he said softly, "I promise. I'm very proud of you and I love you very much."

She kissed him, and in a soft, lovely voice began singing *Sur le pont d'Avignon* until Guy joined in. Then he told her a story about *grandpère* Palafox who, like himself, had been a soldier for his country, and was now a farmer raising cattle and horses and good things to eat. And he told her about the vineyards and olive groves and brooks so clear you could drink from them, and when he saw that her eyes were closed he carried her to bed and tucked her in.

After hanging her small robe in the closet he turned and gazed at his sleeping daughter. She is the child of my seed and Consuela's womb, he thought, and I want her to have all the good qualities of her mother and those of mine that are worth passing on. I love her very dearly, and if I never have a son she will be son and daughter to me and I will never ask for anything more.

He turned off the table lamp and tiptoed from her room, closing the door. In the sitting room he turned on the television set and watched a news program. Across France

139

weather was deterioriating. In mountainous areas travelers were urged to avoid roads and highways. Most metropolitan airports were closed.

The maid came in and asked if she could bring him something. Salad, perhaps? Cold meat? Wine?

"Cognac," he said, and looked at his watch. After nine. Evidently Connie was dining elsewhere. Well, she'd return eventually; meanwhile, he'd relax in comfort.

Carrying his glass he wandered into his wife's *atelier* and turned on the light. On the easel a half-finished abstract painting. Oil paints on the palette were dry. Brushes uncleaned. He stuck them in a jar of mineral spirit. Obviously she hadn't painted for days. He wondered how serious her devotion to art had become.

On a stand beside the wall stood the life-sized portrait of a man. He wore a loose, open-necked blouse over an apparently muscular torso. His face and eyes had a Slavic cast. The mouth suggested a propensity for brutality. A thoroughly *male* face, he reflected, with no suggestion of refinement or breeding. A model—or one of Connie's acquaintances?

The telephone rang and he decided to answer, thinking it was probably Connie calling to check on their child. Instead he heard the voice of Roy Stoner. "Guy? Glad I finally caught up with you. There's something on the fire you ought to know about—especially since you're in Europe."

"What is it?"

"Before I get onto that, how are things going? In Lyons?"

"About as well as expected. What's on your mind?"

"An attorney who represents mostly European financiers spent time with me today. One of his major clients is a Swiss banking consortium headed by a man named Edouard Drach, and they're interested in purchasing control of RyTech. Fifty-one percent of your voting stock was the proposal—for any price you'd care to name. I said I didn't think you'd be interested, but agreed to inform you."

"You're right, I'm not interested. RyTech's not for sale."

"All right. But if you want to hear more about the proposal, Drach is in Geneva. He has a reputation as a very persuasive man who perseveres until he gets what he wants. You're going to Switzerland, aren't you?"

"I may." He didn't want Stoner to know his plans. Didn't want anyone to warn the subsidiary he was coming. Surprise was an excellent battle tactic. "Anything else?"

"Your friend Needham's coming back from the Caymans tomorrow."

"Good. As soon as the Lear can fly I'm sending it back. I don't need it here. Not in this weather."

"Pretty bad, eh? Well, I'll see you when you return. We need to talk."

"Right." And you won't like what you'll hear, Guy thought as he replaced the telephone.

He refilled his liqueur glass and switched off the studio lights. He was changing TV channels when a key turned in the door lock, and he looked around to see his wife coming in. Behind her, wearing Homburg and fur-trimmed coat, came the man whose portrait he had seen.

Consuela halted, stared in astonishment at her husband. *"Ave María,"* she cried and came toward him. "Guy!"

141

Eleven

Her embrace was dispassionate, almost perfunctory, he thought—as though inhibited by her companion's presence.

Moving back Consuela said, "When did you come? Why didn't you give me some—"

"—warning?"

Her cheeks colored. "Advance notice I was going to say. Then—" She turned to her escort. "This is my husband," she said in French. "Guy, Serge Kedrov."

They shook hands briefly. Guy said, "I've seen you before."

His eyelids flickered. "Oh? Where might that have been?" His voice was guttural, grating.

"Your portrait."

"Ah, yes." He removed the black hat. "Excellent resemblance, don't you think?"

"Quite recognizable," Guy agreed.

"Consuela has a great deal of talent; her progress has been remarkable." He looked at her momentarily. "I myself am an art professional. I deal broadly in paintings and sculpture . . . provide encouragement to worthy aspirants."

"Which I'm sure my wife appreciates. Care for a nightcap?"

Kedrov glanced at Consuela, whose immobile face gave

him no clue. "Ah—I think not," he said slowly. "Perhaps another time. You'll be in Paris now?"

"Indefinitely," Guy replied.

Consuela said, "Thanks so much for dinner, Serge. It was so thoughtful of you."

"My pleasure," he said with a slight bow. "You'll not forget the Daumier exhibit?"

"I'm looking forward to it, Serge."

"Marquesa, M'sieu Ryan—" He backed to the door. *"Bon soir."* The door opened and closed. Guy was alone with his wife.

"Well," she said, removing her coat, "this is quite a surprise."

"Though not unwelcome?"

She shrugged. "You've always been—unpredictable, Guy."

"Cuts both ways. Drink?"

She nodded and he poured cognac for her. After sipping she said, "Congratulations on your good fortune."

"RyTech is a mixed blessing." He sat on the sofa, took her hand and drew her beside him. They kissed, but she drew away, frowning. "Did you forget to shave?"

"I shaved this morning at La Rocha. Since then I've been traveling."

"I see." She touched her cheek as though assessing damage.

"Your father's well, so is your sister."

"Yes, she does seem to be accommodating to widowhood rather well."

"Cristina thinks she'd like to spend some time in New York with us."

She gazed at him. "Are we going to New York?"

"I'll be located there for the foreseeable future. Seems logical my family should be with me." He sipped from his glass. "You disagree?"

"I—I haven't thought about it. This—" She waved one

hand at the room. "I mean, I've become accustomed to living here—to a way of life . . . do I have to decide this minute?"

"No. But I'd like our daughter to learn English—she *is* American."

"Actually, Gloria has Spanish citizenship as well. So you've seen her."

"We spent a pleasant hour together before bed. The nurse wasn't around."

"I gave her the night off—some family difficulty." Her eyes narrowed. "You feel I shouldn't have?"

"Not if the maid's an adequate substitute."

"She is, and I don't think you should burst in here and begin criticizing my domestic arrangements. Really, Guy, you can be quite insensitive."

"So you've told me. But I'm very pleased with our daughter. She's as affectionate as she is lovely." He gazed at his wife's profile and felt his throat thicken. Even more beautiful, were that possible. He took her unresisting hand. "I want us to start over, begin again, the three of us. You can choose where we live, have as much money as you want."

"Just as long as it's in New York? I'm not sure I'd enjoy New York—one hears dreadful things about it."

"The European press tends to sensationalize."

"True. Tell me, how did the treasure hunt turn out?"

"Successfully. There was some difficulty with the Haitians, but that's been resolved."

"And you have the treasure?"

"All that we recovered."

She sighed. "You're amazing. I thought it would be a wild goose chase, but I'm glad it was successful. How is your stepmother bearing up?"

"Rather well."

"I wired condolences. I suppose I should have come for

144

the funeral, but Gloria had a cold, and I've never been one for impromptu journeys.''

"Hundreds attended," he told her. "I doubt you were missed—except by me.''

She drank from her glass.

He said, "Is Kedrov your agent?''

She laughed briefly. "Oh, nothing like that. More a patron of the arts. Serge appears to be quite wealthy.''

"His French is flawless.''

"Yes—a rather unusual background. His father was a highly placed Soviet official who managed to send Serge to the Sorbonne. After graduating Serge declined to go back to Russia. Evidently reprisals were taken against his family.''

"Wasn't that rather selfish of Serge? Insensitive?''

"I suppose you could say so. His version is that he chose freedom and individualism to the collectivism of the Russian herd." She eyed him. "You're not holding the foolish notion that there's something between Serge and myself?''

"Not at all—beyond a common interest in art.''

"That's where it begins and ends. Because I have an occasional dinner with someone, you have no right to feel threatened.''

"I don't—if you say I shouldn't be.''

"That's all there is to it. He's very well connected in artistic circles, and I enjoy meeting fellow artists.''

"Of course you do. How long have you known him?''

"Oh, three months or so.''

Three months ago Sean's illness had begun to drag him down; he'd never returned to RyTech. Coincidence? He brushed the thought aside. "Did Kedrov commission the portrait?''

"Hardly—it's to be a gift.''

"A nice gesture," he said. "You do a good deal of painting?''

"Almost every day—depending on the light.''

He thought of the palette with its dry, cracked paints. "Then you've enjoyed living here, gained by the experience."

"Very much—so it's hard to contemplate an abrupt change." She regarded him thoughtfully. "You told Serge you'd be here indefinitely."

"He's not entitled to my confidences—and my stay *is* indefinite. From here I'll go to Geneva. When, is largely up to you."

"There must be many people who would like to meet you—bankers, financiers, industrialists. I should arrange a *soirée*."

"Please, no. I came to see you and our daughter, not exchange pleasantries with strangers." Suddenly he felt tired. From the tensions of Lyons, the unexpected encounter with his wife's escort, her diffidence. He got up and stretched. "I need a bath—and a shave."

"I'll look in on Gloria."

He carried his bag to the bedroom and unpacked. After turning on the tub he got out his shaving gear. As he lathered his face he noticed a thin round plastic container on a shelf below the mirror. He picked it up and saw it was divided into numbered sections for pills. Half the compartments were empty.

Midmonth.

He replaced the container, feeling leaden inside.

Slowly he shaved, preoccupied with the thought: Consuela was on birth-control pills. Was it too late, after all, to pick up the pieces?

Suddenly he felt as though he was in the bathroom, the apartment of a stranger. He nicked the corner of his jaw, wiped away the red line and finished shaving. The cuts from the Mercedes wreck had healed, leaving two faint pink scars on his face. Connie hadn't asked about them.

While he was in the tub his wife came in, busied herself

at the mirror and left. When Guy got out to dry himself he noticed that the pill container was gone.

He pulled on pajamas and got into bed beside his wife, who was propped up, scanning a French fashion magazine. When she continued he reached over and switched off the bed lamp. "Guy!" she protested.

"I came here for a reason, Connie. Are we to be man and wife again—or not?"

"You're so abrupt, impetuous. After eighteen months away you suddenly appear and expect me to welcome you to my bed, be warm and loving—isn't that a little extreme? I need time to—get used to you."

Taking her arm he drew her to him. "How long did it take to get used to Kedrov?"

Her mouth twisted. "How insulting! There's been absolutely nothing between us. I have dinner with an artistic gentleman, and you decide we're lovers."

"You're not? Why the birth control pills?"

She sighed. "Guy, don't think I—let me explain."

"I don't want to hear it, Connie." He released her arm. "I came here bent on reconciliation. If it's not to be, then let's make other arrangements. We're not the people we were when we married, and—"

"What couple is?" she said. "You changed when you left the army. I changed, too—but that doesn't mean I don't love you. Or want to be your wife. To preserve our marriage I came to Paris while you worked in Seville. I found creative fulfillment here, you found the treasure you were looking for. Now we're together again, Guy, but we still have to find out who we *are.*" She moved aside, hand across her mouth as though to ward off a blow.

"If I had an identity problem before, it's been resolved. I'm head of RyTech and I have more problems to solve than you could imagine. So, don't tell me you can't figure out who we are. We're husband and wife." He turned from her. "For now."

"Don't go, Guy. Don't leave me again."

"In the morning I'll see Gloria to school, come back and then we'll talk." He went to the guest room, and pulled down the covers. Had Kedrov lain there with her? He wondered. Well, what had he expected of a wife living half a world away? Who was it who said virtue is pristine until tested? He slid between the sheets and turned off the light.

His virtue had been tested, and his wife would never know how hard it had been to reject her younger sister. But, he had grown up in a far more demanding, more disciplined way than Connie had, accustomed to a self-denial that was uncongenial to the hotter Spanish temperament.

Memories kaleidoscoped through his brain. Connie holding their firstborn to her breast, radiant in the dullness of the hospital room. His joy at fatherhood. His silent vows to be with them always, protect them forever . . .

An hour passed restlessly. Two. Sleep came.

In the darkness—how much later he never knew—she came to him. The sloping of his bed as it took her body wakened him. He started up, but her hand touched his face and she whispered, "I couldn't sleep. That scene was all wrong—it shouldn't have been that way—and everything I said, everything you said, was wretched."

"I don't feel great, either."

"Don't say anything. Just let me say what is on my mind before you make up yours. What I said about preserving our marriage was true and heartfelt. What you said was true, and I understand your resentment. You can divorce me and I won't contest it—nor will I ask for money. But we have our daughter to consider. It's our fault, equally, that she's been deprived of her father, and I want you to consider that, too."

"I've missed her."

"And, whatever else you may think, I've missed you. I'm Spanish and Catholic and my place is with my hus-

148

band. I love you, Guy. I've never loved, or cared for, anyone else.''

Her body moved close to his. As though in a dream he found her lips, kissed them and felt the stirrings of desire.

His wife returned his caresses with growing passion, and soon her thighs parted to receive him. The core of her matrix dissolved as they made love.

The maid brought a breakfast tray; warm, flaky croissants, strawberry *confiture,* and hot, French coffee. As they ate in bed, Connie said, "If you still want me there, I'll come to New York.''

"More than anything I want you with me.'' His lips brushed her cheek. "How soon will you come?''

"As soon as I can, Guy. I've been months preparing for my first exhibition, and I'd be very grateful if you'd let me stay for it—early March. Then there's Gloria's schooling to consider.''

"There are French schools in New York.''

"I'm sure there are. But wouldn't it be kinder to let her finish the term with her friends? In New York she'll have none to play with. And you must remember how hard change is on children.''

"I remember.''

Gloria came in, dressed for school. She kissed her mother, rounded the bed and kissed Guy. "Papa,'' she said in confidential tones, "when I woke I was afraid I only dreamed you'd come back.''

"No dream, it's true. And now we'll always be together.''

"Will you come with me to school?''

"I'd consider it a privilege.''

Connie was smiling at the two of them. "You've got about five minutes, dear—don't make her tardy.''

He shooed Gloria from the bedroom and dressed quickly.

149

Before leaving he kissed his wife. "Any commitments to-day?"

"Lunch with my husband."

"He'll be there."

The driver took them down the crowded Champs Elysées past the Tuileries gardens, and just beyond the Hotel de Ville crossed the river onto the Ile St-Louis. There, nearly in the shadows of Notre Dame, was Gloria's *jardin d'enfants*. She guided him to the headmistress, who bowed graciously and took his hand. "She's a wonderful child, *m'sieu*. So attentive and polite."

"We thank her mother for that," Guy said. Then Gloria was bringing up her little friends, each curtseying in turn and offering a small hand. With a final kiss he left his daughter and went back to the car, wondering how he had survived so long without her, resolving to smother her with attention and love.

When he returned to the apartment Consuela was in her *atelier*, wearing a paint-stained smock, squinting at the clear light, her palette shiny with fresh daubs of oil paint.

Over a second cup of coffee, he watched her work to complete the easel painting, noticing that a cloth now covered Kedrov's portrait.

Maybe things will work out, he mused. There's so much to gain that I have to make every effort to succeed. Aloud he said, "Let's discard the past. Today is the first day of the rest of our lives. Agreed?"

She glanced around. "Gladly."

He looked at his watch. "I have some things to do—where shall we have lunch?"

"Crillon Grill—before it's crowded. Noon too early?"

"Noon will be fine." They kissed, he put on his coat and went down to the street. He walked up Avenue Foch to the Etoile and rode the Métro to the Madeleine station. From there he walked to the American Embassy, entered and asked the receptionist for James McGrain. She requested his passport, and phoned his name to McGrain's office. Returning the passport she said, "Three-oh-four."

He walked across the marble floor to the elevator and got off at the third floor where a pleasant looking black man in his thirties greeted him. "I'm McGrain, sir. Honored to meet you. I was advised you might stop by and told to cooperate fully." He ushered Guy through an unadorned reception space, then into a small, soundproofed office. When they were seated he said, "How can I be of service?"

"I'd like a couple of name checks. One is Serge Kedrov, who claims to have defected some years ago while a Sorbonne student." He spelled the name. "The other is Edouard Drach, nationality unknown, located in or around Geneva, supposedly a large-scale financier. I'm going there within the next few days and may see him. Yesterday he made an open-end offer to buy control of RyTech."

McGrain exhaled sharply. "I've heard of him. We don't keep much here by way of files—just current cases—but I'll check if there's anything beyond what comes back from Washington." He studied the end of his pencil. "With Drach I seem to recall an Arab connection."

"Arab oil or Arab terrorism?"

McGrain shrugged. "Is there a difference? No—I shouldn't have said that—but I've had buddies blown up in Beirut, assassinated right here in Paris."

"As someone said, it's war without boundaries. Carry a piece?"

"Of course. And I hope you do—you're a significant figure in the military-industrial complex. We couldn't afford to have you kidnapped or killed."

Guy smiled. "I couldn't afford it either." He wrote down the apartment phone number and gave it to McGrain. "I'm staying at my wife's place—Avenue Foch. When you call I'll come here."

"Good telephone discipline," McGrain said. "Do you have any reason to believe her line is tapped?"

"No."

He cleared his throat. "Is there anything else, sir?"

"When will I hear from you?"

"Tomorrow at latest."

"Thanks for your help."

"Glad to, sir—it's what I'm here for." As he rose he said, "If you'll forgive a personal observation, Mr. Ryan, I always thought you should have gotten the Heisman Trophy."

"So did my father." They shook hands and parted at the elevator.

From the embassy Guy walked up the Boissy d'Anglas, whose shadowed gutters were choked with thawing slush. At the Faubourg St. Honoré he crossed over to Hermès. There he selected a set of matched luggage for his wife, a smaller set for his daughter. The salesman said he would take care of monogramming and promised delivery tomorrow.

At Burberry's nearby store Guy bought a raglan topcoat and found a tweed suit for rough shooting. He considered other needs and continued on to Sulka's, facing the Louvre. There he was measured for an evening jacket, and selected swatch material for four business suits. He ordered a dozen shirts, picked out several conservative ties and realized it was time to meet Consuela at the Crillon.

While waiting, he had a Scotch at the bar, and after a few minutes saw his wife come in. She was wearing a tailored gray suit and a marten throw, matching hat and gloves, and looked the fashionable young Parisian matron she'd become. Paris-style, they touched cheeks, and he said, "Stunning."

"Then you'll forgive my being late."

"Hora española. Our table's over there." Taking her arm he led her to it and the captain drew back her chair. "Will Madame la Marquise take an aperitif? Vermouth *glacée?"*

"Perfect, Freddy."

As the captain snapped fingers Guy indicated his Scotch. "I'll hold."

Consuela sighed. "For the moment I'm better known than you, dear. In New York all that will change. Then it will be Ryan Le Grand—and his nameless spouse."

"Unlikely," Guy remarked, and took her hand. "But would it bother you?"

"Oh—perhaps for as much as a minute. Then I'd remember when you were the Assistant Military Attaché few people knew—and I was the popular young *Marquesa."* Her tone was light. "The papers were so *bad* about it, Guy—so *affronted."*

They laughed reminiscently and he said, "It was your father who told me to ignore it all. Without him I'd have abandoned hope."

"I know."

"Before you come to New York you should visit La Rocha, let him see how gorgeous his grandchild is."

"I shall," she said as the iced vermouth arrived. "Nicole phoned—very upset over your visit yesterday."

"Because I didn't stay?"

"Because you savaged Thibaud."

"Hmmm—that what I did? Nicole wanted you to intercede?"

"No—just to call you bad names. Frankly, dear, I was *not* a sympathetic listener."

"Good training," he said, "for there'll be much special pleading in years ahead." He described some of his personnel changes and then menus arrived. Consuela chose jellied bouillon and shrimp salad with capers. Guy, a mixed grill and a *démi-bouteille* of Montrachet.

Eating together seemed to close the gap of their apartness.

They spoke of Gloria's education, her possible future—his plans for RyTech, what living in New York would be like, incidents in the lives of common friends, her desire to continue painting. Then luncheon was over and he walked Consuela to the exit where her car and driver waited.

In their bedroom they made love, slept and woke when Gloria returned. Guy helped her with homework and walked with her to the Arc de Triomphe for a view of Paris from its roof, where she had never been before.

On the way back he stopped at a *glacerie* for ice cream treats, bought balloons and bon-bons at a *chocolatier,* arriving at the apartment ruddy-cheeked and glad of the inside warmth. The nurse scolded them both for keeping Gloria in the cold, but Guy paid her no heed, hugged his radiant daughter and went off for a hot bath.

That evening the three of them dined at Maxim's in great splendor, the captain showing special deference to the well-dressed child whose manners he rewarded with a special sweet.

Afterward, Guy stood between them at the curb, holding them close while waiting for the car. And feeling new contentment.

At the apartment a message waited. From James McGrain.

Twelve

Gray morning light filtered through slatted blinds in McGrain's office. Guy had left the apartment while Consuela was sleeping, takèn Gloria to school and gone back to the embassy. The DSA officer scanned a Telex printout and said, "Serge Kedrov has come to security attention before. He may be who and what he says he is but there's no way to verify his background by independent means. We can't ask the Soviets about him, and if that were possible we could hardly rely on their response."

"Doesn't CIA have a continuing interest in Russian émigrés?"

"In principle, yes—but press exposure of CIA officers abroad, and the Agency's wholesale firings in the late seventies were one-two punches the Agency hasn't recovered from. MI-Six has no traces on Kedrov—by that name, at least—and the French internal service, the DST, is chronically crippled by politics and corruption."

"Bunch of blind men stumbling around in the dark."

"Unfortunately—but DST provided a minor note. It seems that Kedrov, in addition to his artistic *persona,* also functions as an unofficial representative of the Bank Narodny—that's Russia's state bank—in Paris."

"What do you mean 'unofficial'?"

"He's not listed as a bank officer but his name has surfaced on banking documents—as a loan guarantor, for example. The surmise is that Kedrov steers individuals and corporations in financial difficulties to the Bank Narodny, and takes a commission."

"So he's not on hostile terms with the USSR."

McGrain shrugged. "Obvious. More to the point, the bank gives generous terms to selected borrowers who of course then become vulnerable to Soviet influence."

Guy nodded thoughtfully. "He's got the look of a *banquier*. What else?"

"There's suspicion Kedrov funnels Soviet funds to left-wing activists and institutions, newspapers that aren't usually considered pro-Soviet. Again, DST should be on top of that, and twenty years ago it would have, but what resources it has are concentrated on terrorism. That's high-profile stuff, see, whereas tailing and bugging a Kedrov is on the dark side with no public payoff for the government."

Guy gestured at the report. "Anything about my wife?"

McGrain swallowed. "She's been seen with Kedrov at art shows, gallery exhibitions, that sort of thing."

"With the intimation they're lovers?"

"Doesn't say that," he said uncomfortably. "But if Kedrov is KGB or GRU he's one of the post-Khruschev breed—a 'joy boy' in security jargon. Educated, linguistically accomplished, competent in ballroom dancing, well-mannered and able to move in social circles that would reject a badly dressed oaf on the Khruschev pattern. Charm rather than menace. And it's paid off around the world."

"I can imagine—but Kedrov's never been fingered as a Soviet agent?"

"Not beyond what he may do for the Bank Narodny."

"Is he married?"

"At the Sorbonne he married a French girl—they were later divorced. After he received French citizenship."

"Marriage of convenience, eh?"

"Perhaps more. She came from a prominent Communist family, and three years ago was killed in Lebanon with a Syrian paramilitary team attacking an Israeli outpost." He set aside the report. "That's what there is on Kedrov."

Guy cleared his throat. "My wife is not politically sophisticated—and artistic circles tend to the liberal. Now that I'm back I don't expect to see Kedrov around."

"So you don't think Kedrov was ingratiating himself with your wife as a means of getting to you."

Guy shook his head. "Far-fetched. When they met, my wife and I were living apart; neither of us anticipated reconciliation. Not even the KGB could predict I'd take over RyTech."

"Unless your top echelon is penetrated."

Guy recalled the words he'd overheard through the heating vent at Eastover. "It's a possibility," he acknowledged, "but I'm not aware of anything more than internal corporate jousting. What about Drach—the man who wants RyTech?"

McGrain picked up several Telex printouts stapled together. "This is a—I hardly know how to describe him. A modern-day Zaharoff, we might start with."

"The old, original 'merchant of death'? The arms dealer?"

"Right. Drach—that's the name he currently uses—is a fascinating figure. When he sells arms to the Israelis he poses as a Jew. To the Libyans, Saudis, Iranians and Iraqis, he comes on as an Arab. Sort of a chameleon, though munitions and armaments are just a sideline with him now. His current persona is that of investment banker. In Switzerland he's gained a certain degree of respectability—one thing money *can* purchase, and he has plenty of it. Sir, how much of his background do you want to know?"

"What have you got?"

"Well, it's shadowy and unsupported for the most part—there's not even a consensus among Western security ser-

157

vices about his birthplace." He looked at the printout. "Was he born in Cyprus as Andreas Gülen, or Bulgaria as Kiril Dankov? He's used both names at different times. Then for a period he was traveling as Josip Dumic, a Yugoslav. Before becoming Edouard Drach he called himself Istvan Varga, a Hungarian refugee. Whatever his origin, Drach came from a humble background somewhere in Europe and learned to profit from war and conflict. For instance, during the Spanish Civil War, when he couldn't have been thirty, he was selling ships, food and munitions to both sides. The Nationalists caught him trying to break the Barcelona blockade with one of his ships, but Gülen—as he was then known—slipped away and turned up in Holland trying to sell the Dutch bombs and machine guns the Loyalists had paid for but never received." McGrain turned a page, read briefly and smiled. "After King Farouk was kicked out of Egypt, one Kiril Dankov concluded a deal with Mohammed Naguib to purchase Farouk's collection of pornography, then the most comprehensive in the world. He managed to get it out of Egypt before Nasser took over, and apparently never got around to paying for the collection. The Egyptian Government didn't think it would be good PR to sue over Farouk's smut, so Dankov/Drach was the beneficiary."

"If you like that sort of thing."

He read further. "Jesus, *this* is bizarre. He's rumored to be impotent, but has a letch for children. Drach gets them from refugee camps in the Mid-east and Central America when he travels there on business. There's a report from Paraguay that he filmed a snuff movie showing him killing a little boy and girl after torturing them sexually." He looked across at Guy. "No one's seen the movie so he can't be prosecuted for murder."

Guy shook his head disgustedly. "Charming fellow—I should sell RyTech to *him?*"

"Like Farouk, Drach is grossly fat, indulges an insatiable appetite. The obesity and impotence suggest a glandular

158

problem, but it doesn't interfere with his brain. In financial transactions very few have bested him—and they didn't live long to enjoy victory." McGrain turned a page. "For two years he was headquartered in Monaco, but he wore out his welcome. Seems a young *artiste*—euphemism for whore— was found torn apart by his guard dogs—after he'd used and abused her. Nothing was proved against him, but the Grimaldies like a clean store and got him out of the Principality. After that he lived in Beirut supplying arms to rival factions, but when the destruction of Beirut began, Drach moved to Switzerland."

He turned to the last page. "Since then he's adopted a patina of respectability, developed friends and supporters among bankers grateful for the money he brings in. Every time OPEC meets in Geneva, Drach throws huge banquets and parties for the sheiks and princes, and includes the more presentable representatives of the PLO." He looked at Guy. "One gets a sense that Drach gravitates to where the big money circulates, regardless of its source."

"Seems evident. And what are the sources?"

"Considering his interest in RyTech and the unlimited offer, that amount of money—let's say a billion dollars— would have to come either from oil-rich Arabs, or the Soviet Union."

"What's your guess?"

"Well, the Arabs have a lot of interest in Western consumer goods, especially expensive automobiles and aircraft, but they sink a lot of their loot into schools and hospitals. High technology isn't their bag, though it may be in a few more years when they produce their own technocrats. The Sovs, however, are famished for advanced Western technology. Considering RyTech's significant Defense role, acquiring your controlling interest would satisfy their wildest dreams. Soviet gold is mined by slave-labor at small cost to the Kremlin. When the USSR needs hard currency, they sell gold on the international market, usually through Bank Narodny branches in London and Zürich.''

"So you think Drach's principals are the Soviets."

"It's my informed guess." He laid the report in an Out box and stretched muscular shoulders. "One other thing, aside from his corpulence Drach is personally vain. In Switzerland he underwent hair transplanting from neck to pate. It doesn't curl or lie back, stands up as though electrified." McGrain chuckled. "Keeps it cropped, Prussian-style."

"Sounds like an old horror movie."

"Are you planning to see him in Geneva?"

"Only if he makes the overture. I'll go out of curiosity, form my own opinion." Smiling, he got up. "It's obvious I've been leading a sheltered life."

McGrain opened a desk drawer. "Your life is very important, sir." He produced a holstered automatic and offered it to Guy, who shook his head. "It's a nice piece but I'd feel uncomfortable wearing it around Europe."

"At least carry it in your luggage—never know."

Reluctantly, Guy took the weapon and drew it from the holster. A short-barrel Walther P-38K, 9 millimeter pistol. He extracted the magazine and found it loaded.

"Insurance," McGrain said.

He liked the solid feel of the grip. The muzzle barely extended beyond his knuckles. Close range only. "All right," he said, "if you're that concerned I'll take it along."

"It's a hell of a piece—hope you never have to use it."

Guy holstered the pistol and pocketed it. "Much obliged for the information," he said. "I'll use it with prudence and circumspection."

McGrain rose and extended his hand. "How long will you stay in Paris?"

"Another day or two." He shook McGrain's hand.

"Traveling to Geneva? In this weather I'd recommend the ultrafast train you may have heard about. *Train à Grande Vitesse,* the TGV. Next thing to flying."

"I know," Guy said. "By the way, ever play football?"

McGrain smiled. "At Pitt. Blocked for Marino—until a kneecap broke. But I got my degree, that's why I played in the first place."

Guy nodded. "Ever consider a career change, let me know."

As he left the Embassy he recalled McGrain's references to the Bank Narodny and wondered if the DSA officer was implying a possible link between Kedrov and Drach. All in all it had been an interesting hour. He turned onto the Boissy d'Anglas and stopped at a *brasserie* for a *fine café*—hot coffee with a shot of cognac. Miserable day, cold, with the kind of dampness that chills the bone. Pewter skies. The cognac warmed and cheered. He taxied to the apartment and found Consuela at breakfast reading *Le Matin*.

He had coffee with her, and when she put on her painting smock he settled down with the telephone and placed a call to Jake Needham in New York.

That evening the three of them went to the ice show at the Cirque d'Hiver. The spectacle with its lavishly costumed skaters and ridiculous clowns captivated Gloria, but on the way home she fell asleep in the car. Guy carried his daughter up to the apartment, enjoying the privilege of fatherhood while sensing how dependent and vulnerable his daughter was. Well, he would be there to protect her.

Always.

He kissed her cool forehead and left while his wife changed their child into her nightgown.

When Consuela came in for a nightcap he said, "I hate to leave so soon, but I have some urgent matters in New York, and before then I must go over the Swiss operation." He took her hand. "Your Easter visit's firm?"

"Of course it is, darling. Gloria's terribly excited and anxious to see New York. As a matter of fact, so am I."

She smiled, and Guy saw again the face of the Spanish girl he had fallen in love with at first sight. His once and future wife. There were doubts and resentments to overcome, but he wanted nothing more than to make her happy in every way, and so ensure his own contentment in their years ahead.

"I've hired bodyguards for you and Gloria," he told her.

Her eyes narrowed. "Because of Serge?"

"Because of kidnappers and terrorists."

"I wish you'd consulted me first. It sounds terribly inconvenient."

"Consider Gloria's safety if not your own. In Paris you'll either be guarded, or—no Paris."

"I'll take Paris—and your bodyguards."

In his TGV compartment Guy read RyTech papers and made notes, emerging for a hearty luncheon in the dining car, with occasional glances at the drab winter scenery. The express pulled into the Gare in mid afternoon, and after checking into the Hôtel Richemond, Guy hired a limousine to take him along the lake to the plant located off the Lausanne road in the Alpine foothills.

Around it stood tall chain-link fencing topped with sharp accordian wire. Above the entrance a sign lettered in ruby-red: *Société Suisse des Recherches Technologiques.* SSRT for short, Guy thought, as he handed the gate guard his card and asked to see Managing Director Hans Egli.

While waiting, he surveyed the setting. The plant was backed up against a mountainside down which came files of high-tension power lines from some distant hydroelectric source. The skeletal support towers looked like grotesque creatures from another planet descending from cloud-hidden peaks to ravage the lowland.

The guard opened the electric gate and Guy walked into the outer premises. From the administration building hur-

162

ried a heavyset man, tie flapping in the wind, nearly stumbling in his haste. He greeted Guy effusively, capturing Guy's right hand with both of his, pumping up and down as he gasped for breath, until finally he said he was Director Egli and welcomed M'sieu Ryan with all his heart.

In the office hot chocolate was served with small sugar cookies and *nougat*. After brief preliminaries Guy told Egli much of what he had told Thibaud in Lyons, and asked to see what SSRT was producing and researching.

As they walked into the factory, Guy realized that most of it had been dug into the foothill. White-coated technicians worked on laser units of various sizes. These, Egli told him, were used in construction and tunnelling where absolutely true lines were essential. The next section produced laboratory-quality lasers for dentistry, cosmetic and orthopedic surgery. Guy was impressed by the area's unhurried efficiency, and moved on until they reached steel-shod doors that opened to Egli's plastic card.

This was the military applications section. Four technicians were mounting a laser weapon in the mock-up of a fighter nose, and Guy watched with interest. Egli said, "We've succeeded in reducing laser weight to less than five hundred kilos, making airborne mounting feasible."

"What's effective range?"

"This prototype can reach a target six kilometers distant. More than three miles," he added proudly. "Because the beam travels at the speed of light the weapon is much more efficient than air-to-air missiles."

"For space utilization I would think a much longer range is necessary. At least five hundred miles. Maybe a thousand."

Egli nodded. "Until recently that was thought to be impractical."

"Due to laser size?"

"Principally because of power-source weight. At one time our calculations were that a generator for a thousand-mile

163

laser beam would weigh at least fifteen tons. Happily, our researchers have developed a power system weighing less than a ton.''

"Solar power?''

"Exactly. The reflectors of silvered plastic weigh next to nothing, and the weight is further reduced by miniaturized solar energy cells developed here.''

"Patented?''

Egli shook his head. "To patent is to publicize. We depend on plant security to keep the design secret.''

They were moving deeper into the mountain. At the end of the area huge steel doors like those of a bank vault closed it off. At either side of the doors were uniformed men with automatic weapons. Nodding to them, Egli pressed the keys of an electronic lock and the heavy doors slid smoothly aside. Entering, they passed around a baffle and Guy became aware of forced ventilation, as in a deep mine gallery. The doors closed behind them and Egli said, "This is where we conduct neutral-particle beam research.''

The left side, Guy thought, looked like an extremely clean manufacturing plant. There was a short assembly line, beyond it glowing furnaces for glass blowing, and a great many unfamiliar machine tools. In the center, masses of machinery. To the right a metal-shielded tube some four feet in diameter that disappeared in the distance.

"The proton accelerator,'' Egli explained. "It extends nearly half a mile into the mountain.'' He gestured at a large, awkward-looking metal structure surrounding a large glass barrel. "The neutral-particle gun. It's taken nearly five years to develop this far, and we anticipate another three years before producing a prototype useful to the military. In comparative terms, the beam generator is as rudimentary as the pencil was to the computer, or a waterclock to a digital wristwatch. There is quite literally no precedent for this work; we learn as we proceed, pause to develop new hardware and go on again. Short steps at a time.''

"How far have the Soviets progressed?"

Egli shrugged. "No one knows."

"*They* know."

"Of course. I thought—"

Guy cut him off. "How much has this research cost RyTech?"

"Oh, I'm not a bookkeeper. The required reports go to New York—the comptroller, Farley Johns."

"He's not here. Suggest a figure."

Egli looked upward, squinted. His cheeks were flushed. Finally he said, "Perhaps thirty million Swiss francs, perhaps more."

"Around twelve million dollars, then."

"I believe that's a reasonable estimate."

"And the research is unique."

"So I understand—aside from the USSR."

"All of which makes it essential to preserve absolute secrecy on everything that's produced here—don't you agree?"

"Of course, sir." His pudgy fingers moved, reminding Guy of the Haitian lawyer, LeSeur. Guy said, "Who's your security chief?"

"Franz Baumstern, he was once a police inspector in Bern."

"Perimeter security looks vulnerable. Tell him it needs improvement, and fast."

"Yes, sir."

"Does he keep files on all employees?"

"You mean, in addition to personnel records?"

"That's what I mean."

Egli swallowed. "He may—I don't know, I never inquired."

Guy heard the rising hum of current. The accelerator tube door opened. Six men slowly rolled the particle gun into position while others made electrical connections. From a shielded booth a technician watched closely. Egli said,

"At the far end is a lead target six feet thick. To date, particle beam penetration is only a foot. Our scientists want complete penetration of six feet of lead before enhancing the gun toward its planned capability."

"Which is?"

"Target disintegration."

From the top of the gun a small laser shot pencil-thin red light into the mouth of the accelerator tube. For alignment. The six men pushed and shoved the structure until the booth technician was satisfied. They moved away, and the hum of current increased.

From the particle beam gun came a *pop* hardly audible over the sound of current. The technician left the booth and motioned the movers to reposition the apparatus. A roller belt was activated, drawing the lead target toward the tube mouth for inspection.

Turning back to the managing director, Guy said, "Tell me about LDC development."

"What do you want to know, sir?"

"How close to prototype are you?"

"Within three to four months, sir. The system is based on green-light laser, a radical enhancement of commercial laser communications."

"Where is the work area?"

"Farther into the mountain, sir." He gestured.

"How many personnel involved with LDC?"

"Twenty-eight, thirty."

"Out of how many employees overall?"

"Two hundred and—yes, seventy-three. Two hundred seventy-three." He nodded in satisfaction.

"With positive vetting for each one?"

"Sir? What is that?"

"It means field investigations, confirmation of birthplace, checking police files, political affiliations, sources of income, whether relatives are Communists. Has that been accomplished for all employees?"

Egli wet his lips. "I—I can't say."

"Then I'll ask Baumstern."

"He's not here today—attending the wedding of a relative, I believe."

"I'll look at his personnel file."

The massive lead target had reached the mouth of the tube where the booth technician was inserting a measuring rod into the latest hole. Drawing it out he shook his head in disappointment. From where Guy stood, penetration seemed to be slightly more than a foot. "We'll go back to your office," he said, and followed Egli through the plant.

Baumstern's file showed education ending at *gymnasium*, high school level. Years of foot patrolling, then criminal investigations until retirement. Widowed, two married daughters. Age sixty-four.

Guy tossed the file on Egli's desk. "He won't do."

"May I ask why not?"

"He's a cop—this isn't a cop's job. The work is highly classified, which calls for compartmentalization. There should be only fully reliable workers to avoid hostile penetration and theft of secrets. The security chief has to be sensitive to the threat of foreign and industrial espionage, and ruthless with personnel who can't meet security standards. The position requires an investigative background, experience in foreign intelligence, and a thorough knowledge of physical security. What's needed is a senior man—military officer, say—who's young enough to approach the challenge with enthusiasm and realize it's not a nine-to-five job. But the problem with military pensioners is that when you call reveille too many stack arms. So I'm thinking of someone from London—Special Branch, not MI-Five, which has yet to clean up its act." He stared at the managing director. "Am I getting through to you, Herr Egli?"

"Yes, yes, sir."

"Have a candidate in mind?"

Slowly, dejectedly he shook his head.

"Until I find one, say nothing to Baumstern. He'll be discharged when the new chief arrives—without notice. So, compute what's fair for Baumstern and have the papers ready."

"Yes, sir."

"When I arrived I told you what I learned at Lyons. Your plant also ships products to shadow firms, and it's to be ended now. Anything scheduled for East Bloc intermediaries is to be halted. Return all advance payments, and if they sue, let them."

"But—my government—"

Guy waved a hand disparagingly. "If they object to the measures my response is this: I'll close down the plant and pull out the equipment. Leaving two hundred and seventy-three unemployed Swiss. Plus you. Seventy-four. I have a place in mind in northern Australia for relocation. So, we do things my way or not at all."

Elgi's breathing was labored.

"I will expect daily reports from you on meeting my requirements. Personnel security is my immediate concern, and that includes you. I'll take your file with me."

He paled. "You mean—I'm under suspicion? But—"

"Everyone is. Your position is the most responsible, so I'll have you vetted independently."

Stiffly he said, "I assure you, my qualifications are of the highest."

"That's not what I'm talking about. We're talking loyalty. If you don't understand that, here's an example: Klaus Fuchs was highly qualified in the atomic field; he worked in Britain, Canada and the US. Unfortunately for the West he was also a Soviet agent, a stealer of atomic secrets. And that was avoidable had anyone bothered to find out that he and his parents were old-line Stalinists. Got it now?"

Egli swallowed. "Yes, sir. But it's not fair to compare Fuchs and me."

"Life isn't fair," Guy told him and stood up. "I expect

168

to be at the Richemond through tomorrow. Any questions, you can reach me there. Good day, Herr Egli.''

He left the office and walked through the yard. The gate guard gave him a casual nod and opened the exit gate. Hell, Guy thought, I could be bringing out a whole laser and he wouldn't know. We need metal detector screening. The whole set-up reeks of complacency.

The plant whistle blew as Guy got into the waiting limousine. The sun was behind the mountains, darkness falling. As the driver backed around, Guy saw employees filing from the plant, and wondered how many would pass screening.

From his room he telephoned Jake Needham and told him to start locating a plant security chief and outlined qualifications. ''I've checked the classified directory, and Geneva has several international executive search firms. London, too.''

''What about the US?''

''Sure, but French is an absolute must here.''

''Right. Are you finished with Geneva?''

''Pretty much. Did the Lear get back to New York?''

''Not yet. When can I expect you?''

''Couple of days.''

''Then I'll get on down to Houston, check things out there. Have a report when you arrive.'' He paused. ''How did you find things today?''

''So vulnerable it's scary.''

He took a hot shower, stretched out on the bed, wondering if he ought to return by way of Paris, see his family again. Gloria's Easter vacation was weeks away, and he wouldn't see them until then. Now that they were a united family he wanted no more separations; the last had almost destroyed them. And—there was Kedrov to consider. Would he get the message or would he try pursuing Connie in her husband's absence?

A knock at the door. Guy wound a towel around his hips and called, "Who is it?"

"Message, sir."

He opened the door and found a uniformed *chausseur* with a large cream-colored envelope on a silver tray. Guy took the envelope and tipped the boy.

It was addressed to him in heavy calligraphic script. Inside was a card bearing an engraved coat of arms below which was the name *Drach* in Germanic script. The handwritten message said:

> *Cher Monsieur Ryan,*
>
> *To my regret I have only just learned of your presence in Geneva. Unless you are otherwise engaged it would be my honor and privilege to have you dine with me tonight.*
>
> *Unless I learn to the contrary, a car will be at your hotel at eight o'clock.*
>
> *Edouard Drach*

Why not? Guy thought. It's better than dining alone, and I'll have a chance to see the man who wants to buy me out. The man of many names. The Chameleon.

At eight o'clock a silver Rolls drew up at the curb and a uniformed driver got out. He opened the rear door for Guy who got inside. Almost noiselessly the limousine pulled away, taking the road north for a short drive along the lakeside. The Rolls turned inland and passed through tall postern gates from where the road slanted upward. Ahead stood an illuminated *schloss* of gray stone with tower corners and

170

crenelation. The entrance steps were marble, the arched doors slightly smaller than those of a cathedral. Above them, carved in granite, was the same coat of arms as on the invitation.

The doors opened and a footman came down to open Guy's door. Guy went up the steps.

Thirteen

On both sides of the long entrance hall stood medieval armor, plate and chain mail, some of the figures holding lances and fauchards in their empty gauntlets. Above them glaves, guisarmes, maces, broad-axes, halberds, morning stars and broadswords were arrayed among heraldic shields. Set at the far end of the hall was a barded horse bearing a rider in chain mail. The knight wore a white silk fall blazoned with a crimson Crusader cross. Atop the visored heaume rested a gleaming metal crown.

Guy had visited similar chivalric displays in Madrid's Royal Palace, and he remembered his surprise at how small those knights had been. Perhaps Drach was subliminally implying that his bloodline went back to the Crusades. Or memorializing the early implements of war.

He followed the footman over stone flooring, hearing their footsteps echo through the cheerless hall until, at the end, the footman turned right and Guy went through a wide, arched entrance into an immense room lighted by electric tapers in wall sconces. The high-vaulted ceiling with its supporting timbers reminded Guy of a medieval church, but it was a knight's hall. The walls were covered with Bayeux tapestries showing chivalric scenes. Below them, more me-

172

dieval weapons were displayed: broadswords, daggers, halberds and glaves.

Toward the far end was a recessed fireplace large enough to hold a squad of pikemen. The laid logs looked like long sections of telephone poles.

There were perhaps a dozen upholstered wooden chairs arranged near the center. The largest chair was topped by a bas-relief crest, and in it sat one of the largest men Guy had ever seen.

The width of his girth was at least a yard, and Guy noticed that the chair seat was lower than the others, so that the man's short legs could rest on the carpet instead of dangling. The man wore a long black silk jacket similar to a Nehru coat, black silk knickers and full-length black hose that led into soft slippers of black leather.

All this Guy absorbed in a glance, and as the man's short arms forced his massive body erect, Guy took in his face, unprepared for its ugliness.

His neck was invisible behind broad jowls that seemed to rest on the collarbone. The trimmed beard was so black as to have been dyed. Exposed skin was unhealthily pallid, lips thick and coarse—the lips of a sensualist—nose broad and porcine. Coal black hair was brush-cut. Deepset eyes under heavy eyebrows gazed back at Guy.

"Edouard Drach. Thank you for coming, Mr. Ryan—and full welcome to my abode." His voice was deep and guttural. He extended large hand and Guy took it briefly, surprised by its cold clamminess. "Thank you for inviting me," Guy said as Drach eased heavily into his cushioned chair.

"An apertif? Perhaps champagne?"

"Champagne will be fine." Guy sat down without being asked. Drach clapped and a servant appeared. After ordering, Drach smiled. "Perhaps my name is not unknown to you, sir?"

"Roy Stoner mentioned it—I was in Paris at the time."

173

"Excellent, excellent." His face assumed an expression of satisfaction as his hands rubbed together, merchant fashion. "Since you know who I am, and I know who *you* are, we may dispense with fencing for information." His eyebrows arched. "Does my abode find favor in your eyes, sir?"

"It's impressive," Guy replied, "but as a soldier I'm not accustomed to opulence."

"But you will be—oh, yes, you certainly will be. I can promise you that." He shifted position in the chair and Guy saw his girth roll like a wave in a waterbed. The only other human of similar bulk Guy had ever seen was Jimmy Rushing, the great blues shouter, but Rushing—short as Drach—wore it well. Rushing's girth was jolly, Drach's, repugnantly aggressive.

Guy turned toward the faint sound of music and saw a string quartet partway down the great room. As he watched, the end of the room lightened, and behind a scrim a ballerina began to dance.

Her light brown hair was braided and coiled atop her head. Her eyes were thickly mascaraed, cheeks rouged, and white satin *pointes* strapped to her small feet. She could have been a Columbine to an absent Pierrot, but for the fact that her powdered body was naked. Small, barely noticeable breasts and a negligible *mons* told Guy that the dancer was eleven or so, twelve at most.

She danced with Degas grace and purity, bowing and spinning to the music, moving so innocently that Guy felt like a voyeur. The arrival of iced Cordon Rouge gave him a chance to turn away. Drach's gaze remained on the little dancer, his eyes glittered as he sipped from his tulip glass. Hoarsely, Drach said, "You approve of Sonya? Talented is she not, sir?"

Guy nodded and drank.

Still gazing at the girl, Drach said, "I am a patron of the

174

arts, in particular the ballet. In time Sonya is destined for the Ballet Russe.''

If she lives, Guy thought, but said nothing.

Behind the scrim a young male dancer had joined Sonya. His face was garishly painted in faun makeup, and but for slippers and white satin codpiece he was nude. They began a *pas de deux,* moving simultaneously, he behind the ballerina, his hands seeming to caress her body without profaning it. Her head dropped back on his shoulder and his hands cupped her slim hips, drawing her against his pelvis. In a sense their pairing was asexual, but Guy recognized it as simulated seduction.

Drach said, ''If she appeals to you, I give her to you, sir. For the night—or forever.''

Guy said, ''I appreciate your generosity, but I have a wife—and daughter.''

''In Paris, I believe.''

Guy faced him. ''Is she yours to give?''

''Oh, yes. Indeed, yes. You see, there was a time when I befriended her mother—that was in another country—but when hard times befell her, as so often happens with rash, imprudent women, she bequeathed her child to me.'' He seemed to tear his gaze from the exhibition and gestured for more champagne. ''Thus she is mine to dispose of. You see,'' he went on, ''my tastes are epicurean, though I hardly expect comprehension by the *bourgeoisie.* What are your tastes, Mr. Ryan?''

''Simple ones, I suppose.'' The dance had become overtly passionate; Guy turned from it. ''I enjoy shooting, riding, good wine, physical challenge—and being with my family.''

Drach considered. ''Accumulating wealth, material things, are not to your taste.''

''It will be a new experience.''

''I see. By the way, an old friend of yours lodged with me recently. Prince Ali Mansour—you recall him? At Vezelay?''

Guy nodded.

"Now Resource Minister of his father's kingdom. Like you, he will inherit richly."

"Unless OPEC falls apart."

"An unlikely prospect," Drach said with a sour tone. "Still, the Prince understands how to enjoy the present. So if our little Sonya does not engage your fancy I may bestow her upon your friend."

"Ali always liked fair-skinned females," Guy remarked. "But at school it was only fantasy."

"Which he has since improved upon, I assure you." He glanced at the dancers, and Guy saw the girl reclining on a rose-colored bed, arms and legs moving, writhing as though to invite her partner. The scene was having a profound effect upon his host. Mouth parted, Drach licked thick lips, his breathing quickened in arousal. Guy thought that whatever Ali's sexual practices, Sonya would be better off in his harem than with this depraved pedophile. Drach had defiled her innocence, made her childhood into a prurient travesty of what it should have been.

As faun and ballerina clasped each other, their movements were openly erotic. Music crescendoed, her legs enfolded the faun and darkness cloaked the scene.

After a few moments Drach said, "Well, what do you think of our entertainment?"

"Titillating," Guy replied, "but not really my bag. Tell me, is Prince Ali involved in your consortium?"

"Usually I would decline a reply—but under present circumstances I will be frank. Ali is not a participant. More champagne? No? Then we will dine."

A manservant appeared and began pushing Drach's rollered chair across the floor. Guy drained his glass, rose and followed, noticing that the musicians had retired. Where the scrim had been a large tapestry now hung. From his moving chair Drach said, "You may have noticed that in décor I am much given to the traditional, the enduring. My own

176

antecedents are lost in the swirl of European history, in fire, pillage and revolution, so I have found it useful to acquire lineage to my liking. Does that seem strange to you?''

"Not when one can afford the trappings and embellishments.''

"Precisely. I conceive my primal ancestor as a noble betrayed by his king—or a king betrayed by malevolent nobles. Either version is suitable. In Monte Carlo I encountered a member of the Alsatian minor nobility. The gaming tables had impoverished him, and I acquired—bought, if you will—his ancestry. The Drach name appealed to me, and by right of acquisition it is mine. Now I am the final member of the Drach line, glandular obesity having deprived me of the ability to procreate.''

As they turned into the dining hall, Drach said, "Does my candor affect you adversely?''

"Not at all. I surmised as much.''

"Then you are a man of the world. I like that as much as I abhor feigned morality.''

"D'accord," Guy said. "Hypocrisy being one of the Seven Deadly Sins.''.

The long polished table was lighted with ancient candelabra that cast soft yellow light on the table settings. Drach was wheeled to the head of the table, Guy was seated on his right. Candlelight glinted from gold utensils and golden service plates. Each piece he noticed, was engraved with the Drach escutcheon. The table covering was white lace on which stood a row of wine glasses. Chablis came with the clear bouillon, rosé with the poached salmon, sweet Alsatian with the rice-stuffed spitted grouse, a Bulgarian red with the salad course. Drach's appetite was Gargantuan; as each course arrived his face and eyes glowed in anticipation. Where Guy had difficulty finishing one grouse, Drach consumed three, stripping each small one with his teeth. Were Drach alone, Guy thought, he would have crammed the meal into his mouth with bare hands.

Dessert was a golden bowl of *framboises* soaked in *kirsch* and topped with thick cream. Guy declined the liqueur tray, settling for syrupy Turkish coffee and a Havana.

They returned to the sitting room as they had come, Drach wheeled by a butler, Guy idling behind, noticing more details of the chateau. As they resumed their former positions Drach said, "In addition to a European chef, I maintain a master from Hong Kong, and one who was in charge of cuisine at Beirut's old King George."

"For your Mid-east associates."

Drach nodded slightly. "So on any night cuisine is diverse. And now that we have dined—well, I trust—let us turn to a matter of business."

Guy exhaled smoke from his Upmann and said, "By all means." The enormous meal seemed to have tranquilized his host, whose mass flowed over every inch of his outsized chair. Guy recalled Jabba the Hutt, and smiled. Absent only was the chittering, malicious Salacious Crumb. For that impersonation a skinny dwarf would do.

Drach's voice interrupted Guy's thoughts. "Your hours at the Société Suisse were profitable?"

"Revealing," Guy said. "Changes are contemplated."

"No doubt. As at Lyons?"

Guy felt a sudden chill; he had no idea that his movements were so closely watched. "As at Lyons," he agreed.

"One should never give away what can be sold."

"Or permit it to be stolen."

Drach nodded. "Bringing us to my offer—unlimited— for a controlling portion of your interest in RyTech."

Guy exhaled blue-gray smoke. It drifted lazily upward. "Not at any price," he said.

"Not for a billion untaxed dollars?"

Guy shook his head.

"Two billion? No? Would you care to name a more attractive figure?"

"There isn't one," Guy told him. "What you may not

178

understand is that I've been given a legacy to protect and with good luck, increase. My late father entrusted the responsibility to me; my stepmother expects me to fulfill it.''

''Even though—by your own admission—you have no penchant for business affairs, the acquisition of wealth?''

''We live by standards,'' Guy said, ''a code if you will. Mine requires keeping one's word. I suppose it's a matter of honor.''

''Admirable,'' Drach said, ''in this world of cheating and dishonor. Well then, sir, no more on the subject. I respect your position however much it disappoints and saddens me. I'm grateful for the time you accorded me.''

''And I for the excellent dinner.''

Drach smiled lecherously. ''No second thoughts about Sonya? Aside from her obvious charms she speaks three languages and is knowledgeable of world affairs.''

Guy rose. ''My wife and daughter would find her presence disconcerting. Prince Ali will be a more suitable protector.''

''Very well, sir. The house of Drach is always at your disposal. I wish your onward journey well.'' He extended his hand and Guy took it. The flesh was almost feverishly hot. The man's metabolism was a mess, he thought as he walked from Edouard Drach.

The same footman escorted him to the door and down the broad steps to the waiting Rolls.

As Guy got into the car he noticed guards patrolling the grounds with spike-collared Dobermans. Edouard Drach was obviously determined to safeguard his possessions.

The engine started. Guy glanced up at the chateau façade. There, on the top floor, looking down from a grilled window was Drach's *protégée*, Sonya. He could see her features only indistinctly, but they gave him an impression of sadness and yearning. Drach should be hung for his crimes, he thought, if only a scaffold big enough could be built for his revolting body.

At the Richemond Guy took his key at the desk, aware of the night clerk's lingering gaze. He rode the lift to his floor and opened the door. His room was lighted, and he remembered leaving it dark.

In the far corner sat two men. Staring at him.

Fourteen

Guy's first thought was of his pistol—but the Walther was still in his attaché case—and the case lay on the reading table—open, the holstered weapon clearly in view.

Before Guy could move the older man stood up. "I am Inspector Berenguer of the Cantonal Police. My associate is Sergeant Rurup. Can you account for your movements this evening, M'sieu Ryan?"

He went further into the room, removing topcoat and gloves. "Suppose you show some ID."

"Of course." Berenguer got out a slim leather case and handed it to Guy. The plastic credential consisted of a photo and legend in three languages. He returned it to the inspector. "Beginning at what time?"

"You left the Société Suisse des Recherches Technologiques at approximately five o'clock?"

"The whistle blew as I drove away."

"And did you later return?"

"No." He sat on the end of the bed. "What's the problem, Inspector?"

"From the factory you returned here?"

"I did—by five-thirty. I stayed in this room until leaving for dinner. By then it was eight o'clock."

"Is there perhaps a witness?"

Guy was growing irritated. "A little after six a *chausseur* came here with a message."

"Yes, that has been established. So—between six and eight you were—where?"

"Here." He gestured at the attaché case. "Working."

Berenguer bent over the attaché case, extracted something from it. "On this?" He displayed Egli's personnel file.

"Among other things."

"May I inquire your particular interest in Herr Egli?"

"I'm new to RyTech. So I'm visiting Europe to inspect subsidiaries, meet my executives."

He replaced Egli's file. "And after eight you were—where?"

"Dining with Edouard Drach."

Berenguer and Sergeant Rurup exchanged glances.

Guy had a premonitory sense that something had happened to the Managing Director. "Has Herr Egli left Switzerland?"

"Curious you should ask. In a way he has."

"You're being oblique."

"Am I? Then you know nothing of Egli's movements since five o'clock?"

"Nothing."

"Did you have a dispute with him? An argument?"

He shook his head. "Herr Egli accepted my observations without dissent."

Inspector Berenguer gestured at the Sergeant who rose and picked up his hat. "Please come with us, M'sieu Ryan. Hans Egli is dead."

As they walked to the office door Berenguer explained that a cleaning woman had unlocked the Managing Director's dark office, turned on the light and found him slumped

182

against his desk. She had thought him asleep until she noticed blood and brains on the wall.

The body was still there, covered with a sheet and almost ignored by technicians who were dusting elsewhere for fingerprints. On the floor, not far from the body, lay an old Swiss Army revolver. Berenguer said, "This is how he was found. We presume the weapon is his. You say there was no quarrel?"

"None. I criticized the plant's security arrangements."

"And took his file with you. To what purpose?"

"To learn more about him, his background."

"Did you form a particular impression?"

"He seemed efficient and willing to please. Nothing of a personal nature was discussed?"

"After you left Herr Egli placed a call to the plant security chief, Baumstern. Did you meet him?"

"No. Egli said he was off duty—attending a wedding."

"As his daughter confirmed. Pity," the inspector said, sighing. "The old locked room mystery."

"Isn't the explanation rather simple—suicide?"

"So it appears."

"Then why enter my room, grill me, bring me here?"

"Because of the singular circumstances. For nearly fifty years Egli lives a quiet, productive life. You arrive unexpectedly—his new chief executive—and within a short space of time either he is killed—or takes his own life." He sighed again, shrugged. "We will, of course, inquire into his mental health. Given his unexpected death what will you do here?"

"I assume there is a normal succession of authority, an assistant managing director to act in Egli's place. Tomorrow I'll look into it." The wall clock was flecked with blood and bits of matter. "It's late and I'm tired."

"Of course."

As Guy turned to leave Berenguer said, "This Drach—a mysterious figure, eh? You have known him before?"

"No, tonight's meeting was our first."

"A social occasion?"

"I responded to his dinner invitation—having no other plans. After dinner, matters of business were discussed."

"May I ask of their nature?"

"I wouldn't dream of disclosing the confidence of Edouard Drach. Inquire of him if you care to—but none of that has any bearing on this." He gestured at the sheet-shrouded body.

Berenguer grunted. "One hears that Drach's entertainments have a rather special character."

"I don't care to discuss them. If you're curious, ask Drach."

"I may. Sergeant Rurup, our guest is ready to leave."

Guy slept late, then read of Egli's apparent suicide over breakfast in his room. His own name was not mentioned. Nor that of Edouard Drach. After dressing he telephoned the plant and asked the assistant managing director to come to the Richemond.

Philippe Vosges was in his late forties. He produced an advanced degree from CalTech and a pleasant, self-possessed smile. It was apparent that he was still shocked by Egli's death, but he set emotion aside and listened to Guy reprise the complaints he had addressed to Egli. After a sip of coffee, Vosges said, "I agree wholeheartedly, Mr. Ryan. A new security chief is imperative, and I will immediately see to order cancellation. Since you've already decided to replace Baumstern I feel free to say I never considered him the man for the job. It's not for a superannuated policeman. But—he was Hans' personal friend, and so above criticism."

"Is it at all possible he shot Egli?"

"Possible, I suppose—but not if he has an alibi."

"Nevertheless, I want you to watch Baumstern carefully.

184

Isolate him from anything sensitive. If he takes offense, tell him the orders are mine."

Vosges nodded.

"Expect Pentagon people to authenticate compliance."

"I'll welcome them. Our research is too crucial to be compromised."

"Exactly. Send me daily progress reports. There's a lot of compensatory work to be done. If you want to move up, conduct yourself accordingly."

A pleased smile. "I shall."

"Unless you nominate someone better qualified than yourself."

"I sincerely doubt that I will."

They shook hands and Vosges left the room. Guy poured more coffee and thought of the late managing director. Something had troubled Egli to the point of desperation. Perhaps connections that could not withstand investigation? Something in his background long concealed?

His father had been right. There *was* rot in RyTech—the question was, how far and how deep did it go?

During the afternoon Jake Needham phoned to say that a security chief candidate was flying in from London for an interview. Late that night Paul Whitaker arrived.

He was a tall, muscular man with a bountiful mustache, a regimental tie and a R.A.C. emblem on his flannel blazer. His handshake was firm and his mien respectful. In French, Guy said, "Thank you for coming on short notice."

In French Whitaker replied, "The prospect of becoming associated with RyTech was too alluring to ignore." He handed Guy a typed résumé. Guy glanced at it. Forty-nine years old. French/British parents. Sandhurst. First porting, Royal Fusilliers in Malaya. Combat in Korea and Yemen. Resigned Captain's commission. "Why did you leave service?" Guy asked.

"The fighting stopped. Special Branch took me in and gave me interesting things to do."

"Such as?"

"Counterespionage. Big Tom Skerrit taught me the trade. Hear of him?"

Guy nodded. "The best there was. Why do you want to leave Special Branch?"

"There's no fun nabbing a spy if there's no prosecution. Skerrit's gone now, some of the others as well. I need stimulation, don't want mental decay to set in."

"You can run field checks, file traces?"

"With the back o' me hand—assumin' I've a team of bright lads." His tone had grown confident.

"What do you know about physical security?"

"Considerable. Took the courses. Lived at Ten Downing for a year protecting the Prime. Nothing happened to 'im, right?"

Guy smiled. "Right."

"Also I worked at G.C.H.Q. for a time—that's the Queen's code-breakers. Physical security of the establishment, plus vetting odd bods." He shrugged expressively. "Closing the barn doors you might say."

"Any contacts in the Swiss police?"

"Two. One in Bern, the other in Zürich. Both serving officers."

"France? S-Dec? DST?"

"Well—I know some names, met a few chappies, but to be blunt about things the French Services are helpless as mice in a python's jaws."

"West Germany?"

"Yes—good contacts there. Same for Holland, Belgium and Norway. Italy? Forget it. Good antiterrorist team, but their CE files are a disgrace."

Guy went over to the drink tray. "Highball? Liqueur?"

"Don't mind if I take a spot of brandy." Guy poured from the cognac bottle. He poured cognac for himself.

"What you've told me sounds impressive, and I'll run an independent check."

"I'd expect that, sir."

"What are your arrangements with Special Branch?"

"They know I'm looking around; I can take a few days off now and then." He drank and looked appraisingly at Guy. "The little I know of you inspires confidence. The salary and perks are about what I've been hoping for—assuming performance begets recognition."

Guy nodded. "Family situation?"

"Widower—grandfather by my daughter. Son's finishing medicine at Manchester. If I come, it'll be alone." He sat forward. "What else?"

"If you'll stay another two days I think we can wrap this up. Tomorrow I'd like you to evaluate the plant's physical security, noting all recommendations in a memo to me. Next day I want you to review the personnel situation, see what's been done by way of positive vetting. Portions of the plant work with systems of incalculable value to the opposition. There's a good deal more that needs to be done, but that's a beginning. I'll give you a note to Acting Director Vosges granting you access to all but the most sensitive area. If I hire you, that will be top priority. If I don't, I'll pay whatever's fair for your time and travel."

Whitaker downed his drink. "Good enough. Where will I reach you?"

"New York." Guy gave him a business card. "Telex your memos." On a sheet of hotel stationery he wrote a *laissez-passer* to Vosges and handed it to Whitaker. "Anything else?"

"No, sir, you've covered matters nicely." Rising, he squared his shoulders. "Geneva's an interesting place. If you take me on I think I'll fit in comfortably."

"So do I." They shook hands and Whitaker left the room. Guy locked the door behind him, then wrote a cable to Jake Needham requesting a Washington check on Whitaker's bona fides. In the morning he would send it from the nearby telegraph office.

That done, he placed a call to Paris and heard Consuela answering sleepily. They talked for a while and he told her he'd be arriving next afternoon for an overnight stay before flying back to New York. She expressed pleasure at the prospect, they kissed long distance and Guy got into bed.

Ever since leaving La Rocha he had found his life taking new and unexpected turns. The interlude with Cristina seemed far in the past now, so occupied had he been with other things. And by the time they met in Dublin for the Arab auction, she would have it behind her, too.

The evening with Drach had been revealing—and Guy thought how horrible it would be for a child like Gloria to fall into the hands of such a monster. Unthinkable.

He pushed it out of his mind and considered the end of Hans Egli. As he reviewed their exchanges he decided that Egli had foreseen the end of his employment, either for managerial shortcomings, or because some guilty secret could be exposed.

So it's well that I came, he told himself, or Egli could have gone on forever.

The memory of Consuela's voice warmed him, and he phoned the concierge asking for a compartment on the TGV to Paris. Finally, he fell asleep, the Walther under his pillow.

In the morning Philippe Vosges called to confirm that Guy had written the message presented by the British visitor. Guy acknowledged it, pleased at Vosges' circumspection and Whitaker's early arrival at the plant. A *chausseur* brought his train ticket, and after breakfast in the grill, Guy packed his bag and checked out.

Sunshine glittered on the lake, and the morning looked crisp and clear, so he decided to walk the few blocks to the

Gare by way of exercise. From the lakeside he took the angled street to the Rue des Alpes and began treading its rise toward the almost visible station. At a distance behind him came several well-dressed men talking among themselves. Fellow passengers, Guy thought as he walked on.

Behind him a car slowed, and Guy glanced around to see a taxi pulling toward the curb. For a few moments it stayed even with him, then drew ahead and stopped parallel to the curb, engine running.

Doors opened and three men stepped out, facing him.

Sensing danger, Guy thought of the gun in his attaché case, but the nearest man pulled a machine pistol from his overcoat and pointed it at him. Guy's mouth went dry. "Get in," the man snapped, and as Guy hesitated he heard the action cock, a shell snap into the firing chamber. The short black weapon thrust menacingly.

Guy dropped his luggage. Moved toward the open door.

Fifteen

In those perilous moments time stopped. The only sound Guy heard was the pounding rush of blood in his temples. Stillness enveloped the street. The thought struck him that he had escaped jungle ambush only to be waylaid on a city street.

The man with the machine pistol ordered, "Get his luggage, can't just leave it there," and the man nearest Guy moved to obey. Guy paused at the cab's rear door and saw the man bend down to pick up his bags.

"*In,*" the gunman ordered. "Move, haven't got all day."

As Guy leaned forward a shove sprawled him across the seat. In that instant came a series of whispering *plops* and he saw the gunman drop from sight, heard the gun clatter on the pavement. Whirling around Guy saw a man sprawling beside the bags. The third man was stooping forward, blood gushing from his mouth.

The shooters were the men who had followed him up the street. One of them approached the wounded man and with his silenced pistol calmly blew out his brains.

The cab driver, frozen until then, grabbed the wheel and gunned the engine. Guy, levering himself up as the car moved forward, crooked his left arm around the driver's neck, crushing his throat. The driver's hands left the wheel to claw at Guy's arm. On his knees in the seatwell, Guy wrapped his right arm around the driver's head and wrenched sideways. He felt the snap and crunch of a breaking neck, and the body went limp. The car was moving slowly, tires chafing the curb. Leaning forward, Guy slammed the gearshift to neutral and got out. Looking around he saw his rescuers getting into a long limousine. His baggage was passed inside, then the car sped forward, braking beside him. A door opened and a voice called, "Get in, man, no time to lose!"

With a glance back at the three bodies, the people rushing toward them, Guy made his decision. He got in, wondering who his rescuers were. If enemies, at least they had disposed of the first gang.

Tires screeching, the limousine accelerated toward the Gare, turned onto a broad street and sped along, scattering cars and pedestrians. Huskily, Guy said, "What's this all about?" and turned to look at the three well-dressed men. Two were young. The elder said, "Trust me, Guy," and he recognized the face of a schoolmate.

"Nigel!" he blurted. "What in hell are you doing here?"

"Saving your life, that's what," replied Nigel Palfrey. "Know who those chaps were?"

"No—do you?"

"Haven't the faintest."

The car dropped into a parking garage, shot through to the other side, reversing direction. Calmly Nigel said, "Always fools 'em."

"Always?"

He grinned broadly. "Meet my pals. Ginger's the freckled bloke, Brian's the other. Being senior, I'm team leader." He looked out of the window and spoke to the driver. "Easy, Fred, we're hard by."

Guy shook hands with the younger men, muttered thanks. To Palfrey he said, "Team leader of *what?* What team?"

"SAS—hear of us?"

"Special Air Service. That what you've been doing all these years?"

"Well, after Cambridge I was 'attached Foreign Office' for a while—six years, actually—got bored with striped trousers, and volunteered."

Guy wet his dry lips. "I thought SAS dealt with terrorists."

Palfrey shrugged. "Hear the SAS motto: 'Kill 'em all, let God sort 'em out.' They were terrorizing you, weren't they? Our brief was to protect you—which is what we did—and are doing."

"Whose brief, for God's sake?"

"Why, your very own DSA that finds you so essential to the West's security." Reaching over, he patted Guy's arm. "Get ready. When we stop it will be fast. We're switching cars." He looked through the rear window. "The chase is not yet organized—but it will be. We'll handle your grips. Pop into the van when we stop. Got it?"

Guy found himself able to smile. "Still giving me orders?"

"Forget your Croesian wealth, you're still a Lower Form scut, and you'll damn well do as you're told. Heads up, hold tight!"

Guy gripped a door pull as the limousine braked alongside a dark blue Mercedes van. "Out and in," Palfrey ordered. A door flung outward and Guy scrambled from one car into the other. He grabbed outthrust bags and moved aside while the SAS team climbed in. Before the door shut the van was moving. "Heads down," Palfrey snapped. "Let's play Invisible Man."

Guy lay flat on the flooring. "Where are we going?"

"Taking you to Bern, old man, whence you board the Paris express—as planned."

"Then you anticipated all this?"

"Not knowing what might happen we stayed close." He took off his hat, freeing the blond curly hair Guy remembered. Palfrey wiped his face. "Warm work for a bit there. Ginger, how many shots expended?"

"One, sir."

"My compliments. Brian?"

"Three, I'm afraid, sir. Bloke wouldn't cave."

"So I noticed. One for me makes five, wouldn't you say? Three Bad Hats for five shots—not a bad exchange." He turned to Guy. "Plus your cab driver. Four. Self help's always in order. Splendid show, scut."

"Thanks," said Guy drily. "You seem to have done this sort of thing before."

"Defense of the realm. Keeping Britain peaceful's the brief."

Guy nodded.

"Here's *your* brief, *cher ami:* a borrowed plane is standing by at Cointrin. It'll hedge-hop us to Bern, and as you've a posh compartment, we'll share until you're safely in Paree."

With a headset Ginger was monitoring police radio calls. To Palfrey he said, "They've found the limo, area's being searched on foot. Apparently the switch wasn't observed."

"That's encouraging," Palfrey remarked. "Guy, why Paris?"

"Wife and child."

"Ahhh—best get them to America. Paris overflows with banditti and brigands. Frightful risk for law abiders."

"I'm only staying the night. Connie and Gloria are flying over at Easter."

"Not sure I'd let them linger. You're on risk notice, y'know. Deadly intent and all that. Wish I knew who's gunnin' for you."

"They could have killed me on the street, so my guess is kidnapping for ransom."

"Reasonable thought." He called to the driver, "Location, Fred?"

"Five minutes off, sir."

To Guy he said, "We'll make it, never fear. Swiss Army pass."

"Authentic?"

"As authentic as the plane."

"You mean the Swiss Army's helping you?"

"Reciprocal favor. I helped train their antiterrorist squad—taught fast reaction, something that runs counter to Swiss grain."

The driver called, "Airport ahead."

Brian began pulling a tarpaulin over them. In darkness they lay flat. The van slowed, stopped. Voices. Guy heard the barrier lifting. The van moved ahead, accelerating. Fred called, "You may uncover now, gentlemen."

Sitting up, Guy wiped dust and perspiration from his face. The others did the same. Palfrey said, "If the Swiss are lethargic, they're also reliable. There's the ruddy plane as promised."

The van pulled alongside a high-wing monoplane painted red with a white cross. Wheels extended through landing skis, and the side door was unusually wide to load stretchers. An Alpine rescue craft.

A gray-uniformed officer saluted Palfrey, who returned the salute and said, "Two passengers to Bern." He beckoned Guy from the van, went back to issue instructions to Brian and Ginger, then brought Guy's luggage to the plane.

They entered the cabin, and strapped into canvas seats. The pilot started the single engine and let it warm. As Guy looked around he was reminded of night takeoff from Port-Au-Prince.

The plane vibrated as it moved toward the flight line. There was plenty of sunshine, but the mountain peaks were shrouded in clouds and mist.

After a brief clearance wait the pilot gunned the engine and the plane lifted into sunlight, then gained altitude to cross the Jura range. Palfrey pointed out the Jungfrau, then Mont Blanc and the Chamonix valley. Skiiers looked no larger than black dots. Soon, Fribourg lay below on the frozen river, and beyond it the pilot skimmed needle peaks and brought the plane down on the Bern runway. The pilot summoned a staff car, accepted their thanks and wished them a safe onward journey.

Half an hour's wait in the Hauptbahnhof and the TGV rolled in. They boarded, found the reserved compartment, and ordered drinks. After touching glasses Guy said, "I could do without more surprises today." Palfrey drew out his pistol with the thick black silencer and placed it on the seat. "Now," he said, "tell me what you've been up to."

"For the next hour Guy related what had happened to him since his father's death—including the threatening overheard conversation, the sabotaged Mercedes and the suicide of Hans Egli. "Then, of course, today's snatch attempt."

Palfrey nodded solemnly. "Mind you, I'm not asking what this Sceptre device is, but it may be the enemy's ultimate goal. You've thought of that?"

"I have. Because it's essential to our Missile Defense Shield."

"Companion piece to what you're developing in Switzerland?"

Guy nodded. "That item will eventually replace laser weapons. Overall guidance depends on Sceptre."

"The Soviets must know enough about Sceptre to covet it, mount an effort to acquire it." He lighted a Caporal, exhaled at the window. "This Drach sounds abhorrent. Can't say I've heard of him, but Central Europe's filled with front men for bad people. Be sure to tell DSA what you gleaned while dining."

"I plan to. By the way, I'm thinking of hiring a new security chief for my Swiss plant. Sandhurst man, now Special Branch—Paul Whittaker. Know him?"

"Not personally, but his reputation's good. One of their best interrogators, tenacious. If you like I'll ask around."

"I have a few days to decide."

"I'll do my best."

The steward came by and they booked a table for lunch.

Afterward, drowsing through the afternoon, Guy wondered how much he should tell Consuela of the Geneva episode. He wanted her and Gloria out of Europe and in New York where he could protect them from danger.

Before the express pulled into the Gare, Guy invited Nigel to dine with them, but his friend declined, saying he had to report to London before nightfall. From Le Bourget a service plane would take him there.

So they parted at the taxi stand, and Guy reached the apartment in time to play with Gloria before dinner.

That night he urged his wife to come with him to New York, saying he'd lived too long without her and their daughter. He needed them both, he said, and Europe was increasingly dangerous for the well-to-do.

"Now, Guy, we agreed on Easter—and before then I'm having a gallery show. That's something I've been working toward. I can't just abandon all that effort."

"Kedrov the impresario?"

"No, I managed it on my own. Talent, not influence. Don't you see? With a Paris show I'll have much better credentials for New York. That's how things go in the world of art."

He sighed. "If you say so. And after that, you'll come?"

She kissed him. "Anything to keep my husband happy."

On the way to De Gaulle Airport they left Gloria at her school, Guy promising to see her very soon. As as they walked toward the Concorde counter he said, "It was bad enough being away from you these past few days; the weeks ahead will be worse. I'll miss you."

196

She hugged him tightly. "Strange," she murmured, "I thought I'd learned to get along without you—now I know it was only an illusion. You're as necessary to me as my hands, my eyes."

"I feel the same—so please be careful where you go, what you do. Even though you'll be guarded."

"We'll be all right—I assure you." She kissed him again. "Time to board, darling."

A final embrace, and he passed through the gate, began walking down the corridor. Looking back he saw her wave goodbye, blow a parting kiss. Guy waved back and boarded.

From his seat he thought he saw her among the spectators watching on the upper level. His throat thickened and he turned away. He'd never considered himself emotional, but parting was hard to bear. Especially from the wife he'd found he still loved.

Halfway across the Atlantic a steward roused Guy with a radio message from Paul Edmonds. Marguerite had been killed in a helicopter crash.

BOOK THREE

Sixteen

A RyTech helicopter had been flying Marguerite from Eastover to the piers of lower Manhattan where she was to have boarded a liner for a round-the-world cruise. The crew of an Eastern LC-1011 reported a chopper exploding off Jones Beach in a ball of orange fire. The co-pilot thought the rotors might have locked before the explosion, but was unwilling to swear to it at the NTSB inquiry. Wreckage of the helicopter was recovered from ten fathoms, remains identified by personal jewelry and dental charts.

Through the funeral Guy was traumatized, drank heavily and wept uncontrollably until Marguerite's will was read by her attorney. She bequeathed Eastover to Rosemont College, the Catholic institution she had attended, noting that she was the last of the Hillyer line. Guy thought: and to avoid a clawing dispute between Gant and Nicole. Her RyTech shares, so recently increased by Sean's bequest, were left equally to her two children. Between them they now owned forty to Guy's controlling sixty percent.

On uppers, Gant giggled through the reading, punctuated by his sister's sobbing. Nicole was also given her mother's jewelry, all but a pear-shaped diamond pendant left to Guy's daughter, Gloria.

A nice gesture, Guy thought, as he dried his eyes and felt Jake Needham's hand on his arm.

Final generous bequests to servants and retainers concluded the reading of the will. Nikky came to Guy and embraced him, sobbing brokenly, while Gant weaved unsteadily away. For a while they talked, exchanging reminiscences of Marguerite, Nikky finally acknowledging resentment over the gift of Eastover to Rosemont. "I grew up here," she blurted, "know every inch of the house and grounds, the stables. What will a bunch of penguins do here but live it up? It's not fair, Guy."

"It was her wish."

"I know—and I shouldn't feel this way, but I can't help it. I just *can't,*" she repeated as fresh tears flowed down her cheeks. Guy tried comforting his half-sister but her grief was too deep, too real, and he realized that tears were a therapeutic outlet.

Kissing her goodbye, Guy left with Needham, and when they were in the long RyTech limousine, heading for Manhattan, he said, "If I'd been killed in Geneva, my shares would have gone to Marguerite. Her death would have transferred complete control to Nikky and Gant."

"Occurred to me." Jake looked out of the window at the bleak winter scenery. "But that didn't happen. Nor did the NTSB find evidence of sabotage."

"Perhaps there wasn't enough wreckage for full evaluation. I can't persuade myself it was mere coincidence."

"I know the thought's in your mind, Guy, but without proof of sabotage there's no point in torturing yourself."

"The cruise was *my* suggestion; but for that she'd be alive."

"You can't hold yourself responsible in the least degree; you're in emotional turmoil and guilt's part of it, but you mustn't become obsessed."

He nodded. "I guess work is the best medicine—so where

do we stand on executive replacements? The sooner a new team's in place the better off we'll all be.''

"First, I think you should let Stoner know where he stands. By now, he must have guessed I'm to replace him.'' He paused. "Or do you want me to tell him?''

"I'll do it.''

"I have his entitlements computed, Edmonds', too. The headhunters have come up with three top-level candidates. I'll pass you their résumés at the office.''

Guy nodded. "Unless one is exceptionally outstanding I'll fill the job myself.''

"Good idea—*if* you want to work yourself to death at an early age.'' He gestured at a snow-covered cemetery beside the road.

"I could try it for a year—I want to get on top of everything, develop corporate momentum. So far I haven't been told of any new product research—except for military hardware.''

"It's a small section now—you want it expanded?''

"I want an imaginative man in charge—one with a proven record, and he doesn't have to be a scientist, just creative.''

Needham made a note. "Do you feel Farley Johns will fit in with the new structure?''

"No—he's more accountant than comptroller. Find a man with broad industrial experience. Is Gunderson out?''

"Gave him his final emoluments yesterday morning. He cleared out his desk, Haynes took his pass and had the locks changed. By noon Miss Knox was in place.''

"I imagine she'd like her office suitably decorated—see that she's consulted.''

"Right. My Houston trip report is on your desk but perhaps I can save you some time.''

"Go ahead.''

"The oil exploration part looks good—so good you may decide to become a producer instead of letting Shell and

Exxon snap up the goodies. I can have an analysis and projections run up—take three or four weeks."

"Do it."

"The salvage corporation has five vessels, four of them positioned in the Persian Gulf to work tankers struck by Iraqi or Iranian jets. Lloyd's covers them at war-risk rates, but frankly, I don't see the profits worth the risk. Besides, there's a lot of salvage competition. I recommend you withdraw them from the Mid-east, find something else for them to do."

"Like what?"

"Containment of oil spills on our own coasts and the Caribbean. Conversion to environmental work would cost no more than Lloyd's premiums where they are now."

"Sounds good—maybe position one near Louisiana's offshore oil fields, another off Norway, and a third near Scotland. Needs study, doesn't it?"

"It does—the fifth vessel is in drydock in Malta, having hit a mine off Libya. That doesn't bother me half as much as the Houston section that runs the Executive Protection Training Service."

"What's your concern?"

"First, the facilities are good. There's a thousand-acre nonproducing ranch by the Mexican border—a Dust Bowler with old shacks and buildings for ambush and weapons training. Nissen hut type barracks and admin quarters, a track for defensive driving trainees, airstrip for snatch rescue, and a well-maintained armory. Among the instructors are a couple of Chicago cops, a Hollywood stunt driver, two ordnance sergeants and a handful of former Green Berets. Heading it is a fellow you may remember from 'Nam—light colonel named O'Rourke—the one who was courtmartialed for brutality and excessive, unauthorized killing."

"He was acquitted, wasn't he?"

"Yeah, and boasts about it. Bottle man, Guy. We can do better than O'Rourke."

"Replace him. What else concerns you?"

He cleared his throat. "The snatch plane is a Beaver. However, the strip shows much wider wheel tracks, meaning larger aircraft use the strip. That close to the border, Guy, I'm worried about drug flights. Shall I notify Drug Enforcement?"

"And Immigration. They can observe the strip without interfering with training."

"It's the trainees I'm most concerned about. The present contingent is twenty-two Arabs from three countries: Iraq, Kuwait and Syria. Ostensibly they're learning how to protect their rulers and cabinet ministers from terrorists and revolutionaries, but I saw a lot of mortar-firing and grenade-throwing going on, and that's not executive protection, it's assault training. O'Rourke said the Israeli Embassy had lodged a protest with State, but nothing happened. He liked that. And he doesn't like Jews." He paused. "Guy, at a minimum it's a slack operation. It can be tightened up and should be. There's a place for executive protection in today's world, but I don't think your facility should become another training camp for terrorists."

"I'd rather get rid of it."

"Let me suggest this: ask DSA to survey the place, evaluate what's going on, the end-use of the Arab trainees. If one of them blew up an Israeli school bus I'd feel sick about it. O'Rourke may be the bad apple, but who knows? Ex-soldiers with the right skills aren't hard to hire."

"I get the feeling the place isn't worth the trouble, Jake. Let's just close it down, pay off the hands and sell the spread." A thought came to Guy. "Is the land good for anything? Cattle? Horses?"

"My Kansas farm boyhood tells me there's too much soil erosion for cattle grazing—but with shelter and hay you could raise a lot of horses."

Guy nodded thoughtfully. "Hold off selling until I can talk with Cristina—she's in horse breeding, and we might want to establish the line here. There's an exceptional Arab stallion named Al-Emir she plans to buy at a Dublin auction. If she succeeds I'll be part of the syndicate.''

"Good tax shelter—but that could change. Next year IRS could lower the boom.''

"I'll take the chance. That do Houston?''

"It does.''

For a few moments Guy was silent, then he said, ''Not that I don't trust Cristina's judgment, but I'd like a private evaluation on Al-Emir. If there's some reason she shouldn't buy she ought to know about it—so should I. Can you check it out?''

"Doesn't sound difficult. There's an Arab breeder in my former law firm. I'll start with him.'' He paused. "DSA gave Paul Whitaker a clean bill of health, so I hired him for Geneva.''

"You did right.''

"He'll be on the job in a few days. And from the reports he submitted he's badly needed. They're on your desk, by the way.''

"I'll read them with interest.''

"Eventually you ought to look in on the Korean subsidiary, if only to show the flag. Seems to be doing well on its own. Next time you get to the British Isles you should get a firsthand briefing on the medical research in England and Ireland. It's too abstruse for me, quite frankly, and it's been running at considerable loss.''

"Yes, I should get the facts.''

"Well, let's see . . . that leaves the Institute for Strategic Research in Frederick, Maryland. The ISR is located in what used to be a small bible college that went bust. Ry-Tech bought land and buildings, all in good shape, and set up the Institute. I've talked with the Director by scrambler phone and learned that in addition to making the Sceptre processor chip, they're working on an antigravity concept originated by Einstein. Albert was going to present it to

206

FDR with a request for developments funds, but FDR died and Truman was too busy ending the war to pay attention to science fiction. With the A-bomb he wasn't interested in anything more."

"How wrong he was," Guy remarked.

"One computer is doing the work of a thousand men, so there's little cost involved. The theory can be proved on a video screen—or disproved. Imagine what Einstein could have done with computer science had he lived. Boggles the mind, eh?"

"Boggles mine."

"The other ISR research area suggests the Occult: Distant viewing, if you've heard of it."

"ESP? Where you sit in a room and guess whether a card in the next room is a king or a trey?"

"Roughly. Here's the example Dr. Hodges gave me: a man stands in front of the Casino at Monte Carlo at a preset time, and does nothing but stare at it. Simultaneously a man in Bangkok tunes out all external stimuli and concentrates on receiving 'brain waves' from the distant man, not knowing where he is. He records his impressions, and if they have to do with, say, a stone palace facing the sea, the test is repeated, seeking more detail. ISR has done this with fifty pairs using outlandish locations—a Welsh coal mine, top of the Eiffel Tower—and come up with some unusual correlations. The insensitive transmitter/receivers have been weeded out, leaving ISR with six exceptionally accurate pairs. Hodges has everything documented and is anxious to secure your interest. The security implications are obvious."

"A coast-watcher who doesn't need a radio to communicate with headquarters. Let's give our research to the Pentagon and tell them to carry on—or pay us to do it for them."

"That's reasonable. By the way, Sotheby's has a treasure appraiser in George Town. He'll report to the New York office, and they'll let us know their estimate of how much the loot will bring."

"Any static from Haiti?"

"*Rien.*" He smiled reminiscently. "What a night *that* was, Guy. Me and the voluptuous Manette; your pistol at the throat of subsecretary Coulou." He shook his head. "More than once I thought we were about to buy the farm."

"I only thought so when we drove onto the pier. A concealed guard could have changed the script. But I was going to finish Coulou. Now—it's corporate combat and financial decisions, nothing as final as death."

He thought of his stepmother and hoped her death had been instantaneous and painless. The only mother he had ever known . . . with Sean, now, the husband she adored. He said, "When NTSB releases the chopper wreckage, I want an independent airtech lab to conduct microscopic examination; I don't care how long it takes or how much it costs. I have to satisfy myself one way or the other. The blow-up was too coincidental, given the Geneva episode the day before."

"But if there was a conspiracy aimed at getting the stock in your siblings' hands it depended on you pre-deceasing Marguerite. You lived through Geneva so there was no reason to kill your stepmother."

"Suppose the two sequential events were activated by a distant controller. He learned I'd survived, but couldn't stop the chopper sabotage. That's not unthinkable."

"No, but it seems far-fetched without evidence of sabotage. We'll see what the lab turns up."

"And I haven't forgotten my 'accident' the night of Sean's wake where someone punctured the brake cylinder." They passed Patchogue and turned onto Route 454, connecting with the Long Island Expressway at Central Islip.

After a while Guy said, "When I overheard those voices I had no idea who they were. Well, when Farley Johns spoke to me at the funeral I decided one voice was his. Probably."

"And the other?"

He shook his head. "I could guess Stoner or Edmonds, but since we're cleaning house it doesn't make much difference. Johns doesn't strike me as one who does dirty work on hands and knees with a cold chisel, but he could certainly hire it done."

Roy Stoner took his firing badly. "I don't deserve this," he said bitterly, and his face reddened. "I was completely loyal to your father and I've never been anything but supportive of you—tried to be helpful during transition. Can you give me one solid reason why I'm getting the axe?"

"Sure—I'm more comfortable with my own people around me. That's it. Be satisfied with your golden parachute, Roy—you've made a lot of money at RyTech and as far as I know you deserved it. Your deferred termination payments are secure, with this condition. If I hear of you bad-mouthing RyTech, me, or anyone in my employ the payments end."

His eyes widened. "That's part of my contract—you can't abrogate it on a whim."

"If you can't ease out gracefully and bottle your resentment, you can sue me. Those are your alternatives. Clear out your desk, turn over your pass and keys on your way out."

Stoner swallowed and his face was pale. "Can I keep my car?"

"No. It's the general counsel's car, and you're not General Counsel."

"Will you tell me who is?"

"Jake Needham."

Stoner's mouth twisted. "Old school tie, eh? You'll regret it, Guy. He's a neophyte, not up to the job."

Guy looked up at him. "The interview is over."

Sullenly, Roy Stoner strode away and Guy rang for Jenny

Knox. In a few moments she entered and looked around. "What a pleasant change, sir. Clean functional desk, attractive curtains, new carpeting, bright paintings on the walls. I think it suits you a lot better."

"So do I. I'd like you to issue a press release announcing Jake's appointment as general counsel. Consult him for background data. As for Stoner, keep him out of the press release and if you're asked about the change, say it was for personal reasons. Don't say the reasons were mine."

"I'll get right on it." She hesitated. "May I ask who's next to go?"

"That's something you don't need to know."

Her face colored. "Of course—the old inquisitive reportorial instinct. Henceforth repressed."

When he was alone he read Paul Whitaker's security survey, appreciating his keen insight into the problems. An experienced professional like Paul was all too rare, and RyTech was fortunate to have him.

So far Guy was satisfied with his appointments. Edmonds would be fired when he returned from an industrial convention in Toronto. Finding the proper replacement would take time, but in the meantime Guy could form his own appraisal of the job and what it required. Then he could better select a new executive vice president or decide to combine the position with his own.

Maryanne Paskow, the senior secretary who had served his father, entered with a bulging folder in her arms. She was a pleasant efficient woman in her early fifties, with blue-tinted hair and a formal manner. "Sir, this correspondence has been accumulating ever since you joined RyTech, and some of it should be answered."

"What is it?"

"A variety of social invitations to balls, fundraising affairs and banquets; invitations from the major networks to appear on Sunday talk shows. Donation requests from twenty-odd charities."

210

"How did my father handle it?"

"With a series of appropriate form letters."

"I want courteous responses to go out, of course. Whatever charitable requests my father honored I'll continue—for the present. When there's time, I'll look at them closely. I have no time for social activity—until my wife joins me. As for talk shows, I don't want personal publicity—route those requests to Miss Knox for reply."

"Gladly."

"Do we need someone full-time to handle this sort of thing?"

"I don't believe so. I've managed it in the past. If it gets out of hand—and I think this is the bulk of it—I can always hire a temporary girl."

He nodded. "Did Sean belong to the Racquet Club?"

"No, the Metropolitan Club."

"I need a place where I can work out and dine comfortably. The Racquet's nearby, so perhaps you'd look into membership for me."

"I'm sure there will be no problem. Mr. Needham can propose you. By the way, Mr. Conor Counihan has been calling for an appointment—an old friend of your father."

"What does he want?"

"Doesn't say."

"I don't care to talk with him, much less see him. We have nothing to discuss—you can tell him so."

"From time to time your father used to give him expense money."

"No more," Guy said flatly, "that's finished."

"I understand. I should have mentioned two letters from Europe." She opened the folder. "I thought you might want to see them. One from London—a Mr. Nigel Palfrey, the other from Geneva—one Edouard Drach. Both expressing sympathy on the death of your stepmother."

"Ignore Drach's. I'll answer Nigel's letter myself."

She placed it on his desk and left. Nigel's address, he saw, was "The Wattles," Dorset.

When he finished writing, the winter evening had closed in. He walked to his apartment, had a drink, made dinner for himself and watched the evening television news. A finance committee meeting was scheduled for the next day, and Guy turned in early by way of preparing himself for a long, boring and incomprehensible afternoon.

The telephone woke him after midnight and as he reached for the receiver he thought it must be Connie, then realized in Paris it was close to dawn.

The voice was Rob Hoskins', saying, "There's been a fire at ISR. Can you meet me there in the morning?"

"If it's important—mind telling me why?"

"Because the fire wasn't spontaneous—it's arson."

Seventeen

Guy had breakfast aboard the Lear as it flew to Baltimore. From the airport a chartered helicopter took him fifty miles west to open fields near Frederick and set down on ISR's helipad.

From the air he had seen the brick Georgian buildings, the wire-fenced perimeter, the guard posts and searchlight towers—and the destroyed, still-smoking ruins. The Institute was set in the center of broad, plowed fields that extended half a mile in every direction. From Route 70 a narrow access road led to the gate, and Guy noticed shallow ditches on either side. Firemen were still coiling their hoses as Hoskins emerged from a group of official-looking cars, and shook his hand. "I felt you'd have a better appreciation of the situation if you saw it firsthand. At night the area's illuminated, and there are sensors planted in the fields. Not even a rabbit can approach undetected."

"You said arson."

Turning, Hoskins pointed to a distant clump of briers and leafless trees. "We found a mortar over there. Guards heard the first round fired, the shell dropped into the pond and exploded, without further damage. The second round hit the machine shop with the results you see. It was a thermite shell that had to burn itself out. Luckily for us, that

213

ended the bombardment. Whoever fired the mortar took off, leaving it behind. If he'd corrected windage, the next round or two would have hit the gym building where Sceptre work is being done." He shook his head. "We have radar to warn of saboteurs parachuting in, but no one anticipated shell fire. So the attack was well-planned."

Guy looked beyond him at the ISR complex, counted nine undamaged buildings grouped around what had been a small college campus. Ice was re-forming across the center pond where the mortar shell had destroyed a fountain and birdbath. "Why not close down this place, move everything to the Mojave—there must be abandoned military sites that would be a lot more secure."

"True, but—" he pointed at what had been the gymnasium—"the crucial manufacturing sections are sixty feet down and resting on bedrock. Nitrogen tanks for zero Centigrade conditions, the etching lasers—it would take six months just to disassemble and move to another location. Another four months to reconstruct. Allow two months' margin and we're talking a year from now. The time loss is crucial—so we're stuck here. We'll just have to protect the place more thoroughly; expand the perimeter, put choppers in the air around the clock." He squinted at the machine shop's smoking ruins. "An antitank battalion with 40-millimeter rapid-fires and howitzers."

"That should stop anything," Guy remarked.

"May have to." From his coat pocket he drew a small sheet of paper and handed it to Guy. "This was left with the mortar."

Inked crudely on the sheet was the message; *Death to nuclear murderers and warmakers. Direct Action Army.* Guy handed it back. "That's the enemy?"

"That's what the enemy *says* it is. *Action Directe* is a French terrorist group that specializes in kidnapping industrialists and murdering Western diplomats—claimed two victims from our own Embassy. Whether the mortarman belongs

214

to a Yankee branch of *Action Directe* we don't know—but will."

"You know who he is?"

"Rather obligingly he left finger and palm prints in the mortar's cold grease. If they show in any Government file—FBI, local police, Immigration—we'll identify him." He tucked away the message. "Silently."

A man in knit cap and ski jacket approached Hoskins, who introduced him to Guy as Tom Felberg and said, "Fire Chief on board?"

Felberg nodded. "He's saying oily rags caught fire—demerits to ISR. That will be the official explanation."

"Excellent. Guy, if you've time to spare, Dr. Felberg will show you the premises."

"As long as I'm in New York by one o'clock."

He had coffee with the institute director, Dr. Horatio Printz, whose comfortable, book-lined office had once been that of the president of the vanished college. To Guy's surprise, Printz was his own age, and the youngest of the scientists Guy had seen so far. He had unkempt brown hair, an untrimmed mustache that joined with runaway chopwhiskers. His deepset eyes wore thick, steel-rimmed lenses. "I'm sorry your visit was occasioned by the sneak attack; still, it won't affect us much. The theoretical work goes on without interruption."

"Good. DSA will be enhancing security."

"Obviously it needs improvement even though measures already in force seemed stringent to all of us. With personnel living here in former dormitories we tend to think of this as a small Manhattan Project—although our eventual products may prove vastly more important." He sipped from his cup, blotted his mouth whiskers. "I didn't know Hans Egli, but Philippe Vosges was an acquaintance at CalTech. I think he'll be a quantum improvement over the late Egli.

His forte is the practical application of pure science where mine is theoretical development." He gazed analytically at Guy. "I'm here because ISR was willing to fund expansion of Einstein's basic antigravity work. If we're successful—and I expect us to be—the result will prove a boon to mankind. I understand you have no specialized scientific background, so I'll summarize the undertaking by alluding to the time-space continuum and certain proton/neutron phenomena we plan to harness. The computer programming work is confined to Building C. Another few months and we'll be ready to develop a prototype apparatus. Before then, I'll submit a proposal with funding estimates." With a wry smile he reached for a blackened cob pipe, began filling it. "To be honest I have a fundamental dislike and distrust for the military-industrial complex, but I set it aside in reciprocity for RyTech's generous funding. Neither foundations nor academia offered help, so where was I to turn?" He lighted a match, held it over the pipe's charred rim.

Guy said, "My father was a farsighted man."

"Indeed." He exhaled a smoke jet. "Some hold him a visionary. I saw him only twice in New York and once here at ISR and soon learned he was interested in hearing results, not a tally of obstacles."

"In that respect I'm much like him. Is the Distant Viewing project expensive?"

"It involves travel and fees to the participants. I regard it with tolerant amusement—as more of Rhine's hocus-pocus. Still, the correlations have proved out astonishingly. Sceptre, of course, is ISR's *raison d'être*. It occupies Building G, the former gymnasium, now much altered from the original." A wristwatch alarm buzzed and Printz said, "Dr. Felberg can contribute more than I, and I have a conference at 'C'. If you'll excuse me, Mr. Ryan."

"Of course—I appreciate the briefing." Guy rose and followed Felberg from the room. They crossed the chilly campus past the damaged pond and went up the gymna-

216

sium steps. Inside an anteroom were two guards. Felberg said, "This is Mr. Ryan, the boss." He inserted a plastic card in a metal slot and security doors slid aside. They went around a baffle that blocked vision and wind, and Guy saw that the entire gym floor was covered with what looked like the blueprints of geometric roadmaps. Above, on the indoor track moved groups of technicians. High in the I-beam rafters were tracks for four immense cameras. Glancing at them, Felberg said, "Improvements on the old U-2 Fairchild cameras for our special requirements. What you see spread across the floor is the design of the Sceptre chip. A section is photographed and infinitely reduced for photolithography. To give you an idea of comparative size, a four-by-eight-foot design section reduces to fifteen hundred microns, the width of twenty human hairs. We can etch a much larger section onto the coated wafer, as you'll see in the ultracold area below."

"How large is the finished Sceptre chip?"

"About one quarter the size of a playing card. Theoretically it could be reduced another seventy-five percent, but because the system will be integrated into a space platform package, further miniaturization is not essential—nor feasible at this stage, because it would require molecular beam epitaxy application to transfer this huge design to a chip the size of a postage stamp. There is, after all, a point at which ultraminiaturization becomes futile. An inch-long automobile is engaging to see, but it can't perform a useful function such as transporting a human being. A roach, yes, but we're not yet providing roaches with recreational vehicles." He smiled faintly. Science humor, Guy thought; at least Felberg was human.

Felberg moved to a closed door, punched an electronic sequential lock. Guy followed him into an air-lock where, as they waited for antistatic cleansing, the Assistant Director said, "The next level down is the computer section. The equipment is organized into parallel processors. They know what's been done and what needs to be done. Operating simultaneously as a super-computer they solve problems instantaneously—for example, re-routing blocked signals much as police detour traffic to open roads."

The former gym basement was filled with a variety of large and small computers, some producing printouts, others plotting graphics on large video screens. Guy counted six programmers at their consoles.

"For discrimination purposes Sceptre stores images and flight characteristics of every known ballistic missile and satellite: Soviet, Chinese, British, French, Japanese—and ours. Of course, with Sceptre integrated into MDs, we'll no longer need to build more nuclear missiles, and can, in fact, greatly reduce our own missile arsenal with consequent savings in the cost of manufacture and manning. To me that justifies the High Side concept. But if I believed Sceptre to be an aggressive weapon I'd do all I could to speak out against it, even destroy it."

Guy said, "The trouble is many scientists aren't convinced High Side can prevent nuclear war."

Felberg grunted. "No persuading them, either, they live in a vacuum. Want to inspect this level?"

"No, let's go on down."

In the next pressurized airlock, they got into lined, helmeted suits that reminded Guy of astronaut gear. In a muffled voice Felberg said, "We need these to keep motes from the air—and to keep warm." Another sequential lock and the door opened onto a moving *pater noster*. As it lowered them Guy felt increasing air pressure. With his guide he stepped off and entered the lower airlock where pressure diminished as an ultraviolet bath sanitized their jump suits.

The door opened into a large area whose walls and ceiling were thickly insulated. Vapor hugged the clean floor near insulated tanks of liquid nitrogen. Frost coated the surface of a long metal tube the size of a tank car. At one end a battery of computer-driven robot arms clustered around a built-in laser gun. Along the side, observation ports blinked an eerie green glow. Guy counted a dozen or so technicians clad like himself moving at their work.

In a muffled voice Felberg said, "The coated wafer is suspended in the tank where the laser will etch a conducting design into the chip. The laser beam is guided by robotics because the work is micro-fine. The beam is just under seven microns in diameter, or one-tenth that of a human hair— which is why not even the slightest vibration is tolerable. We're on, and under, bedrock to prevent it. Conventional bombardment shock would have no effect here, though an earthquake or a nuclear explosion would. The ultracold ambience is essential to control molecular velocity." One gloved arm gestured broadly. "This is the womb of Sceptre. Without it, no functional MDS. All the Sceptre microprocessors we've produced are stored here for eventual mating with the space platforms under production at Rockwell. The first unit will be tested during a classified shuttle flight. Until then, our six identical chips are kept in that titanium safe." He pointed at what looked like the gleaming face of a bank vault. "So now you see what so much RyTech development money has been paying for."

"To me," Guy said, "this is all a form of magic. No wonder DSA is so eager to protect the installation." He watched robot arms begin to activate the laser gun. "Suppose the Soviets acquired one of the Sceptre chips—could they duplicate it?"

"They *could* read it and develop countermeasures. And to read it they would have to reverse our miniaturization process." He pointed upward with his thumb. "Enlarge it back to the design original. That they could probably do. The Soviets have ample money, time and technical skill—even though their own R and D on a similar system has been faulty and flawed." He went to the safe, worked two dials and opened the door.

Except for what looked like a small black drawer the en-

219

tire interior was filled with foam insulation. Felberg pulled out the drawer to show Guy a slotted container. From one slot he carefully drew out a microchip edged in protective metal. Guy bent over to view its varicolored face.

"Next week we'll finish Number Seven," Felberg said, and eased the chip into its container. He closed the drawer, swung shut the heavy door and twirled the dials. "We like to think it's as secure as Fort Knox. Ventilation comes from a distant, concealed vent. If poison gas were ever inserted, sensors would detect it and venting would reverse. Simultaneously, air tanks would cut in and supply everyone below surface for forty-eight hours. Any questions?"

"I'm overwhelmed."

"Well, you've seen the guts of the operation. I trust it's satisfactory."

"So long as you're meeting schedule."

"We're ahead of schedule—it's the platform manufacturer that's fallen behind." He smiled behind the plastic mask. "Promises, promises."

"Could one of the techs walk off with a chip?"

"We don't leave ISR unless we're searched and X-rayed. Besides, only two of us have the vault combinations: Dr. Printz and myself. Every day one of us checks the contents." He wrote his name and the hour on a security sheet. Then they returned to the surface.

Fire engines and Hoskins had departed. Felberg walked Guy to the waiting helicopter, where they shook hands. The chopper flew over snow-swept fields back to Baltimore airport, setting down beside the RyTech Lear.

Guy was lunching at his desk when a call came on his scrambler phone, and he heard Hoskins say, "I thought you'd want to know the nocturnal bombardier was picked up at Dulles Airport a few minutes ago. He had three passports: French, Libyan and Cypriot, each in a different name. We'll match his paper and pen-ink to the Direct Action Army note; with that I'm reasonably sure he'll talk. We identified him through his prints as Achmed al-Maghrebi.''

"Fast action," Guy said.

"We need to know how much the enemy knows—or guesses—about ISR, and whether further attacks or harassment are planned. The uncomfortable thing, though, is what he carried in his coat pocket a completion certificate from that executive training program RyTech runs near Houston. Makes you wonder, eh?''

"It's being closed down on Needham's recommendation.''

"Glad to hear it. Too much mercenary training going on as it is. This Achmed—the alleged suspect of ours—is going to talk, Guy. I have to know who sent him, what's behind the shelling.''

"Who's interrogating? FBI?''

"Not a chance—he's been well-briefed, began yelling for the ACLU—so Wilke and a couple of stout fellows have him en route a mountain retreat. There they can all focus without distractions.''

"My kind of direct action," Guy remarked. "Thanks for letting me know.''

He finished lunch and went into the board room where Needham, Farley Johns and a number of department heads were waiting. After three hours of graphs and profit/loss projections Guy's brain was numb. He deferred decisions pending consultation with the general counsel and went back to his office. Farley Johns came in and faced him angrily. "I'm not accustomed to being humiliated professionally. Your father accepted my recommendations, and for you to take them up with a lawyer who knows nothing about financial planning is demeaning to me.''

Guy cleared his throat. "No offense intended, Farley, but

if you feel you can't work with me I'll take your resignation."

The comptroller's face paled. "I—I wasn't suggesting that," he backtracked. "I've been a loyal RyTech employee for seven years; your late father found no fault with my financial management."

Guy leaned back in his chair. "Difference in style, I suppose. After hearing facts I decide—and who I consult in making decisions is my sole concern, not yours." He flicked a pencil at the lucite wastebasket. "I think it will be better for both of us if you pack and go quietly. Today. You've had a long run at RyTech and I'm willing to say you left for personal reasons. Personnel will compute your entitlements and send them to you. Good day, sir."

Johns gasped, "But I didn't—you'll *regret* this. Believe me you'll regret discarding me so casually."

"So Stoner said—but I don't believe it. You see, I haven't been comfortable with you since I overheard you at Eastover—talking about an 'insider' taking over, getting rid of me. Who was your partner? Edmonds? Stoner?"

"You can't prove a thing," he said sullenly.

"I don't have to. C'mon, it's over with—who was your fellow conspirator?"

"You'll never know."

Guy smiled lazily. "That's insubordination. You've got an hour to leave—don't come back." He picked up the phone and asked Mrs. Paskow to come in. She opened the door as Johns angrily strode through, closed it behind him. Pad in hand she said, "Sir?"

"He's finished. Advise Personnel and Security."

"Yes, sir."

"Then place a call to Paris. I want to speak with my wife."

Connie assured him that except for persistent bad weather all was well. The bodyguards were burdensome, but plans for her painting exhibition were almost complete. She missed him as did Gloria, who was to take part in a school St. Valentine's Day pageant, and wanted him to attend.

"Since I can't, please send pictures."

"Of course, dear. Are you house hunting?"

"So far we're screening two large apartments facing Central Park—and a townhouse in the East Sixties. Four floors and an English basement for servants. Gloria could have the top floor to herself, have any number of doll houses and such. At present the place belongs to a prominent publisher who's getting a divorce—which is the reason for the sale. Of course, others will come along before you arrive. And I think we should have a country place, don't you? With pool, stables and tennis courts?"

She laughed happily. "By all means, dear. Isn't it wonderful to have so much money—and be able to enjoy it?"

"Wealth still confounds me," he said. "Especially when I think that a few months ago I was scraping bottom—quite literally. For myself I don't care about money. I don't value it except as it contributes to our happiness."

"Really, I never thought I could develop so much enthusiasm for the move."

"That encourages me," he told her. "Wish you were here."

"So do I—and will be. Otherwise, how are things working out?"

"I'm learning the job—and finding it's not all desk work."

"You're happy, though?"

"Not until the two of you are with me."

When Jake Needham came in Guy told him of firing Johns, and said, "Anyone in line for the job?"

"Not around here—he delegated very little; his assistants

223

are competent accountants not up to industrial financial theory. But with his departure out in the open, the headhunters will be able to fill the job more easily."

"Anyone we hire has to pass DSA screening."

"That's understood. I have some reports for you: Vosges, de Neuville and Whitaker."

"Read them?"

"Progress appears satisfactory. Your brother-in-law took your admonitions quite seriously."

"He knew he was within an inch of unemployment. So long as he functions on my terms he can stay."

Needham said, "I'd like to hear about your morning trip, but not here. The office hasn't been audio-swept since refurbishing, and it's scheduled for early tomorrow. Until then—"

"It'll keep."

"Sotheby's can auction the treasure in October. That'll allow time for specialized appraisals and the preparation of a photo booklet for potential buyers. The suggestion is to hold the auction in a free port to avoid customs difficulties and possible taxes. I think that's excellent, because if the Haitians lodged a claim in New York there could be years of litigation. But extra-territoriality leaves nowhere to sue."

"I like that," Guy acknowledged. "We've worked too hard, come to far to lose to the likes of Auguste Coulou."

"Absolutely. Well, I'll firm things with the auctioneers for October. As for the earlier meeting, those decisions can wait on a new comptroller—I'd be more comfortable with his opinions than Johns' leftovers."

"Me, too."

"Next item: a crash-investigation firm will be trucking the helicopter wreckage to their lab at Teterboro. They're experienced in this kind of work, do it for insurance companies, and promise a thorough analysis. Might take as much as a month."

"Thoroughness is what I want, Jake."

"So I told them. It's in their hands now. They'll let us know."

"You accomplish a lot, Jake, and I depend on you. Are the hours too long? Complaints at home?"

"Sally says I'm a new man—tired *all* the time."

Guy said, "Why not take Sunday off?" and grinned.

Jake smiled. "You're all heart, boss . . . Seriously, I'll be moseying—unless there's something . . ."

Guy shook his head and watched him leave. Outside, darkness had fallen. He worked for another hour, going over reports, signing letters and reading material flagged for his attention. A memo from Jenny proposed sponsoring a PBS documentary on protecting coastlines from oil spills. A good deal of file film was available, and PBS was negotiating with Heston for the voiceover. Cost to RyTech, $200,000. "The exposure is well worth it," she wrote. "We'd pay that for ten minutes of network prime viewing, and I feel it's a start on softening the corporate image. Moreover, it can be shown repeatedly by independent TV stations, so it's a long-term investment."

At the bottom of the page were two boxes, one labeled *Concur*, the other, *Forget It*. Guy smiled as he checked the former and initialed it. This was how Eisenhower liked staff work presented—the Army way. Boil decisions down to *Yes* or *No* alternatives and get on with other things.

Getting up he stretched, realizing that he was hungry. As he left the office he saw Mrs. Paskow at her desk. "Staying late?" he asked.

"Your father wanted me here until he told me I could leave. I assumed you would want the same."

"Oh, no. I'm not going to be a slave to the office and I don't want you to be one."

"Well—thank you, Mr. Ryan."

Walking toward a nearby restaurant he felt a sense of loneliness. After months of mealtime camaraderie with his boat crew Guy was unaccustomed to solitary dining. Still, he had Easter reunion with his family to look forward to; until then he would have to bear enforced isolation.

At his banquette table Guy sipped Black Label over ice and pondered the scientific wizardry he had witnessed that morning at ISR. He understood more fully why the installation had to be protected, and wondered if the mortarman would break under DSA grilling. Was the shelling related to the Geneva shootout? And how ironic—and disturbing— that the perpetrator had been trained at a RyTech facility.

During dinner he thought about the future of the closed-down spread. Cristina ought to look it over, appraise its potential as a stud farm and range for the foals of Al-Emir. But what of Cristina's infatuation? Her desire to win him over? He didn't like to think how he'd bear up under the onslaught of her affections.

One solution might be to have her accompany Connie and Gloria at Easter; then Cristina would see for herself the futility of her juvenile dream.

After leaving the restaurant Guy strolled up Park Avenue, breathing deeply to fill his lungs with cold night air. The sidewalk was patched with ice, traffic at a lull now that theatre performances were underway.

As he neared his apartment entrance, a man stepped from behind doorside shrubbery and barred his way. "Guy Patrick," he said loudly, "Conor Counihan has disprit need o'ye." And Guy recognized him as one of Conor's Irish bhoyos.

"That's of no concern to me." Guy started around him but the man's left arm shoved him roughly back.

His right arm thrust out a revolver.

Eighteen

"It's the concern of ivry honest Irishman when Conor Counihan's in gaol and needin' bail for freedom."

Guy's upper arm pressed against the holstered pistol, McGrain's gift. "Jail? For what? Public drunkenness? Panhandling?"

"For workin' in the service of Ireland. Will ye do what's right—or no?"

"Get lost," Guy snapped. "I have no time for hoodlums."

The man waved at a curbside car. "Ye'll not defame the Brotherhood." The car pulled even with them, stopped, engine running. The rear door opened and Guy remembered Geneva. With a glance at the waiting car Guy said, "How much does Conor need?"

"The thousand'll set him free."

As the weapon gestured, Guy moved slowly toward the car. "I'll post bail," he said, "if Counihan leaves this country tomorrow. It's worth that to me—and more."

"To that he'd not agree. Get in."

Bending over to enter the rear seat Guy let his coat hang open. Back to the gunman, he drew out his Walther and slid across the seat. As the gunman began to get in, Guy shoved the pistol muzzle against the driver's head. "We're not going anywhere, Paddy," he announced. "Put down your piece or it's brains on the windscreen."

With a Gaelic curse the gunman lowered his revolver. Guy pushed the Walther against his chest and pulled the revolver from his hand. As Guy got out the streetside door the weaponless gunman hissed, "Bloody Orangeman!"

"Let the Brotherhood take care of its own. Tell the old man I'm no part of your ancient quarrels. Threaten me again and I've a bullet for your belly." He slammed the door shut and smashed the window with his pistol butt. The engine gunned, the car shot away.

Guy walked into the lobby and stopped at the guard's desk. Setting the revolver on it he said, "Found this outside. Better have the police collect it."

Without touching it the guard stared at the revolver. "That's an old one," he said. "British Webley—lanyard swivel and all. Don't see many such these days."

"One is too many," Guy said as he headed for the elevator.

In his apartment he poured a long shot of Armagnac and wondered how Nigel Palfrey would rate his street performance. There was much to find fault with, but he had escaped without assistance—unlike Geneva where Palfrey had intervened.

While undressing Guy turned on a news channel, and after a while heard the name of Conor Counihan. The old man was shown manacled between Federal agents who had flushed him out of a warehouse in lower Queens, where, it was alleged, the IRA militant was overseeing the crating of automatic weapons for shipment abroad.

Let him rot in prison, Guy said half aloud, without any feeling of assurance that he would. The search warrant would be found defective, or the inevitable defender would assert absence of probable cause. Or an underling would have neglected to read Counihan his rights. Case dismissed.

As he thought of Counihan he found himself wondering

how Sean would have responded. Doubtless with a check and a defense attorney, so rooted was his fixation on the Auld Sod. Or was more than nostalgic affection involved—guilt perhaps, because Sean Ryan lived affluently in the New World while thousands of his countrymen writhed under the brutish British boot? Supporting Counihan as a conscience-easing move? Well, Sean was dead, he'd never divulge the reason.

Guy finished his nightcap and went to bed.

A week later he hired a new comptroller. Frank Purcell had gone with AMF after Wharton and spent the last decade with Dynamic Technologies as assistant comptroller for finance. Purcell's broad experience in government, contracting for a defense-oriented conglomerate qualified him to replace Farley Johns. Needham's opinion, and Guy agreed.

On Edmonds' return he stormed into Guy's office demanding to know why Johns and Stoner had been fired. Guy had his discharge papers ready, and gave them to the former executive vice president with the same admonition he had given Stoner: backbiting will cost your deferred compensation. Whitefaced, Paul Edmonds took his final paycheck and departed without a word. Personnel distributed his staff and secretaries where they were needed most, and Guy turned to more pressing things.

By telephone Hoskins reported that Pentagon compliance inspectors sent to Lyons and Geneva indicated initial satisfaction over improvements in plant security and end-use certification. "That's thanks to you, Guy. You're doing a fine job shaping things up."

"There's only slight satisfaction in locking barn doors."

"Better late than never—had to be done."

"Reminds me—last time we spoke that mortarman was being driven off for interrogation."

"That's so. Well, he was taken up on the mountain, so to speak, and given a choice. He talked for several days, and named principals in France and Tripoli. Unfortunately for him we determined he was fabricating. Except for admitting that he'd borrowed the Direct Action name to conceal his true backers. That much we believed. But the poor fellow was pathological, couldn't tell the truth to save himself. So, while he was being choppered back from the hospitality lodge, guilt overcame him and he took a dive over the Blue Ridge Mountains."

Guy suddenly felt strange. He hadn't expected that such extreme measures would be necessary. But perhaps there was only one way to deal with fanatics. True Believers. He heard Hoskins saying, "You knew Conor Counihan was arrested?"

"Yes, and I hope he's still in jail."

"Hardly—something called Sons of the Shamrock posted a fifty-thousand dollar bond and the old rascal was set free. By nightfall he was on a plane to Lisbon from where, one supposes, he'll make his way to Erin. If spry enough to outrun Scotland Yard. We could have stopped him but it wouldn't have been cost effective. The fifty G's will pay two agents' salaries for a year. And of course, we got his weapons. They were stolen from an armory near Boston, and not returned—despite demands by two Congressmen. As it happened, the missing ordnance was dropped from accountability—but I hear the weapons are on their way to Afghanistan. If true, that's bad news for the Sovs."

"My kind of bad news," Guy said.

"While you're on the line," Hoskins continued, "we've been advised that those three Geneva 'gunshot victims' were mercenaries of no detectable political bent. The girlfriend of one told the Swiss police he'd been contacted by a stranger 'to do a job,' hired two pals and disappeared. The Geneva Sûreté worked her over but that was all they could get. Irish lads, by the way, hired in Dublin; they flew in the night before your encounter. Having heard mention of Geneva, the lass went there only to learn she was alone in the world.''

Hoskins did have a fondness for sarcasm, Guy thought.

''The set-up means you were being watched.''

''Never doubted it. Did my name surface to the Swiss police?''

''Witnesses described the intended victim, but no one suggested a name.''

''That's encouraging. I may have to return one day.''

''Not for another *soirée dansante.*''

''One was enough.''

''Right now Edouard Drach is on the road. MI-Six is deeply interested in his moves. Because travel involves considerable inconvenience to his person, Drach seldom leaves his castle. So when he does Six attaches significance to it. Drach stopped in Vienna, where he consumed a mountain of Sachertorte *mit schlag,* then on to Istanbul. All by chartered aircraft.''

''Playboy of the western world, eh?''

''He'd like to think so. Take care, Guy.''

As Guy hung up he reflected that the mortarman had learned the ultimate in direct action—from DSA.

With Jake Needham he rode to the PanAm Metroport and boarded RyTech's new replacement helicopter, a Bell Long Ranger, model 206 L-1. Guy took the controls across Manhattan and the Hudson River, relinquishing them to the pilot as they entered Teterboro's traffic pattern. Wind skittered snow across the tarmac as they made their way to the old hangar.

The interior was vast, gray, bleak and very cold. A heavily sweatered man introduced himself as Bill Sonetsky, the chief technical investigator. He led them into a large tent warmed by quartz heaters. Partly on the floor and partly on board tables lay the recovered wreckage of Marguerite's helicopter. Sonetsky said, "Mr. Ryan, this may be painful for you, but you hired us to get at the truth, so I assume that's what you want to know."

Guy nodded, felt Jake's hand on his arm.

"I don't blame the Transportation Safety Board guys for missing what we found. Used to be with FAA myself, and what's generally looked for is rotor-lock, control cable failure—something mechanical. We looked for that as well—with what we had to work on—and like the other investigators found nothing culpable. That was more or less expected because qualified witnesses had seen the helicopter explode. So we concentrated on what initiated the explosion. Obviously, the gas tank caused the fireball—but what ignited the gas?" He drew Guy's attention to the blown-apart tank. "See how it gave way like a fully-opened tulip? Also, the multiple perforations—like shrapnel, right?" With tweezers he held up a small piece of gleaming metal, pointed out others embedded in the tank's metal wall. "In a way it *was* shrapnel. Under metallurgical spectro-analysis these bits were identified as a tungsten steel alloy that's not used in the fabrication of this Bell or any other helicopter. In short, a foreign object. From previous experience we realized it was probably some sort of bomb."

From a table drawer he drew out a grease-stained booklet whose cover read: *Ordnance Manual. U.S. Army. Restricted. No-Forn.* To Guy he said, "You won't tell on me?" His thumb riffled the pages, stopped at one showing four cylindrical devices, each somewhat different from the others. "These exemplars were picked up in Grenada, Lebanon or Afghanistan. Czech manufacture, and their tungsten alloy casing is identical with the fragments I showed you. Very nasty items. They hold improved RDX explosive and can be detonated in several ways. This one's time-delayed to three days; that is a tailpipe trembler, and this one's radio-activated. A bit of radio crystal in the tank's neoprene lining gave us the bottom line. Which is, I'm sorry to say, gentlemen, that a line-of-sight radio signal detonated the bomb, and with it the tank and chopper.''

Guy felt his throat thicken.

In a lowered voice, Sonetsky said, ''The scenario could be this—the bomb is planted surreptitiously, perhaps long ago. Anyone anticipating the flight path along the coast of Long Island could wait along the route with his transmitter—or track the helicopter by car. At the right moment he points the transmitter at the chopper and sends the detonating signal.''

Guy gazed at the metal wreckage. He had seen the remains of choppers in 'Nam, but none as thoroughly destroyed as this. He closed his eyes, remembering the love and affection his stepmother had so selflessly given him, and for a few moments he said nothing. The hangar was still as a mausoleum. When he finally spoke, he said, ''I'm very appreciative for your work and your findings. Can it be kept private?''

''Afraid not, sir. I have an obligation to make a report to NTSB, and I feel they'll refer it to the FBI. That doesn't mean publicity, just that the competent authorities have to be officially informed. And you may want to refer the insurors to me.''

''I'll handle that,'' Needham said brusquely. ''The death of Mrs. Ryan was tragic enough for the survivors without having to see speculation in the check-out tabloids. We'd welcome your cooperation to avoid that.''

''You can count on me,'' Sonetsky said, ''and I'll pass the word along.''

They shook hands and Sonetsky walked them to the waiting chopper.

After they were airborne for Manhattan, Guy remained silent until the 60th Street heliport was in sight. He felt hollow, depressed, and bursting with rage at the killers. Whoever did it had made exquisitely careful plans. And they must have been for the most powerful motives.

"Why?" he said despairingly. "Who killed her, and why?" Anguished sobs wrenched from his throat and his shoulders shook uncontrollably.

As the chopper settled down on the pad Guy dried his eyes. "If I learn who did it," he said in a leaden voice, "I'll kill him."

"Easy, Guy, you're distraught."

Ignoring Nedham's words, he said fiercely, "I learned killing from the Cong—saw enough to tear out your guts. Men skinned alive, left to the ants . . ." He shook his head. "More than ten years ago, but I still remember—I'll never forget."

Head bowed against the freezing wind, he strode up the landing ramp.

Somewhere, someone would pay for her murder.
If it took the balance of his life.

Nineteen

Five days later Gant presented himself at the building and demanded entrance. Guy asked Mrs. Paskow if his half-brother customarily visited their father during business hours.

"Only to ask for money, sir. Mr. Gant was not particularly welcome on the premises."

"I think it's best to continue the precedent. Cool him for half an hour and have him brought up under escort."

"Yes, sir. And travel arrangements for your party are complete. Three round-trip First Class tickets to Seoul. You're to leave the heliport at eighteen-fifteen hours."

"In my absence Mr. Needham is in charge."

"I understand. He'll be back from Washington tomorrow."

Guy pointed at a clear area on the wall. "At Eastover there's a large portrait of my late stepmother. I want it brought here, perhaps reframed—use your discretion."

"I'll see to it, sir."

He spoke with Jake at the Washington office, and after a while Mrs. Paskow brought in Gant.

Guy's half-brother was less disheveled than usual, wearing a fleece-lined coat, ski gloves and a striped muffler from

Middlesex. Without asking him to sit Guy said, "What's on your mind?"

"I want my rights, that's what's on my mind. I've been treated like the runt of the litter."

"What kind of rights?"

He pulled off his gloves. "I happen to own twenty percent of RyTech. With Nikky's twenty, that's forty percent, Guy, and—"

"You have Nikky's proxy?"

"Well—not actually, but she'll vote with me."

"Don't count on her."

He looked enviously around the office. "Still, my twenty percent entitles me to an office."

"You're thinking of taking an active role in managing RyTech? You couldn't even get a prep school diploma. Middlesex booted you for peddling drugs."

"Damn it, don't hold the past against me. I was eighteen then—and like I said at the time, I was framed."

"I see. Suppose I send for your transcript and ask the headmaster for a statement regarding your expulsion? That will be the first item in your personnel file."

Gant looked uncomfortable. Guy said, "You'll start at the bottom, of course."

"The work isn't important, the office is."

"We have work rules customary in any enterprise. No personal business. In your case that means no rock musicians, singers or punk entertainers during office hours."

"Damn it, you're being shitty with me."

"Happens we're not hiring entry-level help, so taking you on is an exception called nepotism."

"Guy, I want my *full* rights. RyTech makes millions, and my stock entitles me to twenty percent of the profits."

"That's not how it works. Our policy is to reinvest profits and avoid taxation."

He stared at Guy. *"You* get paid."

"Because I work here. Sean's job, remember?"

236

Gant scratched the side of his face as Guy said, "I'm trying to accommodate you, don't be difficult."

After a while Gant sighed. "All right—what I really want is an office I can work out of, okay? Desk, chairs, a telephone. I'll settle for that."

"All right," said Guy, "the position is this. I'll spell it out for you. We're as dissimilar as two men can be, but we have the same father, and we have this in common—both of us, in different ways, were disappointments to him. That's the bond between you and me, however tenuous it is. Marguerite was your blood-mother and the only mother I ever knew. She loved you, Gant, put up with your nastiness, your failures, your laziness and self-indulgence as long as she lived. She'd be doing it still, but now there's me acting in her place."

Surlily Gant said, "So, what are you going to do?"

"Much as it goes against my better sense, my impulses, I'm going to set aside dislike and replace it with some of the compassion Marguerite felt for you. You'll get your office and a reasonable drawing account—"

Gant brightened. "Great! That's—"

"With two stipulations, Gant. One is that you don't try to interfere in company business."

Gant shrugged. "Okay with me."

"The other is that you sign a document renouncing any effort by you to contest our father's will—or Marguerite's."

He smirked. "That's cool—my lawyer already told me I didn't have a good case."

"Then you got good advice."

"How about Nikky? She's not too happy about the way things are."

"Nikky? Her husband's job is hanging by a thread. She understands that if she tries to break Sean's will Thibaud goes."

"Did she sign a paper?"

"I didn't ask her to because she has more sense than you. Where do you want to be located?"

"I was thinking of Soho."

"Then find an office for yourself and advise our office manager, Mr. Haynes. He'll take care of renting it."

"What about my allowance?"

"I'll come up with a figure—you won't starve, but if you want upscale living you'll have to promote it for yourself." He made a note on his pad. "Mr. Needham will contact you when our memorandum of understanding is ready to be signed. Are we in agreement?"

"Yeah—sure. This is gonna work out good."

"I hope so. Meanwhile, try to stay out of trouble."

Gant stared at him, turned abruptly and went quickly out. Guy dictated a memo for Haynes and Needham, and when he was alone he thought about his half-brother.

Gant was getting a lot more than he deserved . . . For Marguerite's sake he hoped his brother would get his act together and make something of himself in the entertainment world. But Guy would never forget his foul outburst at the reading of their father's will.

With the Department Head and a marketing expert, Guy flew to Seoul, Korea, playing blackjack and gin rummy between periods of sleep. He was met at the airport by senior officials from South Korea's Ministries of Commerce, Foreign Relations and Finance. At the Embassy Residence, Ambassador Jenkins hosted a buffet-reception for Guy and his companions, after which they slept overnight at the Seoul Plaza Hotel.

In the morning they flew KAL to Cheju Island off the tip of Korea in the South China Sea. Thick snow covered the central mountain, and on level ground the snow pattern showed heavy crosswinds.

The plant manager, Mr. Chon, spoke good English, having been educated in Hawaii, where he had been taken as a war orphan. "After the university," he told Guy cheerfully, "I had almost to relearn Korean, but it's been worth the effort."

The company van was taking them through wretched-looking villages whose low buildings were constructed of field stones and boulders. The countryside was sectioned by low stone walls. The manager said, "There are plenty of stones on Cheju. It's a volcanic island, you know. The natives—I mean my countrymen—make the best use of them."

"This is such an isolated, bleak place. I wonder why the plant was located here?"

"My government offered construction help to RyTech, and installed fishing piers, provided a fishing fleet. Seoul wanted to give the island population employment beyond raising cabbage for *kimchee*."

Guy had heard of the evil-smelling national dish. His nose wrinkled and Chon laughed. "Don't worry, I won't inflict it on you. You like shooting, Mr. Ryan?"

"Depends."

"Pheasant shooting?"

Guy nodded.

"Good. Today we'll accomplish briefings and the plant inspection. Tomorrow morning there'll be a shooting party."

"You mean there are pheasant here?"

"Thick as sparrows on the mainland. The population doesn't kill or eat them, so the birds' only natural enemies are foxes, which are now hibernating. I promise you a good shoot tomorrow."

After a seafood luncheon in the plant cafeteria they were briefed on the plant's activities. Conversion of the ocean's riches into low-cost protein for human consumption was the goal of the plant's experimentation. Trawlers netted schools of "trash" fish that were machine deboned and processed into a gel called *surimi*. To it were added spices and a high

239

vitamin protein derived from green algae. Conversion of *krill,* the tiny crustaceans that formed the baleen diet, was a separate process undertaken during the summer when northern waters could be seined.

"The UN is interested," Mr. Chon claimed, "and the World Health Organization considers our process as a possibility in overcoming the kind of widespread famine that affects such places as central Africa. The problem seems to be in getting people of other cultures to change their eating habits. The classic story happened in China when the rice harvest failed. UNRRA supplied thousands of tons of corn, but the Chinese were unfamiliar with corn as human food and starved rather than consume it. Whether starving Africans will accept our product remains to be seen. We've supplied WHO with substantial quantities for experimental feeding, but the officials have neglected to inform us of results. That is difficult for us to understand."

"Probably bureaucratic bumbling. I'll have it looked into."

"Thank you—our workers would be glad to know their efforts are beneficial to mankind."

There were further briefings on enhancing myofibrillar protein concentrations, and examples of Japanese exploitation of *surimi* in Western markets as simulated shrimp, crab legs and lobster tails. A tour of automated processing followed, and Guy was impressed by the extreme cleanliness of production lines with their white-uniformed attendants, each woman hair-netted to avoid product contamination.

During dinner in the company cafeteria Guy sat beside Mr. Chon at the head table and was pleased to see the employees and their families filling the other tables. After the tempura course Chon introduced him to charcoal-broiled slices of marinated beef called *bul-go-gi,* served with garlic and onions. From a chafing dish came *sinsollo,* a simmered mixture of meat and shellfish, bean curd, black mushrooms, water chestnut and sharp spices. After that, Chon asked his opinion of the plant's product—cakes of processed *surimi,* deep-fried a golden brown—and Guy acknowledged that they were tastier than Gloucester codfish cakes.

The marketing specialist remarked that it would be difficult if not impossible to overtake the Japanese in Occidental markets, and the department head agreed. His thought was to concentrate on sales to protein-poor countries as soon as consistent product volume could be achieved.

There followed rounds of *sake* that left Guy with an unpleasant headache. He turned in early, leaving his companions to enjoy geisha-style entertainment provided by plant talent.

In the morning Guy was outfitted with felt-lined boots, a fur-lined parka, snow mask and a 12-gauge Remington pump gun. Mr. Chon carried an old Japanese double, and accompanied by two volunteer beaters they set off across frozen fields. Wind from the South China Sea blasted his back, and the first birds to break hedgerow cover were swept away even before Guy could shoulder his gun. Stepping over the frequent boulder fences was tiring, and Guy began to regret expressing enthusiasm for the shoot. The beaters circled around in a pincer movement and disappeared behind a low hill. Mr. Chon signalled Guy to proceed slowly, and when they came over the brow the beaters jumped up and down, yelling and waving their arms, and from thick bracken burst a wave of frightened pheasants.

Confused by noise and wind, they hurtled upward, wings frantically beating while Guy sighted and fired repeatedly. Wind hurled the survivors away, except for a crippled bird finished off by Mr. Chon. Guy tallied his kill: four fine ringnecks and two golden Orientals. Mr. Chon applauded politely and the group moved on through thickening snow that spattered the back of his parka like gravel. Guy reloaded with fingers that had grown stiff despite lined deer-skin gloves.

The flat, boulder-strewn landscape and the extraordinarily strong wind gave Guy an eerie feeling of being on a distant, hostile planet. Occasional rock mounds contained crocks of rotting *kimchee* cabbage, but the wind kept the stench from his nostrils.

Another bracken-filled draw produced twice as many pheasants, and Guy dropped another six, Mr. Chon killing two. The weather was deteriorating, light diminishing, the wind blowing with undeflected velocity. Guy's toes and fingertips were numb, so through cupped hands he yelled to Chon, "I've had enough—let's go back."

Chon nodded, but pointed ahead. "Just one more batch? The beaters are already in position."

They divided and Guy walked off to the left. Twenty feet from Chon he could hardly make out the man's form. He struggled over another rock fence and started up a gentle rise. Twelve birds were enough and he begrudged the effort to get more—but it was his fellow hunter's turn to fill his bag.

Remington cradled, Guy topped the rise and looked down. Huddled amid the briars was a pheasant covey sheltering from the wind. One of the beaters frightened them into flight and he heard Chon's barrels explode. Guy shouldered his gun for final shots at the nearest birds, when from the corner of his eye he saw the second beater kneeling in the gully, pointing a twin-barrelled shotgun not at the fleeing birds—but at him.

Guy reacted instinctively, dropping flat as the shell exploded. He turned his hooded head from the shooter, and scrabbled backward. Pellets struck the hillside, some glancing off his hood, but wind deflected the main charge, which would have blown his head apart. A second shotgun blast, more pellets impacted the frozen earth, and Guy raised his head to see the beater hastily breaking his gun to reload.

He had one shell in the chamber when Guy charged down the slope, Remington at his hip. He was deciding whether to fire when the beater closed his gun.

Through face screens their eyes met, and in the other's, Guy saw arrogant challenge. As Guy neared the man, covering him with his Remington, the beater pointed his barrel skyward, set the gun butt on the ground and dropped his chin over the muzzle. *"Don't,"* Guy shouted, *"I won't kill you,"* but his words were lost in the shotgun's roar. The man's face vanished. A chunk of scalp lifted into the wind and whirled away in a rain of blood. Guy halted as the corpse toppled forward.

He was still staring at it when Chon began yelling from the ridge.

His scalp lacerations treated, Guy sat in Chon's private office, warmed by hot tea and Japanese brandy, while the manager scanned the dead man's personnel file. Chon hissed occasionally and made notes. Guy thought about the morning shoot. Sixteen pheasants were being dressed and flesh-frozen, and Guy intended sending half a dozen to Ambassador Jenkins in Seoul by way of appreciation for his courtesies.

After a while Chon closed the folder. "This man Seukeun Kim defected at Panmunjom three years ago. He was processed through our government reception center and given employment at the Choongju fertilizer plant. He applied here saying he wanted the higher wages, and because of his chemical experience we hired him." Chon's hands spread apologetically. "It is not easy to have qualified helpers on Cheju."

"No one's blaming you," Guy told him. "Obviously, he remained loyal to the North."

"As a bachelor Kim stayed by himself. He listened to shortwave programs on his radio and was unsociable. The file says he did his work well, but was not easy to give instructions to, and once created trouble after losing a game of *go*. Otherwise, nothing is known of him.'' He swallowed. ''Mr. Ryan, do you know why Kim would try to kill you?''

''No, but it wasn't the first attempt. His radio could bring in transmissions from Pyongyang?''

''Undoubtedly. Many employees listen to those broadcasts, hoping to hear mention of families or friends. Otherwise, the Communist propaganda programs would have few listeners in South Korea.''

Guy added more brandy to his cup. ''How long ago did you plan the pheasant shoot?''

''As soon as I was sure you were coming. Four days ago, perhaps five.''

''And Kim volunteered to help out.''

''Yes, and I was grateful. As you saw, beaters are essential to get the birds up.'' He sighed. ''The body is still out there. Frozen. I should report the happening to the police.''

''Aside from you, me and the other beater, who knows Kim is dead?''

''Nobody. I cautioned the beater, Mr. Rhi, to say nothing. Is it your wish to keep silence over this?''

''Until I leave Korea. Perhaps Kim's body could be discovered in a day or so, suicide ascribed to brooding over his defection. In this isolated setting that would be understandable.''

Chon nodded. ''Because this man was an infiltrator, perhaps our national security organization should be informed.''

''If you can do so in a private way.''

''With the utmost discretion. How sad,'' Chon said musingly. ''A man comes South in the guise of seeking freedom and democracy. We open our hands and hearts to him, make him welcome, only to find him a liar working traitorously for Communist masters.''

''Perhaps pressure was placed on his loved ones,'' Guy

said quietly, "so he did as ordered. If I'd captured him he could expect reprisals on his family. By killing himself he set them free."

"If so, it was an act of personal honor. I will see that his ashes are returned to the North."

"My companions will stay here to form a comprehensive plan. Once back in New York they'll follow up with WHO to see if we can get some action. It's criminal that populations starve when your plant can do so much to feed them."

Chon's face brightened. "Your words relieve me. I was afraid you would find this operation needless in your scheme of things. Now everyone will be encouraged to work hard."

Guy took the afternoon flight to the Seoul airport, dispatched the frozen pheasants to the Embassy and bought reading material while waiting for the Bangkok plane.

Next day he visited the Thai Celadon shop and ordered a number of graceful lamps and celadon figures he thought his wife would like in their new home. And that night he boarded a round-the-world Concorde for New York.

At Honolulu International Airport, copies of the *Bulletin* were brought aboard; Guy read one over breakfast. An AP story caught his attention: Maryland National Guard units had been activated to disperse a mass of protestors demonstrating against a nuclear weapons plant near Frederick. The story described ISR as a subsidiary of RyTech, an international conglomerate with close ties to the Department of Defense.

During the confrontation, guard troops had employed tear gas against the demonstrators, who were described as a mix of concerned citizens, university students, clergy and environmentalists. Shots had been fired and one of the demonstrators killed. The victim had been a thirty-three year old assistant professor in the sociology department of the University of Baltimore. State police were investigating the shooting to determine responsibility, although two Congressmen and a Maryland Senator thought a National Guardsman had fired the fatal shot.

Guy pushed away the paper. Echoes of the sixties, he thought. If there's no victim, they'll provide one and wave the bloody shirt.

During refueling in San Francisco, Guy telephoned Jake Needham, who said, "They've wasted no time, Guy. The House Armed Services Committee has announced it's going to hold hearings on the incident, and DSA informs me a subpoena will be issued for you to testify."

Twenty

Five hours later, tired and unshaven, Guy conferred with Jake in his office. The attorney said, "The situation is deteriorating but not desperate. Defense failed to persuade the Committee Chairman not to call you. He and certain of his colleagues see headlines and TV cameras, so a subpoena has been issued for you. A Committee aide will bring it from Washington tomorrow, and I'll accept service.

"I suggested that the Department of Justice either represent you at the hearing, or make an appearance implying Executive Branch support. However, the White House is taking a hands-off stance—according to his military aides the President has more than he can handle trying to get defense appropriations through Congress. So the White House doesn't want to expend good will by appearing to back RyTech."

"Meaning me." Guy looked at the dark windows. "Well, no one said this job was going to be easy. Who killed the Baltimore professor?"

"Culprit not identified, and probably never will be. There were about a thousand demonstrators trying to enter ISR, and no witnesses have come forward. One thing, though— the shot wasn't fired from a Guardsman's M-14. The bullet came from a thirty-two caliber pistol—a weapon even cub reporters know isn't carried by troops. That didn't deter the Coalition Against Military Murder from claiming that Professor Förster was a victim of provocations by the National Guard. The Coalition position is that if the troops had given way and let the demonstrators destroy ISR there would have been no violence against humans." He shook his head. "*You* figure it out, Guy, too profound for me. Unfortunately, that's the tone TV commentators and East Coast editorialists are copying. The subtheme is that 'the people' have a right to know what goes on at ISR. Away with secrecy that threatens world peace. The whole move is aimed at annihilating Sceptre."

"So I'll be asked about ISR?"

"Afraid so. And to give you maximum protection I've retained that sly Washington super-lawyer, Roland Pyne."

"The old hired gun."

"And always effective. Helped LBJ through innumerable minefields, maintains close relations with everyone of consequence on Capitol Hill. The cost will be brutal, but I'm glad he's in our corner for this one."

"Good move."

"As I'm sure Pyne will explain tomorrow, you and our other witnesses will be facing some very hostile questioning. The Committee includes three members who loathe the President and abhor anything involving national defense. Some of the Committee lawyers and investigators are, at the least, pacifistic; at worst, concealed Marxists. As anti-Pentagon zealots, they'll do their best to defame you, and because Committee rules have nothing to do with courtroom limitations you can be asked any question that comes to their minds. This is the new McCarthyism, but I've not found the hive media saying so."

Leaning back, Guy stretched shoulders still cramped from the long flight. "This wasn't quite the homecoming I expected."

"I imagine not."

"Suppose they ask me about ISR's work? Sceptre? I signed a secrecy agreement, Jake. I can't talk about Sceptre in public. Wouldn't if I could. Or reveal anything else about RyTech that's classified."

"I hope that won't become a problem, but if Chairman Patruzzi gets carried away by the publicity he may well lose his common sense."

"And if that happens?"

"You could be cited for contempt of Congress. But I rely on Pyne to prevent that—so let's not borrow trouble in advance."

Guy got up and walked over to the window. "Until now I never realized I'd led so sheltered a life. Agitators storm a RyTech installation, a man drops, and suddenly I'm the target of a Congressional investigation."

"Politics," Needham said bitterly. "Makes no sense at all."

"Well, you got on top of it fast, did the right things— retained Pyne. But the White House is shortsighted. Congressional investigations have a history of developing a life of their own, no matter what the facts."

"Facts are the last thing they deal with. Jenny Knox has been responding 'no comment' to the media all day. So I asked her to stand by—in case you decided to put something on the wires."

"I think it's premature. What's to say at this point? Let Jenny go home."

Needham called on the intercom and replaced the phone.

"Any idea when I'll be called before the Committee?"

"I think they have to give you forty-eight hours' notice, so they'll probably lead off with 'witnesses' from the Coalition, including the Congressmen who were there: Reinthaler, Morak and Senator Markham. Then, Drs. Printz and Felberg. That'll set the stage for RyTech's president and chief executive officer—you."

Guy tugged the lobe of his ear. "Do Printz and Felberg have Counsel?"

"Our Washington office retained their attorneys."

For a time Guy was silent. Then he said, "I'll see Pyne and size him up. Then decide whether to appear before the Committee."

Needham looked horrified. "Guy, you can't ignore a Congressional subpoena."

"Under these circumstances I think even my father would. Now, let's get some sleep."

As they left the building Needham said, "I haven't had a chance to thank you for those pheasants. Guess you got lucky in Korea."

"Luckier than you can imagine." He opened the street door for his friend. "Which reminds me, I have something for Hoskins while we're in Washington."

The law offices of Roland Fillmore Pyne occupied the top floor of a building on H Street; Pyne's suite overlooked Lafayette Park and the White House. The floor was thickly carpeted and the wax-rubbed, walnut walls were hung with hunting prints. One large color photograph showed Pyne posed with the Potomac Hunt.

Coming from the private elevator Guy had counted only six other offices along the corridor, and the number seemed disproportionately small compared to the degree of influence Pyne was thought to wield in Washington. Then it occurred to Guy that Pyne needed only a few attorneys, for he was said to operate most effectively in the cloakrooms of Congress and over luncheon tables at the Cosmos and Metropolitan Clubs.

After greeting Guy and Needham expansively, Pyne sat down behind a desk that could have been a Jefferson original. He was a large and imposing figure. His hair was pure white, thick and carefully barbered. His cheeks held the glow of post-massage health and his deep voice was resonant as he said, "Mr. Ryan, it does me honor to have you as a client. I admired the accomplishments of your late father, and I have always felt, as regards RyTech, that corporate size and profits are not to be despised as Original Sin.

"Personally, I consider the episode at ISR to have been tragic and unwarranted. You and I know the confrontation was provoked by agitators too cowardly to act alone—and with little difficulty we can discern their ultimate goal. That is for the three of us to know and acknowledge within the confines of this room. But we must none of us become emotional and blurt forth the truth. For the unfortunate fact is that Hill hearings are as carefully choreographed as a ballet, as ordered as a game of chess.

"Some who wish our country ill seized on the Frederick demonstration as an opportunity to handicap our country's defense system, but—bear this in mind—few members of the Armed Services Committee are hostile to you *personally*. Ex-Major Ryan, USA, is of no concern to them. It is RyTech President Guy Ryan they wish to abuse and humble before them, and so gain stature in the public mind.

"To put it more concisely, the effort is to destroy a symbol. You are the embodiment of RyTech, and in petty minds RyTech epitomizes the so-called military-industrial complex. Those who envy success, wealth and industrial achievement are your opponents no matter how they camouflage their sentiments." He half turned his chair, displaying his leonine profile while gazing over the park below.

Guy said, "I thought it would have been in the Administration's interest to head this off."

"It is," replied Pyne, "but the Executive Mansion has fish of its own to fry. I can tell you that concern was voiced, some effort made to spare you—but it was insufficient. So they are letting the Committee serve you up instead. The White House is confident you will bring it off relatively undamaged. I know you to be a highly intelligent man," he went on, "capable of conducting yourself with grace under fire, and I sincerely urge you to do so, no matter what the discourteous provocation or snide remark. The proceedings will be recorded by network cameras and one slip of tongue, one resentful outburst will be seen by forty million countrymen, and around the world as well. If I dwell on this aspect it is because I want you to fully understand the position. The hearings were convened for Committee benefit, not yours. The cameras are there for the aggrandizement of the members. Your position gives the whole charade its *raison d'être*. You will be attacked as a villain, scolded as though you were some refractory brat. Take it in as good form as you are able, for it is one of the least appetizing aspects of our democratic republic."

"One thing," Jake remarked, "is they haven't had time to question you beforehand. They won't know what to expect from you."

Pyne nodded agreement. "The hearings are being held at the Rayburn House Office Building in the hearing room of the Armed Services Committee. It is a large chamber with seating for press and spectators. We will be at a table, Mr. Needham and I at your side. Facing us from an elevation will be the members, ranged along a wide, quasi-judicial rostrum according to seniority. The space between will be filled with photographers. Cameramen will be to the right and left. The Chairman conducts the hearing. Each member is entitled to question you, plus Committee counsel and assistant counsel. The three members most hostile to our cause are Representatives Alegro, Hastings and Nouri."

He took white legal-length sheets from his desk and passed them to Guy and Jake. "You will be allowed an opening statement, which we have prepared for you. Once that is on the record the inquiry will begin. Between sessions you will be badgered by the media. Say nothing, permit me to respond for you," and for the first time Guy saw him smile. "I've been doing this since before you were born, sir, and

252

with more than a little success. You see, most lawyers deal with the law and law books. My forte is people. I deal *in* people, *with* people. What law I once knew is long forgotten. In its place I stored experience, the knowledge of pleasing and influencing people. FDR's mentor, Jim Farley, was my early idol and role model. He knew and remembered everyone—never forgot a name—and ended his career an honored and revered gentleman. It is my hope to follow Jim's example." He rose, thrusting his large frame against the sunlit background. Guy rose slowly as Needham said, "Thank you, Roland. We appreciate the briefing and Mr. Ryan will respond to the subpoena." He faced Guy expectantly.

"No," Guy said. "I won't play clown in their circus."

Pyne said, "You understand the probable consequences?"

"Sure. And to avoid, or at least postpone them, have your staff engineer legal remedies—an injunction, a writ, whatever."

Pyne wet his lips. "The courts try to avoid confrontations with Congress."

"We pay their salaries," Guy said, "let them sweat this one." He turned to Needham. "Let's go, Jake."

Pyne took an involuntary step as though to detain them, thought better of it and said, "What can I tell the Committee chairman?"

"You'll think of something. And you can tell the White House I'm not going to be this year's sacrifical lamb."

Before returning to New York Guy met Hoskins in RyTech's K Street office. While Jake listened, horrified, Guy recounted the attempt on his life at Cheju Island. "Seukeun Kim is the assassin's name, though probably not his true one."

Hoskins nodded. "Unlikely. Kim is as common as Jones,

making it a good cover name, but we'll ask South Korean intelligence for a closer reading. It's important to know whom he was working for, who ordered him to kill you."

Needham said, "Chinese?"

"Heretofore they've shown no interest in RyTech. It was the Soviets who trained and sustained the North Korean leadership, so KGB influence is the more likely." He cleared his throat. "Staying over for the hearing?"

"I've opted out." He got up. "Sceptre is the target of this fabricated hysteria, and Defense is RyTech's partner in Sceptre. So tell the Secretary I expect his considerable help as regards the Committee."

Hoskins swallowed. "SecDef's already pled your case at the White House, and got turned down."

"That was before I declined to testify. Describe the evolving situation and suggest he try again."

Hoskins said, "That may not motivate him, Guy. He can be damn bullheaded when he wants to be."

"So can I."

Twenty-One

In his office Guy watched the evening TV news, seeing Committee members welcome vituperative testimony from three members of the Coalition Against Military Murder: a defrocked priest, the hippie rabbi of a homosexual congregation, and a storefront pastor whose sideline was antinuclear activism. But when it came to Drs. Felberg and Printz the Committee treated them with the suspicion and contempt usually accorded prisoners in the dock. Guy was proud of his scientists' calm demeanor and replies that cited their security obligations to the nation. Silence earned them the threat of a contempt of Congress citation, and jailing unless they talked.

Guy turned off the TV and called Jake on the intercom. "Heard from Pyne?"

"Nada."

"I've been watching the hearings, Jake, and they're getting out of hand. Let's have dinner here and discuss."

"I'll notify my wife, sign a few things and join you."

Jake cut a portion of sauteed veal, swallowed, and sipped red wine. "Felberg and Printz were shaken by the day's events, Guy, though they didn't show it on camera. Took a hell of a beating."

"That's why we're moving into rescue mode." He looked at his watch. "Seven-forty. It's time for Hoskins to pull his oar, so get him on the phone and tell him to get his butt here in a hurry. I don't care what other commitments he has."

Jake wiped his lips with a napkin and picked up an extension phone. As Guy ate he could hear Jake's tone grow sharper, more insistent. Finally Jake snapped, "I don't care that he's meeting with the Secretary—get a note to him. Say it's in his urgent interest to meet with Mr. Ryan as soon as he can fly here. And I'll expect arrival confirmation. We're not going to sit around all night holding our dicks while Rob plays boy bureaucrat." Slamming down the receiver he turned to Guy. "Okay?"

"Couldn't have put it better. Finish your dinner, it could be a long night."

Seating himself, Needham said, "What do you want from Hoskins?"

"Remember how upset you got in Haiti? Leave this to me, Jake. It's *my* men and *my* company, and I'll do what I have to to protect them." He resumed eating under Needham's thoughtful gaze.

After a while the telephone began to ring.

When Rob Hoskins entered the office Jake and Guy were watching the eleven o'clock news. He pulled off his topcoat, tossed his hat at a chair and said irritably, "What the hell is this all about?"

Turning from the TV receiver Guy said, "Seen any of this crap, Rob?"

"Sure—we're keenly interested in what the media are saying—and we're concerned. Including the Secretary of

Defense. And we're sorry as hell about the Committee's treatment of your men.''

"The chainsaw killers," Needham remarked. "You should have been there, Rob—or had an observer from Defense. Mr. Ryan deserved that—and much more.''

Hoskins settled into a chair. "This a post mortem? I'm personally—''

"—Don't say sorry," Guy said in a hard voice. "Past time for regrets.''

"Yeah," Needham echoed. "Doctors Printz and Felberg were challenged and abused by the Committee. They may be jailed for contempt of Congress, along with Guy.''

Hoskins stared at his folded hands. "It's bad—no doubt about it, but the Secretary's not inclined to intervene—he takes his marching orders from the White House, where there is an evident lack of enthusiasm to become involved.''

Guy said, "It may surprise you, the Secretary and the President, to learn that I'm not inclined to suffer humiliation and jail with my two employees because the White House regards the matter as too delicate to become involved in. Rob, you're counting on my love of country to preserve the Sceptre secret, while moving not an inch in my behalf. That arrangement lacks elemental fairness.''

"Of course it's unfair—but I don't make the rules.''

"Rules went out the door—like that fellow who shelled ISR. You know—the Arab asshole with three passports—what was his name?''

"Achmed al-Maghrebi. Why bring him up?''

"I was thinking of his fate—jumped or was pushed from a Defense chopper over the Blue Ridge Mountains a couple of weeks ago. After interrogation by DSA. Remember?''

"Of course I remember," he said irritably. "What's he got to do with anything?''

Guy said, "The difference between us, Rob, is I have no intention of taking a fall.''

"Well, let's hope the Committee doesn't cite you and the others for contempt."

"Exactly. But, let's set aside hope and get practical. Every Congressman wants something for his home district—even Chairman Patruzzi, right?"

"I suppose so."

"You know better than that—they *do*, he does. And it's no secret most Congressman are battling the White House over budget cuts closing shipyards, military bases and airstrips. Patruzzi's been lobbying to keep open a Jersey naval repair facility that employs about six hundred constituents. To preserve it he's practically declared war on the Administration." Guy looked at Needham. "Any reason I should suffer for the President's frugality?"

Jake shook his head. "None whatever."

"I see a possible role in this for Roland Pyne, don't you?"

"Beginning to," Needham replied. "Yes, I do."

Hoskins shook his head wonderingly. "You've lost me. The repair yard's slated for closure, struck from Defense appropriations. Pyne can't change that."

"*You* can," Guy told him. "MDS is considerably more important than Patruzzi's shipyard, right?"

"No comparison. But, the Secretary knows there's no sentiment in the Administration for presenting Patruzzi with a significant political gift. Okay, I understand—you're asking for a tradeoff—Patruzzi wraps up the hearing in exchange for his repair yard, right?"

"Right."

"Not a chance. The Secretary isn't going to go trotting into the Oval Office for a special pleading that will benefit a senior member of the opposition party."

Guy came from behind his desk. "Press ever show any interest in that place where you briefed Jake and me? The Joint Study Committee?"

"Never heard of any."

"Suppose the press became curious?"

"We'd take down the plaque, move elsewhere." His eyes narrowed. "You'd tell the press about it? Who'd believe you?"

Needham got up and lifted the telephone from a small tape recorder. Partly rewinding the tape he said, "Listen."

From the recorder came Guy's voice: *". . . fellow who shelled ISR. You know—the Arab asshole with three passports—what was his name?"*

Hoskins: *"Achmad al-Maghrebi. Why bring him up?"*

Guy: *"I was thinking of his fate—jumped or was pushed from a Defense chopper over the Blue Ridge Mountains a couple of weeks ago. After interrogation by DSA. Remember?"*

Hoskins: *"Of course I remember—"*

Needham shut it off as Hoskins glared. "You tricked me."

Guy said, "This tape in the wrong hands could get some prick reporter a Pulitzer. My guess is the Secretary would prefer that not happen—not to mention yourself and the ensuing complications in your life. So I'm going to suggest you go back to Washington, see the Secretary at an early hour and engage his support. Unless Pyne informs me a deal has been cut with the Chairman, copies of that cassette will be provided free of charge to the major media. When Patruzzi ends the hearings on a favorable note you get the tape."

Hoskins got up and put on his topcoat, retrieved his hat. "I can't promise anything."

Guy stretched and yawned. "I think you understand how our interests coincide."

Hoskins grunted. "Graymail is what it is. And while we're on the subject of bad news, I have some for you. That Kim fellow, your would-be assassin, wasn't working for the NKs, or the ChiComs. His cipher pads and radio frequencies are standard KGB. Thought you should know."

Guy smiled thinly. "So if the Congress don't get me the Russkys will. Thanks for coming, Rob."

After Hoskins left the office Needham handed Guy the tape cassette. "Would you really make this public?"

"I don't know. Perhaps it won't come to that."

"You didn't sound surprised about Kim being a KGB agent."

"It's logical, Jake. If I'm killed the Soviets could work on Nicole and Gant, buy them out, and install their own front man—through Drach, say. Then turn Sceptre technology over to the USSR. It's the only country that wants to neutralize it, or has the ability to use it in their own interest. So I'm not surprised. Just wondering what they'll try next."

In the morning as Guy neared the office building he saw a clutch of reporters and TV cameramen beside the entrance, so he cut around the block and went in by the back way.

Jennie Knox was first on his appointment list, and after seating herself she said, "What I'm going to suggest has Mr. Needham's preliminary approval. Considering the public damage done to RyTech's image, and Committee suggestions that Professor Forster was killed by a National Guardsman *or* a RyTech guard—" She paused. "You recall the word *Gestapo* was used?"

"Painfully."

"Well, in view of the situation I'm recommending RyTech post a fifty-thousand dollar reward for evidence leading to the indictment of Forster's slayer. That should arouse a lot of interest, show RyTech's corporate concern over the tragedy, and illustrate pretty firmly that we think responsibility lies elsewhere than at our door. We'd hardly post a reward if we had any inkling that an ISR employee was responsible."

"I like the idea."

"Furthermore, someone in that crowd must have seen

Forster shot—probably more than one person. The money might well persuade individuals to step forward and exercise their civic duties. Disinterestedly, of course.''

"Do it."

She rose. "Forster left a wife—widow. She should be the first to know. When I phone her I'll suggest she summon the media and make the announcement.''

Guy nodded. "I could have thought of that—but then that's what I pay you for.''

"Mr. Needham suggested depositing the reward in a Baltimore bank account. To be paid on recommendation of the Maryland Attorney General. I just spoke with his office and his assistant said they'd cooperate. Turns out the AG is running for higher office and welcomes the publicity.''

"Let's allow informants to make statements anonymously.''

"Good point." She made a note and looked at Guy. "I know this is very hard on you, thanks to those Committee bastards. Do you think there's any possibility you'll have to go to jail?''

"That's the general direction," he told her, "but at this point anything can happen.''

Late in the day Roland Pyne's call came through. His voice was jovial as he said, "Good news, sir. In an about-face Chairman Patruzzi has decided he's been drilling a dry well. Privately he's told me the hearings will be concluded within two days. Though he can't say so in public he tenders apologies and expressed hope you won't hold it personally against him. Circumstances, he pointed out, often force national figures into situations they would rather avoid.''

"Aside from my lingering impression that the Chairman's a prick I bear him no special animosity.''

"Excellent. I must add that he found your posting so

large a reward very impressive. A brilliant stroke, sir, worthy of you and RyTech.''

''I liked it myself,'' Guy told him.

''And of course, you will not be called to testify. Consider the entire imbroglio at an end.''

Until next time, Guy thought. ''Patruzzi gets what he wanted and I'm allowed to retreat from the headlines. You collect your fee and I'm stuck with paying a fifty-thousand dollar reward.''

''Such are the burdens of wealth and power,'' said Pyne sententiously. ''You are young and I am old. Let me counsel you to become philosophical about such things. I've enjoyed our brief association, sir. Call on me at any time.''

With a thin laugh Guy replaced the receiver. Another three minutes, he thought, and the old windbag would have convinced me the coup was his.

He was preparing to leave when the scrambler phone rang and he heard Hoskins' voice. ''Satisfied, Mr. Ryan?''

''Tentatively.''

''I get the tape?''

''When the hearings end. Satisfied?''

''The Secretary was horrified, but decided the greater good would be served by giving you a helping hand.''

''So I anticipated,'' Guy told him. ''No hard feelings?''

''What do you expect me to say? You sandbagged me and I hurt all over.''

''It'll pass. I trust we'll resume mutual cooperation.''

''We have to. But in light of recent experience I plan to conduct the liaison more circumspectly.''

''At Oxford,'' Guy said, ''a learned don told me life is a continuing learning process. Failing that we vanish like the dinosaur.''

''Sage words.'' He paused. ''That dinner invitation still open?''

''Any time.'' He put aside the phone and breathed deeply, feeling at the end of a long, forced march. The ordeal had been gut-wrenching, the public pillory something he'd never experienced before.

Mrs. Paskow came in and said, "A lady is on the line, Mr. Ryan. At first I thought it was Mrs. Ryan, but the caller said she was your sister-in-law, Cristina."

"Did she say where she's calling from?"

"No, sir, but she sounded quite upset. Will you speak with her?"

He picked up the phone.

Twenty-Two

"Guy! I'm so glad I finally caught up with you. What I've seen on TV is very disturbing, and I need to know that you're all right."

"I'm fine," he told her, "and grateful for your call. In a couple of days the hearing will end, and, no, I won't have to go to jail."

"Oh, I'm so relieved—can't tell you how worried I've been. It's disgusting, what I've seen—imagine, painting you as some sort of villain. I could hardly believe it."

"Had difficulty myself," he said. "How are you? Don José?"

"Well, I'm fine, but father fell while riding and fractured his thigh. I'm in Seville at the hospital where he's recovering from the operation. He's very cross and impatient, and refused to let me notify you and Connie until just now."

"I'm sorry about the fall and glad he's mending. Give him fond wishes from me. Anything I can do to help?"

"I don't think so. The orthopedic surgeon is one of our finest, and a family friend. Between us we'll take good care of Don José." She paused. "Guy, there *is* one thing that's come up, and that's the auction of Al-Emir. Ali Mansour suddenly decided to hold the auction next week, and—"

"—*Prince* Ali Mansour?"

"Yes, the owner. You know him?"

"I did—at Vezelay."

"Isn't that interesting. Guy—when do you think I'll receive our share from the treasure auction?"

"Not for months, I'm afraid."

She sighed. "I'd been counting on it to pay my share of the syndication. Without it I can't properly bid. Guy, could you come to Dublin and back me? There's so much money involved I wouldn't feel comfortable bidding unless you were there. Besides, once you've seen our horse I'm sure you'll agree he's the best possible investment."

He thought it over. After the Committee ordeal a change of scene would improve his morale, and the time was opportune to visit RyTech's subsidiaries in Britain. The trip would combine business and therapy.

"Guy—you there?"

"Uh huh. Tentatively, I'll come. And I want Connie to join us. She might enjoy the show."

"By all means. That's six days from now, Guy, I'm so excited!"

"There's something else for you to think about in the meantime." He told her about the abandoned Texas ranch and its possibilities.

"Sounds marvelous and I'm anxious to see it. Perhaps I'll fly back with you. But—could you reserve a day to visit father? It would mean so much to him if you would."

"Of course," he said, "I'll plan on it."

"The Gresham is the place to stay in Dublin."

"Then that's where we'll see you."

So far so good, he thought as he placed a call to his wife. Cristina had been businesslike, with no overtures or personal implications, so they would make the occasion a family reunion. Besides, it was important for Cris to see how close he and Connie had become.

After the maid's voice, Connie came on and said,

"What's been printed here about RyTech makes me concerned, Guy. Is—"

"That's behind us," he told her, and summarized her sister's call.

Connie said, "Guy, don't you realize that conflicts with my show? I can't possibly get away. Cris wouldn't know, but I really expected *you* to bear it in mind."

"I *am* sorry," he said. "It's on my calendar but I never thought to look. The past week has had me pretty disoriented."

"Of course, and I'm sorry. But you deserve a vacation, and if the timing's right I'll meet you in Seville. It was wretched of Cris not to let me know about father, but she's so thoughtless. And you really should be in Dublin to keep her out of trouble. After all, you *are* the man of the family."

"I suppose so," he said reluctantly. "Well, I'll stay for the auction and come over to Paris."

He was pondering the trip when Jake Needham came in and said, "You did it again, Chief. Committee Counsel just phoned to say you and the ISR officers won't be recalled. He sounded unprofessionally bitter."

"To be expected," Guy said. "I do hate sore losers."

"The icing on the cake," Needham remarked, "would be having our reward produce Forster's killer." He looked at his watch. "Can't remember when I've left here so early. Not quite six."

"Next week I'll be away so you can set your own hours." He told Jake his travel plans and said, "Tomorrow or next day I'll want to go over our medical research facilities, brief myself before leaving."

Jake nodded. "I'll get background papers together." He started to leave but stopped. "We're in much better shape than forty-eight hours ago, thanks to your creative maneuvers. Haiti—the Committee—you're batting a thousand."

Before Mrs. Paskow left Guy dictated his itinerary to the

research facilities, and told her to schedule the Lear for the trip.

Later, walking up Park Avenue, Guy began thinking of the auction. His agreement to attend had assumed Connie would be along. Now he found himself wondering whether being in Dublin with Cristina could be managed without risk. He felt confident of himself—but of Cristina he was far from sure.

Two days later Nigel Palfrey phoned, and Guy met him at the Oak Room for lunch. Over drinks Palfrey said, "Been toolin' around a bit, Guy. Did a security survey of the Queen's Washington premises and told the Ambassador he hadn't a prayer against a determined bunch of nasties. Unlike Whitehall chaps, I examined the Embassy as a terrorist would. Slay the gate guards, hose an automatic weapon for intimidation, and by George, you're in. Files, cipher room, hostages, all at your disposal." He shook his head. "Appallingly simple to bring off. In total candor I'd much rather keep the baddies out than mount a slam-bang later on." He sipped his Scotch and motioned for a refill. "The Ambassador is one of those effete chaps allergic to bloodshed—the thought of same makes him blanch. Exhibits a monstrous aversion to SAS and all our doin's, feels we're cannibals lustin' for human blood." He grimaced broadly. "Took a personal dislike to me, sad to say; feels I'm a traitor to Cambridge and the profession of pacific negotiation." He drained his glass. "Could all be true, alas."

Guy smiled. "I can see you're all broken up, Nigel."

"Cawn't say, rahlly, if ever I'll recover." He grimaced fruitily. "All in a week's work, what?"

"Stay around a few days and fly back with me. I have some work in England, then Ireland."

"Love to—really would, but I'm off tonight. Ah—Ireland, you say?"

"There's a RyTech medical research facility near Galway, another at Manchester. But the main purpose of the trip is to help my sister-in-law buy an Arab stud at Dublin."

"Will you touch base with Consuela?"

"Of course."

Over mixed grill Guy told him about the attempt by Counihan's men, and his near assassination on Cheju Island.

Palfrey listened unemotionally, finally saying, "The Korean's no further threat, but the Irish laddies remain. And yet you're off to Eire. Guy, you don't even now appreciate how fetching a target you are for the crazies."

"What do you suggest I do? Lock myself in a vault?"

"Come off it, mate. What you have to realize is that because the Geneva snatch squad was Irish, it doesn't end there. You'd have no reason to know, but for long years the IRA has been associated with some very creepy blokes. With the PLO they have a fraternal relationship. The IRA's Marxist arm is directly supported by the USSR, and performs surrogate jobs where the KGB doesn't want to be seen. Given related circumstances, I'd say the KGB was behind that Geneva assault."

Guy nodded thoughtfully, reminded of the Korean KGB agent. To change the subject he said, "Remember Ali Mansour at Vezelay?"

"The pampered little prince? Very big in OPEC now—family connections."

"It's his stallion we want to buy."

"Then have it carefully vetted, Guy. Very carefully, indeed. Prince Ali's no stranger to sharp practice. Tried paying chaps to write his terms, I remember. But for his wealth and station he'd have been turned out of Vezelay. Unsavory feller." He sighed. "Longer I live, fewer I like—outsiders, that is."

"Outsiders?"

"Outside the Special Air Service." Glancing at Guy he

flushed. "Your honorable self excepted. By the way, when you're in London a note at the Special Forces Club will always reach me; Herbert Crescent, Knightsbridge."

They parted at the Plaza fountain and Guy walked over to F.A.O. Schwarz where he bought an exquisite talking doll for Gloria.

He carried it back to his office, eager to see her pleased expression when he gave it to her in Paris.

During the afternoon meeting with Jake Needham, the general counsel said, "It's been brought forcibly to my attention that my predecessor let things slide. Last year an Equal Opportunity suit was filed against RyTech by a so-called public interest law firm in Texas. Stoner responded initially but as discovery proceeded, failed to make timely filings. Because of that the plaintiffs—a small and obscure group of Apaches—were almost awarded a default judgment. Fortunately we got back into court in time, thanks to one of my new assistants who recalled a law journal note on the litigation, and took the trouble to determine where it stood. Now the case will proceed on its merits."

"Commendable initiative."

"With that appalling discovery in mind I had the Lexis electronic system searched for other pending litigation and found a scattering of workmen's comp cases that should never have reached court and should have been settled by the insurer with our acquiescence. Those are now being taken care of. SEC inquiries have gone unanswered for months and we're now getting on top of them—after I pleaded with their general counsel to give us additional time." He shook his head. "Just before I took over, another storefront firm filed a class action suit against RyTech alleging overcharges to the Government and fraudulent accounting practices."

"RyTech guilty?"

"I don't know. Frank Purcell is examining the allegations and will render an opinion. If Farley Johns allowed or encouraged fraudulent overcharges and deceptive accounting we have a corporate responsibility to make restitution."

"Of course."

"After which I'd recommend pursuing civil or criminal charges against Johns."

"By all means. Any more swell news?"

Jake smiled. "That's the downside. The good news is we're becoming aware of past deficiencies that I won't let happen again. Now, I'm in touch with the New York FBI office about your stepmother's death. They received the Teterboro sabotage report from NTSB, but without witnesses they frankly hold out little hope of identifying the killer. Anyone with brief access to the chopper and the ability to detonate the bomb could have done it. Or, two people: one to place it, one to explode it. The Bureau has had men fine-combing the route the chase car must have taken, and found nothing. They thought the signal transmitter might have been discarded after use, but apparently not."

Guy said, "If I could determine a motive for her murder that would narrow the field. The bomb wasn't meant for me, because I was in Europe. So it comes down to who gained by her death?" His eyes moistened and he looked away. "Could private investigators help?"

"I don't think so," Needham said sympathetically. "The Bureau emphasized the lack of witnesses, so my only thought is to post a reward for information—as we've done in the Forster case. Maybe some low-level participant would talk for money and a grant of immunity."

"How large a reward?"

"Say a hundred thousand to start—it can always increase."

Guy nodded. "I want to make an all-out effort to get her killers."

"Okay, I'll work out details with the DA, the Bureau

and the insurers; they might want to contribute to the reward. Then announce it in the New York, Jersey and Long Island papers—Jenny Knox can handle that part."

"Anything from Baltimore?"

"A few calls to the police from the usual confessional lunatics. Nothing solid. And Roland Pyne's bill is in. For fifty thousand."

Guy frowned as he considered the demand. "Sounds excessive to me, Jake. What's your opinion?"

"I suggest we pay him ten thousand for briefing you and another ten for dealing with Chairman Patruzzi. Twenty in all."

"That sounds more reasonable to me."

"Even that's a lot of money, Guy, but when you hire a political lawyer, an influence peddler, you're entering a zone that has nothing to do with the normal practice of law, the courts." He made a note.

"Will twenty thousand satisfy Pyne?"

"I think so. After all, he got considerable media exposure at no cost to himself. I'll send a check with a stroking letter."

Mrs. Paskow's voice came through the intercom. "Mr. Ryan, am I interrupting?"

"Go ahead." He saw Needham get up and signaled the meeting was over. "What is it?"

"A man down at the guard desk says it's very important to see you. No one else, only you."

"Who is he?"

"A William Sonetsky from Teterboro—said you would remember him."

"I do," Guy said with quickening interest. "Please have him come up."

When Mrs. Paskow brought in his visitor, Guy rose and went around his desk to receive him. The aircraft technician wore a grease-smudged sheepskin coat and work dungarees. As they shook hands he said, "I apologize for coming like this, but I wanted to make up for lost time." He opened a canvas carryall and paused. "I guess I better explain . . . We were clearing away parts of the chopper wreckage when one of the men straightened a twisted sheet of fuselage metal and found this." He drew out a bulky manila envelope and opened it on Guy's desk.

Marguerite's black velvet handbag. Last seen at Sean's funeral.

As Guy stared at it Sonetsky said, "I'm sorry it wasn't found before, Mr. Ryan, but those things happen. Anyway, from the credit cards inside I knew it was Mrs. Ryan's— and I thought you'd want it right away."

"I do," Guy said, feeling suddenly gripped by sadness, "and I appreciate you bringing it to me."

Sonetsky nodded. "Glad to. Uh—any leads on—?"

"Afraid not—but you never know, right?"

"Right. Well, maybe the Bureau boys will get an inspiration."

"Maybe." Guy thanked him again, and walked him to the door. When Sonetsky was gone, Guy went to his desk and opened the handbag, feeling eerily close to the woman who had owned it. The bag had been with Marguerite at her death and through a strange circumstance come at last to the stepson who revered and loved her.

Slowly he removed the contents: a warped, dried-out leather case for car and house keys; a pair of gold earrings; remains of a lipstick; a small embroidered handkerchief; credit cards from American Express, Lord & Taylor, Bonwit Teller, Neiman Marcus and others; a folder of Travelers Checks for the cruise she was denied, and—a crumpled envelope unsealed by immersion and taped closed. Probably by Sonetsky.

He smoothed the envelope with the edge of his hand and read the address in handwriting now faded and smeared.

His name was there, the address of his apartment, even

the zip code, but no stamp—could have soaked off. He searched the lining for it, found nothing.

Tearing the envelope as little as possible he drew out several folded sheets.

As with the address, Marguerite's writing was smeared and faded, but under his lamp's strong light he was able to make out the date—the day of her death. Then:

Dearest Guy:

Were you here rather than abroad I should not be writing this. Instead, we would have talked as mother and son, you listening respectfully as you always have.

Since Sean's death I've noticed things at Eastover that are causing me growing concern. Interrupted telephone conversations, dogs barking on the grounds when the servants could find no cause. A broken pane in the library window yet the alarm system did not sound. At night I've heard movement in the darkness, though the servants were all in bed.

You know me too well to think me seized of vapors, dear son, or hallucinating in the night. Indeed, I believe there is a basis for all these disconcerting happenings, and that is one reason I decided to go on an extended cruise. Aboard ship and among other people I will feel safer than I do as I write. The extent of my concern may be measured by that fact that I am not trusting this letter to be mailed from Eastover or handled by the local post. I will mail it to you from dockside so that I can depend on its delivery.

So, to the point: As secretary of our holding company, for years I received canceled checks from banking institutions and turned them over to your father. After his death I decided to withdraw from those duties, in preparation for which I began to examine checks and relate expenditures to what I believed were normal recipients. For the first time, to my apprehension, I discovered that large amounts of money had been received by payees I was unfamiliar with. A village accountant helped me with the work, and through directories, phone calls and unanswered letters Glenn Moorsby discovered that half a dozen of these large-sum payees existed only on paper. Ingenuously, I'm afraid, I asked Farley Johns for explanations. He became flustered and told me he would inquire of Paul Edmonds who, according to Farley, had authorized the suspect payments. Edmonds was out of town so I decided to bide my time. It was then that the events I described began taking place. My calls to Edmonds have gone unanswered for reasons I consider specious. Johns is uncommunicative, asserting his need to consult higher authority. Perhaps so, but it is equally possible that Farley needs time to juggle the books and so reconcile and explain the absence of more than three million dollars.

Unless I receive satisfactory explanations on my return I will be convinced that a criminal conspiracy has taken place. Now that you have this information you will know what steps to take.

I feel badly over thrusting this burden on you as I leave for so many weeks away. But having considered all aspects lengthily I believe I must do so, trusting as always that you will know best what to do.

> With fondest love,
> Marguerite

P.S. Please cable me what to bring Gloria from Japan. I'm so anxious to see her on my return.

Rigidly, Guy gazed at the water-pocked pages, realized his face was cold with perspiration. His fingers were stiff as he laid the pages aside and buried his face in his hands.

Silent sobs shook his body until he was able to steady himself. Wiping his face and eyes he stared at the message from the dead; the unsent letter that explained so much, established a motive for her death.

". . . trusting as always," he read hoarsely, "that you will know best what to do."

Refolding the stained sheets he restored them to the envelope.

Her lifelong faith in him *was* justified, he told himself, and thanks to her he now knew what to do.

Avenge her murder.

BOOK FOUR

Twenty-Three

After a restless, vision-haunted night, Guy rose early, drank a glass of orange juice, and jogged briskly to his fitness club. The place was opening when he arrived, and he had the Nautilus machines to himself for a vigorous workout. After Jacuzzi and massage he left feeling revived.

While he was exercising his body, his mind had been reviewing Marguerite's letter and sorting alternate responses to the information it contained. Surfacing her suspicions to Johns and Edmonds was the worst move Marguerite could have made, resulting as it did in her death. But his stepmother had always believed in the essential goodness of human nature and her life had been sheltered. Unlike his own.

Guy would deal with Johns and Edmonds—he had known that before he finished reading her letter. But he would not repeat her error by confronting those once-trusted men directly. He would deal with them on their own treacherous terms. By stealth and duplicity.

A taxi took him up Roosevelt Drive and across the Triborough Bridge. Near Hunts Point market he paid the cabbie and walked to a used car lot. For four hundred dollars he bought a Dodge junker with fair rubber, had a new battery installed and gave the salesman an extra fifty for license plates.

After filling the tank Guy drove across the Bronx and took the Hutchinson River Parkway north to Pelham. Farley Johns' house was off Colonial Avenue in a section of spacious homes half a century old. Tall maple trees, hedges and flower borders, two-car garages, and children with sleds and scooters. Guy drove past the house twice, parked down the block and watched for signs of activity. After half an hour a well-dressed woman left by the rear door and entered the garage. The overhead door opened and she drove away in a brown Cadillac sedan. Guy glimpsed a smaller car in its stall.

At a filling station he used the pay phone and asked for the lady of the house. A maid's voice said she wasn't there, but would Mister do?

"Not unless he wants to take her appointment."

"Oh, she's going to keep it if that's your problem. Just be patient, she's on her way."

"Well, she said it was important, so—"

"You better believe it. Wants to look her very best for that ladies club thing—the Eastern Star election. Last year she only missed Matron by a few votes. It'll kill her if she don't make it tonight."

"I can imagine. Well, thanks, dearie—oh, here she comes now."

He hung up with a thin smile, looked up Glenn Moorsby's number and arranged to see the accountant at his house. Two hours later Guy knocked on the door.

Seated at the accountant's work-laden dining table Guy thanked Moorsby for accommodating him on a Saturday afternoon. Moorsby, who had thin blond hair and a skimpy mustache, said, "Glad to, Mr. Ryan. It gives me an opportunity to say how sorry I am about your stepmother's death—we were at the funeral but I guess you didn't notice me."

280

"Or anyone." He looked around at the file-strewn room. "Do you have those holding company transactions you worked on with her? The canceled checks, what you found out about the phony payees?"

"I do. And I was wondering whether anyone was going to pursue it further." He shook his head. "She was a wonderful lady, so thoughtful, courteous—reminded me of my own mother."

"She had that quality," Guy agreed. "Is the material at your office?"

"No—considering the implications I decided to put it all in a safe place." He got up. "Come with me."

They went down wooden steps into the basement. Moorsby turned on a lightbulb and took a screwdriver from a workbench. He walked over to a disconnected, rusted washing machine and unscrewed the front panel. He reached into the recess and drew out a cardboard box that once held a large doll.

Handing it to him the accountant said, "I'm glad you're not letting it drop. This sort of fraud makes any honest person sick. But what surprised me was the transparency of the scam—except for disguising the payees, no real effort appeared to have been made to conceal the scam. I was with IRS for four years and saw a good deal of corporate hanky-panky, but this type of fraudulent conversion is easy to detect."

"And should have been, right?"

"Except that the financial controls were in the hands of the embezzlers." He turned off the light and led Guy back to the dining room where Guy opened the box. Moorsby took several sheets of lined yellow paper from atop bundles of checks and said, "You'll find the false payees listed here, with a running account of my discoveries."

Guy glanced at the sheets and returned them to the box. "Did my stepmother pay you for your work?"

"No, and I was beginning to wonder where to submit my bill—whether I should."

"If you'll make it up now, I'll be glad to take care of it."

"Great. I'd appreciate that." He consulted a ledger and began figuring.

The charges were less than six hundred dollars. Guy got out his checkbook and said, "Has anyone asked you about working with Mrs. Ryan?"

"You mean, like Mr. Johns or Edmonds?"

"That's what I mean."

"No, but I heard your stepmother mention my name to Mr. Johns when she telephoned him from my office. That worried me, but with her dead I suppose they don't feel threatened." He peered through rimless lenses. "Maybe I *should* mention this, Mr. Ryan. My office was broken into one night, file drawers pried open and two calculators stolen. The loss was less than my insurance deductible so I didn't file a claim. Now—"

"Report it to Chief Weston?"

"Why bother him? Probably a couple of kids from the city stealing stuff they could sell to buy dope."

"Or possibly not," Guy said, "but it concerns me. A theft of three million dollars carries risks to everyone involved. I'd like you and your wife to take a few days' vacation at my expense. Could you do that for me? Is there someplace you'd like to go?"

"Well, we could visit her folks in Albany, but—"

"I'd like you to leave now. Would you mind lending me a key? I want to go over these checks and your notes so I'll understand exactly what went on. It would be a great service to me. Suppose I make out a check for a thousand dollars—that would cover your bill plus gas for the trip."

"And then some," he said enthusiastically.

"If you don't mind I prefer you not mention our meeting to Mrs. Moorsby."

"I understand."

Guy wrote the check and gave it to him. "I'm going out for lunch," he told the accountant, "and when I get back the house will be empty?"

"That's right."

"I'll take good care of things," he promised, and drove to Hampton Bays where he found a year-round restaurant that provided a good seafood meal.

At Moorsby's he pulled his Dodge into the vacant garage and entered the house. For a while he studied the accounting summary and then he dialed the home of Farley Johns.

The maid must have left because Johns answered in an irritable tone. Speaking nasally through aluminum foil wrapped over the mouthpiece, Guy said, "Mr. Johns, I don't think you know me, but I'm the accountant who worked with the late Mrs. Sean Ryan on her holding company checks."

"Let's see—Moorsby, that it? Marguerite once mentioned your name."

"Moorsby it is. Glad you remember, sir."

"What is it you want?"

Humbly, Guy said, "Well, she died before paying my bill for the work I put in, and I thought you might be willing to settle it—your name came up so frequently in my findings."

A long pause. Before he could reply Guy said, "And then there's all those checks made out to paper payees. Let's see, they total up to—three million one hundred thousand and forty-five dollars. I have them in front of me, and if I were you I wouldn't want them to get into the wrong hands."

Stiffly, Johns said, "How do I know you're Moorsby? Could be anyone calling."

"Well, if you want to be sure, look me up in the yellow pages. I'm home now—office shut for the afternoon. Glenn Moorsby—two n's. I'll wait for your call."

He hung up and drank a glass of water in the kitchen. The phone rang before he reached the table. "Moorsby?

Farley Johns here. All right, you're who you say you are. What were we talking about?"

Guy smiled. "About these checks and such. I'd be glad to have them off my hands, but I'd want to be compensated."

"I see." The voice grew chilly. "How large a compensation did you have in mind?"

"Let's say thirty thousand, Mr. Johns. Considering what's involved that's a small sum."

"*Thirty*—? You're crazy," he exploded.

"Why, Mr. Johns, that's not even one percent of the total embezzlement. I didn't think you'd be such a skinflint. You *or* Mr. Edmonds . . ."

"That's outrageous!"

"Well, I can always offer what I've got to Mrs. Ryan's children. I've heard Mr. Guy Ryan is generous where family is concerned."

"Listen here, Moorsby, get such thoughts out of your head. Where do you think I'd be able to get that much money?"

Guy glanced down at Moorsby's reconciliation sheet. "You socked away close to six hundred thousand in that Carbide Specialties account—Tucson, remember? Draw a check on it, Mr. Johns."

Another silence as the former comptroller thought it over. Finally he said, "I'll have to consult Mr. Edmonds and get back to you."

"That's not satisfactory. You'll bring a check to me tonight and get what I have. I've waited too long, Mr. Johns, and now it's show or tell time. I'll send my wife out and expect you here at eight." He described the house and location. "I'll have my bill ready."

"Damn you, extortion is a very serious crime."

"Nothing compared to what you and your partner have been getting away with. Five to ten years in Lewisburg if the Ryans find out about it."

Johns was breathing heavily. In a choked voice he said, "I'll be there, you damn bastard," and slammed down the phone.

Guy poured a glass of sherry and lay down on the daybed for a nap.

When he woke it was after six and darkness had fallen outside. He ate a bowl of cereal, drank a glass of milk and rinsed the utensils in the kitchen sink.

At the basement workbench he found a thick dowel and cut two four-inch pieces, joined them securely with a two-foot length of leader wire. He wrapped the garrote around an iron pole stanchion and pulled with all his strength. Nothing gave.

He coiled the garrote in his outside pocket, got out the Walther he customarily carried and checked magazine and action. Before returning it to his shoulder holster, Guy snapped a shell into the firing chamber and set the safety.

The time was now seven. Both floors of the small house were dark. He pulled down all the shades, and in the dining room turned on a low-wattage work lamp.

He unlocked the front door, moved a comfortable chair into a dark corner of the living room, and sat down to wait.

Soon his ears became accustomed to the silence of a small village after dark. People were in their homes having dinner, watching TV. Kids at MacDonald's, the video arcade. People who led comfortable lives undisturbed by anything except movie violence. An isolated, satisfactory existence, he mused. Then he got out his pistol and laid it in his lap. Occasionally he heard a distant car, but none neared Moorsby's house.

He was beginning to wonder whether Farley Johns was going to respond when he heard stealthy steps across the front porch.

The door pushed open and a masked man entered the room.

Twenty-Four

Closing the door quietly the man called, "Mr. Moorsby, I'm here," but the voice wasn't Farley Johns'.

Reaching into his pocket the man called, "Where are you?"

"Dining room," Guy snapped. "By the light."

Guy's eyes were adjusted to the darkness, the masked man's weren't. Drawing a handgun from his coat pocket, the man began walking toward the light. As he passed, Guy tripped and booted him forward, heard the gun clatter from his hand.

Gripping the Walther, Guy sprang from the chair and kicked the masked man's head as he tried to rise. The man yelped and rolled away, scrambling for his gun. Guy kicked his belly and the man howled.

"Face down," Guy ordered, "you're covered."

Groaning, the man lay flat, hands covering his damaged crotch. Guy set a knee on his lower spine and stuck the pistol muzzle into his collar. With the other hand he jerked off the knitted ski mask, releasing a mass of dark, greasy hair. Then he looped the garrote around the prone man's throat and tightened it. The man gasped and flopped like a dying shark. Guy released tension. "You're not Mr.

Johns," he said, "and I'm not Moorsby, so we'll talk things over."

"Fuck yourself," the man croaked, "you got nothin' on me."

"Try attempted murder."

"Nah, I was only to scare him, take the stuff. Let me up, you can't prove nothin'."

"I don't have to. Carrying a weapon you broke into a house. You could be shot and no questions asked. Where's your car?"

"Around the block. Take it, keys in my pocket."

"Do much work for Johns?"

"Now and then. Pays good."

In the back of Guy's mind something stirred. "How much for the chopper job?"

The man began to struggle until Guy jerked the noose. "Jesus, pal, take it easy, you could choke me."

"Talk—the chopper job."

"That—Christ, pal, that wire's cuttin' flesh."

"How much?"

"Five."

"Five what?"

"Thousand. Okay, I tole you. You Moorsby's muscle or somethin'?" he whined.

"A friend," Guy said hoarsely. A surge of red seemed to blot his vision, his body was icy. He licked dry lips. He wanted to kill Marguerite's murderer, but something kept him from strangling him. With an effort he said, "How much for this job?"

"Five hundred. After I turn over the stuff to Johns. Hey, we could split it?" A sudden lurch unseated Guy who went sideways, loosening the garrote. The man kicked him in the ribs and went for his gun.

Guy rolled away, came up holding the Walther as the man grabbed his pistol. "Drop it," Guy snapped, but the man snarled, "I got nothin' to lose," and aimed. Guy spun

287

aside as the gun went off. The bullet whipped past his head and Guy fired reflexively—two rapid shots. He was sighting a third when the man clutched his throat; rising to his knees, he fell back, head in the fireplace.

Cautiously, Guy went to him, saw the blue entrance hole through the Adam's apple, and with his left hand felt for pulse. The body shuddered and the mouth fell open.

Guy stood up and holstered his Walther. From the floor he recovered his garrote and picked up the man's Colt pistol—a .38. He wiped his face and considered what to do.

From the kitchen he brought paper towels and shoved them under the man's head to absorb blood. He turned on a dim lamp and collected the three ejected shells. With the knitted face mask he dropped them in a plastic kitchen bag and went through the dead man's pockets. One produced an extra Colt magazine, another, eight dollars and change. A scrap of paper held Farley Johns' phone number and street address. Pontiac keys, and a billfold in the hip pocket.

Visible under the plastic insert was a RyTech employee card. The name on it was Dominic D'Angelo. Photo and face matched. Five feet eleven, one seventy pounds. Job: aircraft maintenance.

His jaw muscles hardened. For five thousand bloody dollars this creep had killed Marguerite Ryan, the one human being who had made his childhood bearable. Guy felt like slicing off his face.

This was no time to give way to emotion. There was work to be done, and it was going to be a long night.

He cleaned away signs of the struggle, sifted fireplace ashes until he found his two smashed bullets, searched the far end of the room until he saw the sofa puncture made by D'Angelo's bullet, decided it would go unnoticed.

He locked the front door and walked around the block until he found the Pontiac. D'Angelo's keys fitted, and wearing gloves he drove it behind Moorsby's house.

Taking out the RyTech card he replaced the billfold in the dead man's hip pocket. Quarter to nine.

The large exit wound was dark with clotted blood. Guy pulled the ski mask over D'Angelo's head and carried the body out to the Pontiac, propping it in the passenger seat. He pocketed the Colt .38 along with the spare magazine. Then he drove southeast to a wild, deserted stretch along Moriches Bay.

When headlights showed a thick pinetree ahead, Guy accelerated and bailed out on grass-covered sand. The Pontiac slammed into the tree. Guy got up and brushed himself off.

Headlights were still on, engine groaning, rear tires spinning in the sand. He reached over and dragged the body into upright position behind the wheel. Then he closed the door and walked from the car.

From fifty feet he sighted the Colt pistol on the gas tank and fired twice before the tank exploded. The concussion wave whooshed past him, and in the brilliant light of the burning car he collected the ejected .38 shells. He extracted the partly empty magazine from the Colt and tossed it into the flaming car, then slapped the spare magazine into the pistol's grip. Treading brown sea grass he went back to the dark road.

It took twenty minutes to walk to the house. He went in, rechecked for signs of the struggle, and added shells and bloody paper towels to the plastic trash bag before sealing the top.

From the dining room table he took the cardboard box D'Angelo had come for, left the table, and turned off lights. Moorsby would never know, he hoped, what had gone on in his absence. He set the door lock and was leaving when the telephone began to ring. Family friend, or—Farley Johns?

The phone was still ringing when he shut the front door.

He backed the Dodge out of the garage and closed the doors.

Ten o'clock.

From the quiet village he drove to a commercial dump and tossed the plastic bag among accumulated trash. Then he drove west, picking up the highway near Brookhaven Airport.

On his way to Pelham.

Twenty-Five

At midnight he drove past Farley Johns' house and saw a light in the downstairs hall, another in a bedroom window. The Cadillac was not in the garage. Late voting at the lodge, he told himself.

The gas station four blocks away was dark but the pay phone was working. Farley Johns answered cautiously. "Who's this?"

"Dom, pal, who the hell you think?" Guy covered the mouthpiece with gloved fingers, his voice imitated D'Angelo's coarse accents.

"Listen, damn it, I told you never call me here."

"Well, fuck you, pal," Guy sneered. "I got problems, too."

"You sound . . . different . . ."

"Stress, pal, an' a hoarse throat—it's cold out on the Island." Guy hoped Johns would buy the explanation. "So, I got the stuff for you."

Johns hesitated. "What about the—guy?"

"Taken care of. Where's my five green?"

"It's late, make it tomorrow night—I'll phone you."

"Tomorrow?" he jeered, "don't hand me that *domani* crap. I'm in a hurry, pal, like you couldn't believe. So get your ass off the soft bed an' drag it here. Chevron station. Your car an' mine."

"Listen—where the hell were you when I phoned the house?"

"Gone."

"Nobody answered."

Guy laughed coarsely. "Don't surprise me none. Quit stallin'—it's cold out here. Get movin'." He hung up and drove partway back. He left the Dodge in an alley and jogged to the house, made it to the garage and got into the rear seat of the compact. Kneeling on the floor, he waited.

In a few minutes the back door slammed and he saw Farley Johns hurrying toward the garage. Flattening himself against the floor, Guy heard Johns get in, shut the door and start the engine. He backed out so fast the car weaved from side to side, slid on street ice. Cursing, Johns spun the wheel and accelerated down the street. Guy glanced up and saw his features set and furious.

Four blocks and the compact bounced into the gas station, braked hard, and Johns peered around muttering.

Guy slid the Colt muzzle against the back of Johns' neck. Johns yelped. Soothingly Guy said, "Dom couldn't make it."

He sat on the back seat and leaned forward. "You've ordered your last killing, Farley. Dom's in custody." His left hand shoved D'Angelo's RyTech card in front of Johns' face. "Telling everything he knows about you—the five grand for Marguerite's murder, the Moorsby job that failed."

"He's a damn liar," Johns said defiantly, but his jaw trembled. "Then—it was you on the phone . . . ?"

"I do Bogart imitations, too—*schweethot*—and I wanted a talk with you before the cops come. If you're lucky they'll take you before the Chapter voting ends."

Johns gasped, *"How did you—?"*

"Never mind. Point is I have everything Marguerite and

Glenn Moorsby discovered—before you had her killed. Dom gets immunity for testifying and you take the fall. Where's Edmonds?''

"I—I don't know."

"You cover for him even now? No, you wouldn't have sent D'Angelo to Moorsby without checking with Edmonds. You let him know the accountant wanted a payoff, let him decide what had to be done. Edmonds will be dealt with and you can pare a few years off your sentence by testifying against him—but that's up to you. How long ago did the embezzling start?''

"Four—four years," Johns said after a drawnout silence. "It was Edmonds' fault, *his* idea. He found out my accounts were short, threatened to jail me unless I helped him milk RyTech."

"What was the split?"

"Two-thirds for him."

"And a third for you. One effortless million. No wonder you left my employ without argument. Where's it stashed?''

Setting his jaw, Johns shook his head.

Guy looped the garrote around his throat and tightened. Johns' body jerked upward against the wheel, eyes bulging as fingers clawed at the sunken wire. Suddenly Guy released tension and Johns snapped forward. His throat made dry retching sounds.

"Not worth it," Guy admonished. "The money can be traced. I want the answer now." The garrote pulled Johns back against the seat. "Now," Guy repeated and loosened the wire.

"Royal Bank of Canada," he wheezed. "Toronto."

"All of it?"

"Except for Tucson."

"And Edmonds?"

"Never told me."

"Well, I'll ask him the same question. What made you two think you could get away with it—under Sean's nose?''

293

"Something—Edmonds had something on Sean—your father."

"Like what? Keep talking, this is the time to spill your guts."

"Something in Dublin was all he ever said. When Sean was young. That's why your father couldn't go back to Ireland. Edmonds never said he threatened your father, just that he would if we were found out."

"But Marguerite found out and you had her killed." Rage boiled within him.

"It was Edmonds' order. Paul made me have it done." Tears streamed down his cheeks. "I didn't want to—she was a wonderful woman."

"You sicken me!" Tears welled in his eyes. He blotted them on his coat sleeve. "Edmonds waiting to hear about Moorsby?"

"Yes."

"All right. We're going to walk over to that phone. You'll call him and set up a meeting. Tell him it's urgent, but don't frighten him. Say it can't be done by phone."

"It's late—he may not want to come."

"Impress him with the importance of your information—say you need immediate guidance, understand?"

"Yes," he whispered.

"Imply it has to do with Moorsby, without saying so. Now, where is he likely to want to meet you?"

"Just outside Bronxville there's a bar—the Rustic Cabin—hillbilly music, strippers." His expression showed distaste. "We'd meet there because no one we know would go to such a place."

Guy grunted. "After all you have your standards. Tell him the Rustic Cabin parking lot. What does he drive?"

"Jaguar sedan—or Mercedes coupe."

"Get out slowly."

He followed Johns to the telephone and supplied change. After half a dozen rings Paul Edmonds answered.

Guy monitored both voices to ensure Johns' compliance, and after Edmonds surlily agreed to meet in an hour, Guy ended the exchange. As they left the phone Guy saw a patrol car move slowly by. Johns gasped but Guy said, "Keep moving—unless you want to surrender now and save them trouble." He looked at his watch. "Arrest warrant should be ready. Wonder how your wife and children will take it, Farley? Demoted from comptroller to lifer. I'm glad they don't use the chair in this state. In years ahead I'll enjoy thinking of you behind bars. They say the best way for a skinny fellow like you to survive is to find a big macho protector. That way the other cons don't hassle you. Visiting's once a week—you stare at your wife through Plexiglas and whisper through monitored phones. I hear most wives come pretty regularly the first year—to keep up appearances—but after that visits drop off. Five years and you get a Christmas card, maybe a bag of candy from the kids. By then you're divorced and friendless—except for that big gorilla who treats you like a wife."

He opened the passenger door and got in. Johns got behind the wheel. Half sobbing he cried, "Why don't you kill me, get it over with?"

"Too easy. I want your suffering prolonged. Arrest, trial—the whole sordid scenario. If you ever come up for parole, say twenty-five years hence, I'll use all the influence RyTech has to make certain you die in prison. So, go home, Farley. Pack toothbrush and shaving cream—they'll supply a special razor in jail—and tell your wife what to expect. I'll wait around until the cops appear—wouldn't miss the spectacle." He turned the ignition key, starting the engine. "And if you're thinking of warning Edmonds what lies ahead you'd do yourself a disservice. If he runs to Canada, say, or Brazil, you'd have nothing to trade. Besides, you say he forced you into the conspiracy, so—"

"He *did*, damn him!" he blurted, then fell silent as his gaze searched Guy's face. "You're going to kill him."

"Drive slowly down the street, take a right, a left and I'll get out where I left my car."

Stolidly, face ashen, Farley Johns followed Guy's orders. He stopped the car and Guy got out. "Drive home, Farley," he told him, "I'll be close behind."

When Johns' taillights were far down the block Guy got into his Dodge and trailed Johns home. He saw the former comptroller drive into the garage beside the brown Cadillac. The mechanical door closed but Guy didn't see Johns emerge. After a while he left the Dodge and walked toward the garage.

Inside, a car engine was running.

Guy glanced at the dark house. Johns had decided not to disturb his wife.

He went back to the Dodge and got in. After fifteen minutes he decided Johns was never going to leave the garage. Alive.

Two down, Guy told himself as he drove along the dark street. One to go.

From Pelham he drove through Mt. Vernon and turned north on the parkway to Bronxville. Keeping the speedometer needle just under the limit he pulled into the Rustic Cabin parking lot in time to see Paul Edmonds' black Jaguar arrive.

Twenty-Six

Loudspeakers set high on the wall flooded the parking lot with sound from within. Heavy amplified guitars, shrieking fiddles, rim-shots and heavy washtub bass clashed with strident voices lamenting faithless lovers. A good deal of crowd noise pierced the wall, suggesting to Guy the heavy decibels inside.

From where he was parked he saw the Jaguar nose into a slot. Taillights went out. The door opened and Paul Edmonds emerged wearing a jacket over a tieless shirt. The lot's strong overhead illumination made his white hair seem a brilliant nimbus. For a few moments he stared around, scanning the close-packed cars. Failing to see what he was looking for, he got back inside. The flare of a cigarette lighter briefly showed his face.

Two couples in Western garb weaved happily from the exit, trading brown bottles. They found their pickup and three climbed into the front seat. The driver braced himself against the fender and urinated unsteadily. Then he got into the cab. Guy could see jostling, legs and arms waving around. The engine gunned and the pickup whipped into the turnaround and screeched to the street leaving a plume of dust.

A BMW arrived, two people got out and hurried into the

Rustic Cabin to join the merrymakers. Paul Edmonds watched without interest.

I wonder what he's thinking, Guy mused. Farley persuaded him to come without putting him to flight. But Edmonds was not a man to panic easily. Self-assured, bolstered by years of executive success, confident of infallibility, he was not likely to come apart as his comptroller had. Like a high seas admiral he would defend himself and his possessions until the deck was awash beneath his feet.

In a way, Guy thought, his father had chosen well, for Edmonds was tough, defiant, accustomed to rough play. Shrewd enough to embezzle millions—and kill to protect his gains.

Such a man, Guy reflected might have sensed a need for protection in tonight's encounter; brought muscle to ensure survival.

As time passed, Guy scanned each arrival closely, finally deciding Edmonds had come alone.

By now, Saturday night celebrants were beginning to leave. Before the lot began to empty he had to make his move.

He joined a group walking unsteadily toward where the Jaguar sat, peeled off and opened the passenger door. Moving quickly toward Edmonds he flashed the Colt. "You're punctual, but Farley couldn't come."

Edmonds stared incredulously. "Guy! What are you doing here? Where's Johns?"

"Telling it all to the cops. Competing with Dom to get it all out first."

Edmonds' face was rigid. "Cops? I don't understand. Dom who?"

Guy showed him D'Angelo's RyTech card. "This fellow—the one paid to kill Marguerite, the one who failed to kill Glenn Moorsby tonight."

"Moors—?" He shook his head in wonderment. Masterful control, Guy thought. Let's see how long it lasts. He said, "Moorsby, the accountant who revealed your embezzlements to my stepmother."

"You must be crazy, all this talk of killing, embezzlements." His expression was outraged.

"Oh, it's true enough. When Dom was caught he fingered Johns—and your old partner-in-crime fingered you. I have the proof, you see. Moorsby turned over all the checks, the names of your phony companies." He glanced at the Colt pistol glinting coldly in the light. "When Marguerite was killed I couldn't understand why, thought the bomb was meant for me."

"What bomb? What nonsense is this?"

"The bomb's been identified—radio-triggered by the man who placed it. D'Angelo's confessed and Farley Johns confirms five thousand dollars as the price." The blasting music, the pounding beat was unendurable. "Trivial—compared to the three million you two stole from RyTech. *And* my stepmother's priceless life." Against a car a man was unbuttoning a girl's plaid cowboy shirt. When it parted he began fondling her breasts. Guy felt detached from everything—as though he were looking down from space. Nothing seemed real. Least of all the hard set of Edmonds' face.

Throat thick with hatred Guy said, "Marguerite Ryan asked questions that couldn't be answered. And so you had her killed. Like *that!*" He snapped fingers, and for the first time Edmonds' features seemed tense and drawn.

"Guy, this is bizarre—I absolutely deny these charges. Farley's been under a strain—at his age it isn't easy to find new employment—but to implicate me in murder, hoping to somehow ingratiate himself with you is—more than cowardly. It's insane. Surely you don't believe the man?"

"I believe him—*and* Dom. The only strain he's been under is spending his blood money. Fact is, they've convinced the cops, and by dawn the Bureau will be brought in."

"Nothing I can say or do to persuade you you're being

299

victimized by two cheap crooks? Guy, for years I was your father's right-hand man. He trusted me—I was almost a member of the family."

"Making all the more loathesome what you did. Holding my father's Irish secrets in reserve—" He shook his head. "Sanctimoniously grieving—while plotting to get rid of me. Coming to Marguerite's funeral—standing with mourners who loved her. There can't be a hell hot enough for you." He licked dry lips, stretched stiff muscles. "I'm taking you in."

"Then I'll defend myself, be vindicated."

Tiredly Guy said, "That's bullshit. The evidence is there, it's incontrovertible."

For a while the only sound was the nasal whining of the country singers. Then, in a level voice Edmonds said, "You paint a most unpleasant picture. On what you call evidence you convict and sentence me." His voice rose, "Why did you come?"

"To see whether there was, finally, a shred of decency remaining, a trace of contrition."

Edmonds' mouth twisted. "What are you looking for? The money? To you it must loom large—never having had any before," he sneered.

"A dollar taken or a million is theft," Guy said huskily. "Johns is helping trace it to Canada and elsewhere. We'll recover it—that's not been my concern. The murder of my stepmother and the crewmen is. If this state used its electric chair I'd demand you burn—and I may get that chance. Aircraft sabotage is a federal crime with capital punishment."

Edmonds' mouth opened. "I didn't plant the bomb," he said breathily.

"Easier to hire it done. Let's go. We're driving to Pelham where Johns and Dominic are digging your grave." He gestured at the ignition with the Colt, but the driver remained motionless. "What do you want—a confession?"

"Not particularly."

"If I told everything on tape, what concession would you make?"

Guy shook his head. "I'm content with the evidence I have. It's late, Paul, start the engine." He stared at the man so long trusted by his father. "You have nothing to trade."

"You're wrong. You don't even know who your father was. You don't even know your name."

The flat assertion startled Guy. "My . . . name? What do you mean I don't know my name?"

"I mean your birth name, your father's *true* name. I have that to exchange, Guy."

He swallowed. Johns had alluded to a secret powerful enough for blackmail. Was this it? "Exchange that for—what?"

"For walking away. Giving me a chance to—save my life."

Guy thought it over, said, "If no one else knew, not even his wife, why you? How can I know it's true?"

"Listen to me—your father was an IRA sympathizer—he gave money to buy arms, paid for Counihan's defense."

"I know that."

"But he never went to Ireland, did he? Isn't that odd for an Irish patriot, one born in Ireland?"

"My mother died there—it would have stirred sad memories," he replied, but he wanted to *know*. "If there's so deep a secret how did *you* come to know?"

"Like your father you're Catholic. Who knows more secrets than a priest?"

The words shook him. He gazed with loathing. "Go on."

"You agree?"

Guy's jaws set. If there was a secret to his name and rearing, to his father's self-exile from Ireland, he *had* to know. Edmonds might run but the law would find him. Slowly he said, "Agree."

Edmonds nodded. "I trust your sense of honor to keep your word." He shifted in his seat, half turned toward Guy. "When he was young your father killed a British soldier, took the identity of an Irish militant who'd been killed in the skirmish."

Guy's mouth was dry. "What was my father's name?"

"Liam Degnan. A gravestone bears his name."

"Where?"

"I don't know. As Ryan he married your mother, who died when you were born. He was a fugitive on the run." His lips twisted. "As I'm soon to be. Your father sent you to this country, followed when he could and made a new life for himself as Sean Foley Ryan—the dead man's name. Marguerite never knew."

"You found out from a priest. You bribed him?"

He shook his head, "That's not part of our bargain. I've told you what I know. Your name is Degnan. Do what you want with it, but go."

"Does Counihan know?"

"He does. I'm in a hurry. Keep your word."

Stiffly, Guy reached for the door, shoved it open with his foot. He turned back to Edmonds for a final question and saw a shiny weapon in his hand. The blast blinded him. He felt a hammerblow in his side, another. Deafened, slammed back by the impact he raised the Colt and fired twice at Edmonds. Expecting more bullets he ducked and slid half out of the car, surprised that he felt so little pain. No blood in his mouth. Vision cleared, and he saw Edmonds lying against the door, mouth open, eyes staring.

His right hand held a nickle-plated derringer, twin barrels.

On his knees, Guy stuck one hand inside his coat to feel for blood. The only moisture was perspiration on his shirt. Fingers probed, met metal, and suddenly he understood. The derringer's soft bullets had struck the holstered Walther. Destructed on the hardened steel.

He got up and looked around. As his eardrums normalized he realized the music was playing full blast across the lot. People walked by unconcernedly. He got back into the Jaguar and closed the door. The stench of gunpowder was strong. There were two punctures in Edmonds' chest. They bloodied the white shirt around the heart. A trickle of blood marked the corner of the dead man's mouth. Guy pulled a handkerchief from Edmonds' pocket and wiped it off.

His hands were gloved, but he used the handkerchief carefully on the Colt, and stuffed it under the seat. The derringer he left in Edmonds' hand, and pulled the coat together to hide the entrance wounds. Light glinted dully in the dead man's eyes. Guy closed the lids and positioned the head to simulate sleep.

He turned on the dash lamp and searched for the derringer's two bullets. As he moved, one dropped from his holster, the other lay in a crack of the seat. Both resembled flattened mushrooms. He put them in his pocket and collected the Colt's two empty shells from the ground.

Leaving the Jaguar he walked to his Dodge, feeling sharp aching in his ribs. He wondered if the Walther was still usable. Its steel had saved his life.

Before other patrons left the Rustic Cabin Guy started the engine and steered to the street. Tonight no one was likely to bother the man in the Jaguar. Tomorrow police would assume Edmonds died fighting off a robber. The Colt was D'Angelo's. Let them make what they could from that.

He had learned part of his father's secret, found out his own true name. There was more to be discovered, but not in America. It all reached back across the sea to the Emerald Isle with its bitter, bloody conflicts.

Who was the priest, he wondered, who had breached the Church's most sacred silence? Where was the grave of the real Sean Foley Ryan?

As he drove south into Manhattan his mind gradually began to calm. His stepmother's killers were dead, all three of them—reprisal for the helicopter's bombing victims. Eye for an eye. Forgiveness was not within him.

He felt drained, sapped of strength, barely able to move the wheel intelligently. Emotional reaction, he understood, as after battle when his exhausted body would sleep for hours.

On a dark, decaying Harlem street he left the Dodge, keys in the ignition. He stripped the plates and carried them under his coat, down into the subway where he bent and dropped them in a can of trash. It was a long wait for the next train south, and he was glad no muggers approached. He felt lacking in strength even to fire the Walther.

He got off at Central Park Zoo, trudged east through silence that smothered the city like thick fog, and entered his apartment building.

The guard was nodding at his desk, video screens forgotten. Guy went past him and rode the elevator to his floor.

He poured a tumbler of Scotch, and drank it in four quick gulps. Too tired to stand under the shower, he sat on tile, letting hot water warm his body. There were marks on his ribcage from the bullets' impact, but they would go away.

The liquor took hold. He stumbled into bed, grateful to be alive. Since 'Nam he had not lived so bloody a space of hours.

As sleep began to drag him under, he wondered what revelations the British Isles would bring.

Twenty-Seven

Monday.

At their morning meeting Jake Needham said, "Seen the papers?"

"No time. Worked out, had breakfast and came here. Anything of interest?"

"Damnedest thing. Over the weekend Farley Johns killed himself, and Edmonds was shot by a robber. Almost strains coincidence, don't you think?"

"I don't know what to think. Send flowers, I guess. Circulate an announcement for employees."

"Ah—you won't be attending obsequies?"

"Hardly knew them," Guy observed. "Besides, I'm getting ready for a business trip—leaving tomorrow, you know." For a moment he thought of telling Jake to start tracking the embezzled funds, decided just as quickly this was not the time. "I spent part of yesterday trying to comprehend what our biomedical research labs are doing. I'll have time on the flight to try again."

"Good luck. Biotechnology, gene cloning, engineered hormones, DNA—they're well beyond my scope. The Point didn't prepare us for them."

Guy smiled. "Satisfied with your job?"

"It's exciting, Guy. I'm eager to get to the office, slow

to leave. At Hay Hughes Wriston and Van Wickle the work was routine. And Sally's pleased. Says I whistle in the shower, something I hadn't done since leaving the service." He paused. "Could you have dinner with us tonight? Sort of a bon voyage sendoff."

"Well, I don't like to think of Sally worrying about dinner for the boss—we can dine *en famille* when my wife comes over. For tonight, why not lay on a baby-sitter and we'll take a table at Lutèce or Le Périgord—wherever Sally would like to go?"

"She'd love it—*and* the required new dress. I know you're lunching with the mayor—probably hit you up for a contribution to some pet cultural project, so be warned."

"Consuela will be my artistic and cultural adviser, and I'll tell him so."

During the morning he read and approved recommendations concerning the Cheju Island plant and responded cordially to a note from Nikky saying he would be an uncle in the fall. He received his Congressman and agreed to consider a plea for re-election funds. He declined an invitation to address the Board of Trade, pleading absence abroad, and told Frank Purcell to resolve a funding dispute between two department heads. "That's your job, not mine," he told the new comptroller. "If you don't feel qualified to make decisions, tell me."

"Well, it's not that, sir," Purcell said uncomfortably, "it's more a matter of courtesy—keeping you informed in case you have set ideas."

"I appreciate the thought," Guy observed, "but I don't care to intervene. Spare me those burdens."

Guy called in Jenny Knox and pointed at her memorandum. "Tell *US News* I'll be prepared for an interview a year from now. Same to *Firing Line* and *Face the Nation*. That's a blanket response, Jenny. Here—extract something from these Cheju plans. Fighting famine with low-cost foods is the kind of image RyTech needs."

"Yes, sir."

"Before summer, plan to go to Seoul, hire a camera crew and make a documentary on the entire process—from net to packaged protein. Show it on public television, prints to the World Health Organization, and the embassies of the poorest nations."

"Excellent idea. I've gotten press queries about the weekend deaths of Edmonds and Farley Johns. If you concur I'll say RyTech regrets their untimely demise, deny any connection to their firings."

"Of course—because there is none."

At noon a limousine took Guy to Gracie Mansion, where he lunched with the Mayor and a dozen notables from varied walks of life. Afterward there were press photographs, which Guy found unavoidable, short of rudeness to his publicity-conscious host.

From his office he phoned Hoskins on the scrambler phone and said he wanted to locate Conor Counihan.

"I'll assume you're not getting into the munitions-running business, which is what the MI-Six liaison officer will want to know. Through Special Branch the Brits keep close watch on the old conspirator, but I'm not sure they'll want to inform me."

"I'll be obliged if you'll try. Tomorrow I'll be at Gatwick."

"Not much time. Ah—what's your reaction to the suicide and murder of your former executives?"

"I'll discuss it another time."

Guy called in Mrs. Paskow and said, "Before my father's death I understand he summoned an Irish priest to confess him, administer the late rites of the Church."

"That's correct, sir. Father Dennis Fallon. From the village of Slane in County Meath. Father Fallon is well along in years and quite feeble. Every year your father would send the Lear to fly him over."

"Why Father Fallon?"

"I understood they knew each other in your father's youth. Your father seldom offered explanations for what he did, and after he fell ill he had even less to say."

"Did you keep the priest's address?"

"No, but I suppose the church at Slane would do, sir. Your suite at the Gresham is confirmed for two nights. If you stay longer there'll be no problem this time of year. But they're booked solidly for the May Royal Dublin horse show."

"I won't be attending it."

"So unexpected—and sad—the deaths of Mr. Edmonds and Mr. Johns."

"It's an unpredictable world," he said off-handedly. "Cancel any payments due them had they lived."

"Yes, sir."

"Has my half-brother been around?"

"Not since he was given his office." She tried not to smile. "Your table at Le Périgord is confirmed for eight and the Needhams will meet you there. The pilot wants to know how early you want to take off tomorrow."

"Nine will be early enough."

"Reservations overnight at Gatwick Airport are confirmed."

"I appreciate your efficiency," he said. "No wonder my father esteemed you so."

"Despite anything you may have heard, he could be a sensitive and thoughtful employer. As you are, Mr. Ryan."

He smiled. "I'm glad we get along so well. As before, Mr. Needham will be in charge while I'm away."

Among his mail was the offer of an honorary degree by a Kentucky college he had never heard of. On the invitation he wrote, *Decline politely,* and routed it to Jenny.

At six he was adding final papers to his attaché case when the scrambler phone rang. Hoskins said, "Best I could get from Six Liaison is that Counihan was last seen in County Monaghan near the Ulster border. I gather that Special Branch has an informant in his band, but the man can report only infrequently. Sorry I couldn't do better."

"Appreciate the try. County Monaghan," he repeated, and hung up.

He enjoyed the Needhams' company during an excellent dinner. Jake's wife was buoyant, and Guy reflected that he would have liked to have had Connie at his side. Well, he'd see her soon, and Gloria.

But when he lay in bed waiting for sleep, his thoughts revolved around Cristina. Undeniably, and wrong as it might be, he was eager to see his sister-in-law in Dublin.

At Manchester the work of his biotechnology labs astonished Guy. The concentration was on medicine: countering dwarfism in children, eliminating such genetic defects as sickle cell anemia and Downs Syndrome, and attacking cancer. Advances in the development of monoclonal antibodies against leukemia were high priority, according to the chief researcher. Promise of *preventing* other cancer lay in the realm of protecting the body's proto-oncogenes from mutation into killer cells.

The only saleable product of the facility was antibodies that were expensive to produce and bought by laboratories involved in related work. Profit was far less than the overall operating cost.

"Which makes us fear," said the laboratory chief, "that you may be inclined to reduce the scope of our work—or eliminate it entirely."

309

"Not after what I've seen today. Though I wonder if the Galway installation is necessary."

"My Irish colleagues will speak for themselves, of course, but their focus is on agriculture and energy. As you are no doubt aware the effort is to produce disease-proof grains, increase bovine milk yield and develop sheep that grow more and better wool. Plants that produce combustible fuel—but you'll hear all that at Galway. Here in England we work to reduce human misery; in Ireland my colleagues work to meet human needs. I'm confident you'll find them equally deserving of continued backing."

"I believe I will," he replied, and flew to the Galway airport that night.

Next day he was shown greenhouses for year-round cultivation of rye, wheat and oats; a model dairy where hormone-treated cows gave an additional ten quarts of milk daily, and a shed where cloned sheep yielded three extra pounds of wool per shearing. Guy promised the chief scientist continued funding and in late afternoon boarded the Lear for Dublin. Flying again across the land where he was born, Guy realized he did not even know the place of his father's birth.

From Dublin Airport a limousine took him down Drumcondra Road to Dorest, and then O'Connell Street where he registered at the Gresham hotel.

After a shower he dressed for dinner and was pulling on his coat when there was a knock at his door. Guy opened it and Cristina came into his room.

Twenty-Eight

His sister-in-law was dressed in white wool slacks and matching top. Around her throat was a pendant diamond. A diamond bracelet circled her wrist, and as she raised her arms he noticed that the wedding band was absent from her finger.

Hands on his shoulders she said, "Is a sisterly embrace permitted?"

He took her in his arms and kissed her forehead lightly. "I've never seen you look more beautiful."

"I've had days to prepare," she said standing away, "and I'm glad you approve. Who knows what eligible males I'll encounter at the auction? Already I've met two, and the auction isn't 'til tomorrow."

He felt a pang at her words, but in seeking a husband she was doing no more than what he and her father had urged.

"I'm sorry Consuela couldn't come," she said, "but if you're free for dinner why don't we dine together?"

"Nothing I'd like more." Her dark hair was drawn tightly back from her forehead and braided into a bun pierced with a jeweled Spanish comb. Darkened eyebrows accented her oval face and he realized that he had never seen her wear lipstick before. The shade matched her fin-

311

gernails, a nuance he attributed to a sensitive cosmetician. He said, "You're stunning. I'll be the envy of every man in Dublin."

She blushed slightly. "Family prejudice, no doubt. Since you're not familiar with Dublin let me recommend a small place away from hotel atmosphere—Snaffles on Leeson Street. If you like we can take cocktails here in the Gresham bar. Most of the horsey people put up at the Shelbourne, and we'll see quite enough of them in the next few days."

"Including Prince Ali Mansour?"

"Yes—he arrived yesterday. Flew in from Morocco on his own 747 with Al-Emir—and six other horses. They're stabled at Ballsbridge where the auction takes place. Showgrounds of the Royal Dublin Society."

He took her arm and they rode the lift down to the bar. There in a setting of polished oak and leather, watching a fashionable crowd gather, they drank together—sherry for Cris, Scotch for himself—and brought each other up to date. Guy described the biotechnological work of his laboratories and Cristina reported on La Rocha and her father's fall.

He felt a strong compulsion to tell her of Marguerite's murder and the deaths of her killers. But it would be wrong to burden her with the knowledge, he mused, and doubted he could ever bring himself to tell his wife.

Cristina returned the wave of a young man sitting with a group around a table. He wore a tartan dinner jacket and had curly blond hair longer than Guy liked. "Lord Harry FitzGerald," she said. "We met this morning while we were both admiring Al-Emir. He's one of a British syndicate and will be bidding against us. World-class horseman, member of the Irish Olympic Team." She paused. "Unmarried."

Guy ordered a second Scotch but Cristina said, "I'll need a clear head tomorrow. This and dinner wine will be quite enough." She glanced at FitzGerald and returned his smile. "I do hope my sister's exhibition will go well. Consuela requires the same sense of identity as I do."

"Explain."

One polished fingernail tapped the stem of her glass. "Not being a Spanish male you don't know what it's like to be raised as a Spanish female under watchful parental eyes. In our system our identities derive from our ancestors. I'm Cristina, younger daughter of Don José, Marqués of Palafox y Urriaga. I needed more than that, Guy, comfortable as it's always been. In Spain it's very hard to cut the silver cord. That's why Consuela fled to Paris. It's why I've developed interests that take me beyond the confines of La Rocha. In Ireland I feel like another person and I'm taken for my own worth—that's tremendously important to me." Her head moved reflectively. "I never thought I'd miss convent school—until I returned to La Rocha, where life was equally limited and oppressive. I suppose that's the unacknowledged reason I married René. As a way out."

"The whole world's open to you," he said. "You have all the necessities to do whatever you choose to do."

Her hand pressed his. "That's nice of you, and I do think life will be good to me. You've helped me grow up, you know."

Guy's Scotch arrived and Cristina said, "Would you excuse me? I promised the syndicator office I'd confirm when you arrived."

He watched her walk away in a smooth confident stride that did nothing to mask her femininity. Faces turned to watch her cross the room, females showing envy, men admiration. Without question, he thought, Cristina was the most beautiful woman there—or in Dublin. And, she was his sister-in-law. Lifting his glass he drank deeply.

As she returned, Lord Harry rose and introduced her to his companions. For a few moments they talked. She shook her head and gestured at Guy. Lord Harry nodded disappointedly and let her go. Guy saw that his gaze followed her every step of the way.

Seated beside him she said, "He invited me to dine with

his friends, but I explained I had a date." She smiled impishly. "Unless you care to relinquish me."

"Hardly," he said, "I see little enough of you as it is."

"Precisely how I feel. While at the phone I took the precaution of booking a table. There was some hesitation until I mentioned your name. That brought immediate action."

"Name-dropper."

"Why should I wait in line when I have a famous brother-in-law?" She squeezed his arm. "Besides, the Irish are very accommodating. Dublin's been called the 'dump of illusions' but I find it much more than that."

"But you're not Irish," he objected.

"You are. Will there be time for sightseeing in the countryside?"

"Perhaps," he said. "I'm considering a side trip to County Meath—that's to the north of here. Village called Slane. It's where my father's priest lives—if he's still alive."

"I'd love to go with you."

"About an hour's drive. And we can look over the battlefield of the Boyne, see an abbey or two." He wondered if Father Fallon could tell him where his mother was buried. Before marriage she had been Molly Doyle, daughter of working parents. But his father had never told him more.

At Snaffles there was a small centerpiece of green carnations decorated with sprays of green fern. The captain was attentive without servility, an Irish trait Guy admired.

They ordered oysters from Galway Bay, smoked Donegal salmon, and shared a rack of lamb. Cristina chose an excellent Bordeaux from the wine list, and Guy reflected on her unusual qualifications to grace a husband's table. Which she'll be doing soon enough, he told himself, perhaps for Lord Harry.

Unobtrusively a young woman had begun to play an Irish harp. She wore a plain black dress with a university tartan across one shoulder. Her complexion was light, her eyes deepset, and her lips moved only slightly as she sang, in

Gaelic then English, a sad song of the Uprising. To Guy she seemed the embodiment of Irish womanhood—or widowhood—for such was the history of Ireland. Kathleen ni Houlihan. Had his mother resembled the harpist, he wondered? Had the face of Molly Doyle been plain or beautiful?

She sang again, plucking the harpstrings almost absently as though to keep the song on pitch rather than to supplement the rich intensity of her voice.

Cristina said, "When I first came to Dublin two years ago I was so overwhelmed by the tradition and solemnity of Trinity College that I thought I might stay and study here. But soon I realized that what I'd taken as Irish seriousness was sorrow in disguise. As in Spain every family was bled by civil war; it's always close to their surface thoughts. To Dubliners, Ulster is the tumor in their land, and they speak in low voices and whispers about almost anything. Ask a Dubliner on the street for directions, he'll tell you gladly, but adds, 'Tis not treasonable information I'm imparting.' " With a half-smile she lifted her wineglass and sipped.

Guy was surprised by the sensitivity of her observations and reflected that her sister—as long as he had known Consuela—had never uttered a phrase of social analysis. He added wine to their glasses and silently rebuked himself for the comparison.

She said, "Dublin reminds me of my father's description of Spain after our Civil War—Belfast must be as Barcelona was—conspiracies everywhere and a general atmosphere of treachery. Though Catalonians don't like to talk about that any more."

They ordered sweet tarts and Irish coffee. The harpist played and sang, and when she was done Cristina began to talk about the Arab line. It developed in Libya, she told him, five strains deriving from a single mare. "Al-Emir is Kohl-breed, you'll see the distinctive blue-black color of his skin, especially around the eyes and muzzle. You'll note his stylish front and balanced conformation, the set of his forelegs and the quality of his underpinnings. Among his ancestry are two world champions, Haddan Enzahi and his son Shari out of Hathor, the German female champion. His pedigree is so impeccable I'm surprised Prince Ali is putting him on the block."

"So am I," Guy said, "because Ali certainly doesn't need money. I agree that Al-Emir will be a great addition to your line—I had his pedigree checked out and I'm more than satisfied with the investment. But Ali isn't—let's say—the most ethical fellow around. Before money changes hands you must have the horse carefully vetted."

"I have," she told him. "I brought Dr. Aristegúi to Dublin and he examined Al-Emir today."

"And—?"

"He urges me to buy. So perhaps Ali just wants to reduce his stable."

Guy felt the beginning of a yawn. Smothering it, he said, "Feeling jet lag, sorry."

"I've had a full day, too," she said, "plus all the excitement of finally being able to do what I hardly dared dream of." Her hand covered his. "Thanks to you, *cuñado.*"

He saw Cristina to her room, gave her a brotherly kiss and went tiredly off to bed.

In the morning Cristina turned out in a smartly tailored suit of Donegal tweed and boots suitable for the show ring. Dark derby with a colorful grouse feather, and a yellow silk tie.

In the grill they shared a hearty Irish breakfast, then got into Guy's limousine for the two-mile ride to Ballsbridge.

The showgrounds of the Royal Dublin Society were heavily guarded. Cristina's pass got them through the gate, and as they neared the show enclosures Guy saw armed guards everywhere. Cristina said, "Prince Ali demanded protec-

316

tion to prevent what happened not long ago when revolutionaries stole a prize thoroughbred for ransom."

At once Guy thought of Conor Counihan, and said, "Seems a wise precaution."

Overhead the sky was a dark, unbroken gray. There had been rain to muddy the ground, and as Guy walked toward the show rings his face moistened with nearly invisible mist. Cristina carried a thin, gold-trimmed briefcase and a shooting stick; as they passed a cluster of people she nodded at several members of the fancy.

In the far ring Al-Emir was being walked by his trainer. Each of two intervening rings held three Arab horses and their trainers. Cristina pointed out the auctioneer in morning attire with top hat and a green lapel ribbon. "If this were the May show," she said, "there would be thousands here—like Ascot, really. Instead, I count about forty, including wives, and only a few will bid."

A man left the fencing and approached them, smiling at Cristina. "Hel-*lo*," he said cheerfully, "been waiting for your arrival." Taking her hand he bent over it as Cristina said, "Peter, this is my brother-in-law, Guy Ryan. Guy, Sir Peter Oakshott." They shook hands briefly, and Guy surveyed the Englishman. Oakshott wore a tweed raglan and a hunting cap of the same pattern, riding boots with blunt spurs. Dark locks accented his pale complexion and his lips seemed almost bloodless. To Guy he said, "A'nt she *marvelous?* I mean, a gel biddin' against us chaps. Ha'nt happened in memory. Fact." Turning to Cristina he said, "Who bids in Al-Emir buys champagne for the losers tonight. Prince Ali has taken the Shelbourne ballroom for the party."

Guy said, "I'd think he'd be obliged to buy."

"Oh, well, custom here." He squinted at Guy. "American?"

Cristina nodded. "Guy is President of RyTech and my

317

principal backer. He was good enough to combine the auction with a business trip, and I'm glad of his company."

"Chaperon, uh? I'll mind m'manners. I say, there's Prince Ali himself." His shooting stick waved at a man in flowing Arab robes leaving a long Mercedes limousine. Photographers barred his way until Ali parted them with an imperious wave. Retainers formed a human barrier around him as the Prince strolled to a sheltered stand. He had gained weight since Vezelay, Guy noticed, and Ali's lip had thickened into sensuality, reminding him of Edouard Drach.

Nudging him Cristina murmured, "Not going to greet your schoolmate?"

"Ali wasn't a favorite friend." He thought of Sonya, the little ballerina, and wondered if she was now part of Ali's entourage.

They strolled past the near rings and came to the third. Cristina's eyes glowed as she gazed at the Arab stallion. She opened her shooting stick and sat down as other breeders gathered nearby. Two more British men and a Belgian count greeted Cristina and were introduced to Guy, leaving as loudspeakers announced the beginning of the sale.

In less than an hour Ali's six stallions were auctioned, top price for a three-year-old was over four hundred thousand dollars.

While bank drafts and pedigree papers were exchanged with the auctioneer, tea was served to the bidders. Lord Harry FitzGerald detached himself from a convivial group and joined them, silver flask in hand. "Bit o'Tullamore," he offered, "to ward off the chill."

Cristina declined, but Guy nodded and FitzGerald added whiskey to his cup. "Now comes the main event," he observed with enthusiasm, "though it may go over-rich for my pocket." He looked at Cristina. "Any case, see you tonight?"

"We'll be there," she said as the auctioneer's gavel sounded.

Bidders gathered around the stand while Al-Emir's pedigree was read. Guy noticed Prince Ali watching the proceedings with detached interest.

The auctioneer announced an opening level of one million dollars. Four bids raised it to two million where it lingered until Cristina touched her hat brim, increasing the bid by a quarter million. The Belgian Count brought it to two million five. Lord Harry and Peter Oakshott conferred before signalling two million six.

Cristina whispered, "Guy, how high can I go?"

"As high as it takes," he told her, and she bid two-seven. The Belgian shook his head in disappointment, closed his shooting stick and walked away. Oakshott raised the bid another hundred thousand and looked worriedly at Cristina who brought the bid to two million nine hundred thousand.

"Come, come, gentlemen, ladies," cried the auctioneer, "surely this magnificent animal deserves further consideration from the fancy? Do I hear three? Anyone bid three million?" His gavel sounded once. Cristina clutched Guy's arm and gasped excitedly.

"Twice. Going," cried the auctioneer, gavel poised, "examine your consciences, I beseech you!"

Apprehensively Cristina watched the crowd.

"Thrice!" He banged the gavel and pointed at Cristina. "To the lady in the feathered derby at two million nine. *Thank* you, ladies and gentlemen. That concludes our proceedings." He stepped down and went over to a side table where assistants were busy with paperwork.

"Well," said Guy, "he's yours."

"Oh, Guy, I've *never* been happier." Arms around his neck she covered his cheeks with kisses. "Thank you, *thank* you!

"Let's go claim him."

They went through the departing crowd, many congratulating Cristina, whose face was flushed with victory. Cameras flashed as they neared the table. Opening her briefcase she produced a draft for two million dollars. Guy made out a check for nine hundred thousand. By far the largest check he had ever written.

"Guy—old chap!" Prince Ali neared him. "Had no idea you'd be here. Cristina, congratulations. I'm satisfied Al-Emir will find a welcome home." He hugged Guy, Arab style, and stood back. "So many years since Vezelay, eh? We must take time to reminisce." He glanced at Cristina, busy at the auction table. "Exquisite, is she not? My congratulations."

Drily, Guy said, "She's my sister-in-law, Ali, not my mistress."

"Oh? No offense intended. But as Cristina's escort—you understand?" He posed for another photograph, this one with Cristina, and before leaving said, "Nine o'clock— Shelbourne ballroom."

Guy nodded and moved away until auction formalities ended. Then he followed Cristina hurrying toward her prize.

She took the bridle from the groom and pressed her cheek to the stallion's muzzle. Tears welled in her eyes. "I can't believe it, even now." Her hand clasped Guy's as she wept with joy.

Oakshott, Lord Harry and other young men surrounded her, admiring Al-Emir, toasting her from flasks until she said, "I must get hold of myself," and relinquished her stallion to the trainer.

They lunched at the nearby Berkeley Court Hotel where a dozen or so disappointed bidders had gathered to console themselves with food and drink. Guy was aware of the men's admiring, envious glances at Cristina, who ignored everything while she outlined plans to capitalize on her investment. "After lunch," she said, "I must deal with the syndicating office, then arrange Al-Emir's flight to Seville. He'll be safe at La Rocha until your Texas ranch is ready. And I may breed him to my three best mares. Guy, thank you again for trusting me."

* * *

Back at the Gresham he turned the limousine over to Cristina and bought souvenirs for his wife and daughter; Aran knitwear and an antique gadroon serving plate. Then he telephoned Jake Needham for a status report.

At nine-thirty they entered the ballroom, Guy in dinner jacket, Cristina in white evening gown with seed pearls ornamenting the bodice. Her dark hair touched her shoulders like a parted curtain, and Guy thought her appearance spectacular.

So did Prince Ali, who approached them and kissed Cristina's hand. "Savoring the sweets of victory? Now that Al-Emir is yours I will confide a little secret—I had expected him to bring five or six hundred thousand dollars more. Does that not make the transaction even more *douce?*"

"It does," she agreed. "I'm happy everything worked out to my advantage."

Ali's robe-draped arm made a sweeping motion. "All this is in your honor, *Señora*—décor, food and drink, the tributes of envious competitors. I felt the occasion would help reconcile them to defeat."

"I hope it will," she said graciously, and moved on.

The ballroom had been draped with thousands of flowers and silken banners—the largest bearing Prince Ali's royal arms. There was a dance orchestra and a rock group. At one side a long buffet had been positioned. From the center rose a large ice sculpture of Al-Emir, its pedestal surrounded by small Spanish flags in Cristina's honor.

A seafood bar offered shrimp, oysters, lobster, and pots of caviar. Next, a salad display, then grilled and baked beef, lamb and hams, carved hot by a chef wearing the white mushroom hat of his craft.

Guy led Cristina to the bar, asked for champagne and toasted her wordlessly.

Oakshott came by and swept her onto the dance floor.

Guy watched them for a moment before sampling the sea-food. When he looked again his sister-in-law was dancing with the Belgian Count. Lord Harry FitzGerald eyed them from the bar, emptied his glass and came toward Guy. "What a splendid show," he said acidly. "We buy Ali's oil, he lets us buy his hosses. Sheerly wonderful."

"Have a shrimp," Guy told him. "They're excellent."

"Don't mind if I do." He helped himself and gazed at Cristina. "Absolute, total stunner," he observed. "Astral heights above our local femmes."

Guy nodded agreement.

FitzGerald wiped his dripping chin on his cuff. "Splendid mind and keen judge of horseflesh," he went on. "Marvelous *coup* today—both of you."

"Her doing," Guy remarked. "I came along to see the fun."

FitzGerald grunted, picked up a lobster claw, broke it apart and gnawed the meat. After smacking his lips he said, "Take it you're *in loco parentis*, as it were?"

"As it were."

"Then with your consent I'll invite Cristina for the May Royal Show, stay at the family seat. There'll be hunting, balls, great time for all."

"You have my permission to invite her," Guy said reluctantly, adding, "Thoroughly independent mind."

"Admire that in a woman," Lord Harry said, clapping Guy's back enthusiastically. "Now to rid her of the Belgian menace." He pushed his way onto the dance floor and bowed to Cristina.

Returning to the bar Guy took a glass of champagne and saw Prince Ali sipping fruit juice. Their gaze met and Ali smiled as he came to Guy. "How ironic that alcohol—an Arab discovery—is forbidden us Moslems, yet granted to Christians."

Guy said, "Perhaps for our corruption."

"So it is said. In this abysmal climate one understands

the Irish love of spirits." He looked at his glass and set it aside. "Ever see any of the old Vezelay boys?"

"Infrequently," Guy told him, "though I came across one in Geneva. Nigel Palfrey."

"Palfrey? Yes, I remember—upper form chap. Can't say I cared for him, though."

Guy sipped from his glass. "Nigel's comments were equally—guarded."

"My name entered the conversation?"

"We were discussing a friend of yours—Edouard Drach."

"Drach, eh? Grotesque fellow, but occasionally of use. I now recall him mentioning you were his guest at dinner. How did it go?"

"For me, uncomfortably. We found little if anything in common." Guy thought of mentioning Sonya, decided against it.

"I suppose he had a business proposal to offer?"

"He did—but I found it unacceptable. Just when I've taken charge of RyTech he wants to buy it from me. That would leave me without useful employment."

Ali shrugged. "You could always take up horse breeding."

"That's Cristina's profession."

"Until she marries, eh? Well, this Drach can be an obstinate fellow. Deals *sub rosa* by preference. Dangerous opponent and, of course, a *parvenu.*"

Guy nodded agreement.

"Offered me his child dancer as an inducement to do a certain thing. I told him to remind me ten years hence."

"Offending him?"

"Drach doesn't take offense. Well, this is one of those occasions when people of the better sort mingle without thought or care, and I see that Cristina is drawing a host of admirers. I daresay she will wed before the year is out."

"If she chooses," said Guy and downed his champagne. "This time I think she'll select with greater care."

323

Ali nodded thoughtfully. "Now that you're part of the international scene I suspect we'll be coming across one another from time to time. My advice is not to attempt more than you can accomplish."

"I'll bear it in mind."

The music ended and FitzGerald brought Cristina to Guy's side. His damp face glowed. "Never enjoyed dancing more," he declared and went away.

From the buffet they selected a light repast. Guy drank champagne and tried to be unobtrusive while male guests chatted with his sister-in-law. One young man named Coltrane was disgruntled over his failure at the auction, and was truculent from drink. Guy was uncomfortable in his perceived role as chaperon, so during Cristina's next dance he slipped away and joined a group of Dublin socialites discussing the day's events. A jeweled, attractively gowned lady said, "You've visited Dublin before, Mr. Ryan?"

"Possibly," he told her. "I was born in Ireland and taken to America as a child."

"How interesting. Where were you born?"

"Aughrim, County Wicklow. My mother was a Doyle."

"Ahh—I'm not sure I know the Doyles of Wicklow. Landowners?"

"Cottagers—they worked the land of others."

Her expression congealed. Very carefully she said, "So many of our people found fortune in America."

"Or earned it," he said pleasantly, "as my late father did."

"Terribly admirable. If you'll forgive my remarking it, your sister-in-law is extremely attractive. One doesn't usually associate business acumen with so lovely a face."

"An unusual combination," he agreed, "and I'll convey the compliment to her if I may."

"By all means. Cristina just went off with Kieran Coltrane—I do hope she'll be on her guard," she said archly, gesturing almost imperceptibly toward an exit.

324

"Why so?"

"Kieran's one of our most notorious bachelors, quite un-principled with the ladies, one hears."

"I see. Well, it's probably time to leave. We have an early day tomorrow." He got up hoping his face concealed his concern, and began walking toward the ballroom's side exit, rock music screaming in his ears.

Emotions flooded his brain: anger, resentment that she would go off without telling him, and—he tried to force back the thought—jealousy? No, couldn't be. Cris wasn't his date, he was her evening escort, no more.

To the security guard at the doorway he said, "Where did they go?"

"Go? Who, sir?"

"The man and woman—wearing a long white gown."

"Ah—down the corridor." He cleared his throat delicately. "End suite," he said and stepped in front of Guy. "There's no trouble, sir?"

"Don't be ridiculous." Guy brushed past him, strode down the corridor past an elevator, and slowed, trying to sort out his emotions. Cris had every right to go where and with whom she wanted—no affair of his. Except that Don José would hold him accountable for anything that might shadow the family honor.

A door opened, slammed loudly shut, and he saw Cristina walking rapidly toward him. Seeing Guy, she slowed, and he saw that her face was flushed, angry. Taking her arm he said, "Can I help?"

"Help with—what?" Her gaze was averted.

"Oh, I thought you might want someone disciplined—for making improper advances."

"Is—that what happened?"

"That's obviously what happened," he said. "Now, if you've had enough of this victory celebration let's get some sleep."

Her lips trembled. "Oh, Guy, I had no idea Coltrane

325

would—would try to take advantage of me." She faced him appealingly.

"Then in the future it's best to assume it, avoid those situations—unless that's what you want."

"Guy! You know me better than that."

"But Coltrane didn't." He dabbed her moist eyes with his handkerchief. "Fact is, you brought it on yourself, dear, so learn from a bad experience."

At the elevator Guy pushed the button and Cristina said, "I will, I promise. I have," and managed a smile. "But for this . . . episode I've had a marvelous time. You'll come to La Rocha with me, see Al-Emir settled in?"

"I wish I could," he said, "but I'll go later."

"Father will be disappointed."

"Can't be helped," he said and stood back while she entered the elevator.

At the Gresham they chastely kissed good night and Cristina reiterated her thanks effusively. To Guy it seemed that she had already pushed Coltrane's brutishness from her mind.

They had early breakfast in the grill, after which Cristina set off to complete Al-Emir's paperwork, and Guy returned to his suite. He had finished talking with the plane crew about flying Cristina to Seville when he received an unexpected visit from James McGrain, DSA's man in Paris.

Twenty-Nine

Guy had coffee brought for them, and after McGrain was settled on a sofa he said, "Glad I got here before you left, sir. Mr. Hoskins didn't know where else you'd be traveling, and thought it important to contact you here."

Guy nodded.

McGrain sat forward. "In an unexpected way the deaths of two former RyTech executives attracted security interest. For nearly a year the FBI has had an important Soviet defector under wraps. The man—we'll call him Ivan—worked in the US for thirteen years as a GRU 'illegal.' His network was targeted at our most sensitive defense installations and factories."

"Why did he defect?"

"I'm short on details, but it seems Ivan's wife and son didn't want to return to the homeland when his tour was up. He couldn't return without them—and live—so he made a deal with the Bureau. Resettlement, the whole schmier, in return for full debriefing and cooperation."

"Go on."

"Seems Ivan saw obituary photos of Edmonds and Johns in the New York *Times,* and told the Bureau he'd recruited one of them about ten years ago. Edmonds."

Guy smiled grimly. "The epitome of capitalist bossism. Never occurred to me he had Soviet masters."

"Didn't look the part, for sure, but that's part of being a successful spy. Ivan said it was an ideological recruitment through some left-wing political study group. Ivan tasked Edmonds with gaining RyTech's presidency."

"Didn't happen, though."

McGrain shook his head. "Fortunately. But I guess it could have—if you hadn't taken the presidency yourself."

Guy said, "I was in New York when Edmonds was killed. The police said it was robbery-murder."

"Ivan claims it was a GRU hit squad, the kind that gets busy after a big man defects, to cut any leads to the USSR."

"Fascinating. And Farley Johns?"

"No espionage connection that Ivan knew of. He supposed Johns did Edmonds' bidding without knowing Edmonds was a Soviet agent."

"But we'll never be sure."

"Death shortstops a lot of revelations. Anyway, Mr. Ryan, Mr. Hoskins wanted you to know about Edmonds' Soviet involvement as it may relate to your further travels."

"I appreciate the information," he said, thinking that, thanks to Ivan, there would be no deep investigation of Edmonds' shooting.

"Mr. Hoskins said this should remind you what an important target for the Soviets RyTech is. You, too, sir."

"I'm well aware of it."

"Hiring guards for your wife and daughter was an excellent precaution, Mr. Ryan. Your friend Palfrey mentioned it the other day."

"You know Nigel?"

"Made himself known to me. Said he was doing physical security evaluations at his embassy, and we traded information. McGrain smiled. "Very conscientious gentleman. Said he passes by your apartment building on his way to work, sort of checking on the guards."

"That's like him," Guy said, "and I'm glad to know. Please thank Rob for me, and I appreciate your coming."

McGrain finished his coffee and got up. "I'd like to really see Dublin, but I have a Paris plane to catch."

They shook hands and McGrain left the suite.

Alone, Guy thought about Edmonds. He'd written him off as a mere embezzler, but the man he'd killed had been much more. A professional Soviet spy, whose treachery would have been buried with him but for Ivan's revelation.

Now, he understood that Marguerite's murder had been part of Edmonds' scheme to gain control of RyTech for the Soviets, and Edmonds was not the first Soviet agent to dip into available funds.

It occurred to Guy that perhaps Hans Egli had been secretly involved with Edmonds. Loss of his job would have made him useless to the Soviets, a prospect which, combined with an overpowering sense of personal guilt, could explain his suicide—but that was only speculation.

Who else have they hidden in RyTech? he wondered. He opened his closet and began packing his clothes.

Guy rode with Cristina to Dublin airport and they walked together out to the waiting Lear. Pilot and co-pilot touched their visors respectfully and began doing preflight cockpit checks.

Cristina pushed back her hat and kissed Guy, whispered, "I'll always love you," and quickly entered the plane.

Guy strolled back to the Civil Aviation office, waiting for the pilot to finish aircraft checks and brief him on how to find his way to Slane. As Guy waited he thought of the aged priest he had never seen, and wondered if Father Fallon was still alive. If not too senile to remember the past, how much would Father Fallon tell him about his father?

How much could he tell the priest?

The pilot came in, and using a wall map showed Guy

road directions to Slane, where he had gone before for Father Fallon.

"Take about an hour," the pilot said, "depending on how many sheep you slow for."

Guy looked at his watch. "It's one o'clock. If I spend two hours in Slane I should be back here before nightfall."

"The road's pretty rough and of course not lighted. Hope you don't have any problems."

"I hope not. Weather okay between here and Seville?"

"So far it's excellent. And I'll keep checking Paris weather on the flight back here."

"I'd like to be in Paris tonight," Guy said, "but if the weather turns bad this evening I'd rather stay here at the airport hotel and fly there tomorrow."

The pilot grinned. "My sentiments exactly." He walked out to the Lear and Guy saw the step-door fold up and lock. The plane turned and rolled smoothly toward the flight line.

He wondered what Cristina's thoughts were, what she was thinking at that moment, and decided he was better off not knowing.

He left Civil Aviation operations and got into his rented Rover. His years at Oxford had accustomed him to British left-hand driving and he had no difficulty exiting the airport and locating the narrow road to Slane.

The sky was the color of dull pewter, the cold air heavy with dampness from the Irish Sea. Celtic crosses along the roadside, mortarless stone walls that reminded him of Cheju Island. Clusters of thatched, whitewashed cottages, clothing on drying lines; milch cows, sheep, and red-cheeked children playing with crude barrows. Grim-faced stone churches dominating each settlement; graveyards filled with solemn Celtic crosses. Ireland's uncounted dead.

The Rover bumped up and over humpbacked stone bridges spanning icy streams. He slowed to let a drover move his sheep, and was rewarded by a hearty Irish smile.

As he drove north he saw rolling drumlins crowding the

330

western hills; wayside shrines and ruined abbeys that might have been tumbled in Cromwell's day; crooked trees that could have served as Roundhead gibbets. Guy knew the haunted history of Ireland, but at Oxford he had never thought to tour his native land. For him his father symbolized Ireland and so he'd stayed away.

Now, with Sean in his grave, Guy felt free to find and know the country of his birth, try to grasp its mysticism, understand the endless tragedy of its oppression. Ireland's tragic export was its people fleeing famine and barbarity, desperately emigrating where they could exist above the level of beasts.

He thought of the relict land's long, sad, church-ridden history, its subjugation by a kindred island people, and the vitality of its young that briefly sparked then died. He thought of Irish friendliness and wit, of Yeats, Behan and Joyce—the ultimate expatriate—who called his country an old sow that ate her farrow. A land of opposites and paradox.

Ah, well, he mused, steering around a misplaced boulder, I'll never know or solve it all, not even the smallest part.

Slane 2 Mi. read the English half of the wooden sign below the Gaelic letters. Nearby, an oldster on a stone, sucked a blackened long-stemmed pipe, cap angled sideways, too small to cover the thicket of uncut hair. A lined, drawn face with deepest button eyes. The shabby coat evoking poverty and age.

Perhaps his Degnan grandfather had looked like that.

More thatch-roofed houses, now; stiles for sheep and cows. Furrowed fields lay barren; autumn stubble still remained.

He saw the old church surmounted by its Celtic cross, steered to it and parked beside the churchyard with its plot of ancient graves.

The rear door's boards were warped and weathered. He knocked, heard footsteps shuffling over stone. The door creaked open and a wizened, gray-haired biddy stared suspiciously. "We need no dikshunarys, an' it be tuppence fer th' graveyard walk."

"It's the reverend fayther himself I'm wantin'," Guy said agreeably. "Tell Dennis Fallon it's Sean Ryan's Irish son."

"Guy Patrick, is it? I've thought ye'd come one day."

The old man spoke from a narrow bed, propped up by pillows. His face and hands held barely more color than the sheets. Through rimless spectacles he peered in Guy's direction.

"I've come," Guy said, "to learn more of my father. You knew him in his youth and heard his last confession."

"God rest 'is soul. That I did, to be shure." He plucked at the sheet across his lap. His white-sleeved bedshirt hung like a shroud.

Silently Guy rose and waved a hand before the face of the priest, whose expression did not change. His eyes, Guy now saw, were the color of watered milk, the spectacles mere artifice; Father Dennis Fallon was blind. As Guy resumed his chair the priest said, "What is't I can tell the son of Sean?"

"I think," Guy said, "you mean the son of Liam."

The words hung in the barren room like motes. Fallon's mouth opened and closed as his fingers twitched. Finally he muttered, "Told ye, did 'e? Shrived hisself at last. Ah, lad, the dark an' bloody secret had to out—I told him so." The voice seemed distant, the words mere cover for his hidden thoughts.

"I know my name is Degnan and my father killed a man."

The priest seemed to shrink into the bedclothes.

Guy said, "The secret kept him from coming back to Ireland. It was used against him later in his life."

"Yer dad was not a murtherer—he kilt in combat."

"But they'd have hung him just the same."

"His own dad, Fergus, was slaughtered by the Black an' Tans when Liam was only four." He looked toward the dusty window as though to see the past as it had been. "Orphaned he was by the Rising. Fed, raised an' eddicated by the Brotherhood—but all that ye must know."

"Educated? Where?" He had never thought of his father as having formal schooling.

"At University College, where else? In the early rise o' De Valera. Scarce had 'is degree when he became a soljer."

"Of the Provisionals."

The priest seemed not to hear him; his thoughts were swirling in the ambiguous mists of Irish time. "In thirty-five he fought some troopers on the Dublin quays. Then it was yer father kilt the Englishman an' took poor Sean Ryan's purse—leavin' 'is own fer the police to find." Turning his face slowly toward Guy he intoned, "Without bloodshed, no redemption—the words o' Pearse hisself."

"And you believe them."

"As I believe in God, the Virgin and our holy land." He crossed himself. "He went underground, then, did Liam, an' fought the English through the war wi' ambushes an' bombs."

"Helped by the Germans, I believe?"

"An' Rooshians, too."

"Ah," Guy said, "the Russians fresh from Spain."

"In certayn quarters the anti-Christ hisself wud o' been welcome."

"So German and Russian guerrillas knew who my father really was."

"It canna be denied."

Guy sat forward. "In New York did you meet an officer of my father's company named Edmonds? Paul Edmonds?"

His head moved slowly, negatively. "Not then. Yer fayther was careful I meet no one else."

333

Guy thought for a moment. "You said 'not then.' Meaning you'd seen Edmonds on another occasion?"

Father Fallon nodded. "Four years ago Paul Edmonds brought a gift here from yer fayther."

"What kind of gift?"

" 'Twas money, the best kind of gift."

"For yourself? The parish?"

"Ah, no, I was the mere temporary destination," he sighed.

"Then it was for the Brotherhood?"

The Priest fell silent, his hands working a rosary. Guy said, "And at the time of my father's death you were with my father only at the hospital?"

Father Fallon nodded. "Confession, then the final rites. Liam met God with a shinin' soul." Weakly he crossed himself. "Ye can be glad o' that."

Guy sat forward. "Where's my mother's grave?"

"Molly—Doyle that was? Ah, I remember. She lies in Aughrim churchyard, hard by where ye was birthed. Married yer dad the year the grand Republic was proclaimed. He couldna take her to no hospital because 'e was 'ard sought them days. She bore ye on a kitchin table, the midwife Coughlan there to cut the cord. It was another priest who buried 'er, an' baptised ye the same sorrowin' day."

Guy breathed deeply, felt wetness in his eyes. "Where is the real Sean Ryan buried?"

"I canna say—wher'er the English dumped 'is corse."

The biddy came in with medicine, administered it with a spoon. Gazing hostilely at Guy she said, "Ye're overlong, the fayther's sick an' tired, be merciful an' go."

Father Fallon waved one hand to mitigate her words. "Aught else, Guy—Degnan?"

"Before I leave Ireland I need to see Conor Counihan. Can you tell me where I can find him? County Monaghan, I heard."

"As good a place as any. Now and thin 'e's seen in bloody Belfast, too."

"Was he one of those who fought alongside my father?"

"I've heard it said that he was on the quays, rifle in han', wi' yer dad." He smiled wanly. "The stories fade. Who knows? Another story has it Liam kilt Ryan in black fury over Molly Doyle—but who alive's to say?"

"You heard his confession."

"An' I'll say only this—not ivry Irishman's yer fayther's friend." He looked away. "Ask Conor Counihan, not me."

"If you can get a message to Conor tell him we must talk." He got up and dragged his chair back to the wall.

The priest said, "Yer spirit's Degnan but yer words are Doyle, be glad o' that."

"What can I do for you, father? Do you need medicine? A doctor?"

The withered hands opened. "The Lord sees to my needs. I'm eighty an' three, my son—sometimes I feel I've lived too long already."

Guy spoke to the biddy waiting by the door. "If I can help you must let me know." Then he knelt at Fallon's bedside, bowed his head and felt the chill touch of the old man's fingers as he murmured a Gaelic blessing. His parting words were, "Lead a good life, Guy Degnan, away from Ireland's sorrows." He made the sign of the cross.

Guy left the room, walked through the simple kitchen and pushed open the wooden door.

As he went down the worn stone steps he saw four figures rise from behind his car. Their faces were fully masked and their hands held automatic weapons.

Thirty

They had blindfolded and gagged him, trussed his arms behind his back and shoved him into some sort of van. Guy lay on the hard floor feeling every bump as the tires pounded country roads.

His body ached, his hands tingled from lack of circulation. He wondered where he was being taken. And why.

They had captured him almost wordlessly, efficiently. He was among professionals, he knew; resistance would have meant sudden death. One of the four had driven away his Rover. Another drove the van, and two were somewhere near.

Could the biddy have summoned them to the rectory? Or had some watcher spied his English car along the road? The old pipe smoker by the sign was well-placed to report all strangers. Was it ransom they wanted—or his death?

His teeth chewed the gag. He rolled over on his back to spread the roadbed shocks.

Lead a good life away from Ireland's sorrows, the old priest had enjoined him. Good advice, he'd thought, but he'd had no time to follow.

As the shock of capture began to wear away, his mind grew active. Killing him at the churchyard would have profaned the holy place, involved Fallon in his murder. But any time in the last half hour they could have stopped the van and shot him in a ditch—if killing was their plan.

So his death was not to be immediate. Ransom was their probable purpose, and Needham would pay all that they asked. But would they free him . . . ? He thought of his wife, the daughter he had barely come to know. Cristina, who loved him, too.

Too much remained unfinished; he couldn't meekly die. Had to resist and get away.

They could be taking him anywhere, he mused; like rabbit holes, there were safe places all over Ireland. To Limerick or Cork, Mayo or Roscommon.

County Monaghan, where Conor had his burrow?

The vehicle slowed, turned sharply, bounced over a rise, lurched and steadied before coming to a halt.

Doors opened. Hands lifted him to his feet. His nostrils scented hay.

A kick sent him outward, stumbling onto straw-strewn floor. He lay prone. Hands jerked him upright, untied the gag, shoved up the blindfold.

His eyes blinked at piercing lights.

To right and left stood armed men. Before him, two sat at a rough table. All six were masked.

Above were rafters, a hayloft shelf. Pigeons burbled in the eaves.

He was in a barn. "Loosen my rope," he said, "or my hands will drop from gangrene."

"It's not you gives orders here," said one man at the table. "Your discomfort means naught to me." The Irish accent was less pronounced than Fallon's.

"Suit yourself," Guy told him. "If you're to kill me then do so. I have a priest's blessing, my conscience is clear."

"Is it, now? You stand before us charged with high crimes against the Irish State."

"Do I? Then where's a barrister for my defense?"

"This is a revolutionary court where we follow not the

customs of the bourgeoisie. As a member of the imperialist class you're guilty for its exploitations."

"By what right do you judge me? I was born in County Wicklow. My grandfather fought and died in the Easter Rising. I'm son of Molly Doyle and Liam Degnan, faithful to Ireland to his death. Who are you to judge me?"

The man at the table said, "Be silent," then whispered to the other "judge." Outside the barn a cow mooed plaintively.

Guy said, "I'll play no part in this charade. Kill me and have done with it. But first, ask Conor Counihan."

The man laughed unpleasantly. "How is it you know Conor?"

"My father's lifelong friend. I'm under his protection in Ireland."

"Are you, now? Perhaps we'll see about that."

Guy knew there were IRA factions within factions, co-operating for major anti-English strikes, then following their separate ways. "Ask Conor," he challenged, "or it will go hard with you."

"Why did you go to Slane?"

"To visit my father's priest. Father Fallon can speak to that. If what you want is money, you're no more than extortionists. If you take my life you're murderers and my death will be avenged." Boldness was his only weapon, he'd decided. Confusion his aim.

The leftward "judge" cleared his throat and lifted a newspaper page. One of the guards brought it near Guy who saw a photograph of himself beside Cristina and Al-Emir.

His accuser said, "Ye paid millions for a foreign nag; how much is your own life worth?"

"Ask Jake Needham in New York."

"No one in Europe? Think, man, on your life."

"I've told you what to do."

The man cursed. One of the guards muttered, "Take bloody long."

"This Needham, how can he be reached?"

Guy told him, adding, "Have him come to Europe— Dublin, Galway, Zürich, name the place."

They whispered again and he thought he heard Counihan's name. Finally, one said, "Take him above," and hands gripped his arms from behind. "Loosen my wrists," Guy said, "I have no weapon to fight the six of you."

Grudgingly the man nodded. Fingers loosened Guy's bonds and he was shoved up wooden steps to the left. After tying his wrists to a wooden post they left him lying on a stack of hay.

Below, spotlights went off, the van backed from the barn. They had not counted on so much trouble, he thought, and were uncertain what to do. Would they consult Conor Counihan, or risk reprisal by killing their captive out of hand? He wanted Jake to be in charge of any ransoming—but would they take that course?

The skylight above was dark. By now the aircrew must be wondering where he was. How long would they wait before taking action? What would they do?

Cautiously he backed to the post, began rubbing wrist ropes against a raw corner. Splinters jabbed his palms. Footsteps coming up. He sat still as a flashlight beam played across him. "Water," he said. "I need water—and food."

He heard steps going down again, and after a while the guard brought back a metal cup, held it while Guy gulped thirstily. "That's better," he said, licking his lips, "and I could do with a drop o' the poteen."

"Water's sufficient fer the likes o' you," the guard said nastily, and when he went down again Guy heard him talking to another man.

So there were two of them. Perhaps others in the farmhouse. He rubbed the ropes vigorously, feeling with his fingertips the first parted strands. His heels moved hay aside, and through cracks in the planking he could see dim light below.

He rested aching arms, resumed the rubbing. During the next rest period he looked up and saw stars through the skylight. When he heard footsteps again he closed his eyes and let his head sag forward as though in sleep. Light played across him. The harsh voice of Conor Counihan said, "Guy Ryan, ye're not the airy lad ye was when first we met."

Guy opened his eyes and looked up at the old man. "Call me by my right name, Conor. Degnan—as you always knew."

"Aye. Knew from the first. An' now in yer extremity ye turn to auld Conor, thinkin' I'd return the favors ye denied me"

"Thinking you'd set things right—for the sake of my dead father, Liam."

"Then think again, lad. Ye'll pay fer your snottiness to yer fayther's friend."

"This gang is yours?"

"Nay, lad, but since ye summoned me I'll share from yer misfartune."

Guy grunted. "You blackmailed Liam for years, so it's apt you're profiting from me."

"Aye—yer dad married well, turned his back on the Brotherhood. I did naught but remind 'im he possessed a stolen name an' could be hung."

"A true friend, Conor. How much am I worth to you?"

" 'Tis not for me to say. That's to be set by the furrin gentleman who guides these patriotic lads. I'll now confer with 'im."

"Do that," Guy said testily, "and I'm sorry I spoke your name. Small good it's done me."

"Hist, they be sanguinary lads, impatient to get yer gold. I counseled patience, else they might 'ave joined ye to yer dad."

"You'll be well paid, old man."

"Aye. The Brotherhood is always needin' funds to carry on our work. And funds we'll get, else these brave lads'll slit yer throat, Guy Degnan."

"That might not sit well with the foreign gentleman."

" 'Im? Oh, 'es the bloodiest of all."

"Who is he, then?"

" 'Tis not fer me to say. We 'ave our secrets, lad."

"So you do. But I should get something for my money."

"Yer life'll be sufficient." He turned and shuffled down the wooden steps.

So much for that, Guy thought, and lay motionless until he heard Counihan leave the barn. At first he'd regretted invoking the old conspirator's name, but of all his captors only Counihan might intervene to spare his life. For Guy had no doubt that they would kill him after ransom was paid.

So, I might as well die trying to get away, he mused, and slowly, quietly resumed abrading the ropes that bound his wrists. He shifted to another corner, where rougher wood brought better results. Friction heated the strands and more began to part from steady sawing.

It occurred to him that more guards might come to the barn, and that he would be moved to another holding place under cover of darkness. Tomorrow could bring more difficult circumstances, including death. His best chance was to get out now.

Gradually the strands gave way. Guy rubbed chafed wrists and gnawed a splinter from his palm. He lay face down and peered through the nearest crack. Masks off, two guards sat at the table playing dominoes, a bottle beside them.

For a few moments he considered the next move, then untied the snub rope from the post and wound its ends around both hands leaving a two-foot span. He stretched it tight and grimaced.

He had his garrote.

Crawling slowly he reached the head of the stairs and

stood up, back against the dark wall. The angle allowed him to view one of the guards. Tiles clicked on the table and when the game ended the guard swept them off disgustedly. Tilting the bottle he drank. "Get yer supper," he told the other. "I'll take care o' mister big an' mighty. Save a morsel for me."

Guy shrank against the wall as a tousle-headed young man crossed below and went out the barn door, closing it. The remaining guard, a redhead, drank from the bottle again and began picking up domino tiles.

Guy groaned. The squatting guard looked up at the loft. Guy groaned again, letting it linger.

"You, there, what's the matter?"

A drawn-out moan. "Sick," Guy gasped. "Help me."

"Fuck ye," sneered the guard. "Ye're dead meat anyways."

"Fuck yourself, asshole," Guy gasped. "Dirty Ulster sod."

With a curse the guard rushed to the stairway, came up two at a time. At the top Guy's foot tripped him and sprawled the guard face down.

Guy was on him before he could roll away, crossed hands looping the cord around his throat. Knees on the man's back Guy forced him down, tightened the noose and soon his boots stopped beating.

For another minute Guy maintained tension, relaxing it long enough to feel the carotid. The artery was still.

Before he got up Guy searched the body, pulled an automatic pistol from the pocket. He jacked a shell into the magazine before dragging the body down to the ground floor. He hauled it to the table and lifted it into a chair, letting the torso slant forward on the table. He folded the arms and placed the head on them.

At first glance, the redhead had fallen asleep.

A long sleep, he thought grimly as he closed the staring eyes.

Using the guard's flashlight he began looking through the barn. The second stall was an armory; automatic weapons, grenades, gelignite, tins of black powder, fuse, cases of shells.

He selected a Sterling MkVII machine pistol with a full magazine. There were four handguns with thick silencers. One was a loaded 9mm Browning. He was weighing it in his hand when the barn door swung open and the other guard came in.

Seeing his companion at the table, he called, "Wake up, y'fool," and went toward him. He cuffed the red hair and the head rolled aside. He was staring at it when Guy shot him through the throat and heart.

The sounds were less than the scraping of a chair.

The dying man's legs twitched reflexively, the body shuddered and lay still.

From the armory Guy took two fragmentation grenades and three sticks of gelignite. He shouldered the Sterling, pocketed the silenced pistol, and left the barn.

He waited in darkness until night vision came. The house was less than a hundred yards away. The van was concealed from the road by a wall of baled hay.

He stayed in shadows as he made his way to the house.

The kitchen window was lighted; inside, at a table, six men were eating. From their clothing he recognized two guards and the "judges." The fifth man was Conor Counihan; the sixth, a heavyset man with close-cropped hair, Slavic eyes and cheekbones. He wore gray whipcord livery—the foreign gentleman.

All six were sharing stew and Guinness, listening to radio news.

To learn if the hunt's on for me, Guy thought, as he armed a hand grenade. Stepping back from the window, Guy estimated distance, and lobbed the heavy grenade through the window pane.

He saw the men's startled faces before the blast obliter-

343

ated them. Yells and screams tore from the smoking window. Guy tossed the gelignite inside, then the second grenade. He sprinted toward the van as half the house disintegrated. The concussion shoved him hard against the van. Flames shot through the demolished roof. In a distant pasture frightened horses whinnied and neighed. Disconnectedly, he thought of Al-Emir.

A figure staggered out of the flames, clothes burning, dropped and rolled weakly on the ground, lay still. Guy went to it, thinking it might be Counihan. Instead, the blackened face and charred uniform identified the foreign gentleman, now deceased. Guy toed aside smoking coat fragments and pulled out the heated leather wallet. Under the melted plastic window was a chauffeur's carnet issued to Grigor Fedorovich Filchuk of the Soviet Embassy in Dublin.

Briefly, Guy considered taking the wallet, then returned it to what was left of the inside pocket. Both branches of Soviet Intelligence used chauffeur cover because it gave their agents easy mobility. Wiping soot from his fingers, Guy stared down at the man who had engineered his capture, and remembered McGrain's admonition that the Soviets would try again and again.

Not this comrade, though. Nor Counihan, who, if not a Soviet agent, was on cooperative terms with Filchuk.

Only hours before, Father Fallon had said there were Irishmen who'd work with the anti-Christ against England.

The old house was roaring like a Guy Fawkes bonfire, popping and whistling, explosions roiling flames through shattered window frames.

Counihan's payoff. The old man's body might not be identified, but the Russian's would, and Guy wondered whether the Brits would exploit the find—or cover it up, as was the British tendency when dealing with Soviet embarrassments.

The van started. He turned through the barnyard and

took a narrow road that led away. The bump of the stone bridge told him he was headed in the right direction. Except for the first guard's pistol, Guy tossed the other weapons into the stream. Until he reached a crossing road he kept the headlights off.

He turned onto it and found a sign a quarter of a mile away. *Nobber* pointed in one direction, *Navan/Dublin* the other. Across quiet fields came the scream of a fire engine racing through the night.

Headlights on, he took the Dublin road.

Beyond Fairyhouse Racecourse a sign pointed to the airport. His body ached, especially his wrists and arms. As he drove he brushed dirt and hay from his clothing, wiped grime from his face. He needed a shower, a drink, a bed. Unutterably tired, he recognized the letdown after combat. Ahead, the dark road unreeled.

From above, a plane came down toward an invisible runway. He saw the distant glow of airport lights and continued driving until headlights showed a narrow side road. He turned onto it and got out, leaving the engine running.

As he walked away he noticed that the license plates were missing. Lucky he hadn't been stopped along the way by vigilant police.

Half an hour's hike through chill night air brought him to the main airport building. He walked through to the Civil Aviation side, and asked the clerk for the Lear's aircrew.

"Be ye misther Ryan?" he asked in polite surprise. "Yer crew's alarmed, sent th' authorities searchin' for ye."

"Wasn't necessary," he said, to pass it off. "At Slane my car was stolen. I've been looking for it ever since."

"Yer crew's at th' hotel. I'll let 'em know ye're found."

"Thanks, I'll do it myself."

A courtesy bus took him to the airport hotel, and from his room he phoned the crew. After thanking them for their concern he said his Rover had been stolen and he'd waited too long in Slane, hoping it would be found. "But you did the right thing," he told the pilot. "If I'd been kidnapped it could have made a difference."

"Yes, sir, afraid that's what we thought. What time do you want to leave for Paris?"

"After breakfast," he said. "Let's get a good night's sleep."

With the breakfast cart came the morning's Dublin paper. While eating grapefruit Guy glanced at the first page and felt his body freeze.

Halfway down the righthand column a story was headed, *Paris Kidnapping. Wife and child of American industrialist taken by gunmen in street battle.*

Sick, incredulous he read on:

Yesterday morning the Spanish-born wife of American industrialist Guy Ryan was kidnapped with their daughter by gunmen who killed their guard and chauffeur, and forced them from the sidewalk into a waiting van. A passerby who tried to intervene was gravely wounded during an exchange of shots. Witnesses said the van sped off, and it is understood that it was found abandoned later in the day. Authorities are maintaining silence about the episode and decline to speculate concerning the perpetrators of the abduction. Whether the motive was ransom or terrorism has not been determined. If the latter, it would be the eighth such episode thus far in the current year, although no militant group has yet claimed responsibility.

He stared blindly at the wall as the telephone began to ring.

BOOK FIVE

Thirty-One

On the third day after reaching Paris, Guy went with Jake Needham to the Bichat Hospital on Boulevard Ney. En route, Needham said, "The patient is Paris police Inspector Jean Bourcave. The kidnappers' bullets tore him up pretty bad—lost a third of his liver and a piece of his lower bowel. He was walking to work at his Commissariat when he saw the abduction taking place and tried to stop it. I thought you'd want to thank him, hear what he has to say."

"You're absolutely right," Guy said, "and I wonder if a present of some kind is in order?"

"I'll ask around tactfully."

At the room entrance a doctor warned them not to tire the inspector, and they went in.

The balding man in the bed nodded at their entrance and gestured to bedside chairs. His skin was sallow with a yellowish tinge, and an array of tubes and electrodes was attached to him. A bushy black mustache adorned his upper lip. His dark eyes were deep set and intelligent.

After introducing himself Guy said, "I'll be forever grateful for what you did, Inspector, and to avoid tiring you I won't ask questions. But if you feel strong enough I want to hear just what happened."

Bourcave nodded. "I appreciate your coming, monsieur,

and I extend my sympathy. I will always regret that I was unable to prevent what happened to your wife and daughter." He breathed deeply, seeming to steel himself for the coming effort, then began. "I was walking the Avenue Foch that morning as I always do, and I noticed something unusual—a bakery van idling where it had no reason to be. Then I saw a woman and child leaving the apartment building. There was a man with them—a bodyguard, I realized later—and he looked around before leading them to a waiting Daimler. The chauffeur opened the rear door for them. So far, m'sieu, everything routine. But before they could get in, the van drew even with the Daimler, and gunfire dropped the bodyguard before he could get out his weapon. Then the chauffeur went down. The woman stood frozen while three masked men spilled out of the van. All carried submachine guns.

"By then I had my pistol out, and wounded the gunman farthest from the woman. Another fired at me from behind the van. I fired back and saw the third gunman force mother and daughter into the van. As it moved away I ran into the street trying to shoot the driver. A burst caught me, and I was down, unconscious before I could get the license number." His face twisted.

"Protecting them wasn't your job," Guy said, "but I'm indebted to you for your brave efforts. The van was found, abandoned."

Pain stiffened the wounded man's face, and he made a strong effort to continue. "Right now it may seem little comfort to you, but I take heart from the assault being so well-planned. That means a serious organization, not just a band of fanatical terrorists. And that organization wants something from you—probably money."

"They can have it all. They've killed two of my people, and if they harm my family I'll hunt down those animals and butcher them myself."

"It's early to talk of revenge, m'sieu. Were there any clues?"

"Your bullet hole in the windshield." Guy's voice thickened. "And they found one of Gloria's earrings in a crevice in the floor." He opened his hand to let Bourcave see it. "I didn't wait for a ransom demand. I've offered a million francs for their safe return, or information leading to the capture of the gunmen."

"Excellent. May I ask what else has been done?"

"Consuela's—*my* apartment has become a sort of command post. My half-sister, Nicole, came from Lyons with her husband. He assembled an array of radio communications gear and satellite teleprinters that connect with my New York office, the Embassy here, and your Ministry of Interior, which is supervising the search by the DST, the Paris police and the Special A.T. Squad.

"In the Embassy Ambassador Brook chairs an interagency task force. Everyone has lines out, but nothing's come in."

"It will, it will. This is bad time for you, m'sieu, but don't begin to lose hope."

"My friend here, Jake Needham, is coordinating everything and keeping me sane." He smiled weakly. "His toughest job."

Bourcave said, "These chemicals they stuffed me with— not good for mind or memory. But now I recall something that could be useful."

"Go on, please."

"The gunmen started shouting to each other when I appeared. It was French, but with an Arab accent." His near hand opened and closed. "Algerian, Moroccan, Iraqi, Syrian—no way I could tell."

A nurse came in. "You must leave, Mr. Ryan."

He took Bourcave's hand. "Thank you, my friend." Guy left the room, brushing past doctors waiting to come in.

* * *

In the apartment he told Nikky what Bourcave had remembered, while Jake had gone to the commo center and transmitted the new information to the task force at the Embassy, and the Ministry of Interior. Returning to Guy he said, "That narrows things, doesn't it? Maybe the inspector will remember more."

"He's still on the danger list. You saw the strain on him to talk at all."

"But he did—that's the point. Yesterday I told the hospital to bring in specialists, do whatever's necessary to get him well. Tomorrow I'll visit him."

"I'll go with you," said Nikky. "He more than deserves the whole family's thanks."

Guy sipped coffee laced with Cognac. "Nikky, I'm very grateful for your coming here. And Thibaud. I wouldn't have known what to do."

"Cristina called while you were gone. She's coming within the next few days. I tried to discourage her but she'd have none of it, said it was *her* sister and niece who were missing."

Jake said, "I'll find things for her to do so she won't be underfoot."

Guy suppressed a smile. Those who thought of Cris as a useless butterfly didn't know her well.

The cook entered and spoke with Nikky, who said, "The larder needs replenishing and I should plan some meals. Be back in a while."

After she left Jake said, "Hoskins is coming over by Concorde this afternoon."

"Why?"

"To add muscle at the Embassy, show his support for you. And—he may have some ideas."

* * *

Guy led Rob Hoskins into the studio with Jake and said, "It's time I told you both what I've been involved in recently."

Jake said, "Sure you ought to?"

"Yes, Counselor. I sense things closing in, perhaps I won't live much longer. I've withheld circumstances that may have a bearing on what I'm going through right now." He paused to sip from a glass of water. "It begins with Marguerite's purse found in the chopper wreckage."

Methodically, he told them of Marguerite's letter and how he had trapped D'Angelo. Then he told them of the suicide of Farley Johns, and the shooting of Paul Edmonds. "Because of what Edmonds hinted about my father's Irish background I visited his confessor in Slane. He added enough detail to show me how vulnerable Sean was to blackmail."

Hoskins said, "By whom?"

"Conor Counihan. Leaving the rectory I was grabbed by four masked men," he told them, and described his "trial," the unexpected appearance of Conor Counihan, his escape and the demise of Soviet agent Filchuk.

"A bad lot," Hoskins said. "Glad you erased them, Guy, gladder still you survived."

Jake said, "What's your sense of the episode, Guy?"

"In the little time I've had to ponder it I've concluded that I was grabbed for ransom by a Marxist IRA faction. Their intention was to get the money, then kill me—that would be consonant with Soviet determination to control RyTech. Counihan being a power in the Brotherhood, they cut him in for a share of the ransom. Conor didn't care what happened to me."

Hoskins said, "It's best I not enlighten our British cousins; for one thing, they'd probably not want to know."

Jake said, "Does your abduction relate to Connie's?"

Guy shrugged. "My family was kidnapped before I was. So far, we don't know if they were captured on Soviet orders, or whether it's an independent terrorist action. But the situation is I'm free and my family isn't."

"On that note," said Hoskins, "I'm going to the Embassy, talk with McGrain and find out what the task force is doing."

Guy was drawn to his daughter's room, filled with toys, books and dresses. Gloria's presence seemed almost tangible, but each time he brooded there his emotions overflowed until he finally forced himself to lock the door and stay away.

Inwardly Guy conceded that this was one of the few times in his life when he was not in control of a personal situation. Others, remote and hidden, were calling the shots. They were in charge of his family's lives, and he could do nothing.

His helplessness sickened him.

Jake allowed the two psychics to walk through the apartment, and for a time Guy felt a surge of hope. Then they came back to ask for money and Guy ordered them not to return.

McGrain came to confer with him and said, "Bourcave's recollection opened up another area to explore. The Left Bank and working-class sections of Paris are jammed with refugees from Francophone Africa. The flight of Algerian *pieds-noirs* began the immigration, followed by large numbers of French-acculturated Arabs from Syria, Iraq, Morocco and Iran. Parts of Paris resemble *kasbahs*, everyone crammed cheek by jowl with their blankets and cooking pots. Real misery in some quarters. They take the dirtiest jobs in France, but there aren't enough of those to go around."

"Make your point."

"Crime ferments in these pockets, sir. Offer fifty or a hundred francs for a murder and you'll find two hundred volunteers. In the early days the police and DST tried to exercise control, but the problem flared beyond them. Now they leave the Arab enclaves to themselves, though they employ informers to tell them generally what's going on.''

"Like eighteenth-century Whitefriars,'' Guy suggested.

McGrain nodded. "Through those informers our allies hope to turn up the abductors. And they've been spreading money around. They figure—and I agree—that among so much poverty someone's going to sell what he knows.''

"Bourcave was impressed with the professionalism the gunmen showed. That suggests training and skill beyond that of ordinary criminals.''

"It does, but remember that a good many operated as guerrillas *against* the French for years—and came here when various popular governments didn't suit their tastes. So they live from what they do best—crime. To form a kidnap team would be, I'm afraid, all too easy.''

"The task force doesn't find an ideological basis for— what happened?''

"Not thus far. They're concentrating on identifying the five perpetrators, and they feel that's justified because— surprisingly—no known terrorist group has claimed responsibility. The assumption is it's just a question of time before a ransom demand is made.''

Guy nodded. "I've thought of a means of verifying whether a claimant actually has my wife and child. Ask him to describe Gloria's earrings. I have one—she's wearing the other.''

"That's good,'' said McGrain, "I'll hold that closely, though.''

"You don't trust the DST, the French police?''

"I don't trust anyone outside the task force room.''

That evening Nikky said, "Thibaud's calling from his office, Guy. Can you talk with him?''

Taking the phone, Guy said, "Thibaud? No news here."

"Nikky told me, and I'm very sorry. Especially since I have disagreeable news for you."

"Let's hear it."

"I've discovered some product leakage—if you understand me."

"Eastward?"

"Exactly. I hate to suggest this, but the problem is important enough I feel you should come here. If there's a ransom demand from the kidnappers, Nikky will phone and you can be back in Paris in an hour or so."

"No way, Thibaud. You're in charge there, you know what has to be done—just do it."

Hesitantly, Thibaud said, "If you're willing to trust me."

"If I didn't trust you, you'd be gone. Thibaud, in an earlier conversation you said Sean had told you to ignore American export restrictions and follow French practice. My question is whether you spoke personally with my father and whether he gave you those orders. Think carefully."

For a few moments there was silence. Then, reminiscently, Thibaud said, "Now I think of it, Guy, I didn't actually speak with Sean. I was told those were his orders."

"Who told you?"

"Paul Edmonds, speaking in Sean's name. Said he was authorized to do so. Should I have—?"

Guy expelled pent-up breath. "I thought that might be the case, and I'm not blaming you. One day I'll tell you about the late Paul Edmonds. And—thanks. If you need me tomorrow I'll be here—except for a morning meeting with the Ambassador."

Thirty-Two

Set back from Avenue Gabriel, the American Embassy faced the Place de la Concorde with its tall Obelisk, the muddy Seine, and the gray, ominous-appearing Chamber of Deputies on the Left Bank. French in appearance, and constructed of biege stone that turned roseate in morning light, the Embassy was guarded by smartly uniformed Marines, alert since the Beirut bombings to terrorists and dynamite-laden cars.

Inside, the task force met in a large ceremonial room papered in flowered damask, and trimmed with ivory enamel.

At the end of a long polished table, Ambassador Brook presided over the meeting. Thin-faced and somewhat pale, Brook wore expensively tailored clothing on his slim frame, and wore it well. Originally a career Foreign Service Officer of modest means, Harlan Brook had married the heiress to a distillery fortune and seen his career zoom skyward. His wife enjoyed the diplomatic whirl, and political contributions by her and her family had secured Brook the Paris post through Presidential patronage.

At least, Guy thought, Brook was presentable, well-traveled, familiar with protocol, and, amazingly, spoke

357

passable French. As Guy sat there, his thoughts turned from the Ambassador to what the Legal Attaché was saying:

"The typical abduction pattern hasn't been followed. From that we conclude that the group had never conducted a kidnapping before—or that they were surrogates acting on orders."

He was a large pink-faced man with nearly platinum hair who spoke with robot-like precision. Guy said, "Whose orders?"

"The possibilities are enormous. Europeans who don't like RyTech. Groups that hate America. Plus whatever enemies you may have, Mr. Ryan."

Ambassador Brook said, "By surrogates—you mean the Soviets? Could the KGB be behind this outrage?"

"It's not a possibility we can exclude, but I lean toward Muslim fanatics. They're notorious for causing long range trouble. So do Latin American revolutionaries who need funds for a coup. Peaceniks would have made their demands known by now . . ." He looked at the DST delegate, who nodded slightly. "In France the FBI—my office—has no arrest powers. Liaison is our principal function, and while we're glad to sit in here, perhaps advise, we look to the Ministry of Interior and the Paris Commissariat of Police as action-responsible."

Across the table from Guy, Hoskins and McGrain exchanged covert glances. In effect, Guy realized, the FBI was signing off.

The Ambassador said, "My instructions from the Department are to be as helpful as possible to all concerned, and urge the Quai d'Orsay to bring its full influence to bear on the situation toward a positive resolution. After all, our Tehran people came home safely."

"After fifteen months of hell," Guy said disgustedly. "My daughter is six years old. Even if she's not harmed, do you think she won't be damaged by captivity—by what she's already endured?"

358

The Ambassador said, "Quiet diplomacy—"

"—is for the birds," Guy interrupted. "In 'Nam when we wanted intelligence we sent out a patrol to take prisoners—and I'm personally familiar with the technique. But what I'm absorbing here is a general air of resignation. De Gaulle broke the Armée Secrète by grabbing underground leaders and torturing them before execution. After he got tough the Algerian conspiracy collapsed. He was dealing with thousands of enemies of the Republic—my family was captured by only four men. It seems inconceivable that with all the Ministry's resources not the slightest clue has come in." He stared aggressively around the silent table. "Apparently the situation is this—either four criminals have outsmarted everyone in France—or the Ministry is totally incompetent."

The Ambassador glanced nervously at the DST delegate, then at Guy. "We all understand the emotional strain you're under, Mr. Ryan, but we're guests of the French Republic—all of us—not its critics. The Interior Ministry has assumed appropriate responsibility for the manhunt—our role here is that of clearinghouse."

"Or outhouse," snapped Guy as he got up. "Well, I've heard enough, little as it was. I've been patient, too patient, expecting you 'experts' to recover my family. 'Have confidence, trust us'—sounds like a hillbilly song."

Achille Maundit, the Ministry sub-Commissioner said, "What would you have us do, sir?"

Placing the palms of his hands on the table Guy leaned forward. "The last scene in *Casablanca* the French cop says, 'Round up the usual suspects.' "

Maundit smiled condescendingly. "And having done so?"

"Break fingers, pull teeth—until someone talks." He breathed hoarsely. "Animals, subhumans have my wife and child and you recommend quiet diplomacy. Well, that's insufficient. Do I disturb you? I won't be back."

359

He strode from the room. Pitiful, he thought, a roach has more resourcefulness than the pack of them.

As he left the Embassy he wondered why Serge Kedrov hadn't dropped by to offer sympathy. Kedrov had been inordinately interested in Connie, so his masters must have ordered him to stay away.

Entering the apartment, Guy found Paul Whitaker waiting for him. Rising, the former Special Branch officer said, "I've been reluctant to press my services, sir, feeling you'd let me know if I was needed."

"I would."

Whitaker nodded. "Anything at all. Anything," he repeated. "But I'm here on a different matter. Can we talk privately?"

"Of course." Guy led him into the *atelier* and closed the door. "When the ransom is paid I'll want you on hand."

"Glad to be of use." He cleared his throat. "Not trusting the telephone lines, I thought best to speak with you directly. It's about G–371."

"G—?"

"Ghost."

"Yes, I remember." Hoskins' briefing had been so long ago he'd almost forgotten the radar-absorbing paint. "What about it?"

"I spot-checked inventory and found a half-liter flask missing. The section supervisor said he checks daily, so the substance hadn't been missing long. We'll have to report the theft to Air Force, you understand."

"I understand, but I don't like it." He gazed at the empty easel that once held Kedrov's portrait. "What do you propose to do?"

"Recover the stolen flask, identify the thief—or thieves—and revise section security to prevent more thefts."

"Can Ghost be duplicated from the half-liter sample?"

"You'd know better than I." He grimaced. "Bringing me to point two. The G–371 formula is kept in a wall safe

360

in the manufacturing section. I went over the safe with a magnifying lens and found fine marks in the steel, plus a thin circle of carbon residue. Meaning an effort's been made to get at the formula.''

''Successful?''

''If the formula had been copied the thief wouldn't need to take the sample. Before coming here I removed the formula and stowed it in my own safe. No one knows it's gone, no one knows where it is.''

''Good. What's the carbon circle mean?''

''Suction cup microphone—to amplify tumbler sounds when the dial turns. Old fashioned, but usually reliable—on a three-way tumbler dial.'' He twisted one end of his mustache. ''This is a five-way dial, but the thief wouldn't have known that—hearing three sets fall, and not being able to open the safe must have drove him crazy.'' He grinned. ''If I know anything about thieves.''

''I suspect you do.'' Guy felt reassured by Whitaker's presence, and now that the Embassy task force had struck out he wanted Whitaker's advice. But the Ghost theft had to be resolved. ''What else?'' he asked.

''A competent thief wouldn't have left scratch marks near the dial. That he left the little carbon circle suggests he was working in bad light—after dark when the section was closed down. Soviet Intelligence has the technical equipment to open that safe in minutes, so one of their safecrackers wasn't working it. But assuming GRU or KGB is behind the effort, they'll supply proper gear to their man.''

''An employee?''

''A penetration agent—recruited in place. Otherwise—''

A knock on the door. It opened a foot, and Needham looked in. ''Guy? Sorry to disturb you, but Hoskins and McGrain are here.''

''Be there in a minute.'' To Whitaker he said, ''Listen in and learn what I'm up against.'' He left the *atelier* door partly open and joined his visitors.

"You were pretty hard on the Ambassador," Hoskins told him, "not to mention the Legal Attaché and the Ministry. Good all-around job of alienating everyone."

"Well, hell," Guy said sourly, "they treat the whole thing as an exercise in quiet diplomacy when two lives precious to me are at stake. It's war without boundaries but they haven't grasped the fact. So I'll make arrangements to get things on track—sorry I didn't do it earlier."

Hoskins' eyes narrowed. "You going around shooting up Arab enclaves?"

"Whatever I do I'll be glad if the authorities stay out of the way."

Hoskins' eyes appealed to Needham, who shrugged and said, "Gentlemen, we appreciate your visit, but as Mr. Ryan's made clear we'll strike our own course from now on."

After they left Whitaker grimaced and said, "Bureaucrats—same the world over. Mr. Ryan, may I ask what arrangements you contemplate?"

"I should have gotten you on the case from the beginning, Paul. Needham has his hands full trying to keep RyTech together, and I don't know what to do."

"Not give up hope's the first thing. You'll pay whatever's asked?"

"Gladly."

His eyes narrowed. "I can't say if this connects to the attempt on you in Geneva, but the girlfriend of one of those hooligans talked to the police a bit. Said all three were Dublin layabouts, hired for the job by some anonymous fellow. So I pursued the matter a step further—spoke with one of the victim's widows—a Mrs. Timilty. After a few pounds' encouragement she said she'd been told by her late husband the employer was a foreigner. Swarthy type with a thick accent. Balkan origin, she speculated, possibly Russian, though she admitted neither she nor the deceased had ever met or spoken with a Russian." He looked at Guy. "The description could fit an Arab, too—Libyan, say—"

Excitedly, Guy said, "The kidnappers had Arab accents."

"Ah, that point was unknown to me. But speculation's no use just now. Doubtless the police are combing the warrens for suspects?"

"So they say." Where were his wife and daughter now? Huddling in some dank cellar fearing every moment would be their last? He wanted to slice open their captors' bellies, rip out their guts with his bare hands.

Whitaker's voice interrupted his thoughts. "If it's agreeable to you I'll get back to Geneva and follow through on the G-371 theft." He paused. "To do it right I need an extra hand, Mr. Ryan. The situation is so delicate I don't feel I can use plant personnel in what amounts to a counterespionage investigation."

"I think you're right about that," Guy said. "What do you have in mind?"

Whitaker took a deep breath. "You," he said, "even though the kidnapping is uppermost in your concerns. It's your plant and the Ghost theft is security-critical. Could you possibly come to Geneva for, say, twenty-four hours?"

Guy thought it over. Whitaker was right about the theft being his responsibility, and he understood Whitaker's need. If there were sudden word from the kidnappers or other developments he should know about Jake could summon him and he would be in Paris within two hours. Slowly, Guy nodded. "I'll go."

Thirty-Three

During the flight to Geneva Whitaker had said, "Occurs to me we may be missing a bet if we don't sow a bit of confusion among the Soviets. Let the miscreant open the safe and deliver a formula to his controller." He'd grinned at Guy. "An early, imperfect formula."

"Great idea, Paul."

After the plant closed for the day, Guy and Whitaker stayed behind to rig a closed-circuit video camera focused on the Ghost section safe. The camera's cable fed into a VCR in Whitaker's distant office, where the two men settled in with coffee and sandwiches.

Guy said, "We haven't covered this point before, but after the thief is identified what's to be done with him?"

Whitaker set down his coffee mug and blotted his mustache with a napkin. "Since we want the false formula to reach enemy hands the fellow can't be arrested at the scene."

"Right."

"So, I have two thoughts. One is for me to conduct a security investigation, and polygraph the thief and every section employee. I tell him he's failed the test, and discharge him. Another, simpler, is to see that the thief has an accident, not necessarily fatal, but disabling. A condition preventing his return for many months.''

"I prefer the former," Guy told him. "Who knows? The polygraph might turn up a confederate.''

"So, having gone to this much trouble we maximize our return.''

Guy nodded. "Seems to me the false formula will gain real credibility when the thief is dealt with, and that's what we want.'' He examined a sandwich and put it back on the plate. "Hope he comes back tonight.''

Whitaker picked up a telescopic-lens camera fitted on an infrared flash. Then he went to the open window and focused on the road beyond the gate. "If our man is met by car I'd like a record of its license tag.'' He set down the camera and turned to Guy.

"I don't want to bring up a painful subject, but I know the welfare of your wife and child is never out of your mind. From my experience the dicey part of ransoming is making sure the captives are freed in good condition. So, since you've invited my participation, I'll be bold enough to request that you allow me to handle the payoff.''

"I'll be relieved if you will.''

He nodded thoughtfully. "The Paris police will be more interested in catching the criminals than in your loved ones' welfare, so your interests diverge. But even if the kidnappers are never caught that's none of your concern. You'll have your family out of France and safe away.''

"That's all I want, what I pray for. But shouldn't I have been contacted by now?''

He shrugged. "Cases vary. The criminals may never have abducted before and hadn't thought beyond the capture. If the kidnapping was state sponsored there'll be political implications—they take longer to surface because of protective layering. But your million-franc reward should be irresistible to anyone with knowledge of the snatch. So I suspect we'll soon hear from an informer.'' He looked away from

Guy and studied the dark video screen. "Nothing yet. We may be in for a long wait. Coffee?"

"Sure—and a tot of that good brandy." He gazed at the video screen, and found himself thinking of Cristina. She ought to be reaching Paris soon, taking the place of Nikky who was increasingly miserable with morning sickness.

And with Whitaker in Paris, Jake could return to New York and resume firm control of RyTech.

Guy found himself reflecting that in his earlier ignorance he had assumed that corporations ran as smoothly and uninterruptedly as trains. But each day some branch, division, or operation of RyTech demanded a prompt decision, the resolution of an unexpected problem. The demonstration and death at ISR—who could have foreseen it? Or the ensuing Congressional hearing?

Abruptly his mind focused on Connie and Gloria—how much were they suffering? Had they been brutalized? Did they realize he was doing everything possible to free them? Were they still . . . alive? He felt Whitaker's hand on his arm.

"Mmm—maybe something . . . see what you make of it."

Guy sat forward intently, saw a flicker across the screen.

Whitaker said, "Could be power surge—or a flashlight."

A beam of light angled across the top right section of the screen. "Sure enough," Whitaker said with satisfaction. "Watch the screen, sir—I'll take a look outside." He went over to the window while Guy stared, fascinated, at the monitor.

Suddenly the safe door brightened. A gloved hand went toward it and placed a vacuum cup beside the dial. Guy glanced around and saw Whitaker peering through the eyepiece of a nightvision scope. "No pickup vehicle visible," he muttered.

"Our man's started on the safe," Guy told him. "Better watch this."

Whitaker activated the videocorder and sat beside Guy. Two more cup mikes were placed around the dial. A hand-held readout computer came briefly into view, and Guy saw that mike wires fed into it. "Wouldn't mind having that gadget myself," Whitaker mused. "Take him no time at all to read the combination. I'll have to change that safe to something more sophisticated." He opened his jacket and took out a snub-nosed revolver, broke open the breech and snicked it shut. "Hold on—there he goes."

Guy saw gloved fingers beginning to turn the dial. Five careful moves, back to zero, and the door swung open. The hand entered and began drawing out papers and documents. An envelope marked G-371 came out and the light beam lowered.

"He'll be opening it," Whitaker said tensely. "Pray he photographs the contents."

As if in answer, the screen lighted with two brief flashes. Moments later the envelope was returned, the other contents replaced. The door closed, and as the suction cups were removed a man's face showed.

"By all that's holy," Whitaker gasped. "One of my guards!" Red-faced he stared at the dark screen. "I could shoot him for the embarrassment alone." His fist struck the table, jarring the coffee cups. "There'll be no polygraph ordeal—I'll see to the bugger meself." He looked at his watch. "Shift changes at four and he goes off duty. Meanwhile, I'll pull his file." After turning off the VCR, Whitaker got up and trudged heavily away. Guy sipped coffee and swallowed a bite of smoked turkey before abandoning the sandwich.

When Whitaker returned he said, sourly, "Rubin Foss is his moniker. Three years on the job." He held up a slip of paper. "Address and phone number. We should tail him to verify delivery." He lay down on a leather sofa. "Let's nap a while, follow him from the gate."

367

Guy watched him set a digital alarm clock for three forty-five, and stretched out on the other sofa.

In the dark room his mind relaxed and purged the present. His thoughts drifted back to the months since his father's death. Marguerite's murder, his reprisals against Edmonds and Johns, reconciling with Consuela, his escape from the IRA, and the sickening shock of Connie and Gloria's abduction . . .

It seemed only minutes later that Whitaker was shaking him awake. "There's coffee, sir, time to go."

Groggily, Guy drank down the coffee and stood up to stretch stiff muscles. The clock showed ten to four. The guard shift was changing. Whitaker handed him a Walther automatic and Guy followed him outside the plant.

Lights out, Whitaker pulled the VW off the roadside within sight of the exit gate. Uniformed guards were leaving, most mounting bicycles, a few wheeling off on mopeds. Whitaker said, "Our man Foss is on that ten-speed with reflecting stripes."

"I see him."

"The question is whether he'll head for rendezvous, or go home to sleep." He started the engine, let it idle. Foss began pedaling toward them, turned around and pumped the other way.

Whitaker chuckled. "I see he's had instruction in evasion techniques, but not enough. Chain's only as strong as the weakest link. Brother Foss has drawn his last paycheck from me."

They watched until his tail reflector vanished around a bend, and Whitaker followed at a distance. The moon was behind clouds, road lights widely spaced. They came to the crest of a hill and saw the lake stretched out like a long, dark shadow to the right.

Going downhill, Whitaker swore. "Lost him!" Ahead,

the darkness was impenetrable. Clouds parted, and they saw the bike's tail reflector glinting like a distant ruby.

Beyond it headlights blinked on, off, on, and off. "Rendezvous," Whitaker said exultantly. "Guy, we're in luck."

The bike reflector moved ahead and presently the waiting car's headlights came on, showing the bicyclist dismounting. Whitaker shut off the engine and coasted to the side of the road. Guy estimated their distance as a hundred yards off.

Foss opened his knapsack and held up something. A car door opened and a man came out. He took the article from Foss and handed him something in return. Guy could see Foss's head bobbing. Then he turned his bike around and began pedaling up the hill. Toward them.

Whitaker said, "Before he nears us, get down." In the stillness they heard the other car start up. It didn't turn around as Guy expected, but began moving up the hill behind the straining Foss.

Foss gained the crest, cycled past them without a glance, and began coasting down in the direction of Geneva. The car accelerated over the crest, sped past the VW, and closed with the bicyclist.

They saw him half turn to wave. The car struck with a grinding crash that flung bike and rider high into the air. The car kept going until it was out of sight.

Whitaker cursed, started the engine and drove to where Rubin Foss lay in a broken heap.

Kneeling, Whitaker felt for pulse and shook his head. "Saved me the trouble," he muttered, turned on a pocket flash and searched the dead man's pockets until Guy saw a bloody envelope open at one end. Banknotes protruded from it.

Whitaker continued searching until satisfied there was no film on the body or in the rucksack. Then he wiped the envelope on roadside grass and tossed it into the VW's rear foot well. As he got behind the wheel he said, "I wish some of our starry-eyed idealists could have seen that liquidation. Might have other thoughts about cooperating with our enemies." He shifted gear and began driving slowly toward the plant.

After a while Guy said, "What did you mean, they saved you the trouble?"

"You didn't think I was going to let him off scot-free?" From his pocket he drew out the address slip. "Let's see—Rue d'Alsace, third floor flat. We must pry deeper into his secret life." He floored the accelerator, and the VW chuffed and whinnied through the night.

As Whitaker began working on the door lock Guy whispered, "Suppose someone's inside?"

"Then it's the worse for them—but the file said he's unmarried. No widow to contend with or bar the way . . . There." He pulled open the door and replaced the plastic jimmy in his pocket. Guy went in first, found a wall switch and turned on the ceiling globe.

Whitaker followed, closed the door and propped a chair under the doorknob. "Don't care for surprise arrivals," he said between set teeth, and went quickly through the small apartment. There was a sitting room, bedroom, kitchen, bath and utility room. "Bachelor digs," Whitaker remarked, and pulled off his coat.

They searched the closet, the mattress, probed furniture, emptied bureau drawers and ransacked the utility room. Finally Whitaker stopped and wiped his face on a shirtsleeve. "Unless we tear down the walls, only one other place I can think of, but it's so obvious I doubt Foss would have used it." He started for the bathroom. Lifting off the top of the commode tank, Whitaker looked into it and smiled wolfishly. "Why, there's our little beauty—and after all that work . . ." He reached down and drew out a plastic container. "G-371," he said. "Ghost. Welcome back." He handed the dripping flask to Guy.

The liquid was charcoal gray. The sealed top intact. "Now," said Whitaker, "let's tidy up."

Fifteen minutes later they were out of the place, the recovered flask in a bag under Guy's arm. As Whitaker drove back to the plant, Guy said, "Wonder why Foss didn't sell this sample, too?"

"Likely holding on for top price. Well, he got paid for his treachery, didn't he?" Moodily he stared at the road. "Vicious buggers—wonder who they were?"

"The license plate was taped over."

"So I noticed." He yawned. "Enemies, whatever name and nationality."

When the plant lights lay ahead Whitaker said, "You'll return to Paris now, and I'll fly in tonight or tomorrow. I have to upgrade that section's security with a better safe and video scanners. For decoy purposes, naturally. I'll cache the formula in another place."

Guy felt drained by the tension of waiting, the violence of Foss's death. "I'll sleep on the couch and fly out when the aircrew's awake. In Paris, get a comfortable hotel room for yourself, and come to the apartment."

They stopped at the gate, where the guard examined Whitaker's pass before opening the way. Whitaker said, "Whatever you think, remember that despair is crippling. Never give up hope."

When Guy reached Paris at midday he found Cristina in the apartment, efficiently taking charge.

Thirty-Four

Dressed in a severely cut dark suit, Cristina seemed fully contained and matter of fact. Her greeting was perfunctory, mere cheek to cheek.

"I was surprised to find you were in Geneva," she said. "It must have been a matter of great importance."

"It was," he said without further explanation. "How's your father?"

"Complaining, but actually making good progress from crutches to cane. He's to get a soft cast soon, so perhaps that will improve his disposition."

"And Al-Emir?"

"Earning his keep. Now that he's in the new stable Lloyd's has him fully insured. Father visits him daily." She glanced away. "Already I miss them both."

"It hasn't been—pleasant here."

"I know that. But for me waiting here is better than so far away. And I need to be near you, Guy. Sorrow is easier to bear when shared." Her eyes moistened. "Oh, Guy, it's so awful. I think constantly of Con and Gloria—can't get them out of my mind."

Guy nodded sympathetically as Jake came in.

After they shook hands Jake said, "Geneva problem resolved?"

"Handily, thanks to Paul. After tying up loose ends he'll come here. That'll free you to go back to New York."

"Wherever I'm needed most. You'll be glad to know I've just seen Inspector Bourcave. His wife's staying with him until she can take him home. Some of his drains are out and he's healing nicely."

"Can you make sure his wife is comfortable?"

Cristina said, "Why don't I see to that? I'd like to meet them, and this will be a good chance. Flowers, perfume would make things cheerier for her. May I?"

Jake said, "Of course—it's something that begs for a woman's touch."

"Then I'll waste no time."

When Cristina was out of earshot Jake said, "A remarkable young woman, Guy. I'm impressed."

Stretching, Guy looked around. "We're making no headway, Jake. No contact, no leads, nothing. How long can this go on?"

"Until the abductors feel it's safe to make contact. They went to a lot of trouble to set up the kidnapping, now they need to cash in on it. I'm sure it won't be much longer."

When Cristina returned she presided over late luncheon from the head of the table. To Guy it seemed she had effortlessly adapted her La Rocha role to Paris, and his appreciation was immense.

Jake said, "Guy, I need some of your time for RyTech matters—decisions I'd prefer you make before I leave."

There were shipyard bids to refit the salvage vessels and contracts to let. Sotheby's treasure appraisers estimated a low value of six million dollars, a high of eight. Guy signed acceptance. "What else?"

"The Lyons contracts you ordered de Neuville to cancel will have the plant showing a loss for the first time in its history. Some legal action was threatened, but we made it clear the principals behind those shadow firms would have to surface in court. So that was the last of it. You'll be glad to know the Maryland police arrested and charged a man with shooting Professor Forster. The grand jury indicted him and the informant claimed the reward."

"Pay it."

"There's a little more to the story, Guy. The FBI is interested in the killer. They searched his Baltimore apartment and found a number of agent items very cleverly concealed—secret writing materials, a short-wave receiver and a reception schedule for Soviet Intelligence transmissions. Also a code pad—and the pistol that killed Professor Forster."

"So the demonstration and killing were ordered by the Soviets. Will the Bureau release that information?"

"Unfortunately not. They want to low-profile the whole thing while they work on the agent. They think he can cough up considerable information they'd like to have—his incentive being a plea bargain backed by the Bureau."

"Well, let's wish them luck. I'm willing to let the FBI have their crack at the killer, but fairly soon I'll want Jennie to start publicizing the true facts behind the episode. The public should begin realizing how some of those peacenik demonstrations are organized, and why."

Jake nodded. "I'll stay on top of it. Now, back to the more prosaic. The Korean plant reports negotiating food contracts with WHO and the International Red Cross. The plant manager and department head request half a million for special packaging equipment to irradiate the food against spoilage."

"Okay."

"Final item—consultants for our long range R&D are on the job. Their preliminary report recommends diversification. Now, there's a Scotch distillery available, and a California vineyard."

"The demand is constant," Guy remarked. "Sounds like a good diversifying line, but before RyTech gets into the liquor business I'll want an analysis made—pros and cons, sales and profit projections, the firm's financial positions, who the principals are—you know what I need.''

"There's no hurry about a decision. Plenty of time to hire the right consultants." He looked at his watch. "I've booked a five o'clock flight on Pan American, so I'll start packing now."

"Call me from New York."

That night Guy slept as usual in the master bedroom, and Cristina in hers. In the morning Paul Whitaker arrived, and while Cristina was out shopping Whitaker took a call from the Embassy's Legal Attaché.

The body of Consuela had been found.

Thirty-Five

Later, when Guy could bring himself to look back he realized shock numbed his mind protectively, shielding his senses against further agony so that he was able to move through succeeding days like an automaton.

Grief eroded all but the most vivid recollections: identifying Consuela's decomposing features in the chill dankness of a Paris morgue; the memorial Mass at Notre Dame; flying with her coffin to La Rocha; a final Mass in the family chapel where Consuela had been baptized thirty-one years before. Burial beside her mother amid the anguished sobs of himself, Cristina, and her stunned, uncomprehending father.

Through all, he remembered, he had been supported by Jake Needham and Cristina. Paul Whitaker handled police and undertaker, making quiet arrangements to transfer the coffin from France to Spain.

Derelicts had found Consuela's body in the basement of an abandoned building on the Rue d'Alesia near the Church of St-Pierre. Cause of death was ascribed to the effects of injected anesthetic. Her jewelry was missing, but whether taken by the kidnappers or the derelicts would never be known. Advanced decomposition indicated death had come within two days of her abduction, and the forensic examiner offered the guarded opinion that the amount of anesthetic was insufficient to cause her death—but the complication of a defective heart valve had been fatal.

The explanation, Cristina found from family physicians: in childhood Consuela had contracted rheumatic fever, damaging her heart.

"Which means," said Whitaker, "that her death was in all probability not intended. It's an important finding because it goes to two things: explains why the abductors failed to contact you—out of fear—and gives strong hope that Gloria is still alive."

They were sitting in the great room of La Rocha, Cristina, Guy and Whitaker. Jake had returned to Paris and Don José was under sedation. Guy said, "Why haven't they asked ransom for my daughter?"

"I've never fully comprehended the criminal mind," said Whitaker, "but I'm sure they will. Just a question of time."

Guy looked at Cristina, who said, "We must continue hoping."

The echo of her words faded and Guy reflected that he had lost those who were closest to him by blood and love: his father, his stepmother and now his wife. Remaining were Cristina, and perhaps Gloria. Finding the treasure galleon had been a watershed in his life; since then he had become intimately acquainted with death and sorrow.

Whitaker's voice broke the silence. "I believe I might be more useful in Paris, prodding the police, the DST. But if I can be of help here . . ."

"You've done miracles," Guy told him. "Without you and Cris I don't think I could have held up."

"You're strong and hardy," Whitaker replied. "When my Anne was killed in a car accident I wanted to give up—but the Lord saw it otherwise. I had loved ones to care for—as do you." He stood up. "Permission to leave?"

"Just stay in touch with me. If—when the kidnappers make contact I must know immediately."

"Of course, sir. Meanwhile, I recommend you spend time here, rest up away from grim reminders."

Cristina said, "We'll take good care of him. Thank you for everything, Paul."

They went out to his car, and when he was gone they carried flowers to the graves of Consuela and Doña Mercedes. From there they stopped at Al-Emir's new stable, and after watching him a while Cristina said, "I've lost all joy in owning him."

"Why?"

"Because at night the thought comes to me that Connie's death is retribution."

"For what?" He couldn't understand what she was trying to say.

"For my daring to love you—her husband."

"That's nonsense." He took her shoulders. "My wife is dead, our child is missing. It's taken that, God help me, to show me how much I need you."

She smiled sadly. "Most of my life I envied my sister her title. Now I've succeeded to it I wish it didn't have to be. Guy, I feel so *guilty.*"

"The guilt is on those who killed her—the men who have Gloria. That's how we must see it."

"If only Gloria were with us, safe and free . . ." she mused.

"I *have* to find her," he said grimly, "focus everything on that."

Nights later Cristina took a dinner tray to her father, sat with him while he plucked absently at the food, then carried the tray down to the kitchen. To Guy she said, "He's devastated; not eating. Hardly speaks at all, just lies there. I don't know what to do."

"Perhaps he should return to the hospital—he can be fed there, cared for until he's stronger."

She shook her head. "I can't stay here alone but I'll talk with his doctor, ask for advice."

They dined then, Guy hardly tasting his food or caring about it. Cristina picked at hers, and after a while they took brandy together and she went off to bed.

Guy carried a brandy bottle to his room, drank part of it and lay under the covers begging sleep to come.

An hour passed. Two. Sleepless, he stared at the ceiling. Moonlight seemed to stir the curtains. Through his mind drifted memories of his baby daughter . . .

Quietly his door opened, closed and Cristina was beside him. "I can't bear to be away from you," she whispered. "I need to know you're here—safe . . ."

They moved together, seeking consolation and assurance in each other's presence, clinging like lost children in dark woods. Then some inner dam broke and he kissed her cool lips, lightly at first and then with more conviction. His body that had been dead, devoid of feeling, warmed to an affirmation of life, a gentle miracle of love and passionate renewal.

Next day they rode together, picnicked beside the stream, swam in its crystal water and made love.

Don José's stunned mind was clearing. He ate his meals with wine, descended to his library and spent hours poring over family photographs. They accompanied him to the graves of his wife and daughter, drove him around the *estancia*, and showed him new-born calves of fighting bulls. Soon he complained of his cast and enforced idleness, declared his doctor a fraud and demanded to see another. With that they drove him to Seville for new X-rays and an examination. The last of the cast was removed and Don José was allowed to walk with only a cane. Between therapist visits he took a consuming interest in his vineyard, searching the long trellised rows for evidence of insects and disease.

Needham called daily on business matters; Whitaker had nothing to report.

Guy spent time with Don José discussing La Rocha's future and walking the fields with him as the *marqués* gained strength. Cristina resumed managing the *estancia*, selling horses and ring bulls, negotiating with Arab fanciers for the services of her stud, overseeing house and servants, placating her father—and staying with Guy each night until dawn.

He found himself brooding less on the avalanche of tragic events, and as his thoughts became absorbed in other things Consuela grew gradually remote. Even Cristina mentioned her less frequently. Gloria, though, was ever in his mind. But there seemed no purpose to staying interminably in Paris, staring at silent telephones. If anything happened, he told himself, they would inform him at La Rocha, and in the meantime he was regaining mental health.

From time to time he spoke with Cristina of quitting RyTech and settling at La Rocha. After an acceptable interval they would marry and have their own family. Her firm response was that, desirable as his thoughts were for the future, the fate of his daughter had to be resolved. "It's true we're happy here, but to do what you suggest implies defeat. Guy, you can never be at peace if you symbolically abandon Gloria, accept her loss as permanent."

"What would you have me do?"

"Live one day at a time—as I do."

Prince Ali Mansour telephoned Guy from Seville, saying, "Finding myself so close to La Rocha I'd greatly like to visit my former steed—and have a word with you. Is it convenient, Guy?"

"I'll check with Cristina."

When she agreed Guy told Ali he'd be welcome, and in

380

the interval Cristina busied the grooms washing and currying Al-Emir.

The Prince arrived in a business suit, met Don José and extended his condolences on their recent and continuing tragedy. Then he went to the stable, remarking on its special security features, and spent a few minutes stroking and talking to Al-Emir, who responded to his former owner. Cristina excused herself for household matters, and as Guy walked with his one-time schoolmate, Ali said, "The stallion never looked finer, Guy, but that's not why I came."

"To see how I'm bearing up?"

"No—I was asked to. By a man who says he has information concerning the return of your daughter." He shrugged expressively. "I can't verify the information—I'm merely performing what may be a service to you as an old friend—but the man has never lied to me, and I recommend you see him."

Guy's body tensed. "Who is he?"

"Edouard Drach."

"Ah, Drach—the always available go-between."

"Perhaps, but he's always been a serious person. What he told me was that he had been privately approached by those who are keeping Gloria. His understanding is that they are willing to return her—for a price."

"How much?"

"He may not know. But he urgently wants to see you. As Drach explained to me, the matter is of such delicacy he does not want to seem to be involved, thus, no letter, no telephone call. Instead, he charged me with conveying the message—and considering your continuing anguish, I agreed."

"Ali, I'm very grateful. But who spoke with Drach? What kind of people—?"

"Ah, you must ask him yourself, Guy. Drach's tentacles reach down as well as up. Perhaps some—person from his past. I only speculate. His final words were that it is a matter of great delicacy—and great import. You are, of course, to call on Drach alone.''

He nodded. ''Tell him I'll come.''

Cristina returned and Ali expressed pleasure at all he'd seen, his satisfaction over Al-Emir's care, his gratitude for her receiving him on short notice. Then he was gone in his Mercedes limousine, bodyguard cars ahead and behind.

Walking with Guy toward the house she said, ''You seem preoccupied. Is something wrong?''

''I'm going to Geneva.''

''Because of Ali? Guy, what *is* it? Don't hold back from me.''

He told her then, voice husky with hope and apprehension.

''There could be danger,'' she said. ''Please take me with you.''

''If there's danger I can't expose you to it. I have to see this through alone. If something happened to you I wouldn't want to live.''

She kissed his hand. ''Then I'll stay—and wait.''

In Paris he conferred with Jake and Whitaker, telling them of Ali's message. Whitaker insisted on flying with him, and Jake agreed. Guy would leave the Lear first, Whitaker later in case arrival was surveilled.

Before nightfall they landed at Geneva. Guy checked into the Hotel du Rhône and for an hour lay on his bed, thinking.

When he got up he was ready to see Drach.

Thirty-Six

He drove a Mercedes through the guarded entrance gate toward the illuminated chateau, thinking it resembled a prison more than he had remembered. He parked the sedan in shadows by some shrubbery and was met by a footman at the steps.

As he followed the footman down the entrance corridor Guy ignored the heraldic decorations, looking instead for photoelectric eyes and motion sensors as Whitaker suggested. He spotted several concealed in suits of armor. The helmet of the equestrian king contained a small camera lens.

Photoelectric cells were set into both sides of the arched entrance to the great hall. Inside, behind a massive work table sat Edouard Drach.

This evening his costume was purple silk trimmed with sable. As Guy approached he saw Sonya, the little ballerina, seated on a floor cushion, leaning against Drach's massive chair. She was reading a book. Sonya glanced up at Guy and resumed reading.

"Delighted to see you again," said Drach, extending his hand.

Guy took it briefly and sat in a chair. "Is my daughter alive?"

Drach spoke to Sonya. "Your exercises now, *petite papil-*

lone. '' She laid aside the book and walked lithely away. Partway down the room a *barre* extended from the wall. Dutifully, the girl began exercising her bare, smooth-muscled legs. The upper part of her body wore a tight, translucent leotard that emphasized her maturity.

"My daughter," Guy said. "Where is Gloria?"

Drach's gaze left his protégée as his pink tongue licked dark, full lips. "Not in this country."

"France?"

"No, of that I am quite convinced."

"Then—?"

Drach slid a color photograph toward Guy. Picking it up he saw his daughter's face. The rest of her was hidden behind the front page of a Vienna newspaper. Its date was four days ago.

As Guy studied Gloria's features, tears welled in his eyes. "Thank God she's alive!" He put the photo in his pocket. "How much do they want?"

Drach cleared his throat. "It seems to be not a question of how much, sir, but of what. Permit me, if you will, to relate some circumstances for your better understanding."

"Go ahead," Guy said thickly.

"First, let me say that I have been assured that your daughter is well and in no immediate danger. The death of your wife was inadvertent, I am told. She and your daughter were administered anesthetic to ensure their tranquility while plans were made. When your wife could not be roused her captors decided to leave France with your daughter. To a haven where all could be secure."

"Vienna?"

"Vienna is a way station between East and West. The photograph would not have been given me were Gloria still there. So my assumption is that she is now farther East."

"Prague? Warsaw?"

"Even Moscow—I am unable to say." He took a deep breath and his jowls quivered. "The man—the intermediary who approached me is someone whom in the past I did business with. In those days he represented a foreign power, as he does today. In confidence he revealed to me that between certain elements of his government and a high RyTech official there was—what shall I say?—an understanding. Which terminated upon the official's death. Measures taken by you, sir, were detrimental to his country's interest.

"As you are doubtless aware certain attempts were made to neutralize you so that the former 'understanding' could be restored." He paused. "During your earlier trip to Geneva, for example—an effort botched by British intervention."

Guy nodded.

A butler brought wine and glasses on a silver tray. He poured two glasses and returned with an assortment of delicate sandwiches, a companion tray of sliced pumpernickel and a pot of cheese. Guy sipped wine while Drach stuffed his mouth. The ballerina, Guy saw, was watching both of them.

After washing down his repast with wine, Drach belched lengthily. The ballerina's face stiffened. Drach blotted his mouth and said, "By now you are beginning to grasp the motive behind your family's abduction. It was, they say, a last resort. Tragically your wife is dead, victim of incompetence—but your daughter is alive. What, M'sieu Ryan, would you give to have her back?"

"Anything," Guy said huskily. "Everything." And heard his words echo emptily through the vaulted hall.

Nodding briefly, Drach said, "Now comes the difficult part, the most disagreeable."

"As if there were anything agreeable about it," Guy said bitterly. "What do they want?"

"First, let us be clear concerning *my* role, sir. I assented to being used as a message conveyor—as I in turn employed Prince Ali. All sensitive arrangements must be conducted among men who trust one another. Thus are links established." He paused to devour the last two sandwiches and gulp more wine. "Our common link is Prince Ali Mansour, a disinterested party but deeply sympathetic to your situation." He wiped crumbs from his lips. "As am I."

"Make your point."

"The point being that for reasons which go back many years I enjoy the confidence of elements ultimately responsible for this unhappy situation. That is the extent of my involvement. Though in the future it is not impossible I may receive some indirect acknowledgement of my services. Above all, sir, it is important that we address each other in complete candor. Nothing is to be gained by disguising one's true position. To put things in their most fundamental form, the people who sought my services possess your daughter. You want her returned. For that, a price has been set which you must pay."

From outside came the barking of a dog, muffled by the chateau's thick walls. The dog howled and was silent. Guy wondered what stifled the dog. To Drach he said, "The price?"

From a stack of papers Drach selected one and scanned it. "I know nothing of technical matters," he said, "so it is your comprehension that is relied upon. The specifics are these: a subsidiary of RyTech manufactures a key element of your space defense shield. This is a microprocessor code-named Sceptre."

"So?"

Drach said, "It is pointless to be disingenuous, sir. A Congressional inquiry recently focused on the Institute for Strategic Research, which is the manufactory of the Sceptre chip."

"I've heard of it," Guy acknowledged, "but I don't pretend to understand it."

"No matter. Sceptre exists. Another country perceives it as a formidable strategic menace. It wishes to analyze the technology in order to maintain worldwide strategic balance."

Guy said, "I take it we're not talking about Albania."

"No," he said, with the first trace of irritation, "it is certainly *not* Albania I am discussing. The country in question regards as prohibitively expensive the development of technology equalling what Sceptre represents. Accordingly, they have sought a short-cut to parity. The capture and sequestration of your family is to be understood in that context. The purpose of this discussion is to set forth their terms for the return of your daughter."

"I'm listening."

"In exchange for Gloria you are to supply one Sceptre microchip."

"No money?"

"This is not a mercenary transaction—you don't realize the stature of my principals, who they are."

"I'm not accustomed to playing on the world stage, so you'll have to make allowances. My daughter is somewhere behind the Iron Curtain. Ransom, one Sceptre chip—"

"—in pristine condition, I should add."

"Against whose guarantee that she will be released to me unharmed?"

"Mine, sir. *My* guarantee. I have satisfied myself that my principals are not interested in murdering your child. In fact I refused to undertake this intermediary role without their solemn word on the matter."

"And their solemn word is to be believed?"

"My word, as well. And our mutual friend, Prince Ali, will confirm that I have never broken my word."

"Ali was a schoolboy cheat," Guy remarked, "but I've heard it's possible for men to change."

"As they mature and learn the value of honorable dealings," Drach said. He glanced toward the *barre* and frowned. Sonya was nowhere to be seen.

Guy said, "I wonder if any of you have any concept of

387

the security measures taken to safeguard Sceptre? The project is joint RyTech/Department of Defense. The guards aren't only RyTech employees, Pentagon people guard it as well. If you think that by virtue of my RyTech position I can walk in and take one like cigarettes from a vending machine, you and your 'principals' live in a dream world. The obstacles to removing a microchip are unbelievably difficult."

"My principals have seen hard evidence of your resourcefulness. They believe you capable of accomplishing it—to save your daughter's life."

His body felt leaden. Rage and hatred were nearly choking him. He wanted to seize a broadsword from the wall and vent Drach's guts, collapse the gross apparition like a water balloon. Fighting to maintain composure Guy said, "That's encouraging, I needed their confidence."

Drach was gazing at the empty *barre*. "Did you notice Sonya leave?"

"No, but I suppose she has to pee-pee from time to time." And what about you? he wondered. Hooked up to a relief tube like a fighter pilot? And smiled inwardly at Drach's brief expression of distaste.

"What you are to do," said Drach, "is secure the chip and bring it to the place of exchange."

"Assuming I can do so—where is the place to be?"

Drach's hands spread. "Some place in Europe to be arranged. It might be helpful in your undertaking to view the problem thus: they don't want to kill or keep your daughter; they want the microchip called Sceptre. The microchip is of no earthly use to you, whereas you prize your daughter's life. A simple, uncomplicated barter: gold for oil; automobiles for wheat. Now, to preserve your daughter's life, sir, before you leave here, you must accept the terms. Details to be arranged later."

"Through you?"

"That remains to be determined. You will obtain the microchip?"

Guy pushed back his chair, got up. "You insist we speak in full candor, disguise nothing. You propound an enormous problem and in less than a minute demand I agree to solve it. To say 'yes' would be facile, but because my daughter's life is at stake, in all frankness, what more can I do than agree to try, knowing the price of failure?"

Drach stared thoughtfully at his fingers.

Guy said, "Understand, this will take time. Working alone I have to visit ISR, inspect the premises, form a plan. Maybe it will be simpler than I now believe, but I'll be working against not only my own corporation, but my government as well."

"Similar extractions have been made—codes, satellite intelligence."

"And detected. My daughter's life means more to me than my own. Convey that thought to your principals." Swallowing, he tried to moisten his dry mouth. "When can you get acknowledgement?"

"Later tonight I should think."

"I'm staying at the du Rhône."

He turned his back and walked from the enormous room. Outside a footman escorted him along the hall, Guy reconfirming the location of Drach's security alarms.

When the great door closed behind him he stood on the steps and sucked in a deep breath. At least he knew more than he had on arrival. Four days ago his daughter was alive—thank God—but her ransom was his country's most advanced defense secret.

How could he meet the demands of Drach's masters?

He walked toward the Mercedes, and as he opened the door heard a *hiss* from the wall above and looked up. Squeezing through window bars was Sonya. Familiarly, she fitted her toes into wall crevices, grasped a stout ivy trunk and came down like a squirrel. Guy saw that she had added black tights to her black leotard for near invisibility. Panting, she reached deep shadows and said, "Take me with you, please, m'sieu. You have a daughter—like her I'm a prisoner but my life is unbearable. I beg you—"

"How do you know about my daughter?" he said sharply.

"When she was here I played with her. When she was unhappy I made up stories to cheer her. But is was not easy because her mother was dead. Is that not so?"

"It is. What else?"

Opening a clenched palm, she thrust it into the light.

He gasped. Gloria's pearl earring, mate of the one found in the van. "Take it," she pleaded, "and take me with you."

His fingers lifted the earring from her hand. "I'll take you from this place," he said, "but not tonight. To free my daughter I need Drach's confidence." He thought for a moment. "Will your friend help you—the boy dancer?"

Tears welled in her eyes. "Mikhail. Edouard tortured him, killed Mikhail for his own pleasure. I heard his screams."

Guy's teeth set. "I'll come back for you as soon as I can. Trust me, Sonya."

Her hand withdrew into the shadows. "I do. Because you're Gloria's father."

"Drach missed you at the *barre*. You'd better get back to your room."

With a nod she grasped the trunk and went up with the sureness of an acrobat. Guy got behind the wheel and started the engine to cover whatever noise she made. He saw her squeeze back through the bars and disappear inside the opening. Turning the car, he drove down the broad access road and passed between the posterns. Half a mile from the chateau he pulled over and got out. He unlocked the car trunk, peered in and said, "Everything okay?"

"Tip-top," said Whitaker, unfolding himself from the

cramped space, "except that I'm a size larger than the bonnet." He got out carefully and closed the lid. Seated beside Guy as the Mercedes headed into Geneva he said, "Made a good tour of the grounds. Dobe attacked and I broke his bloody neck." He rubbed his left forearm. "Vicious creature, but it's the trait they're bred for." He glanced at Guy. "Did I hear voices?"

"Drach's ballerina." Under the dash light he showed Paul the earring. "Gloria was there, Paul. And four days ago she was alive in Vienna." He handed Whitaker the photograph. "This gives me the hope I've needed—to do what I have to do."

Whitaker returned the photo to Guy. "We can thank God your child is alive, Guy. But her ransom is going to be unbelievably high."

"That's true—but how would you know?"

"Through a second floor window on the garden side I saw a man pacing back and forth. He looked familiar—someone from London days. Before I could put a name to the face I remembered him as an upper-level KGB agent who used the London branch of the Bank Narodny for cover. His name was Sergei Kedrov."

BOOK SIX

Thirty-Seven

The apartment building where Whitaker took Guy had underground parking with elevator access to the upper floors. "Convenient," said Whitaker, "when I interview hard cases."

The apartment itself had one bedroom and a sitting room. The drabness was somewhat relieved by a few feminine touches—hanging vines that needed watering, wall pictures and a frilled cosmetic table.

"Came across the place somewhat by accident—" Whitaker remarked, as he poured two glasses of Scotch, "—in connection with Egli's suicide." He clinked his glass against Guy's. "Death to our enemies," he intoned, and sat down. "The widow Egli asked for burial money, which seemed out of kilter considering the late managing director's substantial salary. I agreed, in exchange for her help in clarifying a few points—such as where did Egli's money go?" He sipped again. "Develops that Hans was devoted to the gaming tables at Divonne—a twenty-minute drive just across the French border. He also kept a popsie much to the widow's sorrow—and this place was the love nest. Rent was in arrears so I told the ginger lass to pack it, which she did. I gave her relocation money after learning that once a month her late lover met a foreign gentleman here while she

395

stayed in the bedroom and polished her nails. Before the foreign gentleman's arrival Hans was always very nervous, but after he left Hans was much relieved and in funds again. Once when she was taking *schnapps* at a sidewalk cafe she saw the foreign gentleman drive past. His car was a Skoda bearing a Consular Corps tag." He looked at Guy. "Czech agent, wouldn't you surmise?"

Guy nodded. "Hans realized his covert life couldn't withstand scrutiny and killed himself."

Whitaker sighed. "I'm afraid we'll never know how much he sold to the Czechs, but that's history. It's Kedrov's reappearance we need to grapple with. One plausible explanation is that he's at Castle Drach doing Narodny business with the owner. The more sinister explanation is he's there to represent Drach's 'principals'—as Drach described your daughter's abductors. So I take heart that your daughter's not held by terrorists but by Soviet professionals."

Guy drank the room temperature whisky and felt grateful for it. The stress of facing Drach had taxed his nervous system—then Sonya's revelation. He said, "It's obvious Drach is more deeply involved than he admits. That Gloria was his prisoner is unforgivable. I'll deal with him after I get her back."

Whitaker cleared his throat. "By now Kedrov has got to be pretty well placed in the KGB Illegals Directorate. I've been thinking of taking him as a hostage against Gloria's return. But they'd sacrifice him with no more emotion than they'd feel over spilling a glass of vodka. On their scale of things Sceptre is more valuable than a hundred Kedrovs, a thousand. The Soviet Ambassador moves around Bern without bodyguards, so he'd be easy to take. Again, unless he was someone as senior as, say, their Foreign Minister he'd be written off as a battle casualty—and they'd still have your daughter. Supposing we could snatch Shevardnadze we might make a trade. But he always has three or four bodyguards with him in public, plus a strong detachment of local security people to fend off anti-Bolshevik demonstrators. We'd need two squads of SAS lads plus the connivance of local security.'' He stared moodily at the dregs of his whisky. ''I've even thought of going to Moscow, but neither of us speaks Russky. If we did, the chance of finding Gloria is still about one in twenty million, then getting out alive . . .'' He shook his head. ''I guess you'll have to produce the Sceptre.''

''Before that I want to make sure Gloria was taken behind the Curtain.''

''Kedrov would know, wouldn't he?'' Whitaker said thoughtfully. ''Do any of Drach's servants look hardy enough to double as bodyguards?''

''Not the ones I saw. I think he relies for physical security on all that electronic junk—and the Dobes.''

''So it comes down to whether we snatch Kedrov from the castle—or off premises, as they say. I vote the latter. Unfortunately he can't be allowed to resume his profession—after interrogation.''

''Understood. But he may not leave the chateau for days.''

''Not so sure. He has to have radio contact with his Control, and I saw no such antennae atop Drach's place. Which means he must go to the Soviet Consulate to send or receive messages. Hmmm.'' He went off for a phone directory and brought it back. ''Right—Sovs moved to new redoubt. On Rue de l'Athénée—that'd be over by the Athénée Museum.''

He closed the directory. ''Wanted an idea of the likely route he'd take between Drach and the Consulate. Tomorrow I'll hire a couple of circumspect chaps to watch it and notify me when he enters. It's better to let him do his dirty business there, and take him on the way home. Logic being the Consulate won't miss him, and Drach won't figger he's come to harm for hours.'' He pulled the tip of his mustache. ''Giving us time to satisfy our curiosity.''

"Daylight snatch?"

"Why not? Tried it here on you, and the same in Paris. Surprise being the element most desired." He looked around the sitting room. "This will serve as our CP. I'll fetch a few oddments. This place could be the most useful thing Hans Egli left behind."

Guy looked at his watch. "I should get back to the hotel for Drach's call."

"I'll bunk here and make early street arrangements. Should be in place by ten—both of us."

It was after one when the room phone rang. Guy sat up on the bed and answered. Drach's voice said, "Difficulties have been overcome—for the present. How long do you anticipate it will take to resolve your part of the problem?"

"Three to four weeks," Guy told him.

"No sooner? The merchandise is perishable."

His jaw set. "I'm well aware of that."

"No time to waste, sir."

Guy checked out of the Hotel du Rhône and taxied to the Geneva-Cointrin airport, where he woke the aircrew at the Hotel Penta. "You're to fly out as soon as feasible," he told them. "Put my name on the flight manifest, but I won't be aboard. I'll stay here the rest of the night. When you reach Paris, check with Mr. Needham for further instructions. I may need you back here rather soon."

In the morning he took a bus to downtown Geneva and reached the safehouse by an indirect route. Whitaker appeared shortly before ten and began making *espresso* in the small kitchen. "As far as appearances go," he said, "you've left Geneva for Paris. By now watchers are positioned by the Soviet Consulate, another watching Drach's gate. It's conceivable Kedrov communicated last night but more likely

398

he authorized Drach's response to you and will clear it with his Control today. My Consulate watcher has one walkie-talkie, we have the other." He poured two cups of thick coffee and began drawing lines on a pad. "Here's what we're going to do."

The alert came at midday. Driving a brown Fiat two-door, Kedrov had parked in the Consulate lot and gone inside.

Guy followed Whitaker down to the basement and got into an old black van. They crossed the Rhône by the Pont de l'Ile, reached the University and turned onto the Rue de l'Athénée. Whitaker slowed and pointed out the Soviet Consulate. "It's now or never for us and Kedrov. Pistol handy?"

Guy nodded.

Whitaker produced a hypodermic syringe and handed it over carefully. "Don't jab yourself, can't have you taking an impromptu snooze."

They spotted the brown Fiat in the parking lot. Whitaker spoke into the walkie-talkie and the watcher responded.

To Guy he said, "We'll take up station at the museum and prepare to close."

For twelve minutes they waited, engine running. The W/T squawked and Whitaker pulled away from the museum. They overtook the brown Fiat as it entered the broad Rue de la Croix. Whitaker rammed the Fiat's front side joltingly hard, forcing it against the curb.

Dazed, Kedrov sat behind the wheel, looking slowly around.

Guy dropped from the van, covered Kedrov with his pistol and jabbed the syringe into the Russian's upper arm. He tugged open the door and forced Kedrov into the van, sliding the door shut behind them.

The van backed, circled and headed down a narrow side

street. From the van deck Kedrov stared at Guy, his face a mixture of fear and astonishment. He tried to rise but fell back as the drug took effect. The van jolted and turned, running up one street and down another, emerging finally in a lakeside park. Whitaker slowed through the park, reached the quai and took the Pont du Mont Blanc across the river.

The W/T squawked again and Whitaker listened carefully. "Watcher has the Fiat en route to a garage," he said with satisfaction. "How's the passenger?"

"Fully relaxed," Guy replied. Kedrov's head moved unresistingly with the motion of the van. Guy removed an automatic from the Russian's pocket and appropriated his wallet. A few minutes later Whitaker drove into the basement parking area. Aside from themselves the place was empty.

Between them they dragged Kedrov into the service elevator and down the musty hall to Egli's former love nest. Inside, they bound Kedrov to a heavy oak chair. Whitaker moved a radio near the door and turned on a rock-and-roll station.

They sipped Scotch and waited. Whitaker found a paper bag and cut eye and mouth holes into it. He drew it over his own head and blindfolded Kedrov.

Seven minutes later the Russian began to mutter and stir.

"For the first time in your life," Whitaker said harshly, "you're in the hands of enemies. Because of you Mrs. Ryan is dead. Where is her daughter?"

"Safe," Kedrov spat.

"For your sake she had better be." Whitaker pushed up the blindfold and began sharpening a kitchen knife before Kedrov's eyes. The Russian watched with horror as the knife cut into trouser fabric covering his crotch. Whitaker sawed away, pricking flesh unconcernedly as Kedrov tried to shrink into the chair.

"My *question*," said Whitaker, "was *where* Miss Ryan is."

White-faced, Kedrov watched the blade near his scrotum. He struggled violently and screamed.

"I admire courage," Whitaker told the Russian, "but at times it can be misplaced."

"How did you find me?" Kedrov husked.

"Edouard Drach has friends in many places," said Whitaker. "He exercises delicate judgment in considering where his interests lie." He jabbed the knife and Kedrov yelped.

Guy brought in the flatiron that had been heating in the kitchen. He spat on the metal surface and the spittle vanished in small spurts of steam. Face white, Kedrov gasped, "You're doing this because I slept with your wife."

"No," Guy said, "because you helped arrange her abduction—her death." He pulled off Kedrov's shoes and socks and pressed the iron against the sole of the Russian's right foot. Kedrov screamed. The stench of burned flesh filled Guy's nostrils. He felt suddenly weak, nauseated by his task, but it had to be done. "This," he grated, "is for my daughter's agony." He laid the iron against the left foot and Kedrov screamed piercingly.

Presently Kedrov's voice subsided into choking sobs and Guy said, "The question you'll answer concerns my daughter. You remember Gloria—always there when you came for Consuela, when you stayed the night." He licked dry lips. "From Drach we know she was at his castle. Where is she now?"

Kedrov whimpered, "You're going to kill me."

"Actually," said Whitaker, "that hasn't been decided. Mr. Ryan may prefer to release you scarred and castrated. Ugh, the stink of burned flesh. Surprised it don't bother you."

Kedrov muttered unintelligibly. Guy gripped his leg and forced his left sole against the hot iron. More steam, stench and struggling. Finally Kedrov yelled, "I don't know *where* she is," and began moaning. Guy set the iron on Kedrov's thigh and smoke rose from the burning fabric. Howling with pain Kedrov unbalanced the iron. Guy picked it up and set it on the other thigh. Kedrov tumbled the chair backward, striking his head on the floor. "Bugger-all," said Whitaker. "Hangin's too good for him." He knelt, and with pliers pulled out Kedrov's tongue. "Iron still hot, sir?"

"Hot enough." Guy touched the point to Kedrov's tongue. "Just a sample," he said. "The KGB won't have much use for an agent who can't talk." Kedrov writhed in agony.

"Best leave the tongue 'til last, sir—in case he decides to talk. Just move aside, please, so I can cut off his cock and balls."

Screaming, Kedrov tried rolling from side to side, prevented by the heavy chair. As Whitaker ripped open the trouser crotch, he pleaded, "Not *that*, I'll tell you." He sobbed brokenly.

"Be quick about it," snapped Whitaker, "before I stuff your mouth with nuts. Where's Gloria?"

"Moscow. They have her in Moscow," he bleated.

Guy said, "Suppose I give them the microchip. Will they release my daughter—or kill her?"

"Free her." Words thick from his swollen tongue.

"Where is the exchange to take place?"

"I don't know."

Whitaker drew blood with the knife. Kedrov babbled, "Drach's place."

They left him on the floor and went into the kitchen. Whitaker rinsed his knife and said, "True or false, that's all we'll get from him—unless you want to try for more?"

"He thinks Drach betrayed him so he lacks reason to lie." Rage flared. "He seduced my wife and his men killed her."

"We have to kill him," said Whitaker somberly. "Can't let him sound the alarm."

For the rest of the day they kept Kedrov tied to a bed, giving him whisky until he passed out. They stripped him and cut all identifying marks from his clothing before tying it in a trash bag. Toward nightfall Kedrov began to babble incoherently, and they fed him whisky until he quieted down.

Whitaker brought up a platter of sausage and boiled potatoes and they ate in the kitchen, Guy hardly tasting the food. "I've never killed in cold blood," he said, "but that's how they killed my wife."

"Distasteful," Whitaker remarked, "but can't have this chap harming Drach—nor running to the Consulate and telling all. Ostensibly you're in Paris and neither Drach nor his pals know about me. So, when the Russkys finish mulling it over they'll decide Kedrov defected. We'll finish this night's work and say no more about it. Get on to what's important."

At ten they wrapped Kedrov's unconscious body in a bed quilt and carried him down to the van. Whitaker followed the western side of the lake, and when they were near Anières he slowed and steered the van into pinetree cover near the shore. They carried Kedrov down to where a small fishing boat was tied. The moon was behind clouds as they rowed toward the center of the lake. After a while Whitaker said, "This looks to be far enough," and boated his oar.

Together they lifted the naked body from the quilt and eased it over the gunwale. Guy stroked away.

For a few moments they could see the top of his head on the dark surface. Around it rose bubbles of displaced air, then the water was smooth.

As Whitaker grasped his oar he said, "If the body's ever found death will be blamed on alcohol. One less enemy, sir, and to give the bugger credit I do believe he told us all he knew."

On the Geneva road they stopped to leave Kedrov's clothing and bedquilt among trash at a public dump. Guy got out of the van near the Cointrin airport and walked to the Penta Hotel.

Clouds freed the moon, casting stark shadows across the road ahead. As he walked through the chill night air he told himself that Gloria's life was worth a thousand Kedrovs. Freeing her would justify everything he had done.

He slept until dawn and took the express to Paris.

In his compartment he pondered everything Drach and Kedrov had revealed. Gloria was sequestered in Moscow, and there seemed only one way to regain her.

Deliver Sceptre to its enemies.

Thirty-Eight

After a day's rest in Paris Guy summoned Thibaud de Neuville from Lyons, and without explanation to the Embassy task force they dismantled the apartment's communications center. All so useless, Guy mused, as workmen removed boxes filled with equipment and computer gear.

Cristina was eager for news, and Guy told her what had happened in Geneva, withholding the circumstances of Kedrov's death. She gazed emotionally at Gloria's earring before saying, "I feel she's nearer now. My hope is stronger than ever before."

"Mine, too."

Servants boxed Consuela's clothing for donating to a Paris charity, Cristina arranged their severance pay—Gloria's nurse weeping and begging to be recalled when Gloria returned.

Jake said, "Are you going to sell the place now?"

"After Gloria is free I want her to see her room just as she left it. Then we'll never return."

"Makes sense. So much went wrong here."

He took Cristina to dine at Le Berlioz, a nearby restaurant where he was not likely to be recognized. Over aperitifs he said, "Can your father manage things now?"

"He's walking well, and I hired a nurse to cater to his imaginary complaints."

"Then I want you to come with me." Lifting her hand he kissed it. "Will you?"

"I hoped you'd ask," she said throatily. "More than anything in the world I want to be with you, share your life." She looked down at her glass. "To preserve my father's sensibilities I'll tell him I'm going over to see the Texas ranch with Al-Emir in mind."

"Which is true."

"But I'd go if there were no ranch, no Al-Emir, you understand."

After they ordered dinner she said, "You haven't told me what you have to pay for Gloria's return."

"Tentative arrangements have been made. For now it's enough that she's alive and well. In America I want you to marry me."

"Of course, dear, but—isn't it a little soon?"

"We'll do it privately, have a church wedding after Gloria's return."

She thought it over. "It's not necessary, you know. We can just live together. Unless—there's something else . . ."

"If something happens to me I want to be sure you and Gloria have the kind of life you should have."

Her eyes glistened in the candlelight. "Then there's to be more—danger."

"There's always danger." Gently he kissed her hand.

With Jake they flew to New York, and when Cristina moved into Guy's apartment he felt as though he was bringing home a bride.

Jake arranged for the unobtrusive issuance of a marriage license, and the three of them drove up the Hudson for a quiet civil ceremony at the home of a Dutchess County judge Jake had known in law school. Next day Jake prepared a new will for Guy, dividing his property between Cristina and Gloria, making Cristina executrix and Gloria's guardian. Guy signed it in the presence of Jake and Mrs. Paskow, and when she took it away to emboss with her notary seal Jake said, "This all seems very final, Guy. As though you have some sort of premonition."

"Seems normal procedure. What makes you say that?"

Jake shrugged. "Because you've been silent about one very important thing—Gloria's ransom. She's in Moscow, you say, and you're here. You've said nothing about ransom terms, so I can only speculate."

"And what have you been speculating?"

"Well—the Soviets have what you want most. I asked myself what they could want most from you."

"That's enough speculation, Jake. This is one I want you to stay out of."

"With your daughter's life at stake? C'mon, give me a break. Anything I can do—?"

"I'll let you know. Meanwhile, you've got plenty to do to keep RyTech productive and profitable." He looked away. "In the end we had to kill Kedrov."

"I'm not surprised. Is Whitaker involved in whatever you're going to do?"

"Depends what happens."

"Well, I'll be mighty disappointed if you don't let me help."

He lunched with Cristina at Twenty One, then took her to Tiffany's where they selected a four-carat diamond mounted in a plain platinum ring. As the salesman went off to package the diamond she said, "It's beautiful, Guy—but why?"

"For the engagement we never had."

She smiled. "Since I was seventeen I've felt I was your *prometida*—only you didn't know."

During the afternoon he took her on a boat tour around Manhattan and showed her Central Park, beginning to green under the early spring sun. They had afternoon tea at Tavern on the Green, and as he looked at his new wife's face he thought of all the years he had lived without her. Except for Gloria he had nothing to show for them—and even she was gone.

"You must understand," he said, "that from time to time I'll have to be away from you."

"How soon are you going?"

"Tomorrow."

"Then we must make the most of tonight."

He flew by Lear to Baltimore and told the pilot to return to La Guardia for his sister-in-law, *Señora* de Puig.

"To Houston, right, sir?"

"Traveling with her will be one of Mr. Needham's assistants, and two bodyguards. Remind them they're to be with her at all times. After what happened to my wife and daughter I'm through taking chances."

"I'll certainly tell them, sir."

The chartered helicopter flew him to Frederick in twenty minutes, and Drs. Printz and Felberg met him inside the gates of ISR.

Since the mass demonstration, perimeter security had been reinforced. More floodlights and sturdier fencing; two new radar dishes, and a permanent detachment of Armored MPs with half-tracks and personnel carriers. The troops carried gas masks, he noticed.

As they walked toward the administration building Printz said, "I haven't had an opportunity to thank you for supporting us during the Senate hearing."

"Least I could do. None of it was your fault."

"In any case," said Felberg, "I'm grateful, too."

They went into Printz's office and Felberg closed the door.

When the three of them were alone Printz said, "We're glad to see you, Mr. Ryan—is there a particular reason for your visit?"

"Suppose I told you I came to steal one of the Sceptre microchips?"

Felberg began chuckling, broke off as Printz said, "Since you're a serious man I'd take you at your word."

"Good. You gentlemen are among the world's top problem solvers, and what I'm bringing you is a problem I need your help in solving. First, I need your word that nothing will pass beyond this room—not to Hoskins, your security people, nobody. Can I have that assurance?"

Printz considered. "You have my word," he said slowly.

"And mine," said Felberg. "You helped me out of a nasty spot and I'd be an ingrate not to hear you out."

"Thank you," Guy responded, and saw Dr. Printz fill his pipe. Both scientists settled comfortably into their chairs.

"As you're well aware," said Guy, "my wife and daughter were abducted in Paris. My wife is dead, and through a series of events that don't concern you I learned that my daughter, Gloria, had been taken out of France." He handed them the photo given him by Edouard Drach. "She was alive in Vienna. Before then she had been kept for a time near Geneva in the castle of a man now serving as the abductors' intermediary. He told me—and I verified independently—that the abduction was planned by the Soviet Intelligence Service—the KGB—as some of us had already surmised."

"My God," Printz ejaculated. *"Why?"*

Felberg sat forward. "Think, Horatio—Mr. Ryan has already told us. The Soviets want Sceptre."

"That's it," he said, "and my daughter is held in Moscow until I turn over the Sceptre chip."

"But that's unthinkable," Printz expostulated. "Surely you have no thought of sacrificing our country's antimissile defense?"

"I'm not going to answer directly. I'm going to ask you to step into my shoes for a few moments. My wife is dead, my daughter in the hands of the KGB. I own a corporation that manufactures something the Soviets will exchange my daughter for. Before I left Europe, in order to prolong her life, I agreed to deliver the microchip. Am I going to allow my daughter to be sacrificed, or will I do as they desire?" He sat back. "You're both fathers. Your name is Guy Ryan. What are you going to do?"

For an hour he listened to the two scientists broach alternatives, arguing with each other as they discarded ideas and suggested others. Finally Printz said, "We're getting nowhere. Are you familiar with game theory, Mr. Ryan?"

"Generally. It's a theory of rational decision making. I've taken part in computerized strategic war games."

"Good, then you'll understand the approach I recommend. Unfortunately, we have no real-life empirical model to depart from. So, with computer help we're going to factor in the 'players' and the stakes, having predetermined the outcome: Ryan wins, the USSR loses." He went over to a computer terminal and activated it. "We begin with a Mexican stand-off model which, by the way, developed twenty years ago into the mutually assured destruction strategic concept."

Guy said, "How long is this going to take?"

Printz polished his glasses. "Through lunch at least. Cafeteria in the basement if you're hungry." To Felberg he said, "Well, let's begin." He seemed to have evicted Guy from his thinking.

Lunch was a small, tough steak with onions and a salad. Over coffee, Guy watched ISR employees select food and gather in groups to eat at tables. They seemed to be continuing work discussions, and all of them showed signs of strain.

What they need, he thought, is a recreation facility of

some sort—weight room, Jacuzzi, racquet ball. And better food.

He lingered over coffee before returning to the director's office.

They were still inputting the computer, and Guy's entrance was ignored. He sat in an easy chair and closed his eyes, thinking of Cris flying toward Houston.

He was half asleep when Dr. Printz called, "I believe we have a scenario for you."

Rousing himself Guy said, "Let's hear it."

Thirty-Nine

Dr. Felberg said, "We weren't making headway on the program until we decided to combine relevant elements of the Citadel game program. Empirically we represented you as the assault force against an impenetrable Citadel—the Soviet KGB. Ah—I gather you're not concerned with technicalities."

"Just the bottom line."

"You didn't mention having collaborators, so we programmed this as a one-man effort. By discarding a variety of preliminary moves as impractical, we arrived at these premises. First, short of armored assault, the ultimate security of the area housing Sceptre cannot be breached. Second, an authentic Sceptre microprocessor cannot be delivered to our enemies. Third, the KGB must be satisfied that what you give them is the authentic chip. Fourth, your daughter will not be released unless they have that certainty.

"This extrapolates into the following: you will deliver to the KGB a *simulated* microchip. They will believe it authentic because an announcement will be made the ISR premises has been physically penetrated and highly classified material stolen. Eliminating other suspects will reveal you to be the thief. At which point the entire machinery of our

412

Government will be unleashed to apprehend you and recover the critical chip."

He looked piercingly at Guy. "Thereafter the scenario depends upon your skill and resourcefulness in evading capture. If you are successful, and surface at the exchange point able to deliver the Sceptre chip, it will be accepted as authentic. How the physical exchange takes place in circumstances that yield your daughter, will be up to you to devise. But if you're successful in eluding DSA and the FBI up to that point you should be able to formulate an appropriate plan."

After a few moments reflection Guy said, "Soviet belief in the chip depends upon my being a widely hunted fugitive. The chip I take from here will only *seem* to be real, whereas the search for me will be authentic?"

"Has to be," Printz said. "Too many involved to let out the true story. If the truth leaked back to the Soviets I fear that would end things for your daughter. So you actually have to make off with a chip from ISR."

Guy nodded. "Seems the only way."

"It *is* the only way," Felberg said sharply, "and only the three of us will know. Our part is preparing an authentic-appearing replica chip and facilitating your theft of it. Then finding a chip missing and reporting it to DSA. Leaking to the press the fact of the theft, and implicating you as the man responsible."

"How long will it take you to manufacture a simulated chip?"

Printz looked at Felberg. "I think a week is sufficient time. Reprogramming will be required in order to plant nulls in the microcircuits."

"Nulls?"

"Deviations to interfere with logic."

"To make it unusable by the Soviets?"

"Exactly. Though it should take them months to make that finding. Tom, we could safeguard it with another gaff

413

that just occurred to me, but we won't take more of Mr. Ryan's time.''

"So," he said getting up, "when I hear from you I should be ready to come here, steal the chip and disappear."

Printz nodded. "Your lead time will be only the interval between inventory checks of the Sceptre vault, so you'll want to have your escape route planned. The DSA and FBI will expect that—after all, you will have had time to mull over your decision to betray this country—so they'll hardly expect to find you hitchhiking toward Dulles Airport."

Felberg said, "In previous cases of espionage or theft the FBI has gotten cooperation from Interpol as well as the security services of NATO countries."

Guy said, "Suppose I'm never heard from again?"

The scientists looked at each other. "I suppose we'll confess the conspiracy and take our lumps from the Department of Justice. But we'd try to clear your name. When we produce the missing authentic chip that should be a mitigating factor."

"Let's hope things never get to that point. Gentlemen, I thank you both for your help—and your confidence. If I get my daughter back it will be largely due to you."

"It's not going to be easy to bring off, Mr. Ryan. You'll be in constant danger, especially at the point of exchange."

"I know," he said, "but I've a little time to try to improve the odds."

That night Cristina phoned him from her suite at the Dunfey in Houston. The ranch property was for the most part arid and barren—unnecessarily so, because a creek wound through the property as a future source of irrigation. Several buildings were habitable, and corrals and stables could be established with reasonable expenditure. Unexpectedly she had come across a DEA stakeout near the airstrip, and had to identify herself and her escorts.

414

Guy said, "Far better DEA enforcers than drug runners."

"Yes—for a few moments I was afraid of a wild west shootout." She laughed merrily, then said, "There are two proposals I want you to think about while I'm away."

"Indecent?"

"That's the permanent third. I miss you *so* much. But I see the ranch as an eventual Arab horse breeding and show center. Only California has more Arab owners or breeders than Texas, and in five years Rancho Ryan could be to Arab horses what Ballsbridge is to Thoroughbreds."

Guy smiled. "Y'know, I think I'll retire now and let you manage my life from now on."

"*Ticiticitici*—you're much too young to toy with retirement. But proposal number two may catch your fancy. It's to build a large, comfortable ranch house for us—and our children. Pool, tennis courts—everything to keep us together as a family. What do you think?"

"How soon can we start?"

"Construction?"

"A family."

For a few moments she was silent. Then she said, "I think we should wait on Gloria's return, don't you? And for our public marriage. Wouldn't do to have your sister-in-law wandering around with a large tummy."

"I wouldn't mind."

"Father would."

"Ummm. When will you come back?"

"Tomorrow night. I want to spend a full day on the ranch, see it all. Find out about the water supply and whether wells can be dug to supplement it in dry season. I plan to leave orders for soil testing so we'll know what, if anything, will thrive under irrigation. Right now there seems to be a lot of cactus and tumbleweed, cottonwood trees and some struggling *jacarandá*—I don't know the English word."

"It's the same."

"When I come back to the ranch I want you with me. To choose a location for our house, among other things."

"Gladly."

"Did you have a good day, too?"

"It was—interesting," he told her and they said good night.

Later, lying in bed, he reviewed what he had learned at ISR and what had been decided. He was confident that the two scientists would come through as promised. His immediate responsibility was to develop an escape route to Europe—and for that he would need Paul Whitaker again.

Once more he considered whether to disclose the full plan to Jake Needham and decided against it. The lawyer could face disbarment and Federal prosecution, and that was too much jeopardy. Besides, he mused, an unwitting Jake might prove a more useful ally, for the FBI would be monitoring his reactions as the search for Guy Ryan, traitor, deepened and spread.

Cristina. Bubbling with plans and contemplating bearing children. The Bureau would be watching, so her reactions, like Jake's, had to be authentic. He couldn't involve her, just pray that, whatever the outcome, she would understand.

Whitaker flew over by Concorde and Guy met him secretly in his room at the Pierre. With his customary courtesy, Whitaker asked if Cristina was enjoying New York. "Very much," Guy told him, "and she's fitting right in. Tonight she's attending a meeting of the Spanish-American Society. The Spanish Ambassador is addressing the group, and he's a distant cousin of the Palafoxes, so she'll have a touch of Spain to make her feel more at home."

"Admirable lass," Whitaker observed. "I don't suppose she's party to what we're up to."

"Nor Jake, yet. There's four of us: you, me, and the two Sceptre scientists. And you should know that Cristina and I are married."

"Well, my heartfelt congratulations." His smile was of pure pleasure. "Seemed inevitable, and better sooner than later. May she fill the void in your life, sir, give you much happiness."

"Thank you. Among other things I wanted to ensure Gloria's future—in case I don't get back."

"Think positive and all will go well. Now, if you're agreeable let's get the cards on the table."

After Guy summarized the ISR game plan Whitaker nodded appreciatively. "The Sovs will quite understand the cover story, they being accustomed to defectors who depart with code books and such. I don't like making you out a ruddy traitor, but it's essential to credibility. Now—" he began writing on a memo pad—"you'll need spurious ID, funds and safehouses. Where shall we meet? Paris? Geneva?"

"Let's think it through. From Frederick I'll travel common carrier to Baltimore or Dulles airports and fly to Canada. From there to Lisbon. Bus to Madrid, and hole up for a day. Take a train to Zürich, say, or Bern, then get to Egli's hideaway."

"So we'll meet in Geneva."

"Yes. I'll need to contact Drach, lay things on." He looked at Whitaker. "Any rumpus over Kedrov?"

"Deep lake. Corpse gas won't form until the water warms, midsummer. Something will surface then, but not enough for prompt identification."

"How are your studies progressing?"

"I have the chateau fairly well mapped out. Floor plans from the Swiss Historical Institute and my stroll showed me where the power lines run. Four Dobes with handlers, but only two patrol the grounds each shift. You spotted the entrance monitors, though there may be others on upper levels. The ballerina would know, but no way to contact her. By the way, Kedrov's car was crushed up as junk metal so it's no longer in condition to be traced."

"The remaining question is whether Kedrov has been replaced, and by whom. But I won't know that until I contact Drach and learn if the arrangement still holds."

"It will, never fear. No other way for the nasties to acquire the Sceptre."

"Otherwise," said Guy, "we'll be going to a great deal of trouble for nothing." And losing Gloria, he thought in silence.

Whitaker said, "Fabricating your ID will take a few days, so I'd best fly back tonight. While I'm waiting delivery I'll be doing other useful things: letter drop, disguise material . . ." He gazed at Guy. "How will I know you're on your way?"

"When you read it in the papers."

At her meeting, Cristina had encountered several other Spanish acquaintances, and she told Guy the ambassador had gone out of his way to be courteous. "I said I was here in connection with Al-Emir, and he invited me to attend a ball sponsored by the Spanish Embassy at the Kennedy Center—that's Washington?"

"Yes."

"It's in three weeks. I told him I would attend—if I found a suitable escort." Her nose nuzzled the side of his face. "Have I?"

"You have," he replied, aware that he would not be around. The first of many lies, he thought with a sinking feeling.

"Well, you *could* sound more enthusiastic."

"I apologize—I *am* sorry, honey. I was thinking about business problems."

"Didn't we agree that you were to leave work at the office?"

"We did—*I* did, and I promise to do better. No, I'll be perfect." His arms drew her close. "I don't need anything but you."

As she lay sleeping beside him he thought of the long hazardous journey ahead of him, the strain and doubts his flight would inflict on his bride. Until he regained his only child—much as he wanted to remain with Cristina forever—his happiness could never be complete.

Four days later a bank courier brought Guy a package from Whitaker. It contained everything needed for his fugitive journey from America.

All that remained was a signal from Printz that the Sceptre replica was in the vault, ready to be stolen.

Forty

When Jake came in for morning conference, Guy told him Cristina's plans for the ranch and said, "I want her to go back for a few days and get things started. The agriculture agent should begin testing soil for crop suitability, wells need to be dug and an architect commissioned for the house. Plus a secure stable for Al-Emir, like the one at La Rocha. Let's have the lawyer who went there coordinate things."

"You're not going?"

"I'll be looking at some houses here, then I'm going to take a few days in the Adirondacks for some spring fishing."

"Whereabouts?"

"Near Round Lake," he lied.

"Wouldn't mind some of that myself."

"The guide's Iroquois and supposed to be good—I'll let you know." His voice lowered. "Jake, that's the cover story."

His forehead wrinkled. "Cover—for what?"

Guy took a deep breath. "When I was last in Geneva I came to an agreement with the Soviets who have Gloria. I want her more than anything, and they want something only I can provide."

"What—?"

"You'll find out in time. When news breaks you'll be asked where I am, that's why I gave you the cover story—fishing, Adirondacks, Long Lake."

"But you won't be there. Where will you be?"

"Doing everything in my power to regain my daughter."

"I see," he said slowly, "at least I think I do."

"You've become my best and most reliable friend, Jake. I need you to stand by me, lie for me when you have to. But don't ever believe I could betray our country."

"Guy—I know you're not capable of it." He got up and paced the floor. "What about Cristina?"

"For a time she has to believe I've done a heinous thing. She's going to suffer, and I leave it to your judgment when to tell her what I've told you."

Jake shook his head. "Is there no other way?"

"You can't bargain with the Soviets. They made a demand and I agreed to their terms."

"But will they deliver Gloria?"

"Whitaker and I satisfied ourselves they will."

"Then Paul knows about this."

"He'll be helping me. Covertly."

For a while Jake was silent. He stopped pacing and said, "You're putting your life on the line for your daughter, aren't you?"

Guy nodded. "I think any father would. The Soviets counted on that, of course, and they judged rightly." He looked away. "That's the situation for now. I've told you enough to enable you to handle things in my absence, but not enough to implicate you in a criminal act."

"Guy, you know I'd go the distance for you—the whole distance."

"I know that but I'm trying to keep you uninvolved—so you can take care of things if I don't get back—RyTech and especially Cristina."

"Wish it didn't have to be this way, but I have to respect your intelligence, your decision. What can I say?"

"Vaya con Dios."

During lunch at Le Cirque Cristina agreed to return to Texas, saying, "I had no idea you'd be so enthusiastic."

"Lots of things you don't know about me," he observed, quickly adding, "but will in time." He took her hand and held it. "Don't think I've lost hope for Gloria, but talking about her doesn't help. It's better to try to fill our minds with other things."

"I understand."

"And there are difficult days ahead—for both of us."

Her head tilted. "Are you trying to tell me something—without actually saying so?"

"Only that we'll need each other more than ever. Whatever happens, believe in me."

"Of course I do, and always will—nothing can change that." She touched his cheek. "Suddenly this is becoming morbid—and I'm frightened."

"You mustn't be. While I'm away, whatever comes up, go to Jake. Trust him as I do."

"I'll do whatever you say, dear. Always."

After luncheon Guy returned a call to Tom Felberg at ISR. Dr. Printz answered, and said, "A couple of matters have come up that require your attention in the next day or so."

"Can we discuss them in New York?"

"Sorry, but that's not feasible. When can you come here?"

"What's best for you?"

"Would tomorrow evening suit you?"

"Fine. I'll be there." He replaced the receiver, noticing the tenseness in his hand. Well, that was it. Despite inevitable pain to Cristina he had to make this final try for Gloria. The consequences to himself were unimportant, weighed against the chance of success.

That night he took Cristina to the Coq d'Or, heavily aware that it would be their last dining together for a long time, and perhaps forever. She said, "I wish you'd come to the ranch with me and approve my plans."

"I have the utmost confidence in you, *querida*. What do I know about ranch homes and horses? You're the expert." He took her hand. "While I'm away, why don't you fly over and visit your father? We both know how much he misses you. Seeing you will do him good."

She gazed at him thoughtfully. "Since it's your suggestion I will. But, Guy, I have the eerie feeling you're distancing yourself from me. Do you really prefer going off on a fishing trip to being with me?"

"Of course not." He breathed deeply and in a low voice said, "Darling, it's a pretext. That's the only explanation I can give—please accept it."

Her hand tightened around his. "Does it have to do with—Gloria? The Government?"

"Both."

"Then there's a chance . . . ?"

"If I'm to live with myself I must do this. Please understand."

For a while she said nothing, looked away, then back to meet his gaze. "I'll do the best I can," she said and seemed to draw herself together. "We'll go to Seville, won't we, for Feria?"

"Of course we will, I'm counting on it. Perhaps bring back Al-Emir."

"That makes me feel better," she said, but her smile was uncertain and her lips trembled. "I'll—pray for you . . . and Gloria."

His eyes were moist. "Remember, wherever I am I love you. No matter what happens remember that forever."

* * *

In the morning the bodyguards came early for Cristina, and after she was gone Guy went out, buying an inexpensive overnight bag, toilet articles and clothing. He paid cash and went to the apartment where he collected the items Paul Whitaker had sent over from Geneva. Trilingual Swiss passport in the name of Lucien Victor Passier; physical disguise material; ten thousand Swiss francs, four thousand Canadian dollars, and the number of a *boîte postale* in Geneva. The money was in a used wallet of Swiss make that also contained a driving license, business and night club cards and other pocket litter.

Next, Guy went to a travel agency that handled much RyTech travel, introduced himself, and asked for a ticket to Buenos Aires.

"Certainly, sir. Round trip?"

"One way—I'll buy the return in B.A., cheaper in australs."

She smiled. "Much cheaper. How soon do you want to leave?"

"Tonight."

After checking the computer she said, "There's an Aerolineas Argentinas flight from JFK at 11:00 P.M."

"That'll be fine," he said, and paid with a RyTech credit card. Two blocks from the agency he tore up the ticket and dropped the fragments in a trash barrel. It would take the Bureau a day or so to learn he hadn't been on the B.A. flight. By then, if all went according to plan, he should be in Europe.

He spent the rest of the morning routinely at the office, and after Mrs. Paskow left for lunch he took a plain envelope from her desk and addressed it to the Geneva post office box. He wrote in European calligraphy learned at Vezelay.

By phone he reserved a seat on Air Canada's nine o'clock flight from Dulles International to Montreal in the name of L.V. Passier, saying he would purchase his ticket at the airport.

As he left the office Guy reflected that it could well be for the last time.

He had lunch at a small restaurant off Fifth Avenue, and went to the apartment to collect his traveling bag.

At Penn Station he bought a Baltimore ticket on the Metroliner and settled down in the club car with a drink and *The Wall Street Journal*.

From a car agency at the Baltimore station Guy rented a compact Buick for three days, and paid with cash.

Then he headed west, picked up Route 70 at the Beltway and drove through light traffic to the Institute for Strategic Research. From a mile away he could see the floodlit complex, the somber watchtowers. He parked at one side of the entrance gate and noticed the array of military firepower and vehicles, the bivouaced troops, some on perimeter patrol.

Tom Felberg escorted Guy inside, and as they walked toward the administration building Felberg said, "This is the scenario: you came in response to Horatio's urgent request. When you got here Horatio told you we need a specialized computer for the antigravity work at a cost of two million dollars. You said you'd think it over and asked to be taken to the Sceptre area again. We were reluctant—both of us had dinner plans—but agreed—no sense in upsetting the man you've just asked to supply a couple of million dollars. Okay, we go down, suit up, and you look things over cursorily. What you really want is another look at the Sceptre microchip. So, we open the vault, hand you the container holding the seven completed chips. Opening it with your heavy gloves you fumble the container and it drops, strewing the contents. You pick up the plastic boxes and replace them in the container, mumbling apologies. I close the vault, sign the inventory log and we leave.

"During the next check it's discovered a chip box is missing—as one will be—and internal inquiries begin. We don't notify DSA—Hoskins—until dawn. After that we expect all hell to break loose."

"It's going to be hard on the two of you."

"There'll be initial suspicions but we'll play it cool. Why would we expect the boss to steal a chip? By noon there will be a preliminary search for you, and when your absence from office and apartment is noted the focus will be on your whereabouts."

"Suppose they want you and Dr. Printz to take a polygraph?"

"Simple—we'll decline. Citing Fourth Amendment rights and our contracts. We can stall by calling lawyers and so on. That's not your worry."

They reached the director's office and went in. Printz was at his desk. "So far so good," he said. "Before we go to Building G, a few details. I have the nearly perfect chip here." He shoved it across the desk and Guy picked up the thin transparent box. Inside it, protected by a bed of black foam lay the multicolored chip. "You might as well take it now so we can get on with the rest of the charade." He got up and came around the desk. "Sceptre II—this replica— is packed in a vacuum like the others, and for a particular reason. One of the sandwich layers is a hygroscopic compound. When exposed to air—and you must warn the Soviets of this feature—it will absorb moisture and crumble as an Alka-Seltzer tablet does when left out overnight."

"So I'll understand, what's the purpose of that?"

"To discourage opening until they have it in Moscow laboratory conditions." He smiled broadly. "Explain Sceptre is designed to operate in the moisture-free utter cold of space, which is why it is manufactured in those conditions. Now, to the task at hand. You'll take a Sceptre chip and turn it over to me when we're back here. I have safe storage for it until your project is completed. Shall we go?"

* * *

Dressed in protective suiting, Guy toured the Sceptre area, noting that the night shift was smaller than the number of daytime personnel. He rejoined the two scientists and gestured at the Sceptre safe. After some discussion, Felberg opened the heavy door and got out the black container. He handed it to Guy, who made a show of letting it slip from his gloves, then knelt to recover the scattered vacuum boxes from under the vapor that shrouded the floor—slipping one into the cuff of his glove. He returned the closed container to Felberg, apologizing for clumsiness, and Felberg locked the container in the safe. After marking down closing time, Felberg initialed the form, and said, "Let's go, I imagine you'd like to get back to New York."

"That I would."

They left their protective clothing in the air lock and Guy pocketed the plastic box. When they were in the director's office again, he handed it to Printz and said, "Thanks for everything. You've given me my only chance to get my daughter back."

"Glad we were able to do something," said Printz, and they all shook hands. Felberg passed Guy through the gate and walked with him to the Buick. "I don't know what else to say, Mr. Ryan, but we'll be praying for you—and your child."

He drove through darkness to the Baltimore airport, got his bag from the car trunk and left the Buick in an outdoor parking area. Inside the airport he found the men's room and changed into clothing from his bag. He applied a false mustache, altered the part in his hair, put on a gray crush hat, and wrapped discarded clothing and identifying papers in a plastic bag. Before leaving the stall he sealed the Sceptre II box in his preaddressed envelope, and deposited it in a mail slot, hoping it would reach Geneva undamaged.

The clothing bag he left in a large refuse container, then bought a ticket on the Dulles Airport bus.

At the Air Canada counter he paid cash for a Montreal ticket and showed his Swiss passport to the clerk. Returning it to him she said, "Everything in order, Mr. Passier, you can board now through Gate Five."

By one o'clock he had passed Canadian Immigration and Customs at Montreal's airport, and half an hour later paid for a morning flight on TAP to Lisbon. He spent the night at the airport inn.

In the waiting room a flight delay was announced, and Guy looked around apprehensively. Was it a ruse to capture him? He went to the men's room and stayed out of sight until TAP boarding was announced half an hour later.

It was three o'clock local time when the plane landed in the Azores, evening when he deplaned at Lisbon.

Having slept through most of the Atlantic crossing, Guy decided against spending the night in Lisbon and boarded a modern-looking bus for Madrid by way of Cáceres, a six-hundred-kilometer ride. It was not until he crossed the frontier near Badajoz that he allowed himself to think of his Spanish-born wives, each so different from the other, both fiercely Spanish *a la muerte*. When would Cristina learn of his defection? he wondered. Who would tell her? What would she do? He hoped that in the days ahead some spark of trust would glow within her.

As the bus rumbled through the night he regretted not having left an explanatory letter for her in the event of his death, but there had been no secure way to do so. Jake would have been forced to turn it over to the FBI. And he could not trust Cristina to keep unopened a parting message when she was frantic with despair.

Still, the deception was necessary; if his wife believed him a traitor so would the FBI, the press and ultimately the KGB.

As the bus passed through sleeping Spanish towns he

428

thought of the lie his father's life had been; how the legacy that had come with his father's death had been one of deceit. After Johns, Edmonds, and Kedrov had he become inured to it? Was he so indifferent that he could deceive even Cristina?

His father's death had changed him, and it was as though the old man's malevolence pursued him from the grave. Altering the son's character in ways Sean had failed to do in life.

What had RyTech brought him but violence and the loss of Consuela and Gloria? Only Cristina made his life tolerable and now he was betraying even her.

At Oropesa the bus made a relief stop. Guy stayed aboard and fell asleep before the bus departed.

When he woke it was morning and the bus was unloading in Madrid.

Last stop before Geneva.

Forty-One

He took a room in a small commercial hotel on Barquillo off the Gran Vía, soaked in a hot tub to relieve travel-cramped muscles and went out to a department store near the Puerta del Sol. There he bought a change of clothing except for shoes—Spanish footwear being of notoriously poor quality. The lined raincoat was of good cut, though Guy was uncertain whether it would withstand Geneva's rainfall.

Before returning to the hotel he stopped at a sidewalk stand for a Madrid eye-opener—espresso with a shot of Fundador. He munched a warm roll and walked on.

Morning overcast had given way to sunlight. Cars sped along the *paseos*, challenging pedestrians to try their luck at crossing. Winter-brown grass was greening, acacias were in full bud. Children playing in the yard of a small private school recalled Gloria, and he felt a pang of desolation. During Consuela's pregnancy they had visited Madrid and spent a morning at the Prado Museum. After lunching at Horcher's they had toured the Royal Palace with its stunningly opulent chambers, tapestries and paintings, later joining Madrileños trooping Calle Etchegaray for evening *tapa*-and-wine sampling. He remembered strolling with Consuela in the Retiro Gardens, watching her bargain for antiques at

El Rastro, sitting with her through his first bullfight one Sunday afternoon at the *plaza de toros*. Here and in Seville they had shared small candlelit tables, drunk good wine and *coñac* and supped well.

So many memories, he thought, of a time long past that now existed only in his mind.

Perhaps with Cristina, at some future time, he could re-create that happiness for Gloria.

At a kiosk he bought a morning paper and scanned the foreign news. Nothing yet.

In the hotel he sent out his travel clothes for laundry and pressing and took an early siesta to compensate for jet lag.

The afternoon paper carried the story he was looking for. American authorities were concerned over the disappearance of industrialist Guy P. Ryan after visiting a RyTech subsidiary near Baltimore. Company and police officials voiced fears for his safety, citing the growing incidence of executive kidnappings around the world. Only last month Sr. Ryan's wife and daughter had been abducted in Paris, the tragic episode resulting in Sra. Ryan's death. The fate of their daughter remained unknown. Before her marriage, Sra. Ryan was the Marquesa de Palafox y Urriaga. Sr. Ryan was a former Military Attaché at the American Embassy, and a Rhodes Scholar.

Phase One completed.

Phase Two about to begin.

At the airline office on Calle Velazquez Guy bought a ticket for the Iberia flight to Zürich, departing Barajas Airport at six-fifteen. He took the airline bus to the airport, had coffee and *coñac* at a refreshment stand, and surveyed the crowd and the gray-uniformed officials before satisfying himself that he was not yet sought in Spain.

He had chosen to fly to a German-speaking city where airport officials would be less alert to lapses from Genevois

French. Besides, they would be less interested in scrutinizing Swiss citizens than incoming foreigners.

Whitaker having told him nothing about the provenance of the Passier passport, Guy could only hope that it was authentic enough to see him through the Zürich airport. That and his changed appearance, his physical disguise.

As Guy walked toward the *Salida* gate he tensed. Angling in his direction was the DEA agent who had sat on the Paris embassy task force. The agent—Bowers?—was strolling unconcernedly. Five feet away he glanced at Guy's face but Guy avoided eye contact and walked on, forcing himself not to look back.

In-flight dinner was served, and as Guy nibbled at portions on his plate he reflected that the trouble with Spanish cuisine was the overpowering presence of olive oil. Lacking dairy herds and animal fats, the Spanish fried, baked and roasted everything in olive oil, drenched salads with it, used it to permeate cakes and pies with an unforgettable flavor. He pushed the plate aside and drank a glass of Riscal, recalling that at La Rocha, years ago, he had affronted the cook by requesting eggs fried in butter rather than the customary pressings of the olive tree. But after the kitchen accommodated him life at La Rocha had been smooth flowing and untroubled—until Consuela left for Paris . . .

Flaps down, the plane shuddered. Below lay Zürich's twinkling lights, the dark expanses of the Limmat River and the Zürich-See. The plane approached from the northwest, landing gently on the runway, and taxiing back to the terminal.

As he was processed into Switzerland, Guy found the officials more interested in his suitcase than his passport. New clothing? Coffee? Drugs? Scotch whisky? *"Absoulement rien du tout,"* said Guy, and received pitying glances. What kind of Schweitzer would travel abroad and bring back nothing dutiable? Incredible!

"I don't earn a great deal of money," Guy explained as they closed his suitcase. "Every franc is precious."

The immigration officer stamped his passport so indifferently the ink smeared. With a shrug he returned the passport to Guy, who nodded and walked toward the taxi stand. Then, remembering himself he veered toward the bus lane and got aboard the leader.

After stops at Dubendorf and Schwamendingen the bus trip ended at the Bahnhof beside Limmat quai. Zürich was not served by TGV so Guy purchased a second class ticket on the slower electric train for the four-hour trip to Geneva. At Bern he bought beer and sandwiches from an aisle vendor, managed an hour's uncomfortable sleep and reached the Gare de Cornavin long after midnight.

Thoroughly fatigued from travel, Guy taxied to Hans Egli's former hideaway, and trudged up the staircase, the once-light suitcase heavy as stone.

Setting it down, he yawned, extracted the key from his wallet and opened the door. Lugging the suitcase inside, he closed and locked the door, felt for a light switch and turned on a lamp.

The room was the same as when he had last seen it. The site of Serge Kedrov's final hours. He got ice from the refrigerator and added water. Glass in one hand he made his way to the bedroom prepared to fall on the mattress and sleep until morning.

Sunlight streamed through the window. His nostrils scented fresh coffee. Wondering where he was he squinted around.

Genève.

Had he made it all the way? As if on fast forward his mind unreeled a montage of cars, buses, planes, trains and taxis.

"Hey!" he shouted. "Front and center!"

433

From the kitchen, a Sandhurst bellow: *"Sah!"*

Guy sat up with a jolting laugh as Paul Whitaker came in with coffee. "So I'm to be yer dogrobber, is it, leftenant?" He was grinning broadly; mustache handsomely pointed, face freshly shaven, Windsor knot in his regimental tie, perfectly tailored suit. In comparison Guy felt like a hobo. As Whitaker handed Guy coffee he said, "I don't mind saying I'm prayerfully relieved you made it."

Guy ran one hand through tousled hair. "Letter arrive?"

"Checked en route. It's in the postoffice box, which seems a safe enough place to leave it for the nonce. You had no difficulty en route?"

"Everything clicked."

"Then, welcome to Geneva, M'sieu Passier. I'll have a second cup while you rehabilitate. We have matters to discuss."

A long hot shower, shave and fresh clothing improved Guy's spirits. When he joined Whitaker, the Englishman pointed to the morning Geneva paper. "Page six," he said, and began reading:

"Although neither the Department of Defense or the FBI will confirm or deny it, sources well-informed on National Security matters now connect the unexplained disappearance of Guy Patrick Ryan, head of the multinational conglomerate, RyTech, to the loss of a vital electronic device from a RyTech subsidiary, the Institute for Strategic Research (ISR). The missing device is said to be crucial to the projected Missile Defense Shield (MDS). Other sources, who declined to be identified, stated that Mr. Ryan was last seen when he visited ISR three days ago. Since that time his movements and whereabouts are unknown. Should the electronic device, code-named Sceptre, fall into hostile hands, the entire MDS program would be compromised, according to one knowledgeable scientist involved in defense research.

"More about you, your family, your military service and Oxford studies." Whitaker frowned. "Fascinating how fast they tied the can to your tail. If that much has leaked, be sure an extensive search is underway." He looked at Guy. "The KGB must be salivating with anticipation."

"Things quiet at the castle?"

"Relatively. I've had it under spot surveillance. Cars come and go—petro-Arabs, for the most part—and so far as we can tell Drach hasn't left the place." He drained the dregs of his cup. "However, informed sources tell me a new Soviet economic adviser has joined the permanent trade delegation. His passport name is Pastrovsky, Boris—but the sod's dissimulatin'. The Swiss have him pegged as Nikolai Gerasimov, colonel in the KGB, directorate unknown. PNG'd from Brussels three years ago for trying to subvert NATO personnel. Wife with him then. This time he came alone—which suggests a temporary stay."

"Do you think he's Kedrov's replacement?"

"Until we learn otherwise." He reached over and tapped Guy's knee. "So much for Gerasimov. Contact with Drach must be established without him or anyone knowin' where you are. If they did know the buggers would try to snatch the chip without keepin' their part of the bargain."

"You've thought of an approach?"

"I have."

As Whitaker spoke, the pale, vulnerable face of his daughter drifted into Guy's mind. Staring without expression above the Vienna paper. Helpless. Frightened.

Gloria was alive then.

Was she now?

Fatigue left him as he listened. He began to feel confident again—hard, aggressive as on the eve of battle.

His smile was thin. He admired the devious routings of Whitaker's mind.

The last phase had begun.

Forty-Two

In the letter Whitaker took with him to Bern Guy had written:

Cher Monsieur Drach:

I have the desired item. It is in our common interest to make prompt arrangements as a search is under way.
  I await your advice at . . .

Guy Patrick Ryan

The telephone number was left blank for Whitaker to add following Bern arrangements. He would then mail the letter to Edouard Drach.

Guy drank a bottle of Pilsner and made a light lunch. At two o'clock he answered the telephone and heard Whitaker's voice. "You there?"

"I'm here."

"Good, the system works. Letter mailed. I'm at the airport now. See you presently."

Whitaker returned with newspapers from Paris, Bern and London. The updates were nearly identical. American industrialist Guy Ryan was being sought in connection with the theft of a classified device. Inquiries were going forward in Buenos Aires. Ryan's sister-in-law, the Marquesa de Palafox y Urriaga, expressed disbelief as to his responsibility for the supposed theft, and declined other comment.

"So much for that, eh? The atmosphere is excellent for Drach to receive your letter. Now, to explain the telephone system. Through a private exchange service in Bern an electronic transfer has been made whereby any call to that Bern number is relayed here automatically—human intervention not required."

"Can the Bern number be traced to the relay service?"

"I'm told not. Apparently the privacy service is utilized by certain bank customers to shield their transactions. The service caters to anonymous clients."

"In the States," Guy said, "bookies would love it."

"So far so good. Drach will likely phone tomorrow. After that I'll set a watch on the airport for an unscheduled Aeroflot arrival, though I don't think they'll bring your daughter the entire distance by air."

"How, then?"

"Aeroflot to Prague or Vienna, by car to Drach's chateau. Assuming that's where the exchange will be made."

"According to Kedrov."

"Yes, but Kedrov's disappearance may make them so wary they'll select another site. We must be prepared to go anywhere on quite short notice."

"I'd give anything to talk to Cristina, explain."

"I'm sure—but never doubt her loyalty. She's of superior stuff." He looked at his watch. "Tonight we're planting a few noisemakers on Drach's grounds. As you doubtless remember from combat, diversions can spare lives."

"How large do you think Gloria's escort will be?"

"Two to four huskies. Plus a sod from the scientific side to give your Sceptre preliminary vetting."

"And Gerasimov?"

"Likely stay out of sight in the chateau as Kedrov did. I look to Nikolai to make the final judgment."

"On whether to release my daughter?"

He nodded.

Guy said, "It might come to pass that you'll have to explain things to my wife. Tell Cristina I felt my life was less important than Gloria's. She and my daughter are provided for, and I love them both." He looked away. "Tell her I would do equally were she captive."

"That's a commission I trust I'll never have to carry out." He glanced around the room. "You have food and drink. I'll come back in the morning. Let's anticipate an active day."

After making dinner for himself Guy cleaned up the kitchen, working slowly to kill time. He listened to a radio program of classical music while reading the day's newspapers in their entirety. During a late newscast he heard his name mentioned, and learned that because he had not been found in Buenos Aires the search had shifted to Western Europe.

They're getting closer, he told himself and thought of Don José's outrage when *Guardias Civiles* came to La Rocha.

He slept restlessly. Whitaker returned in the morning, and two hours later the telephone rang. Answering, Guy heard the heavy voice of Edouard Drach.

"My dear fellow, I'm extremely pleased you're back in Switzerland. Tribute to your ingenuity. Ah—you have the item?"

"I do. How soon can we arrange the exchange?"

"That, sir, may take a little time."

"It had better be immediate," Guy told him. "If you follow the press you know how urgent it is. If I'm caught that's the end of everything."

"I understand, yes, quite understand. Well, having just

learned of your arrival I'm at a disadvantage. However, I will attempt to move matters along. You may expect a call from me before day's end." He paused. "Until then I strongly suggest you stay out of sight."

"So far I've been lucky," Guy said, "but I don't feel it can last much longer."

"You've done amazingly, sir, and it's to everyone's advantage to conclude the affair without delay. I will call you soon."

Guy replaced the phone. To Whitaker he said, "We wait."

The waiting, Guy reflected, was more injurious to his sanity than physical action. In 'Nam he had always found himself eager to break from concealment and close with the enemy. But prudence had required patience and concern for the survival of his team. Gloria's survival demanded the ultimate in patience and caution. The present was the most difficult test he had ever faced.

Whitaker had gone out, saying he needed to hire and position more watchers, make additional arrangements.

What plans they had, Guy mused, were based on the supposition that the exchange would take place at Drach's chateau. And for that they had only Kedrov's word. Facing death, had the KGB agent decided to lie? Or had he been thoroughly broken as Whitaker believed?"

He read the newspapers Whitaker had brought. The Senate Intelligence Committee demanded a full investigation into the slack security at ISR that had permitted Guy Ryan to walk off with one of the nation's most critical secrets. So far the White House was resisting growing demands for the appointment of a Special Prosecutor. The Director of Central Intelligence refused comment on the matter, beyond saying that CIA had no charter responsibility for domestic security.

The head of the Defense Security Agency was quoted as saying one should not overlook the possibility that recent tragedies affecting Mr. Ryan might well have unhinged his mind. The Director of the FBI said that if Ryan had indeed left the continental US, the FBI was no longer involved in his pursuit; the CIA was responsible for whatever went on abroad. His supposition was that Interpol was employing all its resources to effect the defector's capture. No, he could not predict when that might take place.

Press sources in Moscow indicated that Soviet authorities appeared untroubled by the American problem, although a Foreign Ministry spokesman predicted that the disappearance of the fascist industrialist was likely to produce another wave of anti-Soviet witch-hunts in the United States.

In Britain, Labour leaders were gleeful in their assertions that compromise of the American MDS project deprived the US of another provocative weapon, and in the end could prove a major benefit in reducing world tensions. The head of a left-wing Labour faction was quoted as saying that Guy Ryan should receive the Nobel Prize for Peace.

All predictable, Guy thought as he discarded the papers, and all useful in establishing the credibility of Sceptre II. With so much stir in the international press the Soviets will *want* to believe its authenticity.

And on that Gloria's life depends.

He pulled aside a window curtain and looked out. A rain cloud had moved down from the mountains and was pelting the city relentlessly. Water gushed along the cobbled street. A gray and dismal day. Poor flying conditions. He wondered what Whitaker was doing.

By two o'clock the rain had stopped. At nightfall Whitaker still had not returned and Guy was beginning to feel uneasy. Then, a little before seven, Drach's call came through.

"Final arrangements," said Drach, "will not be made

441

known until some time tomorrow. That will give you ample time to travel to Geneva and establish contact.''

"Everything's in order?"

"That is my understanding."

"And my daughter? Did you ask about her?"

"Most especially I did. I have been assured that she is well and comfortable."

"That had better be so," said Guy, "or I'll destroy the merchandise. Naturally, I'll need to see Gloria before making the transfer."

"Of course. I trust you will have a safe and unimpeded journey. Please telephone when you arrive."

Half an hour later Whitaker arrived with a pot of lamb stew and a bottle of cognac. As they ate he said, "If I were to place a bet I'd say things will come to a head tomorrow night. Here's Gerasimov's photo, by the way—ever see him before?"

The likeness had been Xeroxed from his passport. Guy saw the pronounced Slavic features of a man in his fifties, white patches in his thinning hair. An unsmiling mouth, almost menacing. "Stranger to me," Guy said, returning the photo.

"Around six, Gerasimov left the Russian Consulate for Drach's place. Thereafter Drach telephoned you." He dipped bread in the remains of his stew. "Circumstantial evidence Gerasimov has taken over from Kedrov to manage the transaction at this end. We've got what we wanted from the Bern relay so I'll cancel it and leave the Soviets nothing to trace." He swallowed the gravy-soaked bread with satisfaction. "Earlier today, while it was still raining, Gerasimov made brush contact with a man at the Palais Wilson. The contact drove to the French Consulate where my watcher determined him to be from the Ministry of Interior—a sub-Commissioner named Achille Maundit. Interesting connection, but no affair of ours."

"No? Maundit represented the Ministry on our Embassy task force. He seemed resigned to letting events take their course."

Whitaker nodded thoughtfully. "Still, the contact was probably part of another KGB operation; they like to meet agents in third countries, especially highly placed agents. But the connection does tell us the Soviets knew from the beginning everything discussed at task force meetings. With Maundit listening they didn't have to tail you, they knew your comings and goings."

Another betrayal; Guy felt a wave of nausea.

Whitaker uncorked cognac, poured two small glasses. *"Prosit,"* he said and drank. "Put on your mustache and rain garb and we'll take a drive to the main post office."

The Central Post Office on Rue du Mont Blanc was a large cavernous building occupying a city block. Guy followed Whitaker to the *boîte postale* section where several hundred boxes were set into the wall. "Fourth row from the top," Whitaker said, "third box from the end. Number A-784."

The envelope he had mailed from Baltimore lay inside.

As they moved on, Whitaker said, "We'll leave it there pending developments. You won't want to surrender the box key until you have Gloria. They won't release her until they have the envelope. How we handle the problem will largely depend on Gerasimov. He may decide against Drach's place and choose another setting. Wherever you go, you'll go in alone. I expect they'll search you routinely for the chip then get down to business." They left the building and walked back to Whitaker's car. "Has it occurred to you the Soviets may plan to kill you?"

"It has."

"Because you're the only one who can tell the world why

you were forced to steal the chip. I can't see them letting you go free."

They got into the car together. Whitaker drove toward the Gare de Cornavin and took the Rue de Lausanne past the train yards and beyond the United Nations Palace. As they neared chateau Drach Whitaker said, "That's my man over there—the Fiat parked at roadside. He'll move along in a bit and be replaced by another watcher."

As they idled past the entrance gate Guy could make out only a few lights inside Drach's castle. Some on the first floor, none on the second, but Sonya's room was lighted behind blinds. Pointing at it Guy said, "Remember, I promised to get her away from Drach."

"Never fear, the child is much in my mind."

A darkened car was parked on the other side of the road. As they went past it Whitaker's headlights crossed the face of the man behind the wheel, and Guy felt his body tense.

The driver was a fine-looking man, with dark brown skin and penetrating eyes. Under other circumstances Guy would have been glad to see him, but finding him near Drach's retreat caused a thrill of apprehension.

For the man was DSA's Paris agent, James McGrain.

"Can't have him muddying the brook," Whitaker said as they drove back to Geneva. "Give the whole show away. McGrain has his reasons for being there and that's well enough, so long as they don't involve you."

"When I first came to Paris I asked him for traces on Drach and he provided them. It could be that DSA is covering all my known contacts, hoping I'll show up."

"And he was on the task force?"

"Yes."

"So he'd know Achille Maundit—perhaps that's the connection. Looking for Maundit to show up *chez* Drach rather than you?"

"McGrain's turf is France, not Switzerland, although if DSA is putting on a full-court press I imagine Hoskins is using all available hands. Of course, McGrain has no arrest power here—or anywhere—and contact between a French official and a KGB agent should interest CIA rather than DSA." He shook his head. "Bottom line—he's in a critical location and has to be shooed away."

"Good man?"

"First class."

"Then I'll not have him hurt."

They returned to the apartment by an indirect route, doubling back from time to time until they were certain of no followers. A block away Whitaker pulled to the curb and said, "When you get up to the apartment, tape this mike to your chest. It's wired to this little battery-powered transmitter. Put your shirt and jacket back on and speak in a normal voice from three locations, one by a window. I'll be listening from two blocks away, and when I join you we'll compare notes."

After the test, Whitaker said reception was best from the window though Guy's voice was audible even from the center of the apartment. "You'll be wired when you go to the meeting place," he said, "and the gadget's mostly plastic. So unless you're stripped there's a fair chance it won't be detected. I want to hear what's going on, find out fast if things come apart." He paused. "That's all the edge I can give you."

He poured a shot of cognac and downed it. "Now if you'll excuse me I'd better see to friend McGrain, get him off the byways and into territory that's safer for us all."

Guy drank cognac and got into bed, thinking that whatever happened this was his last night in the apartment. Tomorrow the long weeks of waiting would be over and he would see Gloria again. Once the Soviets had Sceptre they would have no further need of him—or his daughter—so the problem was to get both of them out alive. No—three of them, as promised Sonya.

To go up against the resources of the KGB he needed a machine pistol and spare magazines. What he would go in with was a two-dollar mike and a pure heart.

The imbalance made the whole equation laughable, and he wondered what possessed him to think he could carry it off. The only thing that mattered was freeing his daughter. She was the focus of everything and he was glad Whitaker understood.

Presently he wondered how deeply Cristina was hurt by his deception. If he lived he would seek forgiveness; if not, Whitaker would explain.

Suppose Gerasimov selected another site for the turnover, one where he would be even more vulnerable than at Drach's castle? What had the KGB concluded concerning Serge Kedrov? Guy could be sure of nothing, not even that his daughter would appear.

Less than twenty-four hours, he told himself, and all questions will be answered, everything made known.

Forty-Three

After a restless night Guy left the apartment at dawn and walked to a nearby church. He lighted candles for his father, Consuela and Marguerite, and stepped into a confession booth.

For half an hour the priest listened, mostly in appalled silence, inquiring into the circumstances surrounding the killings and torture. When Guy finished the confessor said, "In all my years I've never heard such a tale, my son, and I hardly know how to respond. But, tell me—are you truly repentant?"

"I regret the circumstances that made my actions seem the only recourse. As to what I did, I'll have to live with it, Father."

"Are you—defiant?"

"No, Father—honest. The life of my daughter outweighs everything else."

"Yes, that counts in your favor. For you to so unburden yourself tells me that your faith must be strong. Yet, you are prepared to kill again."

"If necessary."

"How can I absolve you?"

"I guess you can't," said Guy, "but thank you for hearing my confession, Father."

"May God be with you."

He left the confessional, dropped francs into the alms box and went out on the church steps. Another gray morning, mist in the air, lindens dripping dew. He returned to the apartment and made breakfast, wondering what he had really expected of the priest. Well, he'd prepared himself spiritually as best he could.

The *Journal de Genève* carried a short report from Washington on the sixth page. Sources close to the Department of Defense indicated that the search for missing industrialist Guy P. Ryan was concentrating on Western Europe. The same sources expressed concern over the possibility that Ryan would try to reach Eastern Europe via Berlin or Vienna.

He heard a key in the door lock and laid the paper aside as Whitaker came in. "Stopped by to make sure you were up and around. Any coffee?"

"Help yourself."

After tasting it Whitaker shuddered and sat down. "Last night friend McGrain was braced by highway police. He showed his diplomatic passport but offered no explanation for being where he was. The police warned him against doing anything inimical to the interests of the Swiss Republic and urged him to leave the country." He sipped again. "All that from a phone call. When are you phoning Drach?"

"Around eleven."

"Remind him the transfer can't begin until you've seen Gloria."

Guy nodded.

"So far, no unscheduled arrivals by Aeroflot or LOT aircraft, but it's early in the day. I still think she'll be brought here by car or train. Long drive from Vienna, so train's the more likely. How's your morale?"

"Mediocre."

"Good—don't want you peaking too early." He finished

his coffee and rinsed cup and saucer in the sink. When he came back he said, "You've suffered a great deal, gone through what would break an ordinary man, so you must not enter final negotiations fatalistically. This is the day you've been waiting for. Nothing in your entire life is as important as today's outcome. You'll survive it and so will Gloria. Force yourself into a positive frame of mind."

"After Drach confirms the exchange is going through."

Whitaker looked at his watch. "Nikolai Gerasimov went to the Consulate early, and I take that as a good sign. I expect the Soviet microchip expert to arrive in the party with your daughter. Their expectations are high, they're eager to get Sceptre. If they fail, they haven't much future back in Moscow. All right, I'm off now for reports from my watchers. Meanwhile, don't sink into a comforting slough of despond." He walked away and stopped. "Shouldn't use this telephone. Go to the Gare to call Drach. Trains hooting should convince him you're just in from Bern." He eyed Guy critically. "Don't forget your mustache," he admonished and went out.

At ten-thirty Guy left the building by a rear alley and took a succession of trams to the Gare de Cornavin. There he telephoned Drach, and as the guttural voice responded a train whistle sounded in the background. "I'm here," Guy said, "ready to do business."

"And the merchandise?"

"In a safe place. Where it will stay until I've seen my daughter. Has she arrived?"

"Ah, not yet, but en route, let us say. You appreciate that there will be a technical examination of the item before transfer is completed?"

"If the item were fake would my countrymen and half Europe be trying to capture me?"

"An obvious point. Ah—I anticipate an interval of some hours before everything is in place and final arrangements made."

449

"How many hours? I can't hide forever."

"I quite understand your quandary. By seven the way should be clear. Is there a telephone where you can be reached?"

"I prefer calling you. Tell your friends unless everything is completed tonight I'm taking the item to my Consulate and surrendering."

"And your daughter?"

"I'll console myself with the knowledge that I did all I could. I'll call at seven."

He hung up, aware of a tremor in his hand.

For a few moments he lingered beside the phone, scanning the crowded station. One uniformed policeman was chatting at a coffee bar, another stood by the entrance looking boredly at arrivals. There could be plainclothesmen as well, he realized, and pulled down his hat brim and began walking toward the exit gate.

Coming through the gate in Guy's direction was a well-dressed black man carrying a suitcase. A raincoat was folded over his other arm. James McGrain.

Abruptly Guy changed direction, but too late. He saw McGrain's eyes widen in sudden recognition. Guy's impulse was to bolt but he knew he could never get away in the crowd. Instead, he walked directly to McGrain and thrust one hand in his coat pocket. Stopping so close their bodies nearly touched he grated, "I can drop you here or we can talk."

"I prefer talk."

"Men's room—you lead."

Only a step behind McGrain, he followed him through the crowd. They entered the men's room and walked to the far end. McGrain started to set down his suitcase but Guy shook his head. "Keep holding it," he said. "You're covered and I'm desperate."

"You must be," McGrain said, "and I'm sorry about

whatever drove you to this." He glanced at Guy's pocketed hand. "The piece I gave you?"

"No, I took it from a Russian. A dead Russian."

"Ah," McGrain said in sudden comprehension, "then the Sovs are behind this."

"All the way. My wife's death was a mistake, they tell me. If they now kill my daughter it will be because I don't give them Sceptre in exchange."

"You know what that means?"

"I know what it means if I don't comply." He looked around, saw the washroom was empty. "I've gone too far to be stopped by you or anyone else. Don't try, understand?"

"Hey, I'm always respectful to a man with a gun. No argument from me."

"Here's the deal," Guy told him. "In exchange for your life, forget you saw me. Not a damn word, ever."

McGrain's eyes stared. "How do I live with myself?"

"Your problem, James. Either way I won't be stopped."

McGrain breathed deeply. "You were a hero to me. I couldn't believe you'd turned traitor." He swallowed. "Still can't."

"Then you don't believe everything you read?"

"Not everything." He glanced at a man who had come in to use the urinal. "You must be pretty sure of getting your daughter back."

"Whatever the odds, I have to try. Been looking for me?"

"At Drach's." He grimaced. "And look who pops up when I ain't got a gun. Can I put down my bag?"

"No. Made up your mind?"

He shrugged. "What choice is there? I've got a wife and two kids. Dead, I'm no good to them."

"What's your train?"

"The TGV. I can still make it."

"We'll go together—in case you change your mind."

451

"I've given you my word. Isn't a black man's word good enough for you?"

"It's not your skin that concerns me—it's your sense of duty. Let's go."

Guy stepped back. If McGrain tried any heroics such as flinging the suitcase, he wanted distance between them. The DSA officer said, "When does the game end?"

"It's fourth quarter. Visitors leading."

"Wish I could have helped."

"You have." He followed McGrain into the concourse, saw the TGV gate and slowed his pace to drop back. McGrain continued walking, and by the time he was at the gate Guy had angled off toward the exit.

He glimpsed McGrain looking around, shrugging. The traveler showed his gate pass and disappeared among other boarders. Guy expelled pent-up breath and straightened his hand. It was wet with perspiration, index finger aching from simulating the barrel of a gun he didn't have.

He walked three blocks to a tram stop, changing routes twice before reaching the apartment. When he went in Whitaker was waiting.

After hearing Guy's summary of his encounter with McGrain, Whitaker tugged his mustache fiercely. "Can the feller be trusted?"

"He let me get away."

"True, but he may have second thoughts."

"Without a gun I couldn't shoot him—had to trust him."

Whitaker spiked his mustache points. "And if you'd had a piece, would you have used it?"

"It would have been a tough decision."

"All right, it's over with. So far today no unscheduled aircraft from Warsaw Pact countries. When's your next contact with Drach?"

"Seven."

"May as well phone from here—won't be needin' this place again." He pulled a cushion from the sofa and unzipped its cover. After groping inside the stuffing he brought out a 9mm Beretta. "Kedrov's. Bugger's got no further need of it."

Guy took the pistol and checked the magazine. Full. He put the Beretta in his pocket.

Whitaker said, "I've spent hours figurin' a way to keep you and your daughter alive after they've seen the Sceptre. To be practical the scheme has to work whether the exchange is at Drach's or some other site. Game of maneuver, right? Here's what you'll do."

Forty-Four

The rest of the day was agonizingly long.

To break monotony Guy prepared an early dinner—and found himself without appetite. Whitaker was gone and, as before during the long pursuit, Guy felt utterly alone. His hand fondled Gloria's earrings and he stared at them until tears dimmed his vision. Silently he wept for his murdered wife and captive daughter, for the pain inflicted on Cristina. The only way he could redeem himself was to bring out Gloria unharmed. Then try to make peace with DSA and the FBI. But that was for a distant time . . .

Whitaker's plan could work, but too many imponderables remained to let him feel confident. In the end, he knew, it would come down to his own appraisal of the situation, and his response.

Even now his antagonists were drawing together the cords of their net, bringing to a close a prolonged intelligence operation. To them he must have seemed an almost eager ally, and a sense of shame engulfed him.

The telephone rang. Hesitantly he picked up the receiver.

Whitaker said, "Gerasimov left the Consulate and went to the castle. That's a positive development."

"Any sign of the travelers?"

"Not yet. I'll phone when there is."

"It's close to seven."

"Hold fast."

Easier said than done, Guy reflected as he went to the bathroom. There, facing the mirror, he taped the plastic microphone to his chest and connected it to the transmitter by his lower spine. He buttoned shirt and jacket. No telltale bulges.

He wondered where Whitaker was.

Outside it was dark. By craning his neck he could glimpse Geneva's familiar symbol, the towering four-hundred-foot fountain at lake's end, the Jet d'Eau. Illumination from the base gave the high drifting mist an other worldly glow.

He remembered coming over the foothills in the school bus from Vezelay and catching sight of the fountain's feathery spray even before the rest of Geneva was visible.

After tonight, would he ever see it again?

His mind drifted back to still evenings when mist from the Hudson hovered in the air as he crossed The Plain from Regimental barracks to the Libe. He remembered endless hours studying Solids and Juice, football practice, the games with Michigan, Penn State and Navy, the charge of adrenalin that suppressed pain until the game was over . . . the satisfaction of becoming a Star Man and good athlete . . . the thrill of making Cadet Colonel, the Heisman nomination . . . He thought of dances he'd attended with dates from Vassar, Sarah Lawrence and Smith. Dining at the Thayer.

And he remembered quiet winter nights, looking up at the gray stone barracks when every window showed orange light . . . hearing the Chapel organ's chords reverberate across The Plain . . .

Good years at the Point, he mused; entering as a boy he left a man, and tried to serve his country as he'd been taught.

Duty. Honor. Country.

The fifteenth reunion of his class was due in May. Guy wondered if he would live to go back once again.

Seven o'clock.

He waited a few more minutes, hoping Whitaker would phone—then downed a shot of cognac and dialed Edouard Drach.

Two rings and Drach answered. Guy said, "Everything in order?"

"So I have been informed."

"Where do we get together?"

"I was asked to give some thought to the possibility of holding the meeting here. All things considered—your familiarity with the premises and my desire to be of service in resolving a distressing situation—I agreed. Is that satisfactory to you, sir?"

"It is."

"Then if you will be good enough to indicate your whereabouts I will send a vehicle for you."

"That's generous but I don't feel I should accept. I have no doubt concerning your own motives, but those of your principals . . . I'll get there on my own. Brown Audi sedan." He paused. "My daughter is there?"

"Will be, sir. She will be."

"I'm anxious to conclude the transaction, so let's have no false delays."

"It is my understanding that there will be none—provided the item you deliver is authentic."

"Guaranteed," Guy told him, "by the US Government."

He hung up and stared at the phone. Gerasimov hadn't changed the location—but where was Gloria?

The telephone rang. Whitaker said, "You on with the fat feller?"

"Yes. Any news?"

456

"Clever folks we're dealin' with, resourceful. Private train car from Zürich came into the Gare half an hour ago. Patient taken off by stretcher and transferred into waiting ambulance. Ambulance departed. Not for hospital, no, no. Castle Drach."

Fear clutched him. "Gloria's hurt?"

"Don't believe it—just a canny way of keeping her from prying eyes." He cleared his throat. "You on your way?"

"I'll be there before eight."

"Splendid. I'll set things in motion my end. Best of luck, sir."

"I have no way of thanking you," he said, throat suddenly tight. "Without your help—"

"Say no more. My reward will be the smile on that little girl's face. Daughter myself, y'know. We'll meet later."

But will we? Guy wondered, as he slowly replaced the receiver, then went into the kitchen. Using a paring knife, he pried open the seam on the inside of his belt tip, then inserted the flat, unnumbered key to the post office box. He flattened the edges between thumb and finger, drank a glass of water and left the apartment.

Driving the lakeside route Guy could see the illuminated cathedral of St-Pierre high on a promontory overlooking the city. As a schoolboy he had attended mass there and remembered the finger-numbing cold.

Now, his fingers gripping the wheel were stiff with tension. So many things could go wrong before the night was over.

But no point in thinking of them at this stage. Whatever happened he would have to respond as best he could.

At the UN Palace a reception was under way and the handsome façade was illuminated. Limousines arriving at the entrance deposited their celebrated passengers and moved on.

Behind him the glow of the city faded. Ahead the dark road unreeled. He let his mind go blank until he saw the posterns at Drach's entrance.

The guard inspected the rear seat well, asked him to open the trunk. Satisfied, he waved Guy in.

Parking well away from the castle, Guy turned off the engine. He shut the keys in the ash tray and got out. No other cars visible. No light in Sonya's room.

The entrance doors opened and Guy went up the steps.

Down the long manorial hall past suits of armor as empty as their owner's claim to nobility. Guy turned into the huge hall and found Edouard Drach waiting.

Behind his chair stood two men Guy had never seen before. Their location suggested they were footmen, but bulges under badly cut jackets told a different story.

Near them sat a middle-aged man whose face Guy remembered from a photograph: Nikolai Gerasimov.

Drach said, "Monsieur Ryan, this gentleman is here to facilitate proceedings. For our purposes he is Boris Pastrovsky. He speaks English and French, so language should be no barrier to mutual understanding."

"Let's get on with it."

One of the "footmen" approached with an airport-style metal detector. He ran it over Guy's clothing. It whined at pocket change and the Beretta. Guy handed over the Beretta. The chest mike had not been detected. "You've got my pistol," he said. "Let me see my daughter."

Gerasimov nodded. "That is permitted. Then the Sceptre microchip, correct?"

"Correct." His throat was so taut he could hardly utter the word. His palms were damp. He wondered if Whitaker was following the conversation from wherever he was.

The vastness of the room, he thought, made them all seem insignificant—puppets on a dwarfing stage, responding to the tugs and pulls of invisible manipulators.

Gerasimov spoke to one of the men who then left his

station and walked past Guy. As the sounds of his steps faded Gerasimov said, "You knew Sergei Kedrov?"

"Kedrov? Met him once in Paris. An art connoisseur."

"You saw him subsequently?"

"No," he lied. "His association with my wife—my *late* wife—precluded friendship."

"I thought you might have encountered him in Geneva?"

"Once was quite enough." Would he see Gloria—or had he been lured for interrogation about the missing Kedrov?

Sounds approaching from behind. Turning, he saw the footman walking slowly behind Sonya. She was wearing a short blue frock, and with her arms was helping a smaller girl stay erect. The girl's face was expressionless, eyes vacant. She moved slowly and uncertainly, as though utterly exhausted—or dangerously ill.

Guy shot out of his chair. "Gloria!" he cried. *"God, what have they done to you?"*

Stumbling toward his daughter, he gathered her in his arms.

Forty-Five

Behind him Gerasimov's voice was calm, dispassionate. "Do not be alarmed, Mr. Ryan. Some tranquilizers for the journey, nothing more."

Sobbing, Guy covered Gloria's cool face with kisses. Presently he gained control of himself and saw recognition in her eyes. "Papa," she whispered. "I'm . . . so . . . glad . . . to . . . see . . . you. It's . . . been . . . so . . . long. *Maman* is dead. I saw . . . her . . . die." Tears welled in her eyes. "I—tried to be brave, Papa, I remembered what you said."

"I know you were very brave," he told her. "And you must be brave, sweetheart, for just a little longer. Trust me."

"I do, Papa."

"And Sonya, too."

Gloria nodded. Guy wiped his eyes and guided her to the sofa. Sonya followed and sat beside his daughter.

Gloria was calm now, he thought, and unafraid as Consuela would have been, and he felt a surge of pride in his daughter's strength and composure. Then Gerasimov said, "Now let us examine the Sceptre."

Guy glanced at Drach. "You told him it's not with me?"

"I did," he said solemnly and folded his hands over his billowing paunch.

To Gerasimov, Guy said, "You have a scientist to authenticate the chip?"

The Russian nodded. "Where is it?"

"In Geneva." He was gazing at his daughter. His mind was filled with her. He wanted to run with her, *now*, but he had to keep his mind clear for the final details of the exchange.

From behind him a man walked toward Gerasimov. "This is Doctor Pushkin," he said. "He speaks Russian and a little German. If you speak neither, I will interpret for you."

"Very well. The microchip is housed in a vacuum container."

"Why?"

"As you know, it is designed for the airless conditions of space. The container is transparent, permitting visual examination of the chip. Tell him the container can be opened only in a vacuum. Otherwise, air will react with chip components and destroy it."

Gerasimov frowned and spoke to "Pushkin," who listened interestedly. He responded in Russian to Gerasimov, who said, "He wants to know how he can examine the chip in vacuum conditions?"

"I agreed to deliver the chip, have it examined. If he knows anything about microchip circuitry he should be able to render an opinion without opening the container."

Gerasimov interpreted again. The scientist shrugged. His career was on the line. Guy said, "Tell him to take a flashlight and magnifying lens. For half an hour he can study it backwards and forwards, standing on his head. After that, he is to call here. He will have the Sceptre and I will leave here with my daughter."

There was silence as Gerasimov thought it over. In a low voice Sonya comforted Gloria, whose face was beginning to

461

show expression. Guy ached to hold her, kiss away her fears. Sonya's gaze found his and he winked unseen.

Gerasimov said, "Where is the chip?"

"At a post office in Geneva."

"Which one, Mr. Ryan? Come, come, time is wasting."

"You haven't agreed to the sequence."

"Well, I agree."

"To be clear," Guy said for Whitaker's benefit, "I will give your scientist my key. He will proceed to the Central Post Office and enter from Rue Chaponniere. He will then telephone here to confirm arrival. At that point I will give him further essential information. Within half an hour he is to telephone and authenticate the chip. My daughter and I will leave together."

Gerasimov considered. "I send a—an escort with Doctor Pushkin. Have you objection to that?"

"Send a dozen."

Gerasimov grimaced. He was not accustomed to bargaining, much less making concessions, and it went down hard. His innate wariness asserted itself. "And if the doctor is unable to authenticate the chip?"

"It will mean Pushkin is incompetent to evaluate such advanced technology." He looked at his daughter, immobile on the couch. "Is it likely I would risk her life and mine with a counterfeit? My government knows it's authentic—otherwise they would hardly try to recover it."

Gerasimov spoke at length with "Pushkin," finally pointing at his wristwatch. Turning to Guy he said, "The key?"

With his thumbnail, Guy opened the belt seam and brought out the box key. When it was in his hand Gerasimov said, "There is no number on this."

"That's information I'll give Pushkin when he telephones from the post office."

"You've planned well," Gerasimov remarked and handed Pushkin the key. He gave Pushkin instructions in Russian and spoke to Drach in French. Drach nodded. "My

462

driver will take the doctor to the Central Post Office and wait for him during the examination, then bring him here with the Sceptre. You should know that Pushkin has been given a code word which will indicate that he has been forced to authenticate the device."

Clenching the box key the Soviet scientist glanced nervously at Gloria and left the great hall, followed by one of the "footmen."

Guy went to the sofa, where he put his arm around Gloria's shoulders and hugged her tightly. "I love you so," he whispered as tears blurred his vision.

Gerasimov said, "While we wait, let me suggest you waste no thought on fleeing. The grounds are patrolled and there is a guard on your car. I respect you as an adversary, but you are greatly outnumbered, and it is I, not you, who has a gun."

Drach said, "Let us have no intimations of violence. As host to both of you I appeal to your sense of what is appropriate. So far matters are proceeding without difficulty. Monsieur Ryan is with his daughter and Doctor Pushkin is en route to verify the microchip. I suggest we have something to eat and drink, and pass the time more agreeably. Comrade Pastrovsky?"

Gerasimov shrugged assent.

Drach spoke to the remaining footman, who left his post and walked quickly away. Guy kissed his daughter's forehead and said, "How can I know you didn't poison her?"

"I am not," Gerasimov said irritably, "in the business of killing children."

"Just their mothers."

"A lamentable miscalculation," Gerasimov replied. "Believe me, that was no one's intention. Your daughter received by mouth a series of sedative capsules. Soon, she will be quite herself, I assure you."

"She had better be," Guy told him, "or you'll see me again." He held his daughter's hands protectively.

Trays of sandwiches, cheeses and drinks arrived. Guy offered a sandwich to Gloria but she said, "I don't want it, Papa. Can we go now?"

"Soon," he said and stroked her hands soothingly. Then he sugared a cup of black coffee and made her drink it. Sonya looked longingly at the food but shook her head when Guy offered sandwiches.

Between huge mouthfuls Drach said, "My little ballerina must adhere to a very strict regimen, else she will never qualify for the Ballet Russe."

Guy noticed that even his nose was porcine, with large dark nostrils, the small deep-set eyes ever watchful. Tonight Drach's costume was ivory silk, and to Guy he resembled a pig engulfed in marshmallows. He consumed food with an intensity so repulsive that even Gerasimov stared in disbelief.

As Guy gave Gloria more coffee he said, "I'm glad you sent an escort with Pushkin. I wouldn't want Sceptre to get into the wrong hands."

Gerasimov looked puzzled. "Such as? Whose hands?"

"Why, the Chinese. In exchange for it they'd give him riches and amenities beyond his wildest dreams." He paused. "Neither of us wants that."

Drach and Gerasimov exchanged glances. "That is absurd," Gerasimov said finally.

"Well, you know him, I don't. But that's no more unthinkable than my turning Sceptre over to the USSR. And having gone to so much risk and trouble I want what I came for."

"*Apropos,*" Gerasimov said, "since you will not be able to return to America, where are you planning to go?"

"Oh," Guy said, feeling like a new man now that his arms were around Gloria, "I considered Prague, but I don't like food queues and ration lines. Western Europe is out because Interpol will always be looking for me. That leaves Africa, the Orient, and Latin America."

The telephone rang. Drach lifted the ornate receiver, listened for a moment and handed it to Gerasimov. "Pushkin," he said for Guy's benefit. Gerasimov spoke a few words of Russian, listened briefly, and turned to Guy. "Which box does the key fit?"

"Number A-784." Guy looked at his watch. "He has half an hour, no more."

Gloria murmured, "For what, Papa?"

"To make sure I've paid their price for you."

Softly she began to cry. She must be accustomed to crying, he thought, after all she's been through these endless weeks. He wished Cristina were there to comfort her, impossible as the thought was. The thought of revenge seared his body, leaving it hot and tense.

Gerasimov said, "Edouard, I don't hear your dogs."

"They do not give tongue without reason." Drach shifted his bulk to a more comfortable position. Guy wondered if he slept in the massive chair, and noticed a curious thing.

Behind Drach a wall tapestry depicted a medieval hunting scene. Lancers, mounted and on foot, were thrusting spears into a wild boar. Drach's face blotted out the boar's head, making it appear as though Drach were the dying boar. The fantasy made Guy's skin prickle until Gloria touched his face.

"Papa, will we live in Paris again?"

"No, darling, but we'll find a nice place. You'll have a pony and we'll ride together every day." In lower tones he said, "Are you feeling better?"

"Yes, but I'm still very tired. The medicine—I could hardly walk."

"I know. Are your legs stronger now?"

"I—I think so. Shall I try?"

"Not now." He whispered, "If anything happens, lie down on the floor, Sonya, too. Don't ask questions, just do it."

465

"Yes, Papa," she said, and he silently thanked Consuela for raising an obedient child.

Drach finished his repast, pinching up the last crumbs from his plate and licking his fingers. He downed a glass of red wine. Guy got up and poured a shot of cognac, sat beside his daughter and slowly sipped. Gloria said, "Will the men let us go, Papa?"

"I think so," he told her. "Do you remember your grandfather Palafox?"

"And the great house at La Rocha? Can we go there again?"

"Some day," he promised, and told her about her grandfather's broken leg, his hospitalization and recovery—anything to lend a semblance of normality to the tense situation and lessen her fears. As he talked he saw more animation in her eyes and face. It encouraged him to hope that she would do as told when the time came. If only he had been able to communicate with Sonya, prepare her for what lay ahead . . . He looked at her calm face, the expression of resignation, and wondered if he would be able to fulfill his promise to her.

Unobtrusively he glanced at his watch. Eighteen minutes gone; twelve ahead. He visualized Pushkin examining the Sceptre in the rear seat of the Rolls. Difficult conditions for a scientist. He wondered if Gerasimov had instructed Pushkin to collect the envelope and return with it. Of course, the scientist might have other ideas . . .

Ten minutes remaining. To Gloria he said, "Walk to the table and come back to me." Dutifully she left his side and went slowly to the table. After resting a few moments she walked carefully back, oblivious of Gerasimov's hard stare. She placed one hand in Guy's.

Gerasimov snapped, "Satisfied?"

"I'm satisfied she's alive."

The Russian blinked and looked away. The tension of waiting was affecting his nerves, too. Like Pushkin's, his career was on the line. Like an unseen cloud a sense of death hung over them.

Drach drank more wine, belched. Wine spotted the ruffle under his chin. He said, "Monsieur Ryan, is it indelicate of me to inquire how you were able to obtain a device so closely guarded?"

"Indelicate, yes," Guy said, "but one day the story will come out. The answer is guile—and bribery." He gestured at Gerasimov. *"He* understands."

The Russian muttered, "You did well—for a novice."

The telephone rang. Without haste Gerasimov answered. He listened intently, spoke two words and handed Drach the receiver to replace. Guy said, "Well?"

Slowly Gerasimov said, "The preliminary finding is positive."

"Then everything's complete, all conditions met." Standing he drew Gloria to her feet. "We're leaving."

The Russian said, "Not until Pushkin places the Sceptre in my hands."

Angrily Guy said, "That's not the agreement. Your own scientist has accepted the chip. What can you add?"

"Possession," Gerasimov said thickly. "Sit and be patient. What is another half hour after so long a wait?"

"It's bad faith," Guy said furiously. "You could decide to take it to Moscow for final examination—us with it." He turned to Drach. "You promised no delays, I hold you accountable."

"Please, sir, please, this is not in my hands. Each of you is free to act as he will."

"You've tricked me," Guy snarled at the Russian.

"Why not? You're a traitor to your own country, a thief and a fugitive. Whatever I decide, you can do nothing."

Outside the chateau there was a deafening explosion. Guy pushed Gloria to the floor. Another explosion and the lights went out.

Forty-Six

Guy dropped to the floor, grasped Sonya's leg and dragged her down beside his daughter. "Stay there," he ordered and began crawling toward the wall. Behind him a gun went off, muzzle blast momentarily illuminating the wall and doorway.

In a crouch, Guy ran to the wall, wrenched a five-foot halberd from its fittings and turned around. Outside it sounded as though a battle was underway. Explosions, small-arms fire. Flames climbing the outside wall showed Guy where the armed footman stood. Gerasimov had backed behind the table. Drach sat immobile. His mouth opened and from it came piercing screams.

The head of the halberd was a broad, double-edged blade with spearhead protruding. He threw it at the footman and saw the spearhead disappear below the man's ribcage. The footman yelled in agony and seized the shaft to pull it out. His pistol hit the floor.

Guy jerked a short sword from the wall and flung it at Gerasimov; it hit flat, knocking the Russian back and giving Guy time to reach the dropped pistol. As he scooped it up the footman fell back against the table, blood spurting from his wound. Guy snapped off a shut at Gerasimov, but the

Russian had changed location. The Russian fired at Guy, who took cover in front of Drach.

Firelight showed Gerasimov backing toward the far wall.

Suddenly, from the entrance a powerful beam fanned the room. Gerasimov fired at the source and Guy heard a grunt of pain. The lantern dropped to the floor but its light showed Gerasimov running toward the hall's far end. Standing, Guy leveled the pistol and fired at the fleeing Russian. Fired again. He could hardly make out his target but he sighted and fired two more rapid shots. Gerasimov pitched forward, hands grabbing the fringe of a tapestry. As the Russian collapsed, the heavy tapestry tore free and dropped on top of him.

Outside, the sounds of battle had diminished and Guy could hear Drach still whinnying with fear. From the floor came tremulous sobbing. As he passed the girls he said, "Stay there, I'll be back."

He walked to the entrance for the lantern and saw Whitaker on his knees, bloody hands clutching one thigh. "Hold on," Guy told him, and picked up the lantern.

He went quickly to the far end of the room and played the beam over the fallen tapestry. He found one end and began hauling it aside, looking for Gerasimov.

As he uncovered the Russian he saw a pistol pointing at him. Guy ducked as the pistol went off, and felt a sharp sting by his left shoulder. He kicked the pistol from Gerasimov's hand and saw the animal snarl on his lips, the malevolence in his eyes. Guy raised his pistol to sight at Gerasimov's face but the Russian rolled aside, stumbled erect and snatched another halberd from the wall. He flung it spinning so that the heavy handle caught Guy's midriff and knocked him down. Like a tiger the Russian was on him, clutching Guy's throat with powerful hands, cutting off his air. From underwater diving Guy's lung capacity was immense, but Gerasimov's choking grip was keeping blood from his brain. Before he blacked out he had to free his throat. His pistol was gone, fallen beyond reach. Guy's left hand shot up, clawing at the Russian's eyes. Gerasimov growled, flung back his head.

Colored lights darted before Guy's eyes—he was fading fast. He saw the Russian's upturned head, drew back his right arm and with all its strength shot it suddenly upward, pistoning his hand at Gerasimov's chin.

The Russian's head snapped backward. Guy heard the crunch of broken bone, a hoarse gurgle in Gerasimov's throat. The head lolled sideways, the Russian's body went limp, dropped on Guy.

Gasping for breath, Guy levered the dead body aside and staggered to his feet. Dazed, he looked around for a pistol, saw Drach seated in his throne, a glinting derringer in one pudgy hand, pointing at Guy, who said, "You can still save yourself."

"Only if you die." His face was rigid, eyes shiny as wet opals. From behind Drach Guy saw Sonya rise, saw Drach's trigger finger tighten and dropped to the floor as a bullet sped over his head. Rolling away Guy collided with the halberd and grasped it. He was rising, expecting Drach's second shot, when he saw Sonya plunge a cheese knife into Drach's silk-covered chest. Drach screeched and flung the girl aside as the knife fell out of its shallow wound. Drach was leveling his weapon again when Guy launched the halberd like a javelin at Drach's body. The heavy weapon entered belly suet smoothly, burying its blade in Drach's guts. The derringer exploded upward, and dropped from Drach's hands as the man seized the wooden haft and tried to jerk out the buried blade.

Sonya screamed.

Guy kicked the derringer away, watched life fading from Drach's eyes, strength flowing from hands and arms. Slowly Drach bent forward, his hands dropped away and he seemed to bow submissively until the halberd's end touched the floor. The dwarfish legs kicked futilely—the body's fat rippled in final waves. Breath rattled in Drach's throat as death prevailed.

While Sonya was pulling Gloria to her feet Guy went to the fireplace and opened a container of long ornamental matches. He struck one on stone and ignited the tapestry fringe. Dry, ancient fibers caught and flared, lighting the enormous room. Guy turned back to the girls and took their hands. He strode to the entrance where Whitaker sat against the jamb.

With his belt Guy made a tourniquet around Whitaker's thigh, above the bullet wound. *"Merde,"* said Whitaker as Guy helped him to his feet.

The four of them left the blazing room and went down the long hallway past the equestrian king, the coats of armor, the blazoned shields. A servant stood aside as they passed.

Guy forced open the massive door and saw the Rolls at the foot of the marble steps. Its engine was running but the driver had disappeared. In the rear seat sat Doctor Pushkin.

They opened doors and Whitaker hoisted himself onto the passenger seat. Sonya and Gloria hesitated, looking at the Soviet scientist.

Guy said, "Get out and give me Sceptre," before remembering that Gerasimov had said the man spoke only Russian and German. But Pushkin took the Sceptre envelope from his pocket and handed it to Guy, who said, "You understand English?"

"Some. I study in secret, listen to BBC."

The Sceptre envelope had been opened but the plastic container was there. Guy stuck it in his pocket.

Distantly came the harsh cawing of a fire engine. Flames blanketed one wall of the castle. Through the open door Guy could see fire billowing along the hall. "Who are you?" he asked.

"Anatoliy Zinchuk, member of the Soviet Academy of Science. Please take me with you."

After the girls were seated beside Zinchuk the Rolls glided down the road. As Guy turned the wheel he felt sharp pain in his shoulder. Jacket fabric was soaked with blood. To Whitaker he said, "You've produced miracles before—how about a doctor?"

"We'll ask my watchers."

The Rolls passed unchallenged through the gate and Guy braked beside two cars at roadside. Whitaker spoke to the men, one of whom replied. To Guy, Whitaker said, "We'll follow him."

Both cars turned around. From the direction of Geneva a fire engine bore down on them, then another. Their sounds set Guy's frayed nerves on edge. The rearview mirror showed Gloria covering her ears with her hands. Sonya sat composedly, hands folded on her lap. Academician Zinchuk stared stolidly ahead.

The surgeon was a cousin of the watcher. He gave Guy a gauze pad for his shoulder, helped Whitaker onto the steel table and cut off Whitaker's blood-soaked trouser leg. The bullet had passed through the thigh. The surgeon poured anesthetic into a cone and set it over Whitaker's nose and mouth. He pulled on surgical gloves and selected instruments from the sterilizer.

Guy went back to the reception room where the girls and Zinchuk waited. He put his arm around Gloria, held her tightly and closed his eyes.

In her soft voice Sonya said, "Thank you for keeping your promise."

He swallowed. "Thank you for helping Gloria—and me."

"I'm not sorry you killed Edouard."

"Don't think about it. You're safe now, no harm will come to you." He patted her hand.

After a while the surgeon opened the door and beckoned to Guy.

Whitaker was still unconscious on the table, thigh wounds

472

neatly stitched, plasma flowing into his veins. The surgeon cut off Guy's jacket and cleansed his shoulder with alcohol. On his raw flesh it was like flame. When Guy grimaced, the surgeon said, "Want anesthetic?"

"Can't. Have to stay operational."

He dusted the wound with antibiotic powder and closed it with twelve stitches. While he was bandaging Guy's shoulder, Whitaker groaned and opened his eyes. "Still alive," he muttered. "Thought I'd passed on to my reward."

"Not for a while," Guy replied, "you're still needed."

When they left the office Guy told the watcher to take the Rolls to Cointrin and leave it in the airport parking lot; they would use his car.

Guy drove it across the river to the American Consulate, and led Zinchuk to the door. When a Marine corporal answered the bell Guy said, "This man is a Soviet scientist seeking asylum. His name is Anatoliy Zinchuk. Let him inside while you notify the Consul-General."

The Corporal looked warily at Zinchuk. "A defector?"

"Exactly. Follow procedure, Corporal."

"Yes, sir."

Zinchuk shook hands with Guy and entered the lobby. The corporal closed and locked the door. He was dialing the telephone when Guy walked away.

In his life he had never felt more exhausted, but as he saw Gloria's face new strength flowed into his veins.

He got behind the wheel, kissed her and held her hand, knowing that everything he had gone through was worth this. With his daughter and Cristina he had a family again.

Whitaker said, "I have a plane standing by, waiting for us."

"You're something else," Guy said admiringly, turned the car around and headed for the airport road.

As he drove through the night Gloria's cheek rested gently, securely on his shoulder.

Through the high thin air they flew over southern France and crossed the Pyrenees into Spain, landing at Seville.

When their airport limousine turned into La Rocha's broad lands dawn was tracing the eastern sky. Cristina hurried down the steps into Guy's arms, and for a time they held each other tightly and without words, his long journey over.

Epilogue

On the following day Jake Needham flew in, and with Cristina listening Guy began speaking of the recent past.

For half an hour he told them about Drach and Kedrov, Sonya, Gerasimov, and Academician Zinchuk; the crucial help given him by Drs. Printz and Felberg, and as Needham listened his features gradually relaxed. When Guy finished, Jake said, "I still think you could have confided in me."

"Yes," Cristina said. "Makes me feel you didn't trust us."

Guy took her hand. "Your reactions had to be authentic. The Soviets had to believe I'd stolen Sceptre, otherwise they wouldn't have sent back Gloria."

Jake's fingers drummed on the chair arm. "They didn't get the replica, then, Sceptre II?"

Guy handed over the chip's plastic container. "It's cracked," he said, "probably in transit. The chip's half melted away. Gray ooze. Zinchuk saw that, of course, but he okayed it anyway. That bought Gloria for me and freedom for him."

"He paid his way," Jake said and pocketed the replica. "I'll get this back to ISR without delay—might help cool Hoskin's rage. And the fact that but for you our Govern-

475

ment wouldn't have Zinchuk." He looked around. "Where's Whitaker?"

Cristina said, "Resting upstairs, until he's able to fly to England. He'll stay with his daughter a while, then back to Geneva."

"Quite a man," Jake said. "We're lucky he was around."

Guy nodded. "Without his talents I'd never have brought it off. He thinks he can placate the Swiss police if that becomes necessary."

Jake grunted. "While I have to work things out with Hoskins and the Department of Justice, get your fugitive warrant canceled and the indictments dropped. Sit tight here until I do."

Cristina said, "Depend on me for that, Jake. And come back with Sally for our formal wedding."

"Of course, wouldn't miss it." He looked at them. "Soon?"

"*Very* soon," Cristina smiled. "I'm pregnant."

"That pleases me more than I can say." He kissed Cristina's cheek and rose. "I have to get back—is there anything you haven't told me?"

Cristina said, "Good question, dear," but Guy shook his head, knowing that he hadn't told her of Sean's strange life, the long years of deception or the truth of his own name. Because the legacy was one of violence, vengeance and death. And because there was time ahead for that and many things, years together while their children grew amid love and caring. Cristina would rear them in a way far different from the childhood he had known; giving them everything he had been denied.

He remembered Marguerite and thought that but for her gentle love he would have become a far different sort of man, austere like his father, incapable of showing affection.

He took his wife's hand and kissed it.

Later, after Jake had gone, Guy stood by the window

watching Cristina in the corral. She was showing Sonya and Gloria the proper way to mount their training steeds: toe in stirrup, reins in left hand, right hand on pommel.

As he watched them his throat thickened with a surge of emotion.

He could see them now—all of them—riding as a family in the Easter cavalcade at the *Feria* in Seville.